RADIO

Book Two of the Vinyl Trilogy

SOPHIA ELAINE HANSON

CALIDA LUX

PUBLISHING

RADIO: *Book Two of the Vinyl Trilogy*

ISBN-10: 0-692-85419-3
ISBN-13: 978-0-692-85419-8

Editor: Katherine Catmull
Cover Design: Docshot
Printing: Createspace
Print and eBook Formatting, and Proofreading: Heather Adkins

For Maya

Terra

Mouse

Ronja

Samson

Jonah

RADIO

PART I: SILENCE AND NOISE

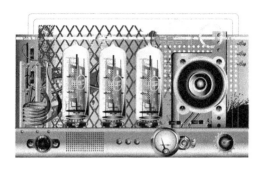

PROLOGUE: MOUSE
Roark

The cold was the sort that no amount of clothing could bar, but the boy hardly felt it as he trudged down the gas-lit avenue. A bitter wind gusted, threatening to yank back his hood. He huffed and tugged it lower on his brow. A rustling to the left pricked his sensitive ears. The hair on the back of his neck stood on end and he scuffed to a halt. He gripped the leather hilt of his stinger, warm with bottled electricity, and slid his gaze toward the source. He let his hand fall, grimacing. "Figures," he muttered.

The wanted poster flapped limply against the brick wall. The words were unreadable, dissolved by the elements, but he knew them by heart.

WANTED FOR HIGH TREASON
VICTOR ROARK WESTERVELT III
REWARD: 300,000 N

Below the blurred lettering was a photograph of the fugitive at a gala in the core. Every inch of him exuded opulence and authority. His silver-trimmed suit and polished shoes. His naked ear, unburdened by a Singer, a public demonstration of his unwavering loyalty to The Conductor. Shinys with diamond crusted Singers crowded around him, clambering to be near him.

If they could see me now, Roark thought with a wry twist of his lips. Skulking around the outer ring in the dead of night, armed to the teeth, the crest of the Anthem tattooed over his heart.

The poster strained against the nails that anchored it, inflating like a sail. Roark squinted at his former self, searching for a crack in his expressionless mask. Thunder rolled overhead. His gaze travelled further down the wall, where a similar flyer was posted.

WANTED FOR HIGH TREASON
RONJA FEY ZIPSE
REWARD: 300,000 N

Roark felt his stomach clench as he drank in the accompanying photograph. Though it was black and white, he could have sworn he saw a hint of green in her eyes. Her wild curls spiraled past her shoulders. Her mouth was pinched into a grim line. He could practically hear her teeth creaking under the strain of her grimace.

The poster billowed, and the girl morphed before his eyes. Her hair was stripped to reveal her white scalp and missing ear, the consequences of his unchecked paranoia. As he watched, her lips formed two words.

Save them.

Roark spun on his heel and stalked down the deserted street. His memories haunted him enough in sleep; he could not allow them to dog him while awake.

The duel winter moons, Carin and Calux, were setting by the

time he reached his destination, an apartment complex on the edge of the outer ring. Half its windows were choked with boards, the others were shuttered. It was the last building before the rings gave way to the slums. Unequipped with electricity, the slums were all but invisible in the weary moonlight.

Roark, his back to the building, squinted out across the shantytown, his chest tightening like a vice as he took in the mammoth black wall at the edge of the slums. Hungry searchlights roamed the tent city, pouring down from the watchtowers. Reminding himself that the cold light could not reach this far, he mounted the steps to the gated door of the apartment building. He jabbed the buzzer labeled *L. Constantine.* No sooner had his finger left the button than the intercom crackled to life.

"Pitch off."

"Open up," Roark commanded, his breath mushrooming in the frigid air. There was a brief pause filled with the irritated hiss of static.

"Password?"

"Come on, Mouse, I know you can see me." The Anthemite leaned around the entry alcove and waved pointedly at the last window on the fourth floor. There was a flash of silver like fish scales as the resident whipped his spyglass back through the drapes.

"Password."

"Fine. Six string."

"That was two weeks ago."

"Sonata?" The lock sprang. Roark popped the metal gate and put his shoulder into the stubborn door. He nearly tripped when it caved with a screech. Cursing, he slammed the door and swiped his hood from his head. His dark eyes flicked around the entry hall, scanning for trouble.

Dust motes swirled in the stagnant air. Four armchairs upholstered in faded salmon crouched around a hearth stuffed with cigarette butts and cans. A naked bulb dangled from a wire above the narrow staircase. The silence was palpable. It played on his skin, raising a mountain range of gooseflesh.

Clutching his stinger, Roark started up the steps at a jog. By the time he reached the fourth floor, he was sweating under his thick winter clothes. He glanced either way down the corridor. Peeling doors stood like soldiers on either side. He turned left and strode to the end, halting before apartment 407. He tapped the frame with a knuckle. "Candy gram." The rolling click of tumblers, the scrape of a deadbolt, and the door flew open.

Roark was greeted by the yawning barrel of a gun. "Put that down before you pull something," he snarked, batting it away and shouldering past the boy half his size.

"Shouldn't you be a bit more concerned about being shot?" Mouse grumbled, slamming the door with a crack.

Roark snorted. "Not if *you're* aiming at me." He surveyed the room, his nose wrinkling. Precarious stacks of documents higher than his waist dominated the studio. The couch and table were drowning in stripped machinery and tangled wires. Debris from abandoned meals littered the floor. The twin bed in the corner was suffocating beneath scraps of paper and books. He wandered to the kitchen table, grimacing as the odor of sour milk tickled his nostrils. "You missed garbage ... year."

"Yeah, well, I've been busy," Mouse grouched, punctuating the final word with the thud of the deadbolt. Roark glanced over his shoulder, a wry smile surfacing on his mouth.

Though Mouse was not a day over eighteen, his hair was stark white. His irises were translucent, his skin a soft shade of fawn that was almost pink in certain lights. A dead Singer clung to his right ear. It had shorted out when he was fourteen, allowing him to pursue his calling as a black market trader. Iris was itching to dissect it, but he was adamant it was safer to leave it intact. Roark was fairly sure that was just his phobia of needles talking.

"Busy getting what you lot requested, I might add," Mouse went on, brushing past the Anthemite to set his revolver on the table. He squinted up at Roark, his expression darkening. "Skitz, when was the last time you slept?"

"Where is it?"

Mouse jerked his chin at the writing desk against the far wall. Roark crossed to it swiftly and found what he was looking for at once. It waited patiently in a clearing of copper wires and chicken bones. Evie had shown him a sketch, but he had expected it to be bigger. "This is the capacitor?" he asked, picking it up and scrutinizing it doubtfully. It was roughly the size of a coin with twin prongs and a flat red base. Nothing special.

"Tell Evie she owes me one."

"Where the hell did you find it, anyway?"

"One of my contacts in the middle ring, goes by the name Cicada." Mouse shook his head in wonderment. "No idea how he gets his hands on all this stuff."

"Are you sure it'll work?"

"Positive." Mouse sniffed, moving to stand beside Roark. They were silent for a moment, their eyes glued to the tiny device, basking in the tangled aura of anxiety and possibility that radiated from it.

This changes everything, Roark realized dimly.

"Oh," Mouse shattered the hush. "I meant to ask, did you ever get that record I snagged for you a couple months back? What was it called?"

Roark felt his blood still in his veins. "The Moor," he answered, pocketing the capacitor.

"Right, what did you think? I thought her voice was a bit ... "

Firelight. Ronja in her black and gold dress. The needle tracing the curve of the record. Evie polishing her rifle. Henry making lists in his notebook. Then the cold bite of manacles at his wrists. Ronja screaming, begging as his father tortured her with The Lost Song. Henry, his voice on the radio. Maybe the stars are alive after all.

Roark crashed back into his body. Mouse was still talking, oblivious. " ... if there were any scratches, they happened after it left my hands."

"How much do I owe you?"

Mouse crossed his arms, settling easily into the mold of businessman. "Fifty."

"Oh, come on. You know father dearest and I had a falling out."

The trader snapped his fingers. "Right, I forgot about my special deal for sob stories. If we factor in your crocodile tears and my apathy that brings us to ... fifty."

"Pitch you," Roark growled, drawing his dwindling roll of cash from the inner pocket of his coat. Mouse held out his blushing palm expectantly. The Anthemite peeled off five notes and slammed them onto the desk. "You're lucky we're friends."

The trader swiped up the bills and folded them into a neat square. "Mmm, whatever you say. If it makes you feel any better, it's for a good cause. I have to go visit Theo in the core."

"Always happy to fund your love life," Roark replied with an involuntary smile. "Theo has been a great help to us, we can never have enough spies up there."

"Oh, he knows it. Barely shuts up about it, in fact."

"I expect not."

"How's your girl?"

Roark tensed, his muscles tightening like springs. "What girl?"

"You know. One ear, about three inches of hair, looks like

she could kill you with her thumb." Mouse jabbed him in the sternum with a finger, snickering. "She has more wanted posters than you do."

"I noticed."

"Jealous?"

"Of course not." Roark glanced toward the window. Dawn was bleeding through the gap in the curtains, gray and sleepy. "I have to get back to the Belly. Wilcox has us on lockdown. Punishment for reckless behavior, or something."

"Lockd ... what are you doing here?" Mouse yelped. "Do you see this place?" He gestured around the studio wildly. Roark shrugged, knowing it would only fuel his agitation. "They break down my door, how forgiving do you think they're gonna be?"

"Please," Roark scoffed. "I wasn't followed. Do you think we would be having this conversation if I was?" The trader gulped, his pupils dilating. The Anthemite chuckled, then offered his friend a lazy salute and started toward the door. "Stay sharp, kid."

"Yeah, whatever. Say hello to your girl for me."

Roark felt his eye twitch. He was thankful his back was to Mouse. "Not my girl."

"Sure." He could still hear the trader chuckling when he closed the door on his apartment. Roark reached into his coat and withdrew his portable radio, grateful for Evie's secure connection. He clicked it and raised it to his lips. "Chimera, this is Drakon," he muttered. "I have the package and am bringing it home."

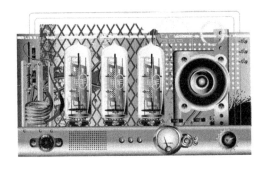

1: BELOW
Terra

Terra Vahl was not the sentimental type, but after two months underground she was starting to miss sunlight. Of course, waiting for the sun in a Revinian winter was like waiting for whiskey to spout from the sink. Still, she would have taken the icy winds over the dank sewer air she now stewed in.

The Anthemite shifted against the wall in a vain attempt to relieve the ache in her left buttock. She let her head loll backward. Her night vision goggles clicked and whirred as they refocused on the curved crown of the tunnel. It looked even slimier through the green lenses.

She was about as far from the surface as she could be, at least a quarter mile below the Belly. Her watch had only started an hour ago, but the minutes were stretched by monotony. Her throwing knives remained sheathed, strapped to her thighs and hips. The only unwelcome guests in the sewer were the rats.

A drop of what she hoped was water struck her on the forehead. She swore, the curse echoing as she wiped away the bead. Sighing, she shut her eyes. Bitter memories stirred behind her lids.

A week after their return from Red Bay, Ito had shed her like an old coat, placing her on guard duty in the sewers. "It was not my idea, Terra," her mentor defended herself after breaking the news. She sat behind her desk, long fingers laced and hooded eyes unforgiving. Terra had stood before her, fighting the urge to scream. Her hands trembled at her sides. She folded her arms to hide them. "Wilcox wants you out of the field, and he certainly wants you off the council. You're lucky he's not exiling you."

"He might as well be."

Ito pursed her lips. Terra glanced away, examining the navy drapes that enveloped the office. They swayed gently as Anthemites ambled by, their voices buffered by the heavy fabric. A lump of pain ballooned in her throat. How many times had she come here seeking guidance, and though she would never admit it, comfort? Terra swallowed the troublesome stone and spoke. "Six years of training, four years as your second ... and you abandon me after one mistake."

It was not a question, but Ito had answered anyway. "You lied to your commander. You went rogue."

Terra snapped her gaze back to the lieutenant. She was greeted by an ivory mask of indifference. That had stung more than any insults or hard truths she could have hurled at her. "*We* went rogue."

Ito rose slowly, pressing her palms to the desk. Strands of her dyed orange hair slipped into her face. Her eyes were scorching. It was in moments like these Terra had wondered why Wilcox was the commander when it was so clear Ito was in charge. "I followed you to Red Bay to save Trip and the others from their conceit and your selfishness."

"Selfishness?" Terra barked a humorless laugh. "You want to talk about selfishness? Talk to Ronja. She risked everyone in this compound for two and a half people who were most likely dead anyway."

Ito considered, tilting her head to the side. "Perhaps," she granted after a beat. "But she was trying to save lives, not destroy them."

"What do you think I was trying to do?" Terra bellowed, slamming her fists onto the desk. The inkwell shuddered, loose papers fled to the floor. The lieutenant did not so much as flinch. "I was trying to make up for my mistakes."

"That doesn't change what you did, and it certainly doesn't excuse you from punishment."

"You want someone to blame?" Terra leaned across the desk until she was nose to nose with her superior. At this distance, she could see the age lines branching from the corners of her eyes. A bolt of twisted satisfaction knifed through her, as if she had discovered a flaw in the masterpiece. "Blame that pitcher from the outer ring everyone is calling the next messiah."

"I do," Ito replied softly. Her head sagged a fraction of an inch, exhaustion seeping through the cracks in her poise. "I blame everyone involved in this, myself included."

"Even Henry?"

Ito lifted her chin, a warning sparking in her gaze.

Terra ignored it. "I know I messed up, Ito, but we have the son of The Conductor locked in a safe house and a new form of The Music that can reach Revinians with or without Singers. We're skitzed and you know it. You need me, now more than ever."

"No," Ito had countered tonelessly. She took her seat and returned her attention to a report held together by a straining clip. She licked her finger, flipped the page. "I do not."

Terra had not spoken to the lieutenant since. In fact, she barely talked to anyone. She kept her head down, her jaw locked, her solitary ear closed to the whispers that trailed her.

Outside Wilcox, no one knew exactly what went down at Red Bay. They knew only what they were told, that the actions of the rash young Anthemites resulted in the death of Henry Romancheck. That Victor Westervelt II had fallen. The commander ordered them to keep their mouths shut about the rest, but it made no difference. The thing about secrets, Terra had come to know, was the harder you squeezed them, the easier they slipped away.

Fact and fiction blended, stories began to swell. Stories of the girl from the outer ring with a voice like wildfire. It was said she could destroy The Music with nothing but her voice. Wilcox was furious, but no matter how he tried, he could not pinpoint the origin of the rumors. The gossip about Terra, he likely fueled himself.

No one knew why Ito had abandoned her right hand. Some called Terra a traitor. Others said she had simply lost her touch, slipped up on a mission and endangered lives. The truth was far worse, and she damn well knew it.

Terra Vahl. The coldest heart and the sharpest mind. Everyone knew that if Wilcox fell, Ito would take his place and appoint Terra her first lieutenant. When the time came, she would lead the Anthem. She was marked for command, the only realistic choice. Roark was too recognizable, Evie, too erratic. In his life, Henry might have been a good option were he not a self-proclaimed pacifist.

No, it had to be her.

Terra knew she was hard to swallow. She was abrasive, confrontational, at times even cruel. But she was trusted, and above all, she was necessary. At least, she used to be.

The scuffing of boots bucked her from her thoughts. Terra was on her feet in an instant, twin blades ready. They felt so natural in her hands. Adrenaline seeped into her palms through the cool metal. She squinted into the greenish gloom. "Show yourself," she demanded. Her voice matched her core, guarded but calm.

"Fancy seeing you here," a familiar voice drawled.

Terra groaned and sheathed her weapons. She would have preferred a strike team of Offs to this. Two glaring orbs flickered into view, the lenses of a pair of night vision goggles refracting off her own. Half a beat later he was before her, a grin plastered across his face. "Where have you been?" she snarled.

"Nowhere," Roark answered in a singsong voice. He started to slink by, but she grabbed him by the bicep and hauled him back in front of her. His waterlogged overcoat squelched beneath her fingers.

"Pitcher," she hissed, pushing him back singlehandedly. The boy stumbled, his heel splashing in the pungent water.

He laid an offended hand on his chest. "Language."

"You were outside."

"I would never disobey a direct order from our commander."

Terra narrowed her eyes behind her tinted lenses. "Where were you?"

Roark shrugged offhandedly, his teeth flashing in the dimness. "Just out enjoying the weather. It was getting a bit stuffy down here."

"You sure it had nothing to do with the plan you and your friends are concocting?"

The boy maintained his blithe grin, but she had known him far too long to be fooled. His jaw tightened subtly, he shifted his weight from one foot to the other. Nervous, a rabbit hearing a twig snap. She had him.

"Tell me what you're up to, Trip."

Roark laughed mirthlessly. "What, so you can go straight to Wilcox?"

Terra shook her head, echoing his brittle chuckle. Her sweat-stiffened braids crunched. She was starting to consider shaving them off to match the right side of her skull. It was not as if she needed to hide her missing ear underground. "Why the hell would I do that?"

Roark cocked an eyebrow, his smile dissolving into a tense line. "You would do anything to get back in his favor, including sell us out."

"There was a time when that was true. Not anymore."

The boy paused, regarding her with a shred of genuine curiosity. "What changed?"

"We warned Wilcox we needed to move against The Conductor before they finish The New Music, but he has his head up his ass, apparently." She took a step forward, swallowing the gap between them. Roark hid his discomfort well, but she could tell he wanted to retreat. "We need to strike now."

"Sounds like someone has given up her shot at command."

"I never said that. We need to prioritize. We have to work together or we all go down."

Roark observed her mutely, his expression unreadable. Terra waited with frozen breath, her heart thrumming like the blades of an aeroplane.

"Pretty words, Vahl," he finally said, sidestepping around her tauntingly. "If only they were true." He clicked his tongue, then moved along down the tunnel. His footsteps lingered long after he disappeared.

Terra stood motionless, her lenses fogging inexplicably. She sat back down on the damp stones and waited for the next rat to cross her path. This one she would nail between the eyes.

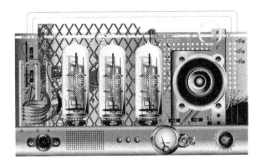

2: WAKE

It always began the same way.

She waited in the center of the room, her knees raw against the rough concrete. Her fingers twitched against her thighs, tapping out a rhythm only she could hear. She felt a searing gaze on her back, but every time she turned around she was greeted by an expressionless wall. She knew it was a dream because she had both ears again, full and round and perfectly symmetrical. Her long curls had returned; her scars were erased.

Ronja took a steadying breath. The room breathed with her, its walls expanding and contracting with her lungs.

1-2-3

2-2-3

3 ...

No matter how many times it happened, she still screamed each time the Offs burst through the door. Their bodies were blurred, only their hands were in focus. She scrambled backward until her spine struck the far wall.

Ronja.

She froze, choking on her own cries.

Henry.

She launched forward, snarling like a feral cat. She reached out, grasping at the disembodied voice of her best friend, her brother. He was just beyond the guards, just out of sight, she was sure of it.

Then they were upon her, tearing at her clothes, her skin. A massive hand closed around her windpipe. She yelled but no sound escaped. He leaned toward her, his breath hot and foul in her face. His eyes were black holes. When he opened his mouth, his gums were studded with needles.

"Ro!" The demonic Offs evaporated. The prison crumbled. Her lungs inflated and her lids snapped open. Ronja shot up, her arm cranked back into a punch. Her assailant reeled backward. "Easy!"

The familiar voice punctured her terror. She breathed a sigh of relief, but did not drop her arm. Instead, she reached up and switched on the lantern hanging above. "Georgie," Ronja rasped, blinking her cousin into focus. The child crouched beside her, her eyes round as records. The pools of light in her irises shivered as the lantern rocked on its hook. "What time is it?"

"About 4:00."

Ronja groaned, kneading her aching eyes with her palms. Her skin was slick with cold sweat. This was the fifth consecutive night her dreams had jolted her from sleep. Iris had prescribed her a draught, but it did no good.

Georgie lay down, scooting closer across the mattress they shared. Ronja flopped back onto her damp pillow with a gust of breath.

"Wanna talk about it?"

"No."

"I just thought ... "

"Nope." Ronja curled the girl to her side, stroking her short hair. "Your hair is growing back fast," she commented.

"Not as fast as yours," Georgie muttered enviously. She reached up and plucked one of Ronja's corkscrew curls. The older girl shook her head, her dark locks whispering against her temples.

"My hair is a beast," she said earnestly. "It can take its time coming back."

Georgie giggled. The sweet sound batted away the reality that loomed over them like a guillotine.

It only lasted a moment before Ronja cut the rope. "Sorry."

"For what?"

"I shouldn't be the one having nightmares."

Georgie did not respond immediately. Ronja turned her gaze skyward, working her jaw methodically. The lantern had stilled on its hook. Chains of dried flowers loped across the ceiling of the tent like telephone wires. Iris had taught Georgie to make them several weeks ago. Now their sanctuary was peppered with shriveled brown petals.

"Ro," Georgie finally said. "We talked about this. I don't remember anything from Red Bay."

"They tortured you, you have every right to be angry."

"I am." Georgie rolled onto her stomach and propped herself up on her elbows, forcing Ronja to meet her gaze. The younger girl's eyes were both stern and compassionate. Neat surgical scars decorated her right ear and temple, all that remained of the mutt Singer Iris had painstakingly disconnected. "But there is nothing for me to dream about. Whatever they did to me and Cos, it wiped our memories."

"Yeah, but ... "

"You remember everything, I know you do."

Ronja did not reply, because she was right. She remembered every second of her time at the lab. She could still feel The Lost Song pounding on the walls of her skull, the razor on her scalp as they cut away her hair, the violent touch of her warden between her thighs. Every time she closed her eyes she saw Cosmin sprawled on the tiles, Roark chained to the wall, his face blazing with panic and desperation. Her mother falling from the airship, a bullet in her brain.

Henry. His voice on the radio. *Maybe the stars are alive after all.*

"What can I do?" Georgie asked, a hint of a plea in her voice.

Ronja offered a tired smile. Her cousin was barely ten and was already twice as brave and ten times kinder than she would ever be. "Nothing. Get some sleep." She kissed her on the brow, then shoved off her quilts and got to her feet. Groaning, she reached her arms over her head, working the sleep from her muscles.

"Where are you going?" Georgie asked, flipping over onto her back.

"Running." Ronja caught her ankle in her hand, moaning again as her stiff tendons creaked. Sometimes, she felt like an old woman at nineteen.

"Again?"

"It clears my head."

"How can you circle the Belly for so long? I'd die of boredom."

Ronja grunted. "Yeah, well, if I don't get out of here soon I just might." She stooped to grab her training gear from the stack of clean clothes in the corner. She peeled off her damp nightshift and crammed it into the overflowing laundry bag.

"Oh," Georgie exclaimed, sitting up partway. Her short hair stuck out at all angles like a stack of hay. "Your meeting with Wilcox is tonight."

It was not question, but Ronja found herself nodding anyway. She shook out her leggings with a snap, then tugged them over her freckled legs.

"You nervous?"

"No." Ronja yanked her tunic over her head, the let her arms flop to her sides. "Resigned."

"He *has* to hear you out. He knows what they're saying about you."

Ronja snorted. "Yeah, sure." She dipped back into the laundry bag and pulled out her hooded sweater. It could survive one more run, she decided. Knotting it around her waist, she retrieved her laced boots from the opposite corner. Shoes were rarely worn in the Belly, but she had quickly discovered running barefoot on unforgiving stone was a bad idea.

"He can only punish you for so long," Georgie mused. "You were just trying to save us, not to mention you brought them Max—"

"Shhh!" Ronja whipped around, a finger flying to her mouth. Her cousin bit her lip, her eyes darting around anxiously. The older girl let her hand fall slowly. "You're not supposed to know about him."

"Who do you think is listening?" Georgie breathed.

Ronja shrugged noncommittally, then plopped down on the edge of the mattress. She crammed her boots onto her feet, keenly aware of the anxious gaze pinned to her back.

The truth was, she had no idea who, if anyone, might be listening. All she knew was that Commander Wilcox trusted her even less than he liked her. The last time they spoke directly was the night of their return from Red Bay. Her memories of that night were shrouded in fog, but there were things she did remember.

Abandoning the Westervelt Industries airship outside the city. The hum of an auto engine beneath her cheek. Roark carrying her on his back through the sewers, her head thumping against his shoulder as she wove in and out of consciousness. Terra leading Maxwell by his bound hands, a black bag over his head. The doors rolling open on the Belly, tears of relief pricking the corners of her eyes.

Then Wilcox was there, stalking toward them. All she wanted to do was go to sleep and never wake up, but the commander had other plans. Iris ferried Cosmin and Georgie off to remove their Singers. Terra led Maxwell to the holding cell. The rest of them were corralled into the debriefing room.

Evie and Roark told their story. Ito chimed in occasionally, her voice and countenance smooth as glass. Ronja struggled to keep her eyes open against the dizzying pain of her stinger burns. Her brain sloshed around inside her skull. Only a handful of words made it through her agony.

The Music. Victor. Tortured. Radio. Ronja. Henry. Sang. Freed.

From what her friends told her, Wilcox did not react immediately. For a moment, he simply sat before them, his expression vacant. Then he laughed. He did not believe them. Ronja understood his doubt. The idea of The Music being able to travel without the aid of Singers was insane enough, but a voice that could counteract it ... she was not entirely convinced it was possible herself. *Real* music was a mode of expression, not a weapon or a shield.

Still ...

No matter how many times she revisited the scene in her mind, she always arrived at the same conclusion. Her voice had in fact stopped The Music. She had seen it. The whip-like arms of The New Music twisting around them, her own song engulfing them like a black hole. She had no idea how music could be seen, and told no one of her visions. But in the end, it did not matter what she saw. What mattered was that her voice was a weapon, and Wilcox was keeping it locked in her throat.

Georgie spoke again, breaking Ronja from her contemplation. "He has to learn to trust you, you brought him so much information."

"Which he refuses to act on," she snapped.

Georgie shank back into her pillow, her expression tinged with hurt.

Ronja sighed, pinching the bridge of her nose between her thumb and forefinger. She felt a migraine budding, and if she did not run soon it would swallow her. "Sorry. Ito promised me ... "

"What?"

That I would be the weapon of the Anthem. That we would destroy The Conductor. That we would silence The Music. That I would have my revenge. That Henry and Layla did not die in vain.

"Ro?"

"Nothing." Ronja attempted to smile, but the result was closer to a grimace. "Go back to sleep. I love you."

"I love you, too."

Ronja turned and brushed aside the entry flap. The dimly lit Belly unfurled before her, still mired in sleep.

She was halfway outside when a tiny voice probed her eardrum. "You have to open up to someone, Ro."

She stepped outside, pretending not to hear.

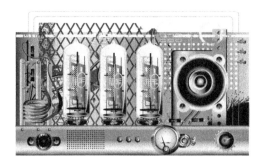

3: CIRCLE TALK

Ronja stood rigid outside her tent. The Belly was as still and cold as a headstone. Most of the blazing overhead lamps were off, only one in every cluster of six burned. When the cook fires were lit at 6:00 A.M., the air would flood with warmth and conversation. Not long ago, she would have welcomed the buzz. Now she reveled in its absence.

Rolling the kinks from her neck, she hopped up and down on the balls of her feet. She glanced left and right down the walkway. It was deserted, just as she had hoped. Keen not to waste another moment of solitude, she took off down the path at a steady clip. With each stride the noise in her brain shrank a decibel. Soon there was nothing but the sound of her heart, the rush of her breath, and the steady drum of her soles.

Ronja had started running two weeks after her return to the compound. She had never possessed the time or calories to do it before. Now, she had more time than she knew what to do with and three solid meals a day. Not to mention, it was the only thing that stopped her mind from ripping itself to shreds.

She reached the end of the station without breaking a sweat, then veered toward the tracks. Tents and huts of scrap metal and plywood whipped past, enveloping families in their shabby arms. Ronja had quickly grown to love the tent she shared with Georgie, despite the thin walls and periodic showers of petals. It was far more welcoming than their decrepit house aboveground. It was stuffed with careworn quilts, pillows, and stacks of unfinished novels. With any luck, Cosmin would join them soon. Ronja knew he would love their sanctuary.

At least, the old Cos would have.

Ronja felt her heart seize at the thought of her cousin. He was still in the hospital wing, a husk of his former self. He could barely speak through his heavy stutter. The left half of his body was numb, useless. Despite her tireless work, Iris remained unsure what exactly had been done to him, what warped forms of The Music he had been exposed to. "You need to be prepared for the possibility that he will not make a full recovery," Iris had told Ronja one night outside his hospital room. "Georgie is young enough that her brain is still quite plastic ... "

"What does that mean?"

"It means it is easier for it to form new connections around the damaged bits," Iris explained patiently, forming a mass the relative size of a human brain with her scrubbed fingers. "Cosmin is almost thirteen, which means many of his pathways are already set." She steepled her fingers before her pink lips. "He may have some very hard days ahead of him."

Ronja poured on more speed. She sprinted along the edge of the platform, pumping her arms as Evie had instructed her. Perspiration beaded on her skin, followed by the dull sting of her healing burns. Most of her stinger wounds had faded from red to white weeks ago, but they still pained her when she exerted herself. Strangely, the sting fueled her.

She was coming up on the western mouth of the subtrain tunnel, which was cloaked in a sheer yellow curtain. The women's bathhouse was just beyond. At this rate, she would need to pay it a visit soon.

A burst of motion hooked her gaze. Ronja skidded to a halt, her boots squeaking on the floor. Her bewilderment dissolved when she caught sight of the dark figure slipping out from behind the curtain. Her teeth gnashed together. She launched into a dead sprint. The boy hoisted himself up onto the platform with feline grace. Climbing to his feet, he raked his long hair from his face, exposing his razor jawline and high cheekbones.

He rounded on her thunder of footsteps, beaming. Ronja screeched to a stop in front of him. A bead of sweat rolled into her eye. "*Again*?" she panted, wiping it away angrily. "You went outside without me *again*?"

Roark considered her with a teasing smile. "Maybe I was just having a morning bath with the ladies."

Ronja punched him in the bicep a bit too hard to be merely playful. He laughed, which only fanned her flames. "I bet you could have found a weak spot in the rubble in *your* bathhouse," she grumbled, peeking over her shoulder to make sure they did not have an audience.

The Anthemite popped up his hands in defense. "Evie found it, not me. Not to mention Wilcox has to clean up, too. How would it look if he found me rooting around in the rocks?"

Ronja snorted. "You could always say you were looking for a bigger place to store your ego." Roark chuckled, a sound that made her heart fidget in her ribs. "You never answered my question," she probed. "You went out without me again?"

The boy sobered. "We both know it's way too dangerous out there for you right now," he replied, shrugging off his dripping overcoat and tucking it under his arm. His black sweater was damp. It hugged the planes of his chest and arms. Ronja fixated on his face pointedly.

"Oh, but not for you?"

"I grew up under the roof of the enemy, I know how to keep them off my trail. Besides, you may have noticed I have the most ears between the two of us."

Ronja barked a laugh. "And whose fault is that?"

Roark smiled, his brown eyes glinting. She knew if she leaned in she would see those unusual gold flecks in his irises. Her stomach cinched. She hoped the sensation did not register on her face. "So," she changed the subject, dropping her voice to a whisper. "Did you get it?"

The boy winked.

Excitement flared in her chest. She took an involuntary half step forward. "Can I see?"

Roark glanced around, then reached down and took her hand, turning her palm to the ceiling. She swallowed, her mouth abruptly dry. His fingertips were smooth and cool as pebbles, so different from her own. He placed something the size of a coin in her hand. She squinted at it doubtfully. "This is the last piece?" she asked, knowing the answer. It was so simple, just like their plan. Was it wise to put so much faith in something so small?

"Yes," Roark answered. "Once we plug it in, it should work."

"If Evie is right."

"When is she not?"

"Good point." Ronja closed her fingers around the device. She looked up at Roark, scanning his features for a trace of doubt. He was so confident, but she knew it was all for show. She had seen him at his lowest point. He had held her at her worst. There was no use pretending they were not terrified, both of what had passed and what loomed on the horizon. There was no going back to the way things were. So why were they acting like there was?

"What happens when Wilcox says no?" she asked.

"He'll say yes, he has to."

"But ... "

"Have a little faith, love."

Ronja rolled her eyes, then offered him the capacitor. He took it and stashed it in his pocket. "Running again?" he inquired. Without waiting for her response, he began to walk, giving a little jerk of his head to indicate she should follow.

"Yeah," she replied, falling into step beside him. Despite her long legs, she practically had to jog to keep up with him. "Nothing better to do."

"That will change soon," he soothed. "For both of us."

"It better," she mumbled.

Roark chuckled. They fell into an easy silence. Silence was something they were quite good at, these days. Ronja had spent the first two weeks in the hospital wing after their return from Red Bay, recovering from her wounds. As if her burns were not enough, she had also suffered a ruptured eardrum, extensive bruising on her arms and legs, and a concussion.

And those were just her physical injuries.

During her recovery, Roark rarely left her side. He slept in the armchair near the head of her bed, only leaving to eat and relieve himself. Ronja was often too exhausted to do much talking, so he learned to read her. He knew when she was in pain, when she was thirsty, when she needed space and when she needed company. Most importantly, he was there to wake her when her nightmares took hold.

Sometimes, when she woke from her dreams in her tent, she found herself wishing he was there to hold her. He would brush her sweaty hair from her forehead ...

"Ro?"

Ronja crashed back into her body, realizing she had been staring into oblivion. Roark was watching her, concerned. "Sorry," she said. "Long night." She scanned the landscape of quiet tents and empty pathways for any eavesdroppers, then spoke in a low tone. "Anything new on Maxwell?"

Wilcox was adamant that the chemi should not be kept in the Belly. It was one of the few points he and Ronja agreed on. Maxwell had been moved to a safe house in the middle ring where he was kept under constant surveillance. Roark sighed, pushing out his frustration with his breath. "Same as always. He eats his meals, sleeps nine hours a night, talks to himself in ... whatever the hell language that is."

"You asked Evie about it, right?"

"Yeah." He scratched the back of his head as he did when his thoughts were whirring. "Samson had her listen and she said it sounded nothing like Arexian."

"How the hell did he learn to speak another language with a Singer?" Ronja wondered aloud. Revinia was not a multilingual society. Everyone under The Music was programmed to speak only the common language. "To prevent confusion and to create unity," The Conductor had explained during one of his rare speeches broadcast into their Singers. Maxwell was equipped with a standard Singer. His ability to speak a foreign language should have been impossible.

"I have no idea," Roark replied.

"Maybe his works differently," she mused.

"None of this makes any sense," he whispered. "Why the hell would the son of Atticus Bullon have a Singer? If I got to grow up without one ... " He trailed off, shaking his head at the stone floor. "We're missing something."

"I know."

"What do you think?"

Ronja peered around at the tents, shooting Roark a meaningful look. He nodded, then slipped his hand into hers, tugging her forward. Warmth blossomed between them, yet somehow it made her shiver. He led her past the final row of huts before the terminus of the main room, then veered off into the low-ceilinged hallway that housed his tent and several others. The secluded corridor was reserved for elevated members of the Anthem, people like Ito and members of the council. Roark was no longer their prized double agent, but she doubted he would be giving up his spacious quarters any time soon.

"After you," he said, sweeping aside the entrance flap with a flourish. Ronja ducked through. Entering his tent was always a bit of a shock. If there was one thing he had maintained from his old life, it was his taste for opulence. Scores of leather-bound books with cracked spines dominated the space. A hammock with a downy comforter and numerous pillows hung from the ceiling rod, swaying gently. A turntable and a sizable stack of vinyl records sat on the patterned rug nearby. Ronja knew if she peeled back the carpet it would reveal the hatch they once escaped through, now sealed with concrete.

"Please," Roark said, gesturing at the low stool near the hammock. Ronja sat heavily, her tired legs sighing with relief. She looked on as he knelt by the turntable. Grabbing a record off the top of the stack, an album labeled *Symphony VI* in curling white calligraphy, he slipped it from its sleeve and set it on the player.

Ronja allowed her eyelids to flicker shut. Static filled the air as the obsidian disk began to revolve. The symphony expanded gradually, trickling in on the mellow notes of a cello. She knew parting her lids would reveal a room full of writhing colors and shapes.

The day she sang at Red Bay and witnessed her voice battling The New Music was not an anomaly. Since then, any type of music drew vibrant colors out of thin air. Drumbeats were cloudbursts of red and white. Piano keys traced rivers of red and deep blue. The cello and the violin spun threads of evergreen and gold and sometimes violet. She had not told anyone about the visions, not even Roark. He and the others were already worried about her enough as it was.

"So?" Ronja opened her eyes. Her breath hitched.

Roark was enveloped in ribbons of gold. They seemed to fuse with his skin and hair, shivering with the rise and fall of the symphony. "Uh ... Ronja?" Warm light spilled from his mouth.

"Could you ... turn it down a bit?" she asked distantly. She raised a hand to her temple, which had started to throb. No matter where she looked, the wavering colors followed. They rode on the waves of the symphony. They might have been beautiful if they did not terrify her.

"It's on three. I was hoping to cover our conversation."

"Please?" Sensing her desperation, Roark clicked the dial on the player. The symphony receded. The gold ribbons lost their effervescence, fading until they were nearly translucent. Ronja blinked rapidly. Fear loosened its grip on her throat.

"Are you all right, love?"

She looked up at Roark, her mouth pressed into a thin line. He watched her in return, his dark eyes shifting as he searched for answers on her face. *Of course not.* "Yes."

"Good."

She shook her head to clear it. "What was the question?"

Roark leaned back on his hands, a tendril of black hair escaping its tie and dripping into his face. The coin he wore on a cord around his neck caught the low light, glimmering faintly as he drew breath. "Do you believe Maxwell is the son of The Conductor?"

Ronja sighed, her shoulders sagging under the question. It was not the first time he had asked her this. He knew her answer. They circled back to the enigma once or twice a week. "He could be," she said. The words were almost a mantra to her now. "Why would he lie about something like that?"

"Atticus Bullon never had any children with his wife, at least that he made public," Roark pointed out at once. It was always his first stop on their cyclical argument. "Why would he hide Maxwell? Why put a Singer on him?"

"Well, Maxwell did say he was a bastard."

Roark glowered at the rotating record, his brow knit with frustration. "The Conductor would never need to hide an illegitimate child. Any judgment cast on him would be suppressed with The Music."

Ronja rested her elbows on her knees, cradling her chin in her hands. Her eyelids drooped. "He ... " She cut herself off with a yawn. Through her lashes, she saw Roark crack a lopsided smile. "He could be telling the truth, could be lying to save his own skin. Or ... "

The boy raised his eyebrows. It was not often they diverged from the familiar pattern of the conversation. Perhaps it was the aftertaste of her nightmare, but this morning she felt the pull of another possibility, one they had not yet discussed. "Maybe Terra made it all up. No one actually heard her interrogate Maxwell."

Roark leaned forward, observing her acutely. "What would she have to gain from a story like that?"

Ronja snorted. "Who knows, why would she tell Wilcox I was a mutt and let us walk into Red Bay without backup? Don't ask me to get inside that twisted mind."

A piano had joined the cello on the record. It sounded like rain on a slow river, far too gentle for her harsh tongue. It left faint red and blue impressions on her vision. She fixated on Roark through their strange beauty.

"I know you hate Terra for what she did," he finally said, holding her steady with his gaze. "But if anyone is lying here, I think it's Maxwell."

Ronja shifted in her seat, crossing and uncrossing her legs. She did not enjoy disagreeing with the boy, but it was bound to happen occasionally. "You don't think it is even a possibility?"

"I think," he replied tactfully. "She is a scheming piece of crap, but in the end, she wants what is best for the Anthem. Making up a story about the bastard son of The Conductor would be a waste of time and resources."

"So was Red Bay," Ronja said in a low voice. "We lost a bit more than time there, Roark." The boy opened his mouth to retort, then seemed to think better of it. Instead, he flopped back onto the lush rug, heaving a sigh that could drown the world.

"Yeah," he finally allowed. "Yeah we did." The comfortable room grew colder in the wake of his words. Ronja found herself shivering beneath her layer of dried sweat. She was seized by the urge to reach behind her and grab the thick comforter from the hammock.

"I should go," she said, shooting to her feet. White lights that had nothing to do with the quiet symphony popped in her gaze. "I should ... "

"You should go back to sleep."

Ronja scowled down at Roark. He was watching her with those damned brown eyes, his strong arms folded beneath his head, his long hair still damp with rain. "I need a bath," she stated with a bit too much conviction.

He grinned, propping himself up on his elbows. "Of course, I would love to." She gave him a solid kick in the side as she stepped over him. He coughed, clutching at his ribs melodramatically. Scoffing, Ronja continued to the exit without breaking her stride.

"Ronja." Her name on his lips gave her pause. She kept her back to him, waiting for him to spit out the words he was obviously chewing on. "If you ever want to talk about ... "

"See you at breakfast, shiny."

Ronja did not wait for his response, but ducked through the door and practically ran down the hallway.

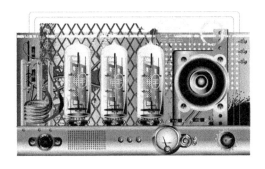

4: FUSE

Though Ronja was not particularly sweaty anymore, she thought perhaps a bath would soothe her nerves. She retraced her steps to the edge of the platform and descended to the subtrain tracks. Ambling toward the women's bathhouse, her mind bobbed like a balloon.

If there was one thing she had learned about herself since being severed from her Singer, it was that she was an open book. No matter how she tried to snuff her emotions, they always crept into her expression. That did not mean, however, that she wanted to discuss them. She knew Roark and the others were just trying to help, but she was tired of being treated like a broken bird.

Ronja brushed aside the yellow curtain and was engulfed by the aromatic, waterlogged air of the bathhouse. The low tunnel was lit by candles and strings of lanterns. A large wood and stone pool stood near the entrance. Beyond that was a line of toilet stalls and further still were the parlor and library. There were no shelves, only stacks of hoarded books that had escaped the burnings decades ago. They stood like paper cairns, just waiting to be read.

The best part was that it was deserted before six in the morning.

Ronja plodded up the steps to the edge of the bath, then stripped down to her underwear. A shiver scampered along her spine when she caught sight of herself. She was no longer rail thin, but lean and strong. Exercise and a steady diet had allowed her to develop muscles and a healthy layer of fat in places Iris was envious of. Those more gradual changes she was pleased with. It was the brutal alterations from her night at Red Bay that unnerved her.

The various scars she had collected over the years were now accompanied by six discoid stinger burns scattered across her torso. Five of them had faded to white, but the one over her heart was still a blistering sun compared to the pale moons. She could not be tattooed with the symbol of the Anthem until it was fully healed. Unfortunately, the self-inflicted wound was almost as stubborn as she was.

Ronja tested the water with her toe. It was perfect, thanks to Evie. The techi had rigged the vents from the nearest functioning subtrain station to pump steam into the water. Glancing around to check that she truly was alone, she pinched her nose and plunged into the bath. A geyser of air bubbles rushed up from below as her feet struck the smooth bottom. Her stiff muscles began to unfurl, softened by the heat. Slowly, she allowed her eyelids to part.

It was almost pitch black below the surface, save for the somehow distant glow of the candles and lanterns. They wavered as the water roiled in the wake of her plunging body. Ronja raked her fingers through her cropped hair. Her thumb nicked the scar marking the spot where her ear and Singer once were. It was no longer painful, but the empty space still felt strange.

Sing my friend,
There and back

Ronja broke the seal, wiping the sting from her eyes. Her chest rose and fell like a hummingbird in distress. She massaged her temples briskly, working the lyrics from her brain. They seemed to sneak up on her when she least expected it. The back of her neck prickled. Heart in her throat, she whirled.

"Terra."

The name escaped her lips before she could bite it back. Terra stood with her back to the pool, halfway down the steps. Ronja kicked herself internally for interrupting the apparent retreat. She would have preferred The Conductor himself to the vicious, arrogant Anthemite.

It was too late. Terra was already making her way back to the platform. Her skin was stained with sweat and filth. A pair of night vision goggles rested on her brow. Half her head was freshly shaven, the other side was heavy with stiff, blonde hair wound into a dozen braids. The whites of her eyes were laced with red.

"Zipse," Terra greeted her tonelessly. Every inch of her radiated reluctance. She looked like she would rather be scrubbing toilets than talking to her. Ronja could relate. "What are you doing here?"

"Guess," Ronja replied tartly.

"Why are you here so early?"

"Avoiding the masses, like you."

Terra swallowed, her throat rippling in the soft light. Her fingers twitched toward the hilt of her nearest blade. Ronja took a half step back, the water parting across her spine. Then the blonde sighed and let her hands fall limp at her sides. "I need a bath; you can stay or go."

Ronja made a noise too harsh and brittle to be a laugh. "You expect me to get out and leave?"

Terra shrugged, slipping out of her overcoat. It hit the steps behind her with a crunch of dried sewage. "Up to you," she replied, bending down to unbuckle the harness that held her knives.

Ronja bared her teeth. Her fingers rolled into fists below the waterline. Rage boiled in her stomach, bubbling up into her mouth. "You sure about that?" she asked tightly. "You might catch some awful mutt disease."

Terra went rigid. She looked up slowly, a snarl distorting her apathetic mask. Ronja matched her expression. She had barely spoken to the agent since her confession aboard the Westervelt Industries airship, mostly because she knew she would not be able to curb her fury.

"Enjoying your time in the sewers?" Ronja asked with a mocking tilt of her head. "I would guess so, a rat ought to be with its kind."

Terra straightened up, leaving her weapons half-hitched to her body. She shook her head. "I am not here to fight you, as much as I would love to see you try." Ronja opened her mouth to retort, but her fellow Anthemite was not finished. "We could pass around the blame forever. You, me, Evie, Trip, Iris, Ito, Wilcox, Henry."

Ronja flinched, the final name like a knife between her ribs.

"Yeah," Terra pressed, taking a reckless step forward. The tips of her boots jutted over the edge of the platform. "I skitzed up. I lied. But guess what?" Her eyes narrowed to slits. "Trip is the one who broke. Iris and Evie enabled him. You are the one who risked the lives of everyone in this compound to save two and half people who were most likely fried. And Henry, he was there for you."

"You pitching piece of ... "

"We are at war, Zipse!" Terra roared, spit flying from her lips. "The sooner you get over your grudge the sooner we can work together and strike!"

Ronja lunged and snatched her by the ankles. Terra swore, shaking one of her legs free and nailing her in the chin. Rust exploded in Ronja's mouth, fueling her rage. With a savage cry she yanked with all her strength. Terra went down, her back slamming into the platform before she was dragged into the pool. They went under, lashing out blindly with fists and knees. Two months ago, Ronja would have been no match for the highly trained agent, but she was no longer the malnourished mutt Roark had met on the subtrain tracks.

She had killed. She had lost. She had been tortured. She had freed minds from The Music with nothing but her voice. She had died.

Two hands snaked under her arms and plucked Ronja from the bath, shouting and writhing. They hauled her onto the platform, her bare back scraping against the rough wood. "Stop!" Evie shouted as she pulled. Ronja registered the command, but it was only white noise. Terra stood waist deep in the water, sporting a ballooning eye and a nasty scratch on her cheek. She was winded and doing everything she could to hide it.

Satisfaction ripped through Ronja. "You better watch your back you pitcher!" she bellowed. "I swear ... " Evie's callused hand clamped over Ronja's mouth. She twisted to free herself. "If you ever come near my family I swear I'll kill you!"

A burst of red and white flooded her vision as a slap exploded across her cheek. Ronja stilled, her sparking brain doused. She looked up. A familiar form loomed above her, scarcely one hundred pounds with a head full of short red curls. "That is quite enough!" Iris shrieked.

Ronja scowled up at her mutely, pressing her hand to her burning face. She leaned around Iris in search of her opponent, straining against Evie's hold. Terra had already hoisted herself up onto the deck on the opposite side of the bath. She stood with her weapons in her hands, bristling like a wet dog. Iris stepped in front of Ronja, her hands on her slight hips. "You're better than this."

"Says who? Evie, let me go!"

The techi muttered something foul under her breath, then released her. Ronja clambered to her feet, wiping her mouth with the back of her wrist. She spat out the wad of blood in her mouth. It landed in the water with a sickening plop. Her eyes never left Terra, who still held her blades at the ready.

"Really," Iris huffed, stepping around Ronja to help Evie up.

"Terra, get out of here," the techi said when she was on her feet. "Go see Harrow for your cheek."

"Please," Terra scoffed, hopping down to the tracks and landing without a sound. She moved with grace that was difficult to ignore. Even her loose harness failed to rattle as she strode toward the exit. "You know where to find me when you need me," she called over her shoulder. "Might want to get your hands checked, singer."

Ronja glanced down. Her stomach bottomed out. Her knuckles were cross-stitched with red welts. They were swollen and bulbous, like smashed plums. Pain came flooding in as she registered the wounds, and she let out a squeak of shock.

"Oh shut up, you deserve it," Iris snipped. She grabbed Ronja by the elbow and dragged her down the steps, trailing blood and bathwater. Evie followed, not even attempting to smother her laughter. "Lucky for you we keep a first aid kit back here," Iris continued as she led her toward the parlor. "Why did you have to start a fight today, of all days?"

"Terra started it," Ronja grumbled as they came upon the first of several vanities. The redhead rounded on her, grabbing her by the shoulders and sitting her on the upturned crate that served as a chair. Evie sidled up behind them. She was carrying the clothes and boots Ronja had left behind. Tossing the bundle onto the floor, the techi hopped up onto the dresser, the waterlogged wood groaning.

"Oh, sure," Iris replied icily. She spun around and squatted before the vanity cabinet. Opening it, she began to paw through the stash of junk inside. "Terra just decided to jump into the water with her radio, knives, and gun. That makes perfect sense."

Evie chuckled from her perch. Ronja shot her a withering look. The surgeon saw right through her, as usual. There was not a person above or below ground who could lie to Iris and get away with it. Shame took root in her. She dropped her eyes to her wounded hands, which were still tucked into fists. The cuts on her knuckles were already beginning to clot.

"Ah," Iris exclaimed triumphantly. She yanked a white box marked with a red cross from the depths of the cupboard and set it on the floor. She turned back to Ronja and took her hands. "Easy," she soothed as the girl sucked in a breath of shock. "I think you might have fractured a knuckle."

"Worth it."

"Was it?" Evie asked. Ronja ignored her, keeping her jaw locked as the surgeon smoothed her fingers onto her legs, then retrieved the bottle of alcohol from the kit.

"This is going to sting," Iris warned as she unscrewed the lid. Her patient grimaced as the sharp odor of antiseptic pricked her nostrils. "On three. One, two ... "

Ronja opened her mouth in a silent scream.

"Easy, easy."

She took a series of deep shuddering breaths. The pain began to dissipate.

"There you go."

Silence fell as the surgeon began to bind her injured digits with clean strips of cloth. Ronja watched the process with a distant sort of fascination. She had always thought if things had been different, she might have liked to be a doctor or a nurse. That idea was about as distant now as it was when she was a mutt.

"What the hell were you thinking?"

Ronja glanced up at Evie. The techi watched her with an inscrutable expression. The glow of the candles drew out the bluish half-moons under her eyes.

"She deserved it," Ronja growled.

"So?" The techi shook her head, her raven hair flickering against her jaw. "Wilcox is just looking for a reason to throw you out, and we need you."

"Do you? Last time I checked, you and Roark were the ones running around topside while I was stuck down here."

"Your time is coming. I know you want to fight, but right now you gotta be patient."

"I am sick of being patient!" Iris gave her bandages a particularly firm tug. Ronja pretended not to feel it. "They're getting closer to perfecting The New Music every day. If we wait much longer, we're going to be too late."

Evie leaned forward, resting her elbows on her muscular thighs. "We make one mistake ... " She held up an ornately tattooed finger. "We'll be caught, and this time they're not going to throw us in prison, they're going to kill us. We have to execute this perfectly, understand?"

Ronja felt a blush creep into her hairline. She felt like a child being scolded for throwing a public tantrum. She gave a brisk nod to show she understood. The techi copied her, then began to hunt for a cigarette on her person. Iris snapped her fingers without looking up from her task. Evie stilled reluctantly.

As Iris continued to bandage her hands, Ronja allowed her mind to wander. Her eyes drifted up to meet their twins in the cloudy looking glass.

It was not just her body that had changed over the past months. Her face had also undergone a dramatic shift. The wardens had shaved her head at Red Bay but her dark curls were returning with remarkable speed. They already reached her temples. Her remaining ear was pierced several times, something she might not have agreed to if Evie and Iris had not forced one too many shots of whiskey down her throat. Her eyes, green shot with gray, were now the eyes of someone who had lost, who knew they might lose again.

"That should do it," Iris finally said. Ronja blinked rapidly to disperse her thoughts.

"Thanks," she said, glancing down at the pristine white wrappings. She laughed softly. The surgeon shot her a questioning look. "This feels familiar," she explained.

Iris gave a tight smile. "If you would just stop grabbing live stingers and getting in fights I could stop turning you into a mummy."

"What should I say, if anyone asks what happened?"

"Just tell them you burned them cooking, or something. No one will believe it, but there were no witnesses."

"Except Terra," Ronja pointed out.

"She'll keep her mouth shut if she knows what's good for her," Evie said. She sprang off the vanity and crammed her hands into the pockets of her cargo pants. "The only person Wilcox wants gone more than you is her."

Ronja itched the bridge of her nose anxiously, ignoring the dull agony that flared in her joints. "I guess."

"Imagine," Iris quipped. "If you could just get a handle on your anger issues, we wouldn't have to come up with a terrible cover story in the first place."

"Imagine, if you could mind your own business."

As soon as the words hit the air, Ronja wished she could retract them. Iris pinched her mouth into a thin line, her eyes unusually bright, and whirled to repack the first aid kit.

Evie reached out and punched Ronja in the bicep. Hard.

"Sorry, Iris," Ronja mumbled. The techi struck her again in the exact same spot. Clutching her now throbbing arm, she pressed on earnestly. "Sorry you had to patch me up again, but thanks for doing it."

Iris slammed the lid on the box. "Mmm."

"Really," Ronja continued, giving her bony shoulder a squeeze. Her knuckles screamed, but she ignored them. "Thanks. I don't know what we would do without you."

Those final words seemed to pacify both Iris and Evie. The surgeon stood up and turned back around, her tranquil mask securely in place. "Bleed out, most likely. Anyway, it's my pleasure. Sorry I slapped you."

Ronja cracked a wry half smile. "I deserved it."

"We gotta go," Evie cut in. "Our turn to collect the morning rations, right?"

Iris beamed, her hazel eyes gleaming. "You remembered," she exclaimed appreciatively.

"Damn right," the techi answered, hooking the redhead to her side. "If we hurry, I was thinking we could ..." She pressed her lips to Iris's ear, lowering her voice to a whisper. Iris blushed brighter than her hair, and Ronja examined her bandaged hands with renewed interest.

"I guess we better be going," Iris said breathlessly, rubbing her cheeks as if she could scrub away the color. "See you at breakfast, Ro. Keep out of trouble until tonight, please."

Ronja waved them off. The couple hurried away. She was left alone with her reflection, which seemed to watch her even when she turned away.

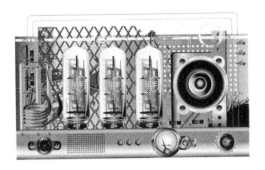

5: LEGEND

Ronja stood on the lip of the platform, watching the Anthemites shuffle by in sleepy packs. To the untrained eye they would have appeared to be wandering aimlessly, but she knew better.

There were fifty cook fires scattered throughout the Belly, each manned by a collection of mismatched chairs and stools. Families and friends chose a fire and stuck to it. Roark, Evie, Iris and their large group of friends took their meals at a circle on the north side of the station. The trio insisted Ronja and her cousins were always welcome. She had yet to decide if that was true in the eyes of their friends.

Ronja guessed she had a solid forty minutes before she had to be at the fire. Breakfast was supposed to begin at 7:00, but the ration line moved at a snail's pace. It was likely that Iris and Evie would be late as it was. She toyed with the idea of going early and waiting for the rest of the crew to show up, but that meant more socializing. If she retreated to her tent, Georgie would doubtlessly wake up and have a meltdown over her hands. The same went for Roark. There was only one chance for peace.

Ronja threw her hood over her damp curls and plunged into

the fray. She moved quickly, the patter of her footfalls drowned out by the babel.

... look at her hands ...

... Ronja

The girl winced as the whispers nicked her ear. Of course, her bandages would draw attention. She tucked her hands into her pockets, but it was too late. Word of her presence was spreading like a plague.

... savior ...

... selfish ...

... how she did it ...

Ronja gritted her teeth and sped up. The words were not cruel, but they were laced with an unsettling combination of awe and distrust.

The incomplete account of the events of Red Bay dredged up mixed reactions from the revolutionaries. Some called her a threat. They saw her only as the selfish girl who chose the lives of the few over the lives of the many. Others labeled her a hero, someone willing to do more than any Anthemite had done in decades. A scattered few did not care if she was brave or stupid, but saw her as some sort of messiah. The mystique only grew as she had not opened her mouth to sing since that fateful day. How word of her voice had gotten out, she did not know.

... counteracts The Music ...

... sounds just like it ...

... human ...

Sometimes she wanted to scream at them all, though most treated her with more respect than she had known in nineteen years. Virtually no one in the Belly knew she had spent most of her life under the influence of a mutt Singer, a fact that would severely damage her reputation were it to come to light. Mutts were not allowed in the Anthem. They were too twisted, mentally and physically, to be brought back from the edge. Mutts were to be pitied, not trusted. When she joined the Anthem, Ronja was not just looking to fight, but to escape the aching loneliness inherent in her status.

You got what you wanted, she reminded herself bitterly. She was no longer an outcast; she was a legend. She was starting to wonder if there was really a difference.

Ronja darted down a narrow aisle between two huts, stepping over stacks of plywood and boxes too large to be kept inside the tiny homes. As she reemerged onto one of the central walkways, a pack of children shot across her path, immune to grogginess. They were young, no more than six or seven. Most had never known the touch of The Music. She wished she could say the same for Cosmin and Georgie.

What would they be like if they never knoned The Music? Ronja wondered as she came upon her destination. Her cousins were children only in body. Their minds were laden with pain and suffering beyond their years.

Her heart was heavy as she approached the red drapes that encompassed the hospital wing. The hangings rippled sluggishly as Anthemites breezed past. Beyond the cloth walls were six quaint rooms shrouded in inexplicable tranquility. One of them had been hers, not so long ago. The thought was jarring. It felt like years ago that she had woken up in the Belly fearing not The Conductor, but the strange boy who had knocked her out and dragged her into the unknown.

Taking down her hood, Ronja padded to the room on the far left and peeked through the drapes.

It was pleasantly cool and dark inside. The only light came from the muted flame of an oil lamp perched on the bedside table. The glow tumbled across the sleeping form on the cot. "Cosmin," Ronja whispered. She stepped inside, allowing the curtain to sweep shut behind her. The form in the bed stirred. "Cos, you awake?"

"I—I am now," came a thick voice.

"Can I stay for a bit?"

Cosmin did not reply, but raised his right arm and stuck up his thumb. Ronja sighed in gratitude and crossed to the worn, upholstered armchair at the bedside. She plopped down and curled her legs to her chest, resting her chin on her knees. She looked down at the boy through heavy-lidded eyes.

Over the past months, her younger cousin had changed as much as she had, perhaps even more. His ear was free of its cage. His wild black curls, shaved during his imprisonment, were returning as quickly as her own. His eyes were still a sharp shade of blue, but the spark they once contained had faded to a tired ember. "W—what the skit—z happened to y—your hands?" Cosmin asked, propping himself up on his elbow.

Ronja groaned. "I was hoping you wouldn't ask."

"Why?"

"Common courtesy?"

"F—fine but you gotta tell me la—ater. Could use a go—od story." Ronja gave him a shove. He smiled, lifting only one side of his mouth. "Hiding f—from Georgie?"

"Yeah."

"Why—y are you up so ear—ly?"

"Maybe I just wanted to talk to my baby cousin."

Cosmin laughed. The sound was unhindered, fluid. "N—not the best con—versation partner. Tr—y the lamp."

Ronja forced a smile. She would never let him see it, but his disjointed speech still cut her deep. He was showing signs of progress; a month ago he could not say a word without breaking it in half. He could now wiggle his left fingers and toes, but recovery was still a long way off. Cosmin put up a good front. For his benefit, she pretended she did not see through it, just as he pretended not to see through hers. They had made a silent pact not to dance around each other like wet sticks of dynamite as everyone else did. "You h—ave your meeting l—ater," he noted.

Ronja lifted a hand. "Can we not talk about that?" she asked, exhaustion bleeding into her tone. The boy nodded, just a quick bob of his head. She thanked him similarly and leaned back into the padded armchair. "Have you seen Charlotte lately?"

Cosmin blushed scarlet and looked down, picking at a loose thread on his white sheets. "Iris is train—ing her to be the n—ext Singer surgeon. S—he comes to spee—ch therapy sometimes."

"Has she mentioned me at all?" Ronja asked, gesturing toward herself halfheartedly. The boy gave a pitying shake of his head. His cousin heaved a sigh and sank deeper into her chair. "Henry asked me to watch out for her, I promised him I would."

Cosmin frowned, his thick eyebrows scrunching. "She—" he began, then huffed and flicked a finger at the notebook and pen sitting on the table.

"Iris says you need to work on your speech," she replied. Cosmin groaned, rolled his eyes, then pointed again. She caved and tossed the items onto his bed. The boy struggled into an upright position, then flipped to a blank page and began to scribble furiously. He was lucky he was right handed. After a few beats, he held up the results for her to see.

She can take care of herself.

"I know," Ronja replied glumly. "I just wish she would let me check up on her now and then." Cosmin gave a rueful smile, then put pen to paper again.

She needs time.

"I know," she sighed, casting her eyes to her knees. Her vision glazed like breath clouding on a mirror. "She blames me for what happened." To her surprise, Cosmin shook his head fervently. He scratched out another message.

You remind her of him.

Ronja felt her throat constrict. How could she possibly remind Charlotte of her brother? He was so selfless, so honest, so good.

Cosmin set his tools aside, observing her keenly. Ronja felt the pull of sleep. Her chin sagged toward her chest. "Do you mind if I close my eyes for a bit?" she asked. The boy nodded. "Get me up in a half hour, would you?" He inclined his head again, then reached out and gave her an awkward pat on the knee. Ronja snorted and returned the gesture. She curled up like a cat in the chair, using the underside of her arm as a pillow. Her eyelids drifted shut as a comfortable fog rolled over her brain.

She dreamed of running through a yawning black tunnel, chasing a sliver of sunlight that knifed through the black. When she finally caught the rays, she cupped them in her hands. They scorched her.

Ronja woke to a pinprick of pain on her knee. She slammed her hand down without cracking her lids, capturing Cosmin by the wrist before he could yank back his pinching fingers. She opened her eyes, blinking sleepily.

"What time is it?" she asked, stretching her arms over her head. Cosmin held up five fingers, then flashed one more on the same hand.

"Pitch," Ronja cursed, scrambling to her feet. "I have to get to breakfast."

"Why?"

"Everyone has to go. We have to be well fed to sit on our asses all day." Cosmin snatched up his notebook, which he had replaced on the nightstand. He wrote out a message while Ronja waited, fidgeting as the seconds whipped by. The boy tossed her the pad. She managed to snag it by the tips of her fingers.

Why eat with people you don't even like?

Ronja shot her cousin an irritated look over the lip of the notebook. "What are you talking about? Roark, Iris, and Evie are my friends."

Cosmin shook his head and curled his fingers at her. She returned the notebook to him, watching mutely as he wrote out another message. This one he held up for her to see.

I mean their friends. You get a weird look when you talk about them.

"What look?" she demanded, slapping the book against her thigh. Cosmin narrowed his eyes and pursed his lips until they were turned white. "Oh, come on," Ronja scoffed. "I do not. Anyway, I like them plenty."

It was not a lie.

The family Roark had fashioned himself was everything she had ever wanted. They were funny, protective, and above all loved each other fiercely. Most were Anthemites by birth, but a few had found their way to the resistance in their teenage years. They were good company, but handled Ronja with a sort of caution typically reserved for wild animals. She did not blame them. For all they knew, she was the reason Henry was dead.

Maybe you are.

Ronja whipped around and grabbed the drapes. As quickly as she had moved she stilled, her clawed fingers digging into the fabric. "Ro?" Cosmin asked from behind her. "You go—od?"

Ronja blinked. Her stiff fingers relaxed "Yeah," she replied, hiking her dejected voice up like a trailing skirt. "I'll be back around lunch. Want me to bring you any more books?"

"No, Trip brou—ght me some."

"Roark did?"

"He brou—ght me some of his fa—vorites. *The Black Ca—stle* is best so f—ar."

"Huh." A smile built on her grim lips. "Not bad for a shiny." Before Cosmin could reply, Ronja bid him goodbye and slipped from the hospital room.

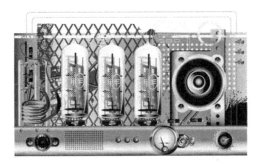

6: BLINDED

The wave of noise that enveloped Ronja each time she left the hospital wing never failed to surprise her. Somehow, the curtains capped the din. The babel was easier to block out than The Music, but she still preferred the quiet. Sighing, the Anthemite lifted her hood and plunged into the throng.

It was a short walk to the cook fire, which was not far from the powder blue tent Iris and Evie called home. She often dropped by before breakfast so they could walk over together, but figured her presence would not be welcome this particular morning.

The fire was situated in a clearing of tents below one of the powerful vents that ferried smoke from the Belly. The atmosphere around the flames was crisp, the closest thing Ronja had felt to fresh air in months. Musical instruments, books, and bottles of alcohol mingled with the small army of chairs that ringed the blaze. How the group continued to get their hands on some of the finest wines Revinia had to offer, she did not know. She was certainly not complaining.

When Ronja arrived, only Samson was there. He sat hunched on his red stool, stoking the embers of a previous blaze. At twenty-four, he was the oldest of their crew. His jaw was square, his blue eyes laughing. He was also, Ronja had not failed to notice, ruggedly handsome. Two years ago Wilcox appointed him captain of the stationary guard, and for good reason. He was level headed and skilled; the Anthemites could rest easy under his watch.

"Morning, Sam," Ronja called as she approached. The man looked up and smiled as she sank into a wooden chair near his. She left a space between them, though she knew he would not have begrudged her sitting directly beside him.

"Morning," he greeted her genially. His grin faltered when he caught sight of her bandages.

"Took a bad fall," she explained before he could ask.

"Into a rabid dog?"

Ronja flushed.

The captain set aside the iron fire poker and leaned toward her. "I saw Terra storm into her tent — you the one who gave her that black eye?"

"Black eye?" she asked, a thread of dark satisfaction in her tone.

Samson's lips twisted into a wry smile. "I would tell you it was a stupid move, but looks like Iris already got to you."

"Why does everyone think I started it?"

The captain guffawed, drawing curious glances from a couple passing by. Ronja shot him a warning look, which he elected to ignore. "Anyway," he said. "I really should punish you for infighting, but it looks like you two already paid your price, so I'll let it slide."

"Thanks," Ronja replied earnestly.

Samson nodded, then dug into his pocket and produced a lighter. He clicked it to life, leaned down, and pressed the shivering flame to the kindling.

"What was it about, anyway?" he asked.

"What?"

Samson returned the lighter to his pocket and straightened up. "Why were you and Terra fighting?"

"Oh." Ronja fidgeted in her seat, itched her nose. "Long story." The answer obviously did not satisfy the captain, but he did not press her. Gratitude spread through the girl. Samson was one of the only Anthemites who did not treat conversations with her as interrogations.

"I see you running in the mornings."

Ronja started, her eyebrows jerking up her forehead. "What?"

Samson reddened, the color traveling down his face and into his neck. "Ah," he stuttered, taking the poker back in hand and jabbing at the logs with fervor. "Not that I was watching, I just get up for my shift around the same time, so I see you sometimes. I mean ... "

The girl threw up a bandaged hand, swallowing her laughter. "I get it. What about it?"

"You look strong." He gazed at her sidelong, his bright eyes pinning her in place. She felt her mouth go dry. "But I could teach you how to punch someone without hurting your hands."

"Umm ... yeah. Sure." Something long dormant in her chest unfurled, shaking off a layer of dust.

"What the hell happened to you?"

Samson and Ronja twisted around in unison. Kala Pent and three other members of their crew were approaching fast. Kala walked at the head of the group. She was nearly as short as Iris, with jet-black hair thicker than rope. Her warm brown hands were dappled with bright streaks of paint, as always. Her dear friend Delilah trailed close behind, her blind eyes the same shade of cream as her skin. The brothers James and Elliot Mason traipsed behind them. Both were members of the stationary guard, but that was where the similarities ended.

"Cooking accident," Ronja explained as they arrived at the edge of the fire. Kala looked to Delilah, who was shaking her head, her chestnut hair rippling.

"Lying," she confirmed, her milky eyes sparking with mirth and curiosity. "Her voice wavered a bit toward the end."

"I knew it," Kala snapped, jabbing an accusatory finger at Ronja.

Ronja batted the digit away with her bound wrist, her contented mood evaporating like boiling water. "Thanks, D," she muttered dryly.

"Happy to be of service."

Delilah stepped around the fire, her hand held out to gauge the heat, then perched on her orange stool. An accident had destroyed her vision when she was a child, but in recent years a sliver of her sight had returned. She was now able to see vibrant hues and vague shapes out of her left eye. As a result, most of her belongings were brightly colored. "If you would just tell the truth once in a while I could stop publicly shaming you, Ronja."

Ronja muttered something foul under her breath, knowing Delilah would hear. She only gave a cheeky smile in response, revealing a small gap between her front teeth.

"Who was it, then?" Kala asked, taking her usual spot next to Delilah.

"I got into it a bit with Terra, no big deal."

"No big deal," James mimicked, pitching his voice up several octaves in a poor imitation. Ronja glowered at him as he stepped over her legs and took the seat between Samson and her. She inched away. She was not fond of the elder Mason brother. He saw the world in black and white and had not cracked a smile in the eight weeks she had known him. "Just breaking one of the only rules the stationary guard has set. But we can overlook it for the *savior*, right, Sam?" He turned to his captain expectantly.

Ronja gritted her teeth and glanced down at her knees, shame prickling under her skin.

"I let it slide when you and Connor got in a fight on duty," Samson replied flatly. "It only seems fair we do the same for a newbie."

Ronja felt her chest expand as James flushed, forcing out the mortification gnawing at her insides. She locked eyes with the captain. He winked at her, quick enough that she wondered if she had imagined it. She wracked her brains, trying to remember the last time someone had defended her before a crowd.

She sat alone in the elementary school hallway, her cold chapped hands curled around a thermos of milk, lost in a world of her own creation. She did not notice the knot of older children approaching her until it was too late. Their dull cruel eyes and grubby hands kept her rooted on the spot, her fingers turning white around the container.

"Stupid mutt, what are you doing in a school?"

"Get back to the pound!"

"Listen to your Singer you dumb pitcher!"

"Leave her alone!"

A dark hand shot through a gap between her tormenters and gripped her wrist. It was so soft, so warm, startlingly different from her own rough palms. Before she could even open her mouth, he yanked her through the mob and pulled her to his side, pressing her face to his knit sweater.

"I got ya, Ro," Henry whispered into her hair. "I got ya."

"Do they hurt?

Ronja blinked. "Huh?"

"Your hands, do they hurt?"

She followed the question to Elliot, who had taken the vacant seat next to Delilah. At seventeen he was the youngest of the group. He was a gentle and sensible boy, the opposite of his short fused brother. Elliot had a rather long nose and protuberant ears, but his eyes were a lovely shade of hazel and his head was full of thick auburn hair.

"A bit," Ronja answered honestly. "Iris said I might have fractured a knuckle, but I think I got lucky."

"Who started it?" Kala asked.

James let out a hollow laugh. "Who do you think?"

Ronja tossed him a black look. He returned it vehemently. "I started it," she admitted, "but she deserved it."

"I bet," Kala replied. "But James is right. Infighting is a serious offense around here, especially for people like ... "

Delilah threw out her elbow and nailed her in the ribs. Kala hissed, massaging her side, but she shut her mouth. Ronja dropped her eyes to the flames, oblivious to the sting of the smoke. Lighter conversations from nearby circles drifted in tauntingly. "People like me," she finished tonelessly. "I get it."

Kala did not respond. Ronja peeked up through her lashes. The painter wore a calculating expression. Elliot and Delilah both appeared pained. She could not see Samson around James, but found herself wondering what he was thinking.

"You know," Kala finally spoke up carefully. "This would be a lot easier if you would just tell us what happened out there."

Here we go, Ronja thought dully. She should have known. Every conversation led back to the night she desperately wanted to forget.

"It would be easier to trust you if we knew your story," Elliot tacked on with a coaxing smile. Kala tossed him an appreciative glance. Ronja fought the urge to reach across the flames to slap him.

"Wilcox would exile me if he found out I talked," she explained tiredly, not for the first time and certainly not for the last. "Roark trusts me. Is that not enough?"

"His judgment is clouded," James answered sourly.

Ronja narrowed her eyes to slits. "What do you mean?"

The guard barked a laugh, his mouth curled into a smirk. "Are you blind?"

"Oi," Delilah mumbled.

"Ronja." Kala was scrutinizing her through the column of smoke. Her eyes were nearly as black as her hair. "You want us to trust you, right?"

Ronja hesitated before nodding.

The painter arranged her mouth into some semblance of a smile. "Then help us to. Tell us what happened at Red Bay, and then maybe we can ... "

"Stop treating me like a bomb about to go off?"

Kala swallowed, her eyes darting around the circle desperately. Again, no one came to her aid. "What I meant was ... "

"How dare you."

"Excuse me?"

"You think you can bait me with friendship? I spent most of my life alone. I have everyone I need." The truth of the words sent shockwaves rippling along her bones, spurring her words. "I am here to fight, and to do that I have to keep my mouth shut. I am not going to risk being thrown out so you and I can braid each other's hair. So, if you would kindly skitz off, I would appreciate it."

It was only in the wake of her words that Ronja realized she had been shouting. The fire crackled cheerily at her feet.

"I ... I ... " Kala stuttered

"I think what Kala means," Delilah spoke up quietly. "Is that it would mean a lot to us if you could tell us what happened to him. How he ... " She raised a hand to her quivering lips.

The rage drained from Ronja slowly, then all at once. She glanced around the circle, but everyone refused her gaze. When she finally spoke, her voice was scarcely more than a whisper. "This is about Henry."

Kala gave a rueful smile, her dark eyes shining. "Of course it is. He was like a brother to us, even after he left the Belly."

"I remember when he was born," Samson interjected. Ronja leaned around James to see him, her eyes widening in surprise. He nodded as if to confirm his own words. "I was five." A low chuckle bubbled up on his lips. "Skitz, he was one ugly baby."

"Please, Ronja," Kala said quietly. "If you could just ... " She gestured helplessly at the intangible.

Ronja swallowed the lump in her throat. A thousand thoughts whipped through her mind, but there was only one conclusion. They were right. They deserved to know why she came home instead of Henry. She took a deep breath, wet her lips, then spoke. "He died protecting us. He stayed behind to make sure we all got out." She shut her eyes as if that would stop her from hearing her own words. "He was cornered and killed himself before the Offs got him."

She allowed her eyelids to drift open and found the focus had shifted from her to Delilah. The blind girl was utterly still, her head tilted to the side as she searched for a trace of a lie. Time stalled until finally she spoke. "She believes it."

Ronja tensed, readying herself for an onslaught. It never came. Instead, Samson loosed an exhausted sigh, then bent down and retrieved a half-empty bottle of whiskey from beneath his stool. He unscrewed the lid and tossed it to the stone floor. Delilah stiffened at the echoing ping. "Sam," she chided. "It is 7:00 A.M."

"7:15," he corrected her. He raised the bottle over his head, the amber liquid glittering in the firelight. "To Henry," he said, his big voice rolling over them like thunder. "An excellent soldier, a loving brother, and a selfless friend." He tipped the bottle back and took a swig, then passed it on to James.

"To Henry," James mumbled, then took his shot. He handed the bottle off to Ronja without so much as glancing her. She took it with both hands, worried it might slip through her bandaged fingers.

"To Henry," she said. "My ... "

My first friend. My best friend. My brother.

She pressed the bottle to her lips, drank long and deep. The whiskey burned on the way down and settled decidedly in her empty stomach. Wincing, she half stood to give the bottle to Kala.

"To Henry," the girl repeated in a thick voice. The rest of the toasts passed in a blur. Ronja stared into the steady flames, searching for something she could not name among the heat and the ash. She felt ill and was certain it had nothing to do with the alcohol.

Did you think you were the only one who loved him? A nagging voice in the back of her mind asked. *Did you think you were the only one who lost him?*

"Breakfast of champions, Elliot."

The younger Mason choked on his drink as Ronja twisted around to see Roark approaching. His hair was dry and tied into a knot at the base of his skull. He had shed his damp shirt in favor of a knit navy sweater, the same one he had worn the night he took her from the subtrain station.

The memory was still fresh, though it was veiled by The Music. She had been terrified of him. How could she have known that days later she would be pressing her lips to his desperately, plunging a stinger into her heart to protect him?

"What the hell happened to you?" Roark demanded as he came to a stop before her. Ronja twisted back around, crossing her hands in her lap as if it would somehow make them less noticeable.

"Cooking accident," she muttered tonelessly.

Roark stepped over the vacant stool next to hers and sat heavily. "Oh, really? Did you get in a fight with a frying pan?"

"Actually, she got in a fight with a certain blonde we all know and love," Kala answered with a breezy laugh. Ronja shot her a glance, both annoyed with and envious of her ability to bury her emotions so quickly. "Apparently, no one taught her how to punch properly."

"I offered to help," Samson piped up. Roark ignored him.

"Well, she did quite a bit of damage to my face a while back," he said with a chuckle, working his jaw as if it stilled pained him. "I imagine Terra looks about as bad as I did."

Ronja snorted. "Not quite."

Roark grinned, exposing his sugar-white teeth.

"Does anyone know where Iris and Evie are?" Delilah inquired. She clutched her stomach as if worried it might digest itself. "They were supposed to bring breakfast."

"I think they had an errand to run," Ronja replied smoothly.

"They better get here soon," James growled, looking first at his watch, then at his captain. Samson was oblivious, staring into space with his chin in his weathered hand. "My shift starts in a half hour; I want to get there early."

Roark snorted quietly. Ronja tossed him a questioning glance. He rolled his eyes at the arching ceiling, then mouthed *suck up*. The girl smiled crookedly. Silence crept up on them, buffered only by the dull hiss of the blaze at their feet and the drone of conversations beyond their circle.

"Do you have your guitar, Sam?" Roark asked abruptly. Ronja arched a brow at him. He winked in reply. "I left my violin in my tent, but I suppose we could make do with you."

Samson flashed his teeth, impervious to the jab. "I do, as a matter of fact." He climbed to his feet and stepped over the stack of firewood. His cherry wood guitar waited patiently in its open case. He grabbed it by the neck and slung it over his shoulder by the leather slap. "Anyone up for a jam?"

Kala and James groaned in unison. The dark-haired girl slid down in her chair like a rag doll.

"I would love a song," Elliot spoke up hopefully. Delilah nodded in agreement, linking arms with him. The boy blushed, the color creeping down his neck. Ronja got the feeling the blind girl knew.

"Majority rules," Sam said.

"What about you, love?" Roark asked, tossing Ronja a crooked smile.

"What about me?"

"I hear music is healing, or something."

Ronja looked down at her bandaged hands doubtfully, and saw him shake his head out of the corner of her eye. "Not that kind of healing."

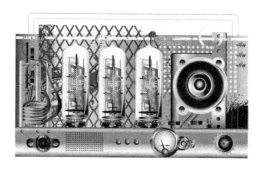

7: WONDER
Roark

He wondered if she knew how beautiful she was, sitting there in the light of the fire. Not the way other girls were, and certainly not in the way everyone would find attractive. She was vibrant and defiant and buzzing with possibility. Her scars did not negate her beauty, nor did they enhance it. They were simply a part of her, like her constellation of freckles, her full lips, her dark hair that was returning so quickly.

And those eyes. Every time she looked at him it reconfirmed he could not hide an inch of his soul from her. More nights than he cared to admit he had imagined her in his tent, her body entwined with his. He would not, could not, ask it of her. Not after what he had watched happen through the one-way glass. She had not spoken of it. Did she know he had seen it?

When she kissed him in the torture chamber, everything fell away. The chains on his ankles. The panic, the desperation, the rage. There was only her. For a fraction of an infinity, he had imagined it would only be her for the rest of his life.

Then she died, her mouth pressed to his, to save him. To save them all.

"Roark."

Roark blinked. All eyes were on him. Ronja stared at him dubiously. That was when he realized he was gawking at her, his jaw unhinged. He cleared his throat. "Sorry, could you repeat that?"

"I asked what song you had in mind," Samson repeated slowly, as if Roark were a bit dense.

"Whatever you like," he answered, shoving an escaped strand of hair out of his face. "I leave the choice in your semi-capable hands." The captain laughed, his weathered fingers scuttling along the neck of the guitar. He began to strum out scales, fidgeting with the tuning pegs. Ronja watched, her lips parted and her eyes wide. Sometimes, Roark forgot how fresh the concept of music was to her. When she had sung to free him from The New Music, it seemed so natural.

"Ideas, anyone?" Sam asked.

Delilah snapped her fingers, a memory sparking in her white eyes. "What about *Sparrow*?"

"By Frequency?" The captain squinted up at the ceiling as if the lyrics were written there.

"Yeah." Delilah licked her lips, then relayed the chorus. "You cannot be the one for me, you need your own damn recipe ... "

"But I wish, oh darling, please," Samson picked up the tune. His singing voice was as ragged as his hair, but it was not unpleasant. "You could make me a part of your disease."

"Nice choice," Elliot commented. Delilah smiled softly and rested her head on his shoulder. Roark felt his lips quirk upward. They had been dancing around each other as long as he could remember. In his opinion, it was high time they stopped.

"All right," Samson said, punctuating the word with a satisfying down strum. "One, two, three, four ... "

He burst into motion, carving out the melancholy rhythm with his fingers. Delilah disentangled herself from Elliot and popped to her feet. She twisted from side to side, arms loose and skirt rippling. Three bars came and went, then the lyrics poured from her.

I think I knew before you said so
But I still broke beneath your words.
You are a child until the day
They go away

Do you miss me in the mornings
When you would kiss me on the brow
Do you miss me in the mornings
When you would kiss me on the brow

Delilah paused, wetting her lips as Samson broke into a complex solo. She spun toward Kala, her hands clasped in pleading. The painter groaned. Delilah stuck out her hand, wriggling her fingers. Sighing, Kala got to her feet. She was a full head shorter than Delilah, a fact that never failed to surprise Roark. Her personality was deceptive. It made her seem ten feet tall.

The solo drew to a close, and the girls picked up the chorus.

You cannot be the one for me
You need your own damn recipe

Kala looked as if she would rather be yanking out her own teeth than singing before a crowd, but Roark saw through her. She would do anything to make Delilah happy. Their voices twined with the rhythmic guitar were infectious. He soon found himself tapping his foot to the beat. The chorus was just ending when he noticed Ronja was mouthing the words.

But I wish, oh darling, please
You could make me a part of your disease

Her eyes were closed, a meshwork of blushing veins sprawled across her lids. When he was a child he saw his mother drop to her knees and pray, her palms bared to the sky. In that moment, it looked as if Ronja were pleading with a deity sure to hear her call.

"Sing," he heard himself say.

Her eyes flew open, her pupils shrinking like violets. He immediately regretted interrupting her. The weight of her gaze was suffocating. Kala and Delilah were still singing. Samson was still playing. Roark could barely hear them over the noise in his head.

Save them. Save them. Save them.

"Samson, oi, Sam!" The captain managed a final defiant strum before he muted the strings with his palm. Delilah and Kala fell silent in his wake. "Sorry to interrupt," Evie said through the toothpick she was gnawing on. Her arms were laden with several loaves of bread and packages of dried fruits wrapped in newspaper. "But we need to borrow Trip and Ro."

"We brought breakfast," Iris chimed in, a large pot curled to her chest. Her short red curls were stiff with sweat, hinting at the nature of the 'errand' Ronja had mentioned. "Save a bit for us, would you?"

"You're not staying?" Delilah asked.

"Nope," Evie replied lightly. Her eyes flashed to Roark. He straightened, his muscles tightening. Anyone else might have missed the twinge of trepidation in her expression, but he knew her far too well. Something was wrong. "We just have something we need to take care of."

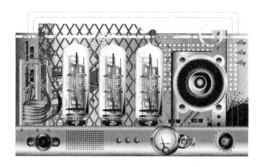

8: TRIPPED

They abandoned the fire in a whirlwind of dodged questions and plastic smiles. As soon as they turned the corner on their comrades, they found an aisle between two vacant tents and ducked into it. They huddled in a tight knot. "What the hell is going on?" Ronja whispered. Her bandages were turning boggy with sweat.

"Wilcox moved up our meeting," Evie replied.

"What? To when?"

"To right now," Iris answered flatly.

Roark and Ronja looked at each other. "Why?" they asked at the same time.

"No bloody idea," Evie replied sourly. She crossed her arms, chewing on her toothpick furiously. Iris peered around, bouncing on the balls of her feet. "He never moves appointments; the man practically schedules his shits."

"When did you find out about this?" Roark asked.

"Five minutes ago," Iris said. "He sent Barty to our tent with the message."

"Thankfully we were already dressed," Evie added under her breath.

"It could be nothing," the surgeon cut in, glossing over the comment. "Maybe something came up this evening."

"Or he could be trying to trip us up," Roark countered darkly. "He'd like nothing more than to watch us skitz this."

Iris stretched out a hand for Evie to take. She intercepted it absently. "If he finds a single hole in our plan ... " the surgeon murmured.

"He'll run it into the ground," Ronja finished, keeping her voice low so it did not shake. The three Anthemites shifted their attention to her, watching the gears of her mind spin through her green eyes. "We can't let that happen."

Roark clapped a bracing hand to her shoulder. She peered up at him, battering down her fear. He squeezed her stiff muscles, lifted one corner of his mouth. "We won't," he promised.

"This is adorable," Evie drawled, popping her toothpick out of her mouth and sticking it in her pocket. "But we have to be on the other side of the station in about thirty seconds."

The quartet was still for a moment, their joint anxiety swelling. Evie and Roark locked eyes, exchanged a nod. They did not wait to see if the others were ready, but shot out of the alley like death itself was on their heels.

Ronja and Iris shared a knowing glance, then followed. Two sharp turns later they exploded onto the central pathway that cut through the station, the Vein. Ronja had not used it in some time; it was far too crowded. It ran east to west across the Belly, and could have easily accommodated two lanes of autos. Thankfully, it was all but deserted in the middle of breakfast.

Snatches of casual conversations and the aroma of sizzling meat roared past Ronja as she ran. She kept her eyes on Evie and Roark, who were a good twelve paces ahead. They moved in perfect synchronization, their neurons knit after years of training side by side. Despite the adrenaline whistling through her veins, she felt a jolt of petty jealousy. She forced it down vehemently. Now was not the time. The west end of the station was approaching, nearly as high as the black walls that encircled Revinia

They arrived with seconds to spare, scraping to a halt before the iron door that led to the debriefing room. Ronja felt her thoughts dissolve as she took in the rusted frame. It was beyond this door that she first learned the truth about Revinia, The Conductor, and The Music. It was here she first pledged herself to the resistance, only to abandon it hours later to save her family. Now, the roles were reversed.

She was here to convince the commander to make a move, not the other way around.

Evie wasted no time approaching the door and hammering on it with her fist. Iris padded up to stand beside her, twisting her hands anxiously.

Roark slipped back to speak to Ronja. "Just like we practiced," he murmured.

The girl nodded mutely. Her hand twitched at her side, yearning for his. She tried to pass it off as a nervous tick, but nothing got by Roark. He curled his long fingers around her bandaged ones. His touch should have been painful, but was not.

The lock clanged, the door flew open. A woman stood in the frame, lean as a sapling with dyed orange hair and prominent cheekbones. She was dressed in a high-necked black sweater and matching slacks. She could have stepped out of the financial district were it not for the automatic pistol strapped to her thigh.

"Ito," Evie greeted her levelly.

"Wick," the lieutenant replied. Her eyes passed over the techi and landed on Ronja, who lifted her chin. She and Ito had not spoken since their talk on the airship. *Welcome to the Anthem, singer.* It was more than an address, it was a promise, one Ronja intended to make her keep. "Come in," Ito said, pressing her back to the door to allow them to pass. "We've been waiting."

"Yeah, for ten seconds," Evie grumbled. She and Iris stepped inside and disappeared around the corner.

Ito gestured for Ronja and Roark to pass, but the girl found she was rooted to the spot. She cast her gaze to the boy. He was already looking at her. He gave her hand a squeeze so quick she thought she might have imagined it. Somehow, it was enough. They approached the entrance together, pulses and footsteps meshed.

"What happened?" Roark breathed as they passed Ito. The lieutenant only offered a subtle shake of her head.

Dank air washed over Ronja as they crossed the threshold. The room was just as she remembered. Low ceiling, featureless stone walls, an oak conference table wreathed with a dozen chairs. The last time she had been here they were filled with council members, men and women there to judge her. Now, only one seat was filled, the only one that mattered.

Tristen Wilcox sat at the head of the table, draped in the glow of a solitary light bulb. He was dressed in his counterfeit Off uniform, the white emblem of The Conductor stitched over his heart. His sharp gray eyes latched onto Ronja as she made her way to the opposite end of the table. Iris and Evie had already chosen seats on the far right, leaving the two chairs directly opposite the commander open. *Thanks guys*, she thought dully as she sat. The door slammed. The lock clicked. Roark slipped into the seat immediately to her right as Ito moved to stand beside her superior.

Silence echoed. The air was thick with the smell of groundwater. Wilcox did not even appear to breathe, staring her down across the wooden surface like a bull about to charge. Iris began to tap her fingernails against the table, but caught herself and started to chew them instead.

"Well, this is all very enlightening," Roark finally said, reclining in his chair and lacing his fingers behind his head to form a pillow. "But one of us should really say something within the next hour. Would you like to start, sir?"

Evie choked on a laugh, disguising it as a cough. Wilcox stiffened, his jaw bulging behind his stubbled cheek. Ronja wracked her brains, trying to remember the last time she had seen the commander unshaven.

Ito stepped up to the edge of the table. "We all know why we're here," she said. Her voice seemed to echo despite the cramped space. "You four are advocating a preemptive strike against The Conductor and His Music. The commander wishes to hold back. I am here as a moderator. I'll set my personal opinions aside and remain neutral during this discussion. The commander ... "

"Can speak for himself, Lieutenant," Wilcox interjected coldly. Ito pursed her lips. A shadow of irritation passed over her elegant features, but was quickly scattered by her poise. The commander opened his arms in what would have been a welcoming gesture were it not for his condescending smirk. "So. The savior has requested an audience with me. To what do I owe the honor?"

"It can't be that much of an honor. This is the third time we asked you to meet," Ronja replied dryly.

"I have a revolution to run, Zipse. I don't have time to indulge your every whim."

But you have plenty of time to sit on your ass. "Of course not, sir. Thank you for meeting with us." Out of the corner of her eye, Ronja saw Roark shoot her a relieved look. It was as if he could smell her blood boiling and knew how close she was to snapping at their superior.

"What is this about?" Wilcox inquired.

"Well … " Ronja felt her mouth go dry. She glanced at her friends, who were watching her expectantly. They had agreed a long time ago that she would take the lead on the pitch. She was, after all, the linchpin of the operation. Now, with the commander staring at her like something stuck to the bottom of his shoe, she was wondering if that was really the best course of action. Too late now. "We … we have a plan. We have a way to take down The Conductor and The Music." Wilcox waited for her to continue in stony silence. "But we need your help."

The commander smiled, a creeping twist of his lips that did not reach his eyes. "Then, as Westervelt so eloquently stated, we are short on time. You have ten minutes to convince me of your plan. If you fail, you will never speak of this again. If I hear that you have been stirring up dissent, you will be exiled. Is that clear?"

Ronja glanced at her friends. The gravity of the ultimatum sank in as she scanned their expressions. Enemies of the state were written into The Music. Every citizen was trained to know their faces, meaning nowhere under the bruised Revinian sky was safe for them. She turned back to Wilcox, eyes simmering with determination and scarcely veiled fear. "Yes, sir."

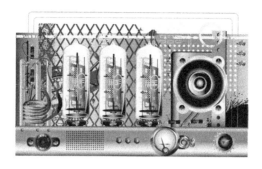

9: THE PITCH

Ronja pushed back her chair with a screech and got to her feet. She kept her hands locked behind her, both to still them and to hide her bandages. The scarred oak table sprawled before her. The commander waited, expressionless and cold. She took a deep breath, swallowed a lump of nonexistent saliva, and began.

"Two months ago, Roark kidnapped me from a subtrain station in the middle ring, mistaking me for an undercover Off." Relief flowered in her chest as her words hit the air. Her voice sounded far steadier than she felt. "The Music spiked in my Singer, triggering The Quiet Song. My mother, as you know, is ... was a mutt." Ronja winced internally at the slip up. It was still natural to refer to her mother in the present tense. She wondered when the impulse would fade, for Layla and everyone else she had lost.

"I know all this." Wilcox sighed. His eyes darted to his watch pointedly. "Clock's ticking, Zipse."

"My family was taken by the government after falling victim to the echo effect," she continued as if he had not spoken. "We infiltrated Red Bay to save them but were captured. Victor

Westervelt II was there. He interrogated us, seeking intel on the Anthem."

Wilcox smiled bitterly and reclined in his high-backed chair, which groaned under his weight. "Yes, I am sure the Anthemites exposed by our own Mr. Westervelt are as familiar with this part of the story as I am."

Ronja watched out of the corner of her eye as Roark flushed. She was seized both by the urge to embrace him and to kick him. She needed him present, not wallowing in guilt. "Roark did what he had to do to keep us safe," she said firmly, returning her attention to Wilcox. "I owe him more than my life."

"What do you mean?" the commander asked, a hint of curiosity in his tone. Ito crossed her arms, her brows knitting thoughtfully.

"Uh ... " Ronja stumbled, a hare caught between a wolf and a trap. She had said too much, hinted at something she wished to keep buried. Roark did not know she knew. She wanted to keep it that way. She shook her head, her brief curls shivering. "Roark was put in an impossible situation. He made the best choice he could."

Wilcox rolled his eyes, but kept his mouth shut. Roark relaxed slightly. Ronja breathed a sigh of relief. Her hands were slick beneath the layers of gauze, the salt working its way into her wounds. She flexed her fingers in a vain attempt to relieve the sting, successfully making it worse.

"While we were at Red Bay, we discovered what Westervelt was working on," she went on, speaking authoritatively. "A new form of The Music that can reach people with or without Singers. For the sake of simplicity, we are calling it 'The New Music.' Both Roark and I felt the effects of these Songs. I was exposed to The Lost Song, which impacts the pain centers of the brain. Roark was hit with The Air Song."

"The Air Song," Ito repeated, a question ringing in her inflection.

"Yes," Ronja repeated eagerly. "It's similar to The Music we know, but way more powerful."

"It drains you," Roark spoke up. Ronja cast her eyes at him sidelong. He stared at the face of the table, but she knew he was not really seeing it. "It does more than just dampen your emotions, it obliterates them. All you have left is your obedience to The Conductor."

Ronja nodded, suppressing the urge to reach out and take him by the hand. "According to our source," she went on. "The New Music will be finished in a matter of months. Before his death, Victor planned to release it on all of Revinia, including the Anthemites. Without a doubt, The Conductor plans to do the same."

"How do you know when it will be finished?" Wilcox asked.

"Our prisoner," Ronja said. "Maxwell."

"Ah yes, the bastard son of The Conductor that no one has ever seen or heard from who just happens to have a fully functioning Singer." Wilcox smirked, leaning back in his chair. It creaked beneath the increased pressure.

Skitz. "Sir," Ronja began carefully. "I agree, it's strange given his supposed status, but Roark and I were both exposed to these Songs and we can assure you, they work. Even if Maxwell is lying about the timeline, it will be released eventually. If anything, our attack on Red Bay may have sped things up."

"I suppose we have you to thank for that." Wilcox ground the words out.

Ronja smiled blandly. "Actually, sir, you have us to thank for warning you about it in the first place."

Evie coughed again. Iris swatted her on the arm.

"Fine," Wilcox said. He checked his watch. "You have five

minutes. Are you going to get around to explaining this plan of yours?"

Ronja felt the blood drain from her face as all eyes fell on her yet again. This was it, the moment she had been waiting for. Her mouth felt like sandpaper, yet somehow she was able to speak. "We want to hack the Singers and play real music," she said. "We want to use my voice to free the city before The New Music is finished. We want to start a revolution."

Wilcox was utterly still across from her, his eyes dull as slate. Ronja continued, reining in her voice as it attempted to rocket through the speech. "I was able to free Roark from The Air Song in just a few seconds by singing to him," she explained. "Even though The Air Song is more powerful than The Music, it will probably take longer because the Revinians have been under The Music their whole lives. But we think it could work."

By the time the final word escaped her lips, Ronja was trembling. Wilcox was silent. The only sign that he was still breathing was the throbbing vein in his temple. Ito broke the bone-deep hush. "Is it possible?" Her voice did not sound like her own. It was childlike, uncertain.

"Yes," Iris said fervently, speaking up for the first time. "Singers are capable of receiving radio waves as well as the waves The Music travels on."

"How do you know this?" Ito probed.

Iris smiled, a bit of pride glinting in her eyes. "I am a Singer surgeon, ma'am. As I was saying, they can receive radio waves. The Conductor occasionally transmits speeches via radio directly into the Singers, a little extra propaganda to fuel the masses."

Ronja found herself nodding. She remembered well the sudden, booming voice that echoed over the erratic notes of The Music. *Passion is perilous. Emotion is treacherous. Disobedience is destruction.* Even now, free from her Singer, those words were ingrained in her.

"I have already tested it using a transmitter and a disconnected Singer," Iris said. "The audio comes through just fine."

Those words were what finally snapped Wilcox from his catatonic state. "Where did you get this Singer?" he demanded. "I ordered you to destroy them all."

"With all due respect, sir, I need the practice," the surgeon said mildly. "It's not often I get to perform an actual surgery."

On the surface, the comment seemed benign, but Ronja felt the potency beneath it. She dipped her chin, smirking at the table. Sometimes, she forgot that Iris was every bit as fierce as Roark and Evie.

"Is this what you have been doing since I ordered your lockdown?" Wilcox growled. "Testing Singers, building transmitters, concocting some insane plan that hinges on the daughter of a mutt and her supernatural voice?"

Ronja slammed her teeth together to pin down a scathing reply.

"Not supernatural," Roark corrected him. His voice was poised, but Ronja could tell his patience was wearing thin. "Science."

"Science is rooted in evidence."

"We have more evidence. I am not the only one Ronja freed from The New Music, sir."

Wilcox opened his mouth, closed it. His face was vaguely purple in the low light.

Roark stepped out from behind his chair smoothly, straightened his sweater, then crossed to the iron door. He looked past the stunned commander to Ito. She nodded mutely. Roark cracked a grin, then flipped the lock. Light and noise poured into the room. A slight figure stood in the doorframe, silhouetted by the glow of the Belly. "Come in, Sawyer, thank you for waiting."

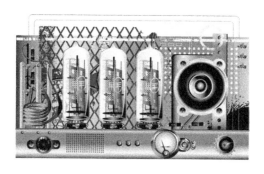

10: WALTZ

Wilcox shot to his feet. His chair rocked violently and would have toppled had Ito not steadied it. "This is a private meeting, get out!" he snapped.

Sawyer Gailes hopped across the threshold, tossing the commander an amused look. Her short hair was a rare shade of dark red, her skin smooth as cream. Her eyes were brown and far too intense for her age. A series of puckered scars decorated her right ear. "Settle," she drawled.

Wilcox took a massive step around the table. Sawyer scuttled back into Roark, who caught her by the shoulders. The crown of her head barely reached his sternum.

"Tristen," Ito warned. "Perhaps we should hear what she has to say."

Wilcox rounded on his lieutenant. For a brief moment, the room was suspended. The cacophony of the Belly drifted in through the door, distorted by the sluggish flow of time. Ronja held her breath. Finally, Wilcox caved. He sat heavily and snapped his fingers at Roark, who shut the door with a triumphant clang.

"Sawyer," Roark prompted. "Will you tell the commander

what you told us?"

"Save it, shiny," she answered, peeling away from Roark. She looked him up and down, snorted disdainfully, then turned her attention to Wilcox. Evie chuckled. Roark shot her a scalding glance. "I was in the middle of eating a perfectly good meal when some kid slipped me a note that said the secret club meeting was about to start."

"Who passed you this message?" Wilcox growled. "Was it Bartholomew?"

The girl put her nose in the air and crossed her arms. "I ain't no snitch."

"Sawyer." Roark sighed, pinching the bridge of his nose with his thumb and forefinger. "Please."

She passed him a sour look. "Yes, yes, all right. Zipse and her voice freed me from The New Music," she said, her voice gravelly with irritation. "It was like clouds parting over a field full of bunnies and flowers. Can I go now?"

Ronja dropped her gaze to her boots, a smile tugging at the corners of her mouth. Sawyer was not doing them any favors, but she had to admire her spunk.

"In a moment," Ito assured the girl, raising a hand. "Tell me what you remember from that day."

Sawyer heaved a sigh, popping her hip to the side. "I woke up in my cell like any other day, smelling like shit and hoping for a bullet to the brain. Then one of the goons came to get me and put me on a stage in front of the entire pitching lab with a mutt and some humans."

Ronja pursed her lips. She was accustomed to her mother being placed in a separate, subhuman category, but it never failed to fray her nerves. Sawyer went on, oblivious.

"Westervelt—the older one, not this one." She gestured to Roark, who shifted uncomfortably. "Was there. He brought Trip up on stage and started playing the … " She wiggled her fingers next to her temple as if she could draw the words out. "What was it?"

"The Lost Song," Roark reminded her.

"Right. He started playing The Lost Song over the speakers, on top of The Day Song. Good thing I was already half deaf, or it would have fried my brains." She flicked her right earlobe pointedly. "Anyway, we were on stage and this girl came plowing through the doors, bald as … well as me and covered in blood." She turned to Ronja and cracked a droll smile. "You looked like a skitzing nightmare."

"I felt like one," Ronja replied dryly.

Sawyer laughed loudly. "Anyway, baldy and her friend, the blonde one, got tackled and Westervelt started up that other Song."

"The Air Song?" Ito broke in.

"Air Song?" Sawyer repeated thoughtfully. She nodded to herself. "Yeah, I guess, the one that can travel without Singers."

"Sawyer." Roark sighed.

"Right, anyway, I blacked out, then I woke up to her singing." She jabbed a finger at Ronja. "She was singing to her boyfriend, but I heard it anyway."

Roark cleared his throat loudly. Ronja bit her lip.

"And then?" Ito pressed.

Sawyer shrugged. "And then you came in through the roof, which was insane, by the way." Ito smiled, an ember of humor igniting in her eyes. The girl must have sensed the glimmer of affection, because her voice softened. "Thanks for that."

"No need to thank me, it was Trip and Ronja who pulled you from the rubble."

Sawyer nodded, but did not appear to be in the mood to thank them.

"Is there anything else you can recall?" Ito questioned. "Anything that might help us?"

"Yeah, there is actually," Sawyer answered slowly, chewing her lip as she rifled through her thoughts. Ronja went rigid. This was not part of the plan. "When she sang, I could still hear The Music, but it was easier to ignore."

"You could work around it," Ronja muttered under her breath.

"What was that, Zipse?" Ito asked.

Ronja did not answer, her eyes still on Sawyer. "It was like you could hear it, but you could work around it."

The teenager nodded eagerly, excitement bursting through her bored mask. "Right," she confirmed. "Exactly."

"Like you could recognize its command, but could refuse," Roark added. Ronja and Sawyer rounded on him, their eyes widening. He ran his fingers through his hair. "I felt it, too."

A memory ignited in Ronja, drawing a quiet gasp from her. "I used to count," she breathed. Roark stepped forward to stand beside her, trying to meet her gaze. She was long gone, her mind reeling back into the past. Her mouth continued to move of its own accord. "It made The Music easier to ignore. 1-2-3, 2-2-3 ... "

Roark whipped around toward Evie and Iris. The techi and the surgeon looked at each other, their brains spinning faster than words could contain. "It sounds like she was keeping time," Evie said, her voice wobbling slightly. "Ro, who taught you to count like that?"

Before Ronja could respond, Roark turned back to face her, his eyes glinting like match heads. "Counting like that, switching the set number for the first number, is distinctly musical. It correlates with a specific type of song called a waltz." He took an eager step toward her, color high in his cheeks. "Who taught you to count like that?"

"I ... I ... " Ronja wracked her brains. She had learned to count in elementary school, like anyone else. But that specific practice ... where had she learned it? Her head began to throb. She kneaded her temples to soothe the ache. Her memories from her years under The Music were muted, sapped of color. Sifting through them was like walking through a maze choked with fog. "I don't know."

"Enough." Dread pooled in her stomach as Ronja turned to Wilcox. She had forgotten his presence entirely. "Gailes, get out."

Sawyer sniffed. "Were you not hugged enough as a baby?"

"Leave," Wilcox hissed. The teenager threw her hands up in defeat, then ambled toward the exit.

"Keep me posted," Sawyer ordered, the command obviously aimed at Ronja and her friends. Before they could respond, she wrenched open the metal door with strength she should not have possessed. A gust of cool air washed over the room when it slammed shut.

"Sir," Roark began.

"Quiet, Westervelt," Wilcox barked. "I have heard enough."

"You have your proof."

"Proof?" The commander laughed hollowly. "You call that proof? She is an outsider; her words mean nothing. You could have bribed her; you could have recruited her for your cause."

"*My* cause?" Roark demanded. "Last time I checked we were on the same side."

"I am your commander," Wilcox reminded him, his voice sinking another octave. "You act like you own this place, running around with your little band of disciples. Your cover is blown; you are no longer necessary." Roark blanched, his shoulders sagging beneath the truth. Ronja gritted her teeth. Only once had she seen him look so defeated, in the presence of his sadistic father. The commander continued relentlessly. "You have endangered this operation for the last time."

"What are you so afraid of?" Several beats of her heart came and went before Ronja realized she had spoken aloud.

Wilcox stiffened. He stared at her blankly, his expression reminiscent of the precarious calm in the eye of a hurricane. "Excuse me?"

"How long have you been in charge of the Anthem?" Ronja demanded. The man seemed to vibrate with rage, though it may have been the flicker of the electric light playing on his skin. "Twenty years? What have you done in that time?"

"You have no idea what you're talking about," he growled.

"I know enough!" Somewhere in the back of her mind, Ronja realized she was shouting, but she could not find it in her to care. Her blood was roaring louder than a subtrain. "I know you've infiltrated the highest Off stations, but you haven't stopped their abuse. You've destroyed Singer shipments, but they just replace them with better models. You had a spy inside Westervelt Industries and it is still standing. When was the last time you brought in a new recruit, huh?" Wilcox maintained his silence. "How many minds have you freed since Roark brought me in? Do you even want to see Revinia go free?"

Ronja forced herself not to flinch when the commander slammed his fist into the table. A shudder ripped through the wood, through her bones. "Do you have any idea what you are saying?" he asked in a hoarse whisper. "I have been fighting The Conductor since before you were born, and do you want to know what I have learned? He cannot be defeated."

"He has to be in His eighties," Ronja shot back, the spark fading from her voice as her confidence wavered. "Even if we don't take Him out, He'll die someday soon. The government will be destabilized and we can ... "

"You think that matters?" Wilcox jabbed a finger at the

ceiling, pointing up at the choked city. "I could kill Him tomorrow. I could string His body up at the palace doors and nothing would change. Do you know why? Because He will live forever in The Music, inspiring fear and reverence and obedience. We cannot win."

"You've given up," Ronja breathed.

"We have everything we need down here to keep living for decades," the commander said, more to himself than to her. "I'll do whatever I have to do to keep my people safe."

"Sir," Ronja said softly. "No one is safe anymore. The New Music is coming for all of us. But I ... I think we can stop it. If you would just give us a chance ... "

"Get out."

"What?"

Several things happened at once.

In one massive stride Wilcox was a breath from Ronja, his hand wrapped around her bicep. He yanked her toward the door like a rag doll and she was too stunned to protest. Evie leapt to her feet, her chair hitting the wall with a ringing crack. Roark launched forward, shoving his superior into the table with one hand and curling Ronja to his side with the other. His familiar musk enveloped her.

"GET OUT! NOW!" Wilcox bellowed, braced against the table.

"Go," Ito implored them urgently. "Now."

Roark ushered Ronja out the door, eyeing the unhinged commander ferociously. Evie and Iris hurried in their wake. They slammed the door on the commander and lieutenant. Just before it closed, they caught the start of an argument that could shake rain from the sky.

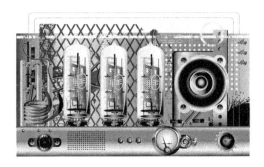

11: RECORDER

They stood in stunned silence outside the debriefing room, their hearts as heavy as their limbs. Roark still clutched Ronja to his side protectively. She let him, fearing her knees might buckle. Her mind was pulsing, her arm still throbbed where Wilcox had grabbed her.

"Well," Evie finally said with a bleak laugh. "Looks like Ronja was right all along. Wilcox is a piece of — "

"Shhh!" Iris exclaimed. She snatched her girlfriend by the hand, her hazel eyes darting around the station. "Not here." Without waiting for their response, she started back down the Vein, dragging Evie behind her. Ronja and Roark exchanged a glance, then followed. Curious gazes trailed them as they traipsed down the path, but no one said anything.

You've done nothing wrong, Ronja reminded herself as an Anthemite with gray hair and weathered skin passed her a scathing look. *Yet.*

They did not speak again until they had arrived at the powder blue tent Iris and Evie called home. Relative calm washed over Ronja as she passed through the entrance. The space was cramped but not claustrophobic, and bursting with color.

Embroidered pillows and quilts drowned the wide cot in the corner. Dried flowers hung from the ceiling. A small dresser that doubled as a writing desk sat in the corner. The air was thick with the smell of soil, dying petals, and stale sweat

Besides her own tent and the hospital wing, Ronja spent more time here than anywhere else. She often fell asleep on the padded floor, up late listening to records on the lowest volume, whispering about things she had never been able to talk about before. The language of young women was foreign to her. Sitting on the rug listening to stories of first kisses and crushes was one of the first times she had felt truly human. Not a mutt. Not a slave. Not even a revolutionary. Just a girl with her friends.

"Well ... " Evie began again. Iris swatted her on the arm, tapped her finger to her lips. The techi rolled her eyes as the surgeon crossed the tent, then knelt before the turntable that sat on a low wooden stool. A record was already in place, waiting patiently to be heard. Ronja craned her neck. No matter how many times she saw a record come to life, it never failed to fascinate her. Iris dropped the needle. Gentle piano music poured from the speakers. Ronja blinked. Colors blossomed from the sound. This time, light blue and a pale shade of green. Relief flooded her. These colors were not particularly distracting.

"Well that was terrible," Evie said dryly

"Yeah," Roark agreed. "I think we all know what this means."

Ronja raised her eyebrows at him. He passed her a weary smile. "Ready to see the sky again, love?"

Her heart stuttered. They had known from the start they were going to follow through with their plan with or without the support of the commander. Still, despite her surface doubts, a part of her always believed they would find a way to make him see reason.

But now she understood. Wilcox had given up on fighting a

long time ago. He was not a general, but a warden cowering below the crust of the planet. Bile rose in her throat. Did the Anthemites still believe they were fighting a war? Did they know there was no endgame, no final battle with Tristen Wilcox at the helm?

"When do we leave?" she asked, struggling to keep her voice steady.

"Are you ready?" Roark asked.

Ronja nodded. She had packed a knapsack weeks ago and hidden it under her stack of laundry. It contained all her necessities as well as the collapsible stingers Evie had gifted her. She had yet to explain to the techi she was about as skilled with stingers as she was at socializing.

"In that case, we leave tonight."

"Tonight?" Iris gasped.

"Yeah," Evie concurred, massaging her chin with her thumb and forefinger. "Wilcox would never expect us to hit eject so soon."

"And for good reason," the surgeon whispered shrilly. "Do we even know how we're getting out?"

Evie tilted her head to the side. "Good question." She sat heavily on the cot, which groaned under her weight. Iris plopped down beside her, chewing on her pinky nail. Following their lead, Ronja hopped up onto the dresser with a loud squeak. The tips of her boots brushed the rug. "Well," the techi started slowly. "The bathhouse exit is out."

"Why?" Iris asked.

"The sewers will be crawling with guards," Roark explained.

"How else can we get out?" Ronja inquired, her eyes shifting between her comrades. Roark began to pace, his footfalls muffled by the thick rug. "We have emergency exits, right?"

Evie nodded. "Six of them, actually." She flopped back onto the mountain of pillows, massaging her eyes with her tattooed palms. "Problem is, they're all sealed off. They're rigged to blow if we ever need a quick exit, but even if we got our hands on the detonators ... "

"We would leave the Belly defenseless," Ronja finished. Evie nodded against the pillows, her hair whispering against the fabric. "So what are we left with? The front door?"

Roark scuffed to a halt, facing the exit. He put his hands on his hips, tilted his head to the side.

"No," Ronja hissed, raising a warning finger he could not see. "No way."

"Are you kidding me, Trip?" Iris moaned.

The boy spun to face them, beaming. Green bands ringed his body, pulsing in time with the piano. Ronja squinted through them. "Hardly," he said.

"It'll never work," Evie said. "This is pitched, even for you."

"It'll work," Roark countered smugly. "If we have the captain of the guard with us."

Ronja blinked. The record continued to spin obliviously. A cello had joined the forlorn piano, casting rivers of gold across the tent.

Evie broke the stream with a chuckle. "You skitzer."

Roark smiled wickedly. "I spoke with Sam a while back. We have his allegiance."

Iris let out a scandalized squawk and aimed a kick at Roark. He sidestepped her easily. "How long has he known?"

"About a month," Roark muttered, massaging the back of his head. When all three girls began to complain, he threw up his hands. "Listen, he and I agreed that the fewer people who knew the better."

Iris folded her twig arms. Evie just shook her head, staring daggers at her blood brother.

"Wait, how much does Sam know?" Ronja inquired from her

perch.

Roark glanced at her over his shoulder, a flicker of jealousy flaring in his eyes. "Everything."

Of course, she thought dimly. It all made sense now. Samson had always treated her gently. He was infinitely more welcoming than Kala and the others. She assumed he was just a kind soul. Clearly, it was more than that.

"How is this going to work, exactly?" Iris asked, her practicality overwhelming her annoyance. "Having Sam with us only takes care of the topside guards. People are still going to see us leaving."

"Not if we leave in the middle of the night," Ronja pointed out.

"So," Evie began, tapping a mocking finger to her lips. "We are banking on the hope that absolutely *nobody* is going to need to take a piss in the middle of the night?"

"People come and go from the Belly all the time," Ronja argued.

Iris shook her head, her brief locks fluttering. "But everyone knows we're on lockdown."

"You three worry too much," Roark said with a weighty sigh. Ronja glowered at him. If he felt the sting of her gaze, he chose to ignore it. "Really, your lives would be much better if you just relaxed a bit."

"Spit it out, Trip," Evie goaded him. "What have you got up your sleeve?"

"Music."

The record skipped like a startled rabbit. Ronja jumped. The colors swimming in her vision shivered in response. A violin had joined the fray, adding a hopeful tinge to the melancholy tune. "What do you mean?" she asked.

Roark beamed, exposing his sugar-white teeth. "I think it's

time the Anthem heard your voice."

Ronja's breath caught in her lungs, her lips parted in shock. "No," she breathed. She could feel Evie and Iris watching her with perplexed eyes, but kept her gaze fixed on Roark. His smile had slipped a fraction of an inch, but he still radiated confidence. "Absolutely not."

Roark dipped into his pocket and pulled out a small black machine. It resembled a handheld radio, though instinct told Ronja it was not. He offered it to her with an encouraging nod. She eyed it as if it might bite her, then grasped it tentatively. It was lighter than she had expected. "What is it?" she asked, turning it over by the tips of her bandaged fingers.

"An audio recorder," Roark answered, peering down at it fondly. "Mouse got it for me a few weeks back, I have a few of them. It records your voice and spits it back out again."

"What does that have to do with getting out?" Iris inquired.

"Everyone has been dying to hear this one sing," Roark explained, jabbing his thumb at Ronja, then holding out his free hand for the recorder. She set it in his palm sullenly, wondering if she could set his hair on fire if she stared hard enough. "She sings into these." He gave the device a little shake. "The recorders have amplified playback. We set them up at three different locations, set them to go off at the same time and ... "

"Bolt when everyone is trying to figure out where all the noise is coming from," Evie finished with a laugh. "Not bad, I like it."

"Why does it have to be me?" Ronja mumbled dejectedly. The three Anthemites raised their eyebrows at her. She flushed, fidgeting on her perch.

"What are you afraid of?" Roark asked after a brief pause. His voice was maddeningly gentle.

"I am not afraid."

"Of course not. When was the last time you sang?"

Ronja gritted her teeth, daring him to push her. "To save your skin from The New Music."

"Why?"

"What do you mean 'why?'" she hissed, sliding off the edge of the dresser. Roark regarded her down his long nose, his expression smooth as glass. "Because you were about to pledge your allegiance to The Conductor."

"Yes, but you haven't opened your mouth to sing since then. Why?"

Ronja tucked her sore fingers into fists, shrinking in his shadow. Suddenly, she hated how he towered over her. "There hasn't been a need."

He cocked his head to the side. "Do you need a reason to sing?"

"Yes!" she barked, drowning the flow of classical music. Iris shushed her, peering around anxiously. Ronja drew a rattling breath, then continued in a softer tone. "Yes, I do."

Roark's dark eyes roamed across the planes of her face. She trembled beneath his penetrating gaze, fighting the urge to reach up and itch her nose. "Why?" he finally asked.

"Because," she whispered. "Whenever I think about singing, I choke. All I can think of is ... " Her words turned to cotton in her mouth. She gestured broadly at the unspeakable. Her bandaged hand passed through a band of green. It rippled like curling steam.

"Why did you agree to the broadcast if you feel this way?" Roark asked. There was no pity in his eyes, only curiosity and devastating kindness. It made her want to scream.

"Because it has to be done. My voice is a weapon; I'll use it when I have to."

Roark smiled ruefully. "Your voice is an instrument of

freedom. It can free you too, if you let it."

Ronja bit her lip until it went numb. She wanted to shout that he was wrong, to shake his shoulders until he understood that nothing short of the destruction of The Music and the death of The Conductor could set her free. But he looked so sincere standing there before her ...

"Fine," she growled, tossing up her hands. "Just tell me what to do."

Roark beamed. "Follow me."

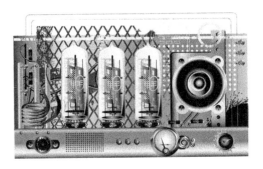

12: THE BRINK

"The best part about living back here is that it's pretty much deserted during the day," Roark told her as they approached his quarters for the second time that morning. "Not to mention, sound doesn't carry the way it does on the platform."

"Yeah," Ronja laughed. "I bet you love that."

The boy laughed as they arrived at his tent. "I just meant you don't have to worry about anyone hearing you sing."

"Sure."

Roark shoved aside the entrance flap, jerking his head to indicate she should pass first. She ducked through the opening, the boy close on her heels. The room was just as she had left it, with one small change. A full pack sat on the floor near the hammock. "You knew we would be leaving," she murmured.

Roark sighed, scratching the back of his skull and eyeing the pack with distaste. "I hoped not, but always better to be prepared."

"You should have told us about Sam, Roark," Ronja scolded him. She crossed her arms, staring him down. He squirmed under her harsh gaze. "We can't be keeping secrets from each other, not anymore."

"You're right," he conceded. He bowed his head, a strand of black hair falling into his face. "I'm sorry."

Ronja nodded brusquely. She had not been expecting an apology right off the bat and was not entirely sure what to do with it. "No more secrets."

"No more secrets," he promised solemnly. "Now." He reached into his back pocket and produced the recorder. "Are you ready, singer?" he asked, tossing the device high into the air and catching it with the opposite hand.

A sudden thought slammed into Ronja. "Wait," she said, holding up a hand. "Wilcox lives back here."

Roark strode back to the entrance, stuck his head through the flaps, then retreated. "He never comes back during the day," he promised, smoothing his mussed hair. "Frankly, I can't remember the last time he came back before two in the morning."

Despite her keen dislike for the commander, Ronja felt a twinge of sympathy for him. He was misguided, perhaps a bit of a coward, but he was dedicated and had given her family shelter. That was worth something.

"Ready?" Roark coaxed, holding out the device for her to take.

"Why can't you do it?" she grumbled as she snatched the device from him. "You could sing, or play the violin."

Roark chuckled. "You do *not* want to hear me sing, love. Besides, like I said. People have been waiting to hear your voice since that rumor struck up."

"Oh, right, the one you definitely didn't start?" Ronja inquired dryly.

The boy groaned. "Are we still on that?"

"Always. How are people supposed to know it's me singing?" Ronja inquired, sitting down on the hammock. She sank deeper into the cushions than expected and fought to keep her dignity as she struggled to plant her feet on the floor.

Roark smiled down at her, his eyes glinting mischievously. "A voice like yours would never go unnoticed down here. Believe me, love. They'll know."

Ronja could not resist a quiet laugh. "No need to flirt with me."

"Please," he scoffed, fluttering a dismissive hand. "That was not flirting. If I was flirting with you, you would know."

"Oh?" She folded her arms in mock scandalization.

The boy winked. Her stomach cartwheeled. "You'll know."

Ronja sobered, letting her wrapped hands fall to her lap. Roark followed her lead, his cheeky smile fading into a dour line. "You know, we never talked," she said, her voice the size of a pinhead. There was no need to elaborate; he knew what she was referring to.

"I know." Roark dragged his fingers through his thick hair, his eyes on the patterned rug. It might have been a trick of the light, but she was fairly certain there was a hint of color in his face. "I know it was just in the moment, and after what happened ... "

"What do you mean?" Ronja asked too quickly, glancing down and away. She could feel his heavy gaze resting atop her curls.

"I saw what the guards did to you."

The girl raised her head despite the immense weight that bowed it. "You were behind the mirror."

Roark looked as if he might be sick, his blush replaced by a nauseated pallor. It was answer enough.

Ronja sighed, reaching up to massage her left temple. Her headache was back. "I guess I knew that. You're the reason they stopped, aren't you?"

"I begged my father," he said, his voice barely more than a

whisper. "When they left I thought you were safe, but when you showed up in the torture chamber I realized he had just changed his technique." Shame bent his spine. "I just made things worse."

"No," Ronja replied. "Torture I can endure. But if they had gone through with it, if they had ... " She swallowed. The words were in her mouth, but they stuck to her teeth like gum. "If they had raped me." Roark flinched as if she had slapped him. "I might have broken."

When he finally spoke, his voice was a husk. "I am so sorry."

"What happened happened," she answered. "I'll never forget it, but I am tired of letting it hold me back." As soon as the words left her lips she knew they were true. She felt strangely light, as if her bones were filled with air. Warmth spread from her core to the tips of her fingers. Charged by the heat, she continued. "Roark." He looked up at the sound of his name. The whites of his eyes were laced with red. "I ... "

"Forgive me."

She shook her head firmly. "There is nothing to forgive."

Ronja felt the world tilt as Roark dropped to his knees, his head bowed. "I swear," he said, his voice so low and raw it was almost unrecognizable. "As long as I'm alive, as long as you want me around, I'll protect you, Ronja."

A part of her wanted to tell him he was being dramatic, that she did not need his protection. But as she gazed down at him, she saw not a warrior in search of validation, but a boy seeking redemption. He needed her. She would be a fool to pretend she did not need him.

Sliding off the hammock, Ronja knelt before him, taking his trembling hands with her bandaged ones. He locked eyes with her, shock rippling across his tortured features. "I'll protect you, too," she whispered, steadying his shivering gaze with her own. "Maybe, when this is all over, we could ... "

"Yes."

Ronja blinked. "What?" The gold flecks in his eyes flared, sunlight pouring through a lattice of leaves. He squeezed her injured hands lightly, careful not to apply too much pressure.

"It might be awhile," Ronja warned nervously, her wrapped hands fidgeting in his. She wondered if it was possible to sweat through the thick wreath of bandages. "I need time, and with everything going on ... "

Roark was shaking his head, smiling softly. He bent forward and pressed his soft lips to her brow. "I'll wait for you, Ronja Fey Zipse. We are on the brink of a new world; I'll wait for you there."

Ronja felt her throat tighten. Her vision clouded, her head buzzed. She floated somewhere above her body, watching as the scarred girl from the outer ring knelt before the heir to the city. Watching as he stared at her like she was the world encased in skin and bone. Confusion and euphoria raced through her blood. *What am I waiting for?* she wondered vaguely.

Then Roark pulled away, releasing her hands. "Do you want to be alone?" he asked.

Her eyebrows knit in confusion. "What?" she asked. He chuckled, waiting for her to catch up. "Oh. Yeah, yeah that would be good."

"What are you going to sing?"

Skitz. Ronja had not even considered that. She had listened to hundreds of songs since her introduction to real music months ago, but singing and listening were completely different birds. "I have some ideas," she lied fluidly.

For a moment, they were still, listening to the distant hum of the Belly, basking in the tentative promise of the future. Ronja was seized by the urge to reach out and touch him again. Before she could, Roark got up. "I should let you focus," he said regretfully.

"Right."

"The rest of the recorders are in the top drawer. Do you know how they work?"

"I can figure it out," she assured him, following his example and getting to her feet. "Just wait at the end of the hall, make sure no one comes back here."

"Of course." Roark turned with the grace of a dancer and strode toward the exit. He stopped before ducking through the door and threw a coy smile over his shoulder. "May your song guide us home, love."

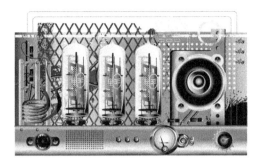

13: CHARLOTTE

Ronja knelt on the luxurious carpet, the three recording devices laid out before her like playing cards. Thoughts darted in and out of her mind like gnats. Some were needle sharp, others soothing. In the end, they belonged to her and that was enough.

We are on the brink of a new world; I'll wait for you there. A smile crept across her mouth, reopening the swollen cut she had forgotten. Something deep in her ribs stirred, long dormant after nearly two decades of solitude. It was not a promise. It was something different, something foreign. It was hope.

Ronja reached out and turned on the recorders with three successive clicks. She knew exactly what she was going to sing.

She finished recording the song as quickly as possible. She had to stop and erase the results twice, once because she could barely hear herself, once due to an unexpected voice crack that would put a twelve-year-old boy to shame.

When she was satisfied, she poked her head out of the tent and beckoned at Roark. He was seated at the mouth of the tunnel, his long legs sprawled before him as he stared into oblivion. She waved frantically until he noticed her and sprang to his feet. He jogged over to her.

"All done?" he asked unnecessarily.

Ronja nodded. Her throat was raw, her stomach felt like it was trying to digest itself.

"You should get some breakfast," he suggested. "Hopefully Delilah saved you some, though with James and Sam around I wouldn't count on it."

She cleared her throat. "Yeah," she agreed lamely. Still, she did not move to leave. Roark looked as if he wanted to say something and was straining to hold it back. "I should go," Ronja finally said. She shoved the curtain aside and stepped out into the alcove. Their elbows brushed, sending heat singing along her nerves.

"We should probably stay away from each other today," Roark blurted.

Ronja peeked back at him over her shoulder, her eyebrows lifting.

The boy smiled regretfully. "If Wilcox sees us, he'll assume we're plotting something."

"We are."

"Exactly."

"Good point."

Go, Ronja urged herself. Still, she did not budge. She sifted through her thoughts like a library catalogue, searching for something to say. "What time are we leaving?"

Roark scanned the empty hall, then refocused on her. "Not sure yet, things are still a bit hazy with the captain."

"Okay." *Get going.* With a heroic mental push, Ronja forced her muscles into motion, striding off down the hall with feigned ease. "See you later, shiny," she called back to him.

"Until then, singer," his words floated after her.

Her journey back to her tent was a blur. She did not even

bother to lift her hood as she wove through the crowds, taking the full brunt of the suspicious stares. Her brain was clogged with a thousand vibrating thoughts, leaving no room for her to care. *We are on the brink of a new world; I'll wait for you there.* Her lips curled into a smile.

When she arrived at her quarters, Georgie was already gone, likely running amuck with her new gang of friends. Without a Singer, Georgie was a social savant. The adults doted on her. The children were enamored with her. Many of them had never seen the light of day. Eleven was the cutoff for leaving the Belly. They fed on her tales of sunlight and rain and plants that grew without the aid of ultraviolet lamps. Though she would never admit it, Ronja knew Georgie reveled in the positive attention. She deserved nothing less after a childhood marred by cruelty and ostracism.

Taking advantage of the abandoned tent, Ronja dove into cleaning like a demon. She was not neurotic about tidiness like Iris but found a certain solace in menial labor. She unspooled her bandages so she could better tackle the project, knowing full well the surgeon would make her regret it. Her knuckles were capped with brown scabs that spidered each time she made a fist. They did not appear to be fractured, though. She had broken enough fingers that she was familiar with the particular ache.

Stripping down to a pair of soft leggings and a tank top, Ronja shoved her mattress and nest of blankets outside. Her neighbor, a woman named Harriet with ashen hair and a sweet disposition, judged her intent and lent her a broom. Ronja thanked her and swept the floor until it was spotless. When that was done, she replaced the mattress, shook out the quilts, and returned them to the bed. She even smoothed the wrinkles from the sheets and tucked them in, just how Georgie liked.

After picking up a quick lunch at the fire, which to her relief was deserted, Ronja hauled her bag of laundry to the bathhouse. She spent the better part of an hour by the pool, scrubbing the oils and stains from her clothes. Several other women were engaged in the same task nearby. They kept to themselves, chattering mindlessly and occasionally passing her uncertain looks.

No matter how she tried to focus on the harrowing night ahead, her thoughts kept bounding back to Roark like a stubborn puppy. *We are on the brink of a new world; I'll wait for you there.*

Would he really? The thought made her wince as she battled a stain, but she knew it was worth considering. There was no doubt in her mind that Roark cared for her, that he would protect her with his life if necessary. Still, he was a notorious flirt. Evie and Iris had spilled the details on his past one night in their tent. To say the shiny was a player would be an understatement. It did not bother her, exactly. Among the Anthemites, relationships were casual affairs. There were several dozen married couples and a handful of steady partners in the Belly, but for the most part, the revolutionaries moved about as they pleased.

"People pretty much do whatever they want down here," Evie had explained one night by the fireside. The techi had taken a generous swig from the nicked bottle of wine they were sharing, then held up a tattooed finger. "As long as it's consensual. I mean, before Iris ... " She whistled long and low, a sound as wistful as it was vulgar.

"What was that, darling?" Iris asked sweetly from the other side of the circle.

"Nothing, dear." Evie leaned toward Ronja, cupping her hand around her mouth. Her breath was heavy with the scent of red wine. "If you ever have any questions or need anything, you just let me know."

Blushing faintly at the memory, Ronja gathered her sopping

clothing and stood with a grunt. She was still growing accustomed to the casual manner sex was discussed in the Belly. Cold droplets landed on her bare feet as she lugged the bundle of garments to the drying racks. She slung the articles over the wooden bars, stewing.

She had never been in a relationship before, though it was not for lack of want. Henry had a revolving door of girlfriends. Despite his good looks and unfailing kindness, she had never viewed him as anything but her brother. She knew he felt the same way. The rest of Revinia saw her as a filthy mutt. Finding love had never been in the cards for her, so she gradually let the idea wither. Now, she was free to love. She was free to have anyone who wanted her in return. That did not mean she had to be naive.

"Ronja."

Her thoughts scattered, dust blown off the cover of a rambling book. The dress she grasped slipped through her fingers and landed on the floor with a wet slap.

"Charlotte," she breathed.

Ronja had only seen the girl at a distance over the past weeks. Charlotte looked older than she remembered. She *was* older, she reminded herself with a jolt. Her baby fat was disappearing, replaced by high cheekbones and full lips. Her corkscrew curls formed a halo around her face; her large brown eyes matched her skin. They were familiar. Steady, never soft. They were the eyes of her brother, down to the thick lashes and inquisitive spark.

"I've been looking for you," Charlotte finally admitted.

The younger girl laced her fingers before her, rocking back and forth on the balls of her feet. The habitual motion sent Ronja barreling into the past. To afternoons spent at the Romancheck house. Studying with Henry at the kitchen table while Charlotte read on the hearth. The soft patter of rain on the roof, the shriek of the kettle. They were treasured memories, some of the only times she felt truly at ease beneath The Music.

"You've been avoiding me," Ronja replied flatly. "For weeks."

"I know." Silence fell, heavier than the waterlogged air of the bathhouse. "I know Henry told you to take care of me, but I was in and out of this place all the time growing up. I have friends, people who look out for me."

"I know," Ronja assured her. Charlotte lived in a tent next to a large family near the tracks. She ate at their fire and looked out for the younger children as if they were her own siblings. "But it was his last wish. Would it kill you to let me check up on you once and awhile?"

Charlotte dropped her gaze to her feet, shame creeping across her features. "Cos told me you think I blame you," she said quietly. Ronja tensed, preparing for an onslaught. "I just wanted to tell you that I don't. I blame Henry. He always had to be the skitzing hero. He ... " She pressed a hand to her quivering lips, her eyes filling with shivering light.

Ronja stepped forward and enveloped her in a fierce hug, rocking her side to side. Charlotte did not make a sound, though her entire form shuddered. "I am so sorry," the older girl whispered into her hair. "I miss him, too."

Charlotte sniffed, pulling away from Ronja and wiping her nose with the back of her wrist. "Yeah," she said thickly. "I just thought I should tell you while I had the chance."

"What do you mean?"

Charlotte tilted her head to the side, an ironic smile splitting her pained mask. She rose on her tiptoes and curled her hand around her mouth. "I know about your voice."

Ronja pulled back sharply, clutching Charlotte by the shoulders with clawed fingers.

The younger girl gave a solemn nod. "So it *is* true. I thought it was just a dumb rumor."

"It is," Ronja blurted.

Charlotte chuckled. "You were always a crap liar, Zipse." Ronja flushed. She snatched her by the hand and tugged her deeper into the tunnel, abandoning her sopping laundry. The girl allowed herself to be towed without complaint, her hair bobbing cheerily. They wove through the collection of vanities until they hit the jagged wall of rubble that marked the edge of the Belly.

"Who told you about my voice?" Ronja demanded.

Charlotte rolled her eyes at the curved ceiling. "Who do you think?"

Ronja groaned, dragging an exhausted hand down her face. Cosmin was a sucker for pretty girls, and Charlotte was as lovely as she was devious. "You have to keep this quiet, you get that."

"Why?"

"Because I said so."

Charlotte gave a harsh laugh, cocking her hip to the side. "Okay, *Mom*."

"Char," Ronja implored her desperately.

"When are you leaving?"

The direct question caught Ronja off guard. Her stomach hit the stone floor as understanding clicked into place. She licked her lips, which were suddenly bone dry. "How did you ... "

"Cos."

"I haven't told him yet."

"Well, he knows, so you might want to get on that."

Ronja swallowed, grappling with the bolt of unwelcome news.

Charlotte shook back her hair with a huff. "You gotta stop underestimating us kids. We see more than you think."

"Does Georgie know?"

Charlotte shrugged. "Probably."

Ronja swore under her breath. Was that why Georgie had been so worried about her? Did she expect her to bolt when the conference with Wilcox failed? The possibility stirred up nausea in her gut, made worse by the fact that it was true.

"When are you leaving?" Charlotte asked again.

Ronja cast her eyes to the ground. "Tonight," she admitted.

"And were you planning on telling your cousins, or were you just going to up and leave like Henry?"

The words slammed into Ronja with the force of a steamer. She locked eyes with the girl when she answered. "I was going to tell them tonight." *Liar*, a voice in the back of her mind whispered.

Charlotte nodded brusquely, as if she heard the truth echo. "Right. Look." She took a step toward Ronja. At this distance, the resemblance to her brother was striking, everything from her nose to her lips to her deceptively calm eyes. "Georgie and Cosmin need you. You don't get to just run off and play hero whenever you feel like it."

Ronja dropped her gaze to her feet again, shame rising in her like a full moon. "I have to do this."

"Like hell you do," Charlotte growled.

The older girl raised her chin, forcing down her guilt and tightening her jaw like a tourniquet.

"You just want to go play solider with Trip."

Ronja heard her composure snap in the hollows of her mind, a branch beneath a boot. Fighting the urge to shout, she forced her words through gritted teeth. "I have to keep them safe."

"They are safe! This is the only safe place in the entire bloody city!"

"Not for long," Ronja growled. Charlotte paused at that, a hint of doubt inching into her face. "Listen," the older girl implored her, taking her by the shoulders. "The Conductor knows about the Anthem. It's only a matter of time before he finds the Belly. I am trying to stop him before that happens, but to do that I need to leave."

Charlotte shrugged her off, her lip curling in disgust. Ronja let her arms flop to her side, dejected. "Fine," the girl said. Her voice was like gravel. "But you need to promise me something."

"Anything."

"Say goodbye to your family. You owe them that much."

Without so much as a final nod, Charlotte spun on her heel and stalked away, her hair bouncing in time with her footsteps. Ronja watched her go until she was out of sight, unable to move.

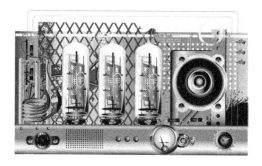

14: SILENCE AND NOISE

R onja knelt on the mattress, her head bowed as if in prayer. She checked her watch. 2:56 A.M. Somewhere far above, The Night Song was flooding homes, bedrooms, alleyways, slicing through dreams like a ship through the waves. She could still hear it sometimes if she listened. It clung to her, a stench she could never be completely rid of.

Movement to her left drew her gaze. Georgie was twitching in her sleep. The low light of the lantern wandered across her round features, highlighting the divot of stress on her forehead. A nightmare, perhaps, or a truth she could not shake.

When Georgie had arrived back at their tent for the evening, Ronja was already asleep. At least, she was pretending to be asleep. She kept her nose tucked under the edge of her quilt as her cousin stood over her, waiting. Eventually, Georgie sighed and lay down on the mattress, curling into a tight ball. She fell asleep at once.

Ronja reached out and tugged the blankets up around her thin shoulders. Georgie shifted, her pale eyelids shuddering, then stilled. The older girl dropped her gaze to her thighs, where a sealed envelope rested. It was blank, expressionless. When she had gone to write their names, her hands had failed. The letter inside was brief. There was no closing. She had not even bothered to sign it. If she had told them how much she loved them or begged for their forgiveness, she would have shattered.

She would have stayed.

Ronja rose on one knee. The letter slipped, landing on the mattress soundlessly. She got to her feet slowly, stooping to avoid the low ceiling. Strands of raven hair dripped into her face, cloaking her vision. Curiosity got the better of her. She padded over to the square mirror that stood atop their tower of books. Her lips parted in shock.

Her eyes were luminous against the long black wig. Iris had dropped it off earlier wrapped in newspaper along with a tube of what she initially thought was paint. A second look revealed it was foundation meant to cover her freckles. The makeup was a shade too dark for her pallor. It altered her features a startling amount. Her cheeks and nose were empty without the smattering of freckles, though the effect was not entirely unpleasant.

Ronja glanced down at her watch again. The long hand had limped through another sixty seconds. 2:57. *Almost there,* she coaxed herself. As the day passed, she had grown increasingly concerned that Roark and the others had somehow forgotten to tell her what time they were leaving. It was only when she went to crumple up the newspaper her wig and makeup arrived in that she glimpsed the note scrawled inside.

Diversion at 2:58. Elevator at 3:00.
— S

Ronja returned to her reflection. The collar of her trench coat rose past her chin, shielding her mouth. Her heavy knapsack was slung over her shoulders, her stingers tucked safely inside. *I look like an Anthemite*, she realized. All this time underground, her voice caught in the back of her throat, she had not felt like a revolutionary but a recluse. Back to her watch. The second hand oscillated around the thirty second mark, then crept onward.

Ronja stooped to set the letter on her pillow. Somehow, it made her side of the bed look even emptier. Three seconds. She turned her back on the sanctuary, on her family, on her unspoken words. Lifting her hood, she closed her eyes as the minute hand locked into place.

Goodbye, Georgie.

Her lips were sealed when her voice ripped through the Belly.

Ronja exploded from the tent. The lights were low, the scattered lamps like exhausted moons above her. She stood thunderstruck outside her quarters as Anthemites stumbled from their homes, blinking in the face of the deafening lyrics. Shouts and curses rang out. They looked around wildly, searching for the source of the voice that beamed down at them from all angles.

Be still, my friend
Tomorrow is so far, far around the bend

Her own voice tickled her ear as she launched into the bewildered crowd. It did not sound as she expected it to. It was steady as a mountain, rough around the edges. It was not beautiful, exactly. It was powerful.

Cast your troubles off the shore
Unlace your boots and cry no more
Because today my friend, I promise you are on the mend

Her words faded out on a sigh she did not remember

heaving. The relative quiet raised chills on her skin. She dipped her head lower, tugging on the edge of her hood. Around her the Anthemites were still struggling to identify the source of the song. They jostled her shoulders, their attention slipping over her as if she were a wraith.

Ronja.

Ronja.

Ronja.

Her name was on their lips. Roark was right, they knew her voice without ever having heard it. Reeling, she moved as quickly as she could without running. Her paranoia burgeoned. It was unnecessary. For the first time in months, no one was paying her any mind. It was working. She cut between two tents and slipped into the Vein.

The elevator burst into view at the end of the wide aisle. Her heart leapt into her throat. She had trained herself to ignore the exit. The thought of leaving had become so distant there was no sense taunting herself with it. Green and white designs spiraled across the metallic doors, a mosaic of farmland viewed from an airship.

Almost there. Perspiration beaded on her brow. She was gaining on the exit too fast. They could not linger outside the elevator waiting for a wayward member of the mob to break ranks. Their only chance was to coast straight through the doors when Samson opened them at 3:00, a blip in the babel. Ronja slowed to a virtual crawl, allowing herself to be jostled by the writhing throng.

She nearly jumped out of her skin when the recorder looped, blasting her voice into the Belly again. The Anthemites redoubled their efforts to discover the source.

Be still, my friend

Tomorrow is so far, far around the bend
Cast your troubles off the shore

A gentle hand touched the space between her shoulder blades. Ronja flinched. A familiar form slipped into her peripheral vision. His face was obscured by his deep cowl, but she would know his swagger anywhere. "I prefer your real hair," he murmured.

Ronja smiled grimly, though she knew he could not see it. "Where are they?"

"On their way."

Unlace your boots and cry no more
For today my friend,
I promise you are on the mend.

Ronja checked her timepiece. "Fifteen seconds," she muttered. She felt rather than saw Roark tense beside her. They were only meters from the elevator. The world was shrinking in diameter, narrowing toward their escape. Behind them, the Anthemites were still running around like chickens with their heads cut off. "How many times is it set to repeat?"

"Three."

As if in reply, the recording began its final loop.

Be still, my friend
Tomorrow is so far, far around the bend

They were only steps away. The harder Ronja stared at the elevator doors, the more the painted patterns seemed to dance. Two sets of footsteps struck up behind them, one light and hurried, the other heavy and sure. Ronja peeked over her shoulder, relief welling in her chest. Evie and Iris were nearly unrecognizable. The techi sported a mousy brown wig and a cracked pair of glasses that magnified her rich brown eyes. The surgeon wore a braided blonde wig and a ratty newsboy cap.

Ronja twisted back around and came to a stop before the elevator. The world shuddered to a halt. For a terrible moment, her breath was suspended.

Then the doors rolled open like a hungry mouth, spilling greenish light across them. Samson stood in the compartment garbed in an oversized bomber jacket and heavy black pants. She knew beneath his coat he was armed to the teeth. Somehow, that did not make her feel better. "Get in," the captain ordered sharply.

Ronja hitched up her bag and stepped across the threshold. Her friends filed in after her. They shuffled around to face the front, tensed for an assault. The Belly sprawled before them, teeming with baffled Anthemites and light and sound. Ronja felt her soul clench. Though it had become something of a prison over the past months, the underground station was the first place she ever felt truly free. It was their first home, their only home. She would protect it and her cousins, no matter the cost.

I promise you are on the mend

"Ronja!"

No.

Ronja felt her legs give, yet somehow she remained upright. Her friends stiffened around her, their hands flying to their respective weapons. Hundreds of pairs of eyes rounded on them as her name echoed in the wake of the song. A wave of devastating silence washed over the Belly. Samson slammed his fist into the button. The elevator doors began to roll shut.

A slight form shot out of the stagnant crowd. Her eyes were

wide with panic and anguish. A crumpled letter was clenched in her fist. She skidded to a halt a dozen paces from the closing doors, her night dress swirling around her knees. "Georgie," Ronja breathed. She took a half step forward but Roark wrapped a restraining arm around her waist.

The doors closed with a polite peal of chimes.

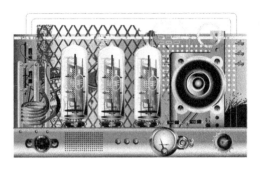

15: ASCENSION

The elevator crawled up the shaft unhurriedly, the gears groaning through the thin walls. Five pairs of lungs drew on the air. No one dared speak. Roark maintained his grip on Ronja, as if she might attempt to pry open the iron doors. She had not so much as blinked since they shut. "So ... do you think they saw us?" Evie finally asked.

"Yeah," Samson replied tonelessly. He swore, slamming his fist into the wall with a reverberating thud. "They saw us."

"I knew this was a bad idea," Iris exclaimed with a scalding glance at Roark. "Going out through the pitching front door ... "

"The sewers would have been crawling with guards, you know that," the shiny shot back, releasing Ronja. She touched the place where his hand had been, only vaguely aware of the argument taking place around her. Her mind was still anchored below. "I'd like to point out it was working perfectly until ... "

An earsplitting screech and the elevator jerked to a stop. The lights winked out. Iris let out a squeak. Samson swore. Ronja crashed back into her bones. She swiped her hood from her head as if it would allow her to see better. Silence fell as the compartment swayed, suspended from dangling cables.

"Are you going to say it or should I?" Evie asked out of the black.

"They must have cut the power," Roark growled.

"You think?" Iris shouted. "Great, now we're all going to suffocate."

Roark made a noise of dissent. "No need to be defeatist."

A flashlight flared in the dense shadows. Ronja blinked as her pupils pulled in on themselves. Samson aimed the cold beam at the ceiling, his neck craned to examine the cheap tiles. "The center panel is an exit," he said. "If we can ... "

Roark scooted Iris aside gently, reached up, and palmed the panel upward, sliding it out of view. The darkness of the elevator shaft was somehow deeper than that around them.

"Yeah, that," Samson said. He turned the flashlight on his face. The beam carved out deep shadows in his eye sockets. "I'll go first, then I'll pull the rest of you up."

"Excuse me," Roark cut in. "I think the strongest of us should go first."

The captain laughed, the sound filling the already cramped space. "We can compare shoe sizes another time." He shed his bulky pack and set it on the floor with a ringing clang. Handing the flashlight off to Evie, he reached up with ease and gripped either side of the portal. He hoisted himself up with a grunt, kicking Roark in the chest.

"Oi!" Roark yelled after him, but Samson was already through. The remaining Anthemites crowded under the hole, squinting into the gloom. The flashlight cut through nothing but air and dust. Heavy footfalls studded the roof.

"We're only a few feet below the door," Sam called down. "I can get it open." A collective sigh of relief swept through the group. There was a charged pause, followed by the unmistakable sound of metal grinding against metal. Ronja shivered as cold air rushed down through the portal, stirring the tips of her wig.

"Don't move," came a voice from above.

Evie clicked off the flashlight. Ronja felt rather than heard her and Roark draw their stingers. She cursed herself internally for storing her own weapons so deep in her bag. "James," Samson said loudly. Ronja stiffened and felt Roark do the same to her right. "What are you doing here?"

"My job."

"I told you I was going to cover your shift."

"And I told you there was no need."

A pause. Ronja held her breath. Sweat trickled down her spine. Iris was shivering nearby, terror rolling off her body in waves. Ronja forced down the urge to reach out to her, fearing making a sound.

"Wilcox just radioed me," James went on, his voice hard as stone. "He told me to cut the power on the elevator, that it was full of traitors."

"James ... "

"This is pitch, Sam!" the elder Mason bellowed.

"Keep your voice down."

"You know Ronja is insane, right?"

Ronja felt her temper flare. She gritted her teeth to keep from bellowing an insult. Roark shifted on his feet. She imagined his grip tightening around the hilt of his stinger.

"That girl is going to get us all killed."

"Or she could save us."

A hollow laugh. "You really believe that?"

Samson paused for a beat. "How much do you know, James?" he asked cautiously.

"Everything." Ronja could almost see his smug smile in the blank slate before her. "Wilcox trusts me, he told me everything."

"Then you know the rumors about her are true."

"I know *she* believes them, but come on, Samson." Frustration saturated his boastful tone. "How can you believe them so easily?"

The captain was quiet for a long moment. Ronja thought her bones might shatter beneath the weight of the pause. "Roark, Evie, and Iris are my family. If they trust Ronja, I do too. I thought you were part of that family."

Time reached out into the darkness, toying with them in the claustrophobic compartment. Each breath felt like twenty. Finally, the suspension snapped. "Get on your knees," James ordered.

"Jim ... "

A resounding click, the safety of a gun being switched off. Roark went rigid. His stinger flared, painting the shadows blue and white. Evie followed his lead. The combined glow was enough to reveal their tense faces.

"Get up here and get on your knees." The elevator swayed as Samson pushed off from the roof. "Hands behind your head." Leather crunched. Static spiked as James flipped on his radio. "Sir, I have them. What should I — "

Crack.

Roark swore, stuffing his weapon into its holster and shoving Ronja and Iris out of the way. Ronja braced herself against the wall as the boy started to lift himself through the portal. A thud like a bag of flour slamming into the ceiling shook the elevator. Roark yelled and crashed back onto the floor, landing on his arm awkwardly. "Sam!" he bellowed, scrambling to his feet gracelessly and clutching his shoulder. "Samson!"

"I'm ... I'm good," came the breathless reply. Evie raised her crackling stinger to the hole in the ceiling. A muscular arm drooped over the edge, lifeless. It was white as the belly of a fish.

"James," Ronja murmured. "Is he alive?"

Iris stepped forward, her confidence snapped firmly into place, and pinched his wrist. Everyone in the compartment ceased breathing until she released him with a quick nod. Ronja sighed, relieved. As much as she loathed him, she did not wish him dead.

"How did you take him down?" Roark shouted up to Samson, admiration ringing in his tone.

"I didn't," the captain replied shortly. A soft thump graced the roof, followed by the whisper of lithe footsteps. The Anthemites glanced at each other in the harsh aura of the stingers. A heavy scraping pulled their eyes skyward, just as James was dragged from view. Another hand, lean and strong, shot through the gap.

"Terra," Ronja spat.

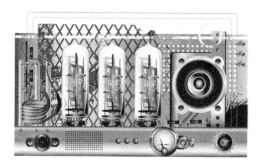

16: BITTER

"Grab my hand," Terra ordered. Ronja bristled. She curled her fingers into fists, ignoring the throbbing pain that resulted. The last thing she wanted was to touch Terra, unless it was to add a broken nose to her list of injuries.

"What are you doing here?" Evie asked.

"Saving your skins, again," Terra replied. The techi chuckled, holstering her stinger and plunging them into darkness yet again. A split second later she flicked on the flashlight and passed it to Roark. "Any time, Wick."

Evie clasped the offered hand. The agent yanked her up fluidly, despite the techi's muscular frame and bag. A moment later, Evie reached down, crooking a finger at Iris. The surgeon stepped forward and was pulled through like a rag doll. Ronja and Roark were left alone in the compartment.

"Go ahead," Ronja said, jabbing her thumb at the portal. Roark shook his head and stuffed the flashlight into his coat pocket. The girl eyed him dubiously. "What are you ... oi!" He had grabbed her by the waist and lifted her as if she weighed nothing at all. Cursing colorfully, she braced her hands on either side of the hole and hoisted herself up. Roark released her just as she clipped the side of his head with her shoe.

"Is this going to become a tradition?" he yelled after her. Ronja was no longer paying attention. Scrambling to her feet, she peered around the shaft. She was alone on the roof save for James, who lay motionless on his side. His mountainous torso rose and fell steadily.

"Ro, come on!" Ronja looked up. Evie knelt in the doorway several feet above, her tattooed hand outstretched. Terra had moved out of sight, much to her relief. Iris and Samson lingered at the door, conversing in hushed tones. The captain glanced down at his fallen subordinate periodically, his face clouded with warring emotions. "Hurry up," the techi said, a twinge of uncharacteristic anxiety coloring her tone. "Wilcox is probably on his way."

Ronja took her hand and allowed the techi to drag her up, pack and all. Her knees scraped the sharp lip of the floor and she hissed in pain. Evie helped her to her feet. Brushing the dirt from her knees, Ronja glanced around the room.

The aboveground station had not improved since her last visit. Heaps of trash and junk littered the dimly lit space. Pale winter moonlight spilled through the slats in the boarded windows, landing in puddles on the stone floor.

Moonlight. Ronja felt her throat tighten. Her eyes flooded, and she was gripped by the urge to reach out and pocket the glow.

"What the hell were you thinking?"

Anger suffocated the bliss enveloping her. Ronja had almost forgotten about Terra. Curling her mouth into a snarl, she rounded on the agent, who leaned up against the wall, her half shaven head resting against the bricks. Even in the faint light, the violet bruising around her eye was visible, though it was not as impressive as Samson had made it out to be. "What are you doing here?" Ronja growled.

"What? No 'thank you?'" Terra inquired tersely. She peeled off from the wall, prowling toward her like a stalking cat. Evie lodged herself between them before things got heated.

"Not now," the techi warned sharply, her palms pressed to their sternums. The two girls glowered at each other but did not resist. They both knew she was right. "Trip!" Evie called desperately. "Get your shiny ass up here!"

Scuffling sounds rose from the elevator shaft, punctuated by a muffled curse. Then two tawny hands appeared at the edge of the floor. Roark dragged himself up, wincing visibly as his injured shoulder strained. "Terra," he greeted the agent as he clambered to his feet. "You're looking terrible. James should be fine, by the way."

"Guys, we need to split," Samson broke in before Terra could respond. Ronja glanced over at the captain. He was as grim as she had ever seen him, his blue eyes drained of their usual mirth. He carried his title well. "Wilcox will be here any second."

"Doubt it." The entire party shifted its focus to Terra. She gave a lazy smile. "Wilcox may have some trouble getting out through the sewers. We should have about fifteen minutes, thirteen since Trip took his sweet time getting up here."

"What did you do?" Evie asked, her thick brows disappearing beneath false bangs. Terra grinned, the first genuine smile Ronja had seen her wear since their escape from Red Bay.

"Another time," she answered coyly. "We still need to get out of here now."

Ronja narrowed her eyes, the comment having lit her short fuse. She crossed her arms over her chest, a challenge. "What makes you think we're taking you with us?"

"Ronja," Roark warned in a low voice.

"You think we should take her with us after what she did?" she demanded, rounding on him. If he was intimidated by her thunderous expression, he did an excellent job hiding it.

"I mean," Iris spoke up tentatively. "She did save us."

"Wilcox will exile her if we leave her," Evie tacked on.

"Or worse," Sam muttered darkly.

Ronja bristled, her nostrils flaring. She was vastly outnumbered and they did not have time to deliberate. She threw up her hands in defeat, then jabbed a finger at Terra. "If you betray us, I'll kill you." Her insides vaulted at the words, especially since she knew they were true.

"And if it turns out your voice is useless, I'll bring you to Wilcox myself," Terra replied easily.

Ronja opened her mouth to bite back but a hand on her shoulder gave her pause. She looked up at Roark, seething. His eyes were steady as a still lake. *Calm down*, he reminded her silently. "Mouse is in a truck at Hill and 61st," he said, turning his gaze on the rest of their group. "We leave in groups of two. Sam and Ro will go first."

"What?" Ronja yelped, turning around to face him directly.

"Thanks," Samson muttered.

"You and I are far too recognizable as a pair," he explained gently. At this angle, their faces were scarcely a breath apart. She could smell the musk of his hair, see the tiny freckles that dappled his cheekbones. "We'll all be safer this way."

Her heart wilted. He was right, of course. Going out alone was dangerous enough. Together, they were a beacon for trouble.

Roark continued. "Iris and Evie will go next, Terra and I will follow last."

"Great," Terra mumbled

Roark shot her a sour look, then moved on. "Keep your heads low, and whatever happens, do *not* run." A wave of nods rippled through the knot of Anthemites. A gust of brutal wind threw itself against the walls of the station. Ronja shivered. It had nothing to do with the cold.

Samson zipped his jacket, then stepped toward Ronja. She practically had to lean back to make eye contact with him. "You ready, partner?" he asked.

No. "Yeah."

Evie reached out and punched her on the bicep. Iris touched her elbow. Roark gave her shoulder another quick squeeze. The ghost of his touch burned through her overcoat. With any luck, that warmth would carry her through the streets unscathed. Ronja glanced over at Samson, who was already halfway to the back door. He had pulled a knit cap over his shaggy blonde hair and was digging for something in his pocket.

With a final glance at her friends, Ronja hiked up her pack and followed.

The exit from the aboveground station was unremarkable to say the least. That was the point. While she understood the strategy, sometimes it shocked her how easy it would be for an Off to break down the wooden door and walk straight in. All that protected them was the power of suggestion, a member of the guard posing as a sap addict, and a keypad with a shifting code that locked the elevator.

A chill passed through her. The faces of her cousins, of Charlotte, flared in her psyche. How much time did they have before the Belly turned from a haven to a tomb?

Ronja came to a halt behind Samson. His callused hand was frozen on the brass doorknob. Unlike Roark, the captain was prized by the resistance for his stability and levelheadedness. He was loyal not only to his cause, but to his commander.

But he was not willfully blind to the threat of annihilation.

Samson twisted the knob and pushed open the door, his hand on the gun at his hip. Silver light yawned, spreading across the floor like encroaching surf. He stepped into the alleyway, peering around suspiciously, then motioned for her to follow.

Ronja felt four pairs of eyes on her back as she passed through the frame, pulling up her hood. The full brunt of the wind struck her and she sucked in a shocked breath. It was frigid. Yet, somehow, it was not as she remembered. She scanned the side street. Nothing but trash bins and frost-sealed crates. She lifted her eyes to the uncommonly clear sky. Carin loomed large and white. Calux, the winter moon, was a bluish afterthought. She had never been able to fully appreciate their majesty under the hands of The Music. Now, they sent shivers singing down her spine.

Samson tugged on her sleeve, pulling her forward. The door shut behind them. Her brain snapped into high gear. She broke away from him, matching his pace as they hurried to the mouth of the alley. She half expected the world to grind to a halt when she stepped onto the main road, but it kept spinning. Her heart thundered as she observed the derelict neighborhood she grew up in.

The cast iron gas lamps. The drab brick houses and cobblestone streets. The gated storefronts and overflowing waste bins. The red-and-white propaganda painted on the sides of buildings and nailed to storefronts.

Passion is perilous.
Emotion is treacherous.
Disobedience is destruction.

"Come on," Samson muttered. He took off down the empty avenue at a brisk pace, his head low. She jogged after him, her footfalls too loud on the damp street. The wind cut at her, stirring her false hair and trench coat, but it was the silence that made her shudder. Had it always been so quiet aboveground?

The unmistakable rustling of parchment pulled her gaze to

the right. Her eyes popped. "Skitz," she whispered. Sam just nodded. There was nothing to say. Dozens of wanted posters bearing Roark's name and her own lined the buildings. More than half bore her image. Many where illegible, leeched by the elements. Others were fresh, their print bitingly clear. "300,000 notes," she said under her breath. When she worked the subtrain and newsstand, her yearly income was 4,500. A wicked grin twisted her lips as a foreign sort of satisfaction flooded her veins. "All this for a mutt from the outer ring."

Then she remembered who had taken her picture. She tore her eyes from the flyers, stared dead ahead. They were approaching 61st. She recognized the deli with the faded green awnings.

Ronja stiffened, her fingers curling around the straps of her bag. "Sam," she breathed, forcing herself not to break her stride. "Did you hear that?"

"You, in the hoods, stop right there!"

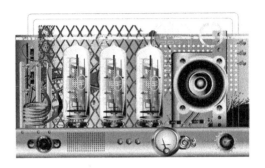

17: HALTED

Ronja and Samson froze, spines rigid and hearts petrified. They did not dare reach for their weapons. For the second time that night the girl unbraided herself for stuffing her stingers into the bottom of her pack. If they made it to their destination, she vowed to ask Evie for some sort of holster she could wear around her waist. "Keep your head down," Samson whispered as a pair of elephantine feet lumbered toward them. "Let me do the talking."

"Quiet!" the Off barked, his footfalls scuffing to a stop directly behind them. "Turn around, nice and slow."

They followed his command. Ronja kept her eyes on the ground, her hands at her sides. She could not see him but she could smell him. Sour sweat and alcohol. The pungent odor called back memories of her old boss, Don Wasserman. Given the labored quality to his breathing, she imagined he was just as obese. "Is there a problem, sir?" Samson asked meekly.

The Officer ignored him. "What are you two doing out this time of night?"

"My sister and I are going to see our aunt, she phoned an hour ago. Her health has taken a turn for the worse." Ronja smiled at the frost-bitten bricks. The captain was an excellent liar, his tone fluid and natural. She had not expected that of him.

The Off was not impressed. "Your sister mute or something?"

"No sir, just very shy."

Ronja bobbed her head in agreement, her eyes still fixed to the ground. Heavy footfalls, then a bloated gut encroached on her vision, barely contained by the uniform stretched across it. A gloved hand snatched her jaw, lifting her face to the sky. Fear spasmed in her chest and she jerked away. Snarling, the Off forced back her hood and released her. By some miracle her wig stayed in place, cloaking her absent ear. She waited for him to raise the alarm, her chin dropped and muscles coiled. Instead, he gave a disapproving grunt. "I was hoping you'd be blonde like your brother."

"Sir?"

"Look at me, girl."

Ronja crushed her disgust in her palm. This was not her first encounter with Offs like this. Her status as a mutt had not always been enough to drive them away. She knew how to deal with them. Steeling herself, she let her eyelids droop, her jaw go slack. She looked up. He was shorter than she expected and twice as wide. His beady eyes were shot with red. She held her breath as he drank her in, waiting for a spark of recognition.

"Papers," he commanded, but the word was drowned out by the series of hacking coughs that exploded from her open mouth. Spittle flew and the Off leapt back, swearing and wiping his ruddy face. "Skitzing hell, does she have the Retch?"

Maybe, pitcher. The Retch was rampant in the outer ring, especially in the winter months. In the past she might have played it off as some sort of fictional mutt disease, but the Retch was just as effective.

"We're not sure, sir," Samson answered, blending with her

facade fluidly. "We're taking her to the doctor tomorrow." Ronja wiped her nose with the back of her wrist demonstratively.

"Get out of here," the Officer snapped, shooing them away with a thick hand. "Go on, scram!"

"Yes, sir, thank you, sir." Without wasting another moment, Sam snagged Ronja by the wrist and began to drag her down the street, coughing and wheezing. She started to look over her shoulder, but Samson tightened his grip on her. "Keep your eyes forward," he warned under his breath. "Slow down."

Ronja slackened her pace, ignoring every fiber in her body that was begging her to run. It was only when the retreating footsteps of the drunken Off faded completely that her stiff muscles relaxed. The captain released her. She wrapped her fingers around the straps of her backpack to keep them from shaking. "That was too close," she said. "What about the others?"

Samson shook his head, his false Singer winking in the orange light of the gas lit lamps. "He was too blasted to recognize you; Trip should be good."

Ronja bit her cheek to hold back her words. The captain had not understood her. Iris and Evie were making the journey to Hill and 61st alone. As formidable as the techi was in a fight, the Officer was a beast ... and he was on the hunt for a blonde.

Iris burst into the front of her mind, her lovely face framed by her platinum wig. The rage she had pushed down came crawling back, digging its claws into her throat. Even if the Off missed Evie and Iris, he would find another victim, one who could not fight back by order of her Singer. Ronja stopped in her tracks, only steps from the deli that marked the intersection. Two large wanted posters were pinned to the double doors, both bearing her photograph.

"We have to go back," she said.

Samson rounded on her. His blue eyes flashed brighter than

the metal piece on his ear. "What, why?"

"We have to take down that Off," Ronja answered calmly, shrugging off her pack and squatting on the cobblestones. She unbuttoned it and dug through the layers of clothing. The cool metal of her stingers kissed her fingertips, causing the wound over her heart to prickle painfully. She yanked the weapons from the pack and stood, radiating reckless confidence.

Samson fidgeted, shifting from foot to foot on the slick avenue. "Ronja," he began uncertainly. "I get it, I do."

"Do you?"

"Yes. You feel like you have to protect everyone."

"I do," she snapped, wincing as her voice bounced down the deserted street. Her eyes darted about. Nothing but sleepy gas lamps and dark windows. Samson sighed. Ronja sucked in a deep breath and blew it out through her teeth, clutching at poise. "We both know what will happen if we let him go."

"I know."

Ronja bristled at the genuine ache in his voice.

"But if we go after him, we'll miss our ride. Mouse is only going to wait so long, that kid is a piece of work."

"Then we work fast."

"Think about it," Samson implored her. "What if he calls for backup before we take him down? One of them is bound to recognize you and this whole thing blows up. Do you see those posters?" He jammed a gloved finger at the posters on the doors of the deli.

Bloody convenient, Ronja thought gruffly. "I am not blind," she growled. "But the next woman he finds, the one who can't say 'no.' We have a duty to protect her. Right, *captain*?"

His title hung between them, a needle hovering over a record. They balanced it for a long moment, watching each other in the strangely warm light of the lamps. Finally, Samson sighed, his bulky shoulders sagging. Weariness seeped from his skin. "If you really want to save this city, you'll keep yourself alive. You have to pick your battles if you want to win the war, Ronja."

The fight leaked from her. She did not speak to the captain. Instead, she shouldered her bag and marched toward the intersection, her shadow blinking in and out of existence as she waded through the puddles of light. Samson watched her for a long moment, then followed.

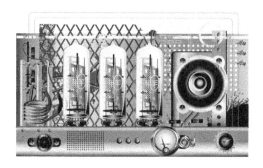

18: STOWAWAY
Roark

"We good?" Roark whispered. Terra did not answer, nor did she give any indication that she had heard him. She was taking her time checking around the corner, one hand on her nearest blade, the other braced against the brick wall. "Oi, Terra." The girl slipped out onto 61st Street, striding confidently across the icy cobblestones. He followed with an impatient grunt and a final glance over his shoulder.

Though he placed a fair amount of trust in Mouse, he had to admit he was a bit surprised when he saw the hulking canvas covered truck waiting in the shadows between two street lamps. He half expected the boy to lose his nerve at the eleventh hour, but for once it seemed everything was going according to plan. *Almost everything*, he reminded himself dully.

"Hurry up," Terra commanded, beckoning at him from several paces ahead.

"You got here thirty seconds ago," Roark grumbled, but he sped up. There was no telling when Wilcox and his agents would bust out of the Belly. He still had no idea what Terra had done to keep them pinned down and was not entirely sure he wanted to.

Not to mention, they had seen a drunken Off stumble by around 59th Street.

His pulse climbed as they approached the back of the auto. It was an ancient truck once used to ferry laborers back and forth between the city and the farms and could seat up to fifty. Many of the workers were mutts, forced to work the fields their ashes would one day fertilize. Roark felt his gut cinch. Had Layla been one of them? Ronja never spoke about her mother, not since Red Bay.

The canvas flaps at the back of the truck rippled as he and Terra came upon them. Wasting no time, they hoisted themselves up onto the rough wooden platform and stepped into the compartment. Blackness rushed over him. The fabric was thick enough to mute the streetlight. Roark stepped forward, vaguely aware that Terra was securing the flaps behind him. As his vision adjusted, the faint forms of his family bled into view. They lined the walls of the truck, seated on low benches. "Everyone here?" he asked quietly.

"Yeah," a knot of voices replied. Relief swelled in Roark when he heard Ronja among them. "You all right, Ronja?" he asked.

"Fine," came her brittle reply. His brow furrowed. He opened his mouth to ask for the truth, but a burst of static cut him off.

"Oi, everybody ready back there?" Mouse demanded over the radio. "I do *not* like just sitting here waiting for ... "

Evie shut him up with the push of a button. "Lock and load, hamster," she snapped.

There was no response from the other end of the line. The engine revved with a guttural thrum. Roark stumbled as the vehicle lurched forward. A hand, callused and strong, snagged him by the wrist. "Thanks, Sam," he said, squinting down at the hunched form.

"What?" the captain asked from the opposite end of the

compartment.

Roark's body worked twice as fast as his mind. He twisted from the iron grip and whipped out the revolver at his side, his stingers forgotten. "Lights!" he bellowed, cocking the gun. "Get the lights!" The sound of stingers igniting and knives singing twined with the rumble of the engine. Bright light flooded the cramped space as someone lit the lantern hanging overhead. For a split second, Roark was blinded by it.

"Easy, fella," came an unfamiliar male voice, heavy with a foreign lilt. Roark rifled frantically through the handful of accents he was familiar with. His formal education had focused very little on the outside world, and he had only ever met foreigners in passing. He was not familiar with this particular accent. He blinked, drawing the stowaway into focus.

He crouched in the corner of the truck bed, inches from the entrance. A hood covered his head. He shook it back to reveal long dark hair and darker eyes. He grinned, flashing blazing white teeth. "Hands where we can see them," Roark ordered as Evie stepped up to stand beside him, her stingers sizzling in her hands. The rest of their comrades pressed against their backs, watching the scene unfold with bated breath.

The stowaway laced his fingers behind his head, still smiling up at them genially. The truck bounced when it struck a pothole, and a strand of hair slipped into his face. He shook it back with a huff. "Guess I need a haircut," he chuckled. "You feel me, pretty boy?"

Roark tightened his grip around his revolver. "Who are you?"

"Jonah, just Jonah."

Evie breathed in sharply. Roark flicked his gaze toward her, startled. Her jaw was set, her hooded eyes flashing in the electric glow of her weapons. "You're Tovairin," she said. Somehow, she made it sound like an accusation.

Of course. Roark kicked himself for not recognizing the accent sooner. Tovaire was the war-torn nation adjacent to Arexis, Evie's homeland. He only knew what he had heard from Evie and her parents, that Tovaire had fallen into chaos after the war. That it was now run by bloodthirsty gangs funded by drugs and human trafficking.

"What are you doing here?" Roark demanded.

Jonah sighed, as if it truly pained him to be answering their questions. "Well, I was having a nap until the truck started moving about an hour ago, then you *fiesters* jumped on board." His smile spread like a plague. "I get it was dark and all but, really? None of you noticed me?"

"This is why we should have gone first, Trip," Terra snapped.

Roark tossed her a glance over his shoulder, passing a warning through his eyes. The blonde girl did not seem to sway despite the constant motion of the truck. She had drawn her largest knives, machetes that could cut through skin as well as bone.

Jonah pushed a low whistle through his lips. Roark turned back to him, his eyes narrowed. As much as he despised Terra, he hated the way Jonah was looking at her more.

"Look at you with those big knives," the Tovairin noted appreciatively. "Someone take a piss in your coffee? Would it kill you to smile?"

Terra bared her teeth, twirling her blades with dangerous ease. "I would, if I was cutting out your tongue."

The vicious words did not deter the rogue. Jonah chuckled, his eyes roaming up and down her body.

"Skitz ... enough!"

Roark nearly lost his grip on his revolver when a blunt force knocked him aside. Evie steadied him as they watched Ronja take his place before the stowaway. She had drawn one of her stingers and held it before her like a sword, painting both their faces blue.

Her hood was flipped back, revealing her onyx wig and searing green eyes.

"What are you doing here?" she demanded. "Tell us right now or this goes in your eye."

Jonah sneered at the crackling end of the weapon. "Trust me," he said, raising his eyes to her face. "I've had worse." Ronja switched her stinger to her right hand and popped the top clasps of her overcoat. The branching knot of scar tissue over her heart was particularly prominent in the violent glow. The stranger arched a brow in surprise.

"You sure about that?" Ronja asked flatly, transferring her weapon back to her dominant hand.

Roark smiled. He loved how fierce she was. She was a river dammed only by skin, a devastating creature forged in hardship and suffering. Not a solider, a survivor.

"Feisty," Jonah noted, leaning toward her. Even kneeling, the top of his head almost reached her shoulders. "I like that." Ronja cranked back her weapon, twisting the handle so it blazed brighter. The stowaway flinched. "All right, all right, easy," he mumbled. "I was just having a laugh."

Ronja did not appear to find the humor in his words. When she spoke, it was with irrefutable authority. "Answer the question."

"If I do, will you please put that down?"

The girl smirked, her eyes glinting with twisted mirth. Roark felt his mouth go dry. "Depends on your answer."

Jonah huffed, shaking his long hair over his broad shoulders. "Fine, fine. We heard you were in a bit of a snare, so they sent me to see what I could do."

"They?" Ronja inquired brittlely.

"Your old allies from yesteryear," he drawled. "The great nation of Tovaire."

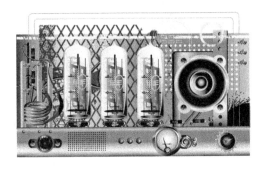

19: THE KEV FAIRLA

The engine coughed beneath them, fracturing the stunned silence. Ronja gaped at Jonah openly. He watched her with an unnerving combination of curiosity and conceit, his face dripping in the violent light of her stinger. She had heard him speak, but had not understood him.

Evidently, she was not alone.

"Wait, what?" Iris asked dubiously. Ronja glanced back over her shoulder. The surgeon stood on her tiptoes, bracing herself against Samson to see Jonah. She was the only one not aiming a weapon at him.

Jonah eyed her with swollen pupils, shaking his head in wonderment. "What is it with this city and beautiful women?"

"You're not my type," the surgeon replied tartly.

"Shame," the Tovairin sighed. Evie made a noise reminiscent of a growl, her stingers blazing brighter as she spun the handles.

"You said you were sent here to help us. Elaborate," Ronja pressed.

"But of course," Jonah answered with mock sincerity. "I am part of a little group of Tovairins called the Kev Fairla." He paused, waiting expectantly for a wave of recognition or excitement. All he got were creased brows and bewildered glances. He grunted, clearly hoping for a better reaction. "Well, maybe the Arexian has heard of us."

All eyes switched to Evie. Trepidation sparked in Ronja. The techi did not look like herself. Warring emotions crowded her face, she looked half ready to brawl, half ready to vomit.

"Evie," Iris said cautiously, pressing a gentle hand to her arm. "What is it?"

The techi swallowed, trembling visibly. "The Kev Fairla are a gang," she said through her teeth. Her penetrating gaze never left Jonah, who continued to smile doggedly. "They murdered their queen decades ago and have been ruling in place of a real government ever since."

"Sounds like you disapprove of our coup," Jonah noted dryly. "You have to admit, Parish was insane."

Evie continued as if he had not spoken. "Arexis and Tovaire have been at war since before I was born. They attacked us unprovoked."

Jonah let out a harsh laugh, craning his head back. "That war ended years ago. When was the last time you were home, *pestre*?" Evie flinched. The Tovairin smirked. "Ah, did I strike a nerve? Have you ever even been to Arexis? Can you even read your own *reshkas*?"

Evie lunged, stingers snapping. Without thinking, Ronja threw out her arm to stop her. A familiar agony kissed her forearm, muted by her leather sleeve. A cry of shock and pain ripped from her chest as she clamped her hand over the smoking fabric.

The techi swore, backpedaling and holstering her weapons. "What the hell, Ronja?" she bellowed.

Ronja let her hand fall from her singed arm, glowering at the techi in the swaying lantern light. Roark and the others were gawking at her as if she had just sprouted a fresh ear in the middle of her forehead. Jonah was silent. She felt his eyes on her. If he was grateful for her intervention he did not say as much. "We have no idea who he is," she said firmly.

"He just told us!" Evie spat.

"Not everything."

Evie barked a laugh, looking around wildly for support. Everyone was either looking at Ronja or the wooden floor. "Ro," the techi pleaded. "You don't know these people."

"And you do?"

"Enough!" Roark barked, striking silence into their throats. The auto lumbered over another pothole, which Ronja barely registered as the shiny stepped up to stand beside her. Their eyes locked. They shared a nod, then rounded on Jonah. The rogue glanced back and forth between his captors innocently, his hands still resting atop his head. "At ease," Roark said, jerking his chin at him.

"How generous," the Tovairin said silkily, letting his brawny arms fall to his sides. He let out a sigh of relief, flexing his fingers and rolling his wrists.

"We're going to ask you one more time," Roark intoned. "What are you doing here?"

The Tovairin chuckled, a low rumbling that meshed with the hum of the engine. "What do you think? We want to help you take down that *fiester* you call The Conductor."

Another wave of stunned silence rushed over the compartment, staunched only by the guttural hum of the engine and the whistle of the wind through the canvas. The Anthemites stared at Jonah as if he were speaking in his native tongue. He gave a bland smile, waiting patiently for their response.

"Why?" Samson finally broke the hush. Ronja glanced back at him. They had not spoken since their argument on the street.

She had almost forgotten he was there.

Jonah straightened up, the humor wiped clean from his dark features. "Wow, you really are cut off. Time for a history lesson, I guess. Tovaire supported Revinia when you decided to break from Arutia during The War of the Ages. In return, you gave us enough ammo to win our freedom from Vinta."

Ronja wracked her brains, sifting through her limited knowledge of the outside world. In school, they had only learned about one war, the one that caused the chasm between Revinia and its parent country, Arutia. This, she supposed, was The War of the Ages. She vaguely remembered reading about Tovaire breaking from Vinta in a contraband book she found in the Belly. Before she could recall why they left, Jonah spoke again.

"We owe you," he said genuinely. "We heard this Conductor fella is a real piece of work. You helped us gain our freedom, we want to return the favor."

Ronja felt the world tilt, and it had nothing to do with the rocking auto. She blinked rapidly to level her vision. Since being freed from her Singer, she had spent a lot of time thinking about the world outside the walls. It had never occurred to her to wonder how others saw Revinia. Did they know about The Music, about the mutts and the lies? Suddenly, she doubted it.

"You expect us to believe you came all the way across the ocean just to pay a fifty-year-old debt?" Roark asked doubtfully.

"Did I say that was the only reason?" Jonah purred. "Our organization"— He emphasized the word heavily, shooting Evie another scowl, which she returned full force. —"is low on weapons. Revinia is one of the last nations on the planet with a full arsenal. We help you take down The Conductor, we get half his weapons." The Tovairin spread his large hands peaceably. "Sound fair?"

"Why not just make your own weapons?" Ronja asked

doubtfully.

"Well, Tovaire is an island, our resources are pretty limited." Jonah cocked his head to the side, considering her, as a blush crept through her makeup. "When was the last time you were outside your walls?"

Two months ago, she wanted to say, but she knew that was not what he meant. She had never crossed the Revinian border and he damn well knew it.

"The world is, how would you say it? Skitzed," Jonah explained. His nonchalant manner was gone, replaced by an aura of bone deep exhaustion. Ronja had no idea if they could believe his story, but she got the feeling he was being candid, if only for the moment. "It all went downhill after The War of the Ages. While you've been sitting pretty behind your walls, the rest of us have been fighting for our lives."

"What have we been doing?" Evie grumbled.

"The larger nations like Vinta and Lestradov have most of the weapons," Jonah went on. "Vinta has been trying to reacquire us for years. We can only hold them off for so long." He hung his head, his hair swaying with the motion of the auto. "If they storm our borders, our country, our culture, everything will be lost."

Ronja cut her eyes to Roark, only to find he was already looking at her. He arched a thick brow inquiringly. She gave an almost imperceptible nod.

"Why now?" Roark demanded, feigning immunity to the tragic tale. "You must have known you were running low for some time, why come to us now?"

Jonah chuckled morosely, lifting his head to look at them. "Smart boy, we *have* known for a while. About as long as we've known about the Anthem."

It took everything Ronja had to keep her expression flat. She felt rather than saw Roark stiffen at her side. He opened his mouth to claim ignorance, but Jonah beat him to it.

"Save it," he said, waving a callused hand. "Did you really think no one was going to hear about a band of freedom fighters in the most secretive city in the world?"

"Well ... uhhh ... " Roark stuttered, for once at a loss for words. "Yeah."

The Tovairin shook his head, a knowing smile twisting his mouth. "The deeper a secret is buried, the more people try to dig it up."

"Stop dancing around the question," Ronja snapped. "Why cross the ocean now?"

"We knew we needed the Anthem in order to take down The Conductor, but you hadn't made any progress defeating him, even after all this time. There was pretty much no chance of us getting our hands on any of his weapons." He paused, genuine excitement winking in his gaze. "Then we heard about the Siren."

The auto rounded a sharp corner, causing those not holding onto one another to stagger. Ronja remained static as a pillar, scrutinizing Jonah through pinched eyes. "The what?" she asked carefully.

"Maybe you have another name for it," Jonah said with an offhand shrug. "Probably something better than some bird from a fairy tale. The point is, we heard you got your hands on a powerful weapon."

"You heard wrong," Roark answered tightly.

Ronja glanced over at him, confusion and fear wrestling in her stomach. Why did he look so upset? The only siren she could think of was a wailing fire alarm. She had no idea how that related to weaponry or fairy tales.

Jonah looked Roark up and down. "Easy, fella. All we want is ammo and guns, you can keep your bird."

"Excuse me," Ronja broke in loudly. "What the hell is a

siren?"

"A siren is myth. Half woman, half bird." Ronja turned around, trusting Roark to guard her against the Tovairin. Terra was watching her boots intently. Her intense hazel eyes glinted in the lantern light. "Their voices can shatter empires, bring men to their knees."

"How do you know that?" Iris inquired, shock ringing in her soprano voice.

Terra shrugged, then looked up at Ronja.

A chill sang down her spine as understanding clicked into place.

I will be your weapon.

Welcome to the Anthem, singer.

"Oh," Ronja breathed. The sound was swallowed by a deafening screech from beneath them. She winced as the truck rolled to a stop, the high-pitched noise scraping her eardrum.

Roark holstered his revolver with a flourish, then spoke to the group at large. "What do we do with this one?" he asked, gesturing at Jonah as if he were a piece of luggage.

"I have an idea," Evie answered at once, eyeing the Tovairin with disdain. "We kill him."

Terra swept her blades across one another with a ringing whistle. "I like it."

"No," Ronja and Roark snapped in unison.

Iris spoke up, ever the voice of reason. "We treat him like we did Ma ... " She bit her tongue, glancing at Jonah suspiciously: " ... our last prisoner and put a bag over his head."

"That may look a bit suspicious," Jonah pointed out dryly.

Pitch, Ronja thought. He was right. Sneaking around in the middle of the night was dangerous enough, but if they were caught with a prisoner, they were pitched. "We take him inside and lock him up." She turned to Roark, abruptly realizing she had no idea where they were. "This place has more than one room, right?"

The boy snorted, rolling his eyes at the canvas ceiling. "Yes, it has more than one room."

"Then we lock him in one and figure out what to do with him later."

"And if he bolts?"

Ronja tracked the question to Terra. Her knuckles were bleached around her knives, her hazel eyes narrowed through her violet bruises. "Then you can do him in yourself."

Terra cracked a smile. Static spouted from the radio Evie had tucked into her pocket, making them all jump. "Oi! You planning a banquet back there? Get out of my auto!"

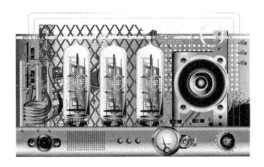

20: THE WAREHOUSE

Terra was the first one out. Roark aimed to beat her, but backed off when she shot him a look that could curdle milk. The Anthemites waited in tense silence as she scanned the area, her silhouette quivering against the tan canvas. Finally, she summoned them with a low whistle.

Iris, Evie, and Samson leapt out next, landing on what sounded like wet gravel. Roark motioned for Ronja to follow but she shook her head, her eyes stuck on Jonah. The Tovairin pondered her with interest, still on his knees with his arms at his sides. "Something you want to say, *loralie*?" he purred.

Ronja bristled. She was not familiar with the word, but his tone was one she knew all too well. "Get up," she ordered sharply.

Jonah complied with a groan. It was only then she realized how long he must have been kneeling. Ronja swallowed as he got to his feet, shaking out his legs. He was massive, taller than Roark and stronger than Samson. Even through his jacket she could see the outline of his powerful biceps. She fought the urge to take a step back.

Roark aimed his revolver at Jonah, glowering at him down the short barrel. "Ronja will go first, you and I will follow. If you take one step out of line ... " He gave the revolver an indicative shake.

Jonah barked a laugh, his dark eyes flashing. "Ever shot anyone with that, fella?"

The shiny gave a thin smile. "I rarely need to."

Jonah shrugged, the tough fabric of his jacket crunching. "Fair enough."

With one last glance between Roark and Jonah, Ronja flipped up her hood and crossed to the exit. She brushed aside one of the flaps and paused at the edge of the platform, squinting into the semidarkness. Bitter wind slammed into her, knocking the breath from her lungs. "What the hell ... " she muttered.

A month ago Roark had informed them that they would be broadcasting from one of his private residences in the city. She assumed he meant some sort of townhouse or apartment, maybe even a mansion. They had agreed not to discuss exactly where they were headed for security reasons.

This was the last thing Ronja expected.

They were parked in a broad alleyway strewn with industrial waste. Scraps of metal warped by time, partially dissected engines, bundles of frayed wires. It was not houses or apartment complexes that framed the street, but huge stone warehouses. They were windowless, roofed with oxidized copper. At the head of each building was the unmistakable emblem of The Conductor, overlaid with the glaring WI of Westervelt Industries. As impressive as the buildings were, they were not what stole her breath.

It was the looming black wall that rose from the ground like a bloated storm, only a couple hundred yards before her. Under the influence of The Music it would have instilled awe and reverence in her. Now, it squeezed her ribs, struck terror into her heart. Her instincts screamed at her to run, to hide. Instead, she stood rooted on the spot.

"Ro, come on," Iris called.

Ronja blinked. The redhead, Evie, and Samson were already halfway down the gravel path. Terra was nowhere in sight. She was likely off stalking the perimeter. Wrapping her fingers around the straps of her bag, Ronja jumped off the truck and hurried after her friends, the soggy pebbles crunching beneath her soles.

"What are we doing here?" Ronja asked. The three Anthemites glanced at each other, clearly weighing their response. An old wound flared in her chest. "You can trust me," she reminded them.

"We know," Iris soothed her. "But it's … "

"Hard to talk about," Evie finished.

Ronja looked at her boots. "Oh."

For a long moment there was only the sound of their footfalls on the gravel, the wind throwing itself against the great wall that was far too close. Iris tugged at the tail of her false braid, her teeth chattering silently. Sam was stoic, his face unreadable. Evie appeared in desperate need of a cigarette. Ronja had never liked smoking, but at that moment it sounded good.

A dozen painfully quiet paces later they arrived at an iron door near the center of the building. They stared at it blankly, as if waiting for it to open itself and invite them in. "If I had known Trip was going to bring us here," Evie finally said. "Skitz. How long has it been?"

"Three years?" Samson guessed.

Ronja cranked her head back, scanning the massive building with a puckered brow. "You've been here before?" she asked. The structure appeared to have been abandoned for years; its stone walls were caked with soot and filth.

"Yeah," Evie replied, her voice oddly tender. She reached out and ran the pads of her fingers across the door. Her tattoos were almost invisible in the waning light of the moon. "This is where Peter and Beatrix Romancheck died."

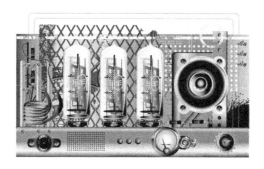

21: MEMORIALS AND MANTRAS

Ronja wanted to speak. She felt she should say something, anything, but all the appropriate words tasted wrong. Evie, Samson, and Iris watched as she digested the information, their faces wrought with empathy.

For most of their friendship, Ronja believed what Henry told her, that his parents died in an auto accident when he was a child. The truth was far worse. Peter and Beatrix Romancheck were agents of the Anthem. Their team was tasked with disrupting a shipment of upgraded Singers that had been delivered to a Westervelt Industries warehouse on the edge of the city. They were ambushed by a squad of Offs and tortured on the floor of the factory for hours before they were beheaded. The building was subsequently abandoned by the company.

It was a sickeningly perfect place to hide.

"You told her, then?"

Ronja whipped around, her expression fractured with horror. Roark was approaching with Jonah in tow. The rogue appeared more at ease than the shiny, drinking in his new surroundings with muted interest. Terra prowled behind them, the moonlight glancing off her exposed blades.

"Yeah, they told me," Ronja rasped as the trio came to a stop before them. "Why would you bring us here?"

Roark did not answer, his mouth pressed into hard line. He did not need to explain. He knew she knew the answer. It was more than just a logical hiding place. It was a tribute to Henry, to his sacrifice and that of his parents.

Roark tore his eyes away from Ronja and started toward the door, digging into his coat pocket and pulling out his collection of copied keys. Terra took his place next to Jonah, pressing the tip of her knife to his kidney. The Tovairin passed her an amused look, which she ignored.

Roark picked through his key ring, his leather-clad back to them. He located the right one and unlocked the door with a satisfying click of tumblers. He shoved it open, his gun raised. The Anthemites tensed behind him. Jonah yawned. Stale air leaked through the portal. Ronja shivered, rising on her tiptoes to peek into the factory. There was nothing to see; it was pitch black.

An auto door slammed and they all spun around. A slight figure with white hair was sprinting toward them, coat and scarf flying. He slid to a stop in front of them, sending up a spray of slush and gravel. "What are you waiting for?" he demanded between huffs. "Get inside and open up the pitching garage!"

"You're Mouse," Ronja realized, her anguish dissipating as curiosity took hold. He was small for his age and eerily beautiful. His skin was a delicate shade of fawn, his eyes nearly translucent.

He fluttered a dismissive hand in her face, not looking at her. "Yes, yes, hello, do shut up." Ronja blinked in shock as Mouse rounded on Roark. "Seriously, the longer we're out here ..." He cut himself off. His jaw dropped when he caught sight of Jonah. "Who the hell is this?"

"Your stowaway," Roark replied, a hint of a threat in his voice.

Mouse floundered, looking back and forth between the shiny and Jonah. "Excuse me?"

"We found him lurking in the back of your truck." Roark folded his arms, considering the black market trader with narrowed eyes. "We were actually wondering how he got there."

"Trip," Mouse all but squeaked. "I can promise you I had nothing to do with this, I dunno how he got back there, but I swear, I had no idea and I..."

"Okay, okay! Calm down." Roark rolled his eyes. "Just, get back to the truck, drive around. We'll open up the north garage for you in a minute."

Mouse shot a seething look at Jonah. "I'll deal with you later," he ground out.

Jonah made a noise too harsh and brief to be a laugh, looking the tiny boy up and down before turning his gaze to the sweeping black wall. Mouse grumbled something foul under his breath, then raced back toward the idling truck, his breaths mushrooming in the air. Roark shook his head, then stepped into the warehouse. They filed in after him. Ronja felt her lungs empty as she stepped inside. The air was thick and musty. It was only slightly warmer inside than it was in the alley. Her footsteps echoed. It felt as if the blackness were listening.

"Trip, hit the bloody lights," Evie complained.

"Trying," came his disembodied reply. "Gotta prime the generator." There was a bit of scuffling, then a noise of vindication. Electric light flooded the space. Ronja shielded her eyes as her pupils contracted.

"Whoa," she breathed, dropping her hand. Somehow, the factory seemed far larger on the inside. The floor was concrete, the walls stitched with exposed pipes. Hundreds of wooden crates were scattered across the room. Some were solitary; others were stacked in towers of six or seven. All of them were branded with the initials of Westervelt Industries and the emblem of The Conductor. "What are they?" Ronja asked no one in particular.

Roark ambled over to her, his arms folded loosely as he surveyed the warehouse. It was a tiny fraction of the estate he was once destined to inherit. "They used to hold Singers," he told her. He switched gears before Ronja could ask why they were still sitting around. "Sam, help me open the garage, would you?"

The captain was in the process of securing the door. He forced the corroded deadbolt into its niche, the grating sound drawing another wince from Ronja. "Sure," he answered. He shrugged off his pack and set it on the floor with a hollow thud. Roark followed suit.

"Trip," Terra spoke up. "Where do you want him?" She stood next to Jonah, the tip of her knife still poised to skewer his vital organs. The Tovairin appeared as relaxed as ever, peering around as if he were sight-seeing.

"The basement," Roark replied, regarding the prisoner warily. He dug into his coat pocket and produced his set of keys. He tossed them at Terra, who caught them with her free hand. "Fourth key in, the big brass one. Put him in the storeroom."

"What should I do with him then?"

The venom in her words was enough to wither flowers. Still, Jonah appeared unconcerned. Roark considered the apathetic man with a tilted head. "Nothing for now," he finally said. "We'll talk later."

Terra inclined her head, then shoved Jonah forward roughly.

"Easy, blondie," the Tovairin grumbled. "That is not what I mean when I say I like it rough."

She gave him another push, her blade inches from his back. Jonah sniggered, then marched forward dutifully. The remainder of the Anthemites watched the pair until they were swallowed by a bend in the forest of wooden crates.

"Sam," Roark called out to the captain. "Mouse is going to have a hernia."

"Right," Samson agreed. They started off across the factory floor at a jog, their footsteps bouncing off the soaring walls.

"Make yourselves at home," Roark shouted back.

"Where?" Ronja asked lamely, turning to Evie and Iris for an explanation. She could sleep just about anywhere, but was hoping to do a bit better than the unforgiving ground. The couple smiled at each other, passing between them a bittersweet glance.

"Follow us," Iris said.

It took them two full minutes to cross the warehouse. As they wove between the maze of boxes, Ronja fought chills she could not entirely explain. Perhaps it was knowing what they once held. Or maybe it was knowing that at any given moment, she might be passing over the spot where Peter and Beatrix and the others were slaughtered. Had their blood been scrubbed away, or did it linger? Where were their remains; were they burned, buried?

A thought struck her with the force of a bullet. What had been done with Henry? Was he incinerated in the oven that had almost claimed her body? Had they kept his corpse for scientific purposes? Red Bay was a laboratory, after all. Nausea clutched her stomach and she swayed. Evie steadied her.

"Easy," the techi said with a nervous chuckle. "You all right, mate?" Ronja shrugged her off roughly, ignoring her kindness. Evie let her hand drop like a stone. "Sorry about your coat. Did I burn you?"

"No."

"Good." Evie fell silent, clearly waiting for Ronja go on. When she refused, she tried again. "Why did you get in my way?"

Ronja halted, the silken tips of her wig swinging. Both Iris and Evie managed another step before they doubled back. Iris was blushing fiercely. The techi looked baffled. "Are you kidding me?" Ronja hissed. "You attacked him unprovoked."

"Unprovoked? Do you know what he called me?" Evie spat. "*Pestre*, it means whore. Specifically, Arexian whore. I may not speak Tovairin, but I damn well know that word."

"So you hit him in the head with a live stinger? You could have killed him."

Evie crossed her arms, anger seeping from her every pore. Red blotches were starting to appear on her neck and cheeks. "We might have been better off."

"Yeah," Ronja shrugged. "Maybe, but we can't just go around killing people who offend us."

"Do you have any idea what you're talking about?" the techi barked. Iris laid a warning hand on her elbow. She might as well have been a gnat. "My family fled Arexis because the Tovairins were slaughtering us. My mother was pregnant with me, she almost died trying to get out of the country. We fled to Revinia and it was sealed a year later."

Ronja considered her friend quietly, her green eyes shifting as she took in her blotchy skin, her straining jaw, her clenched fists. "I'm sorry," she finally said. "I didn't know." She paused, selecting her words with the utmost care. Evie was a stick of wet dynamite. "But that doesn't justify killing a stranger in cold blood."

Evie erupted.

"Tovairins are liars and killers, the whole lot of them!" She stalked over to Ronja and stopped a few inches from her. The singer had to lift her chin to hold eye contact.

"All of them?" she inquired calmly.

Evie opened her mouth, closed it. The stains on her face and neck bled into one another until she was entirely red. "Did you hear what I said? They murdered my people! It was genocide."

"I know," Ronja said quietly, reaching out a tentative hand to touch Evie on the shoulder. The techi flinched as if her skin burned. "But Jonah was probably a child when that war ended, just like you."

Evie knocked her hand away with a brittle laugh. Ronja fought a wince as her bruised knuckles throbbed. "What, are you saying we should just trust him? Do *you* trust him?"

"No, of course not, but it has nothing to do with his nationality."

Evie let out a jarring laugh. She shook her head, her lips parted. Ronja tried again, her voice slow and even. "I am not asking you to trust him, or forgive him, or even talk to him. I am asking as your friend ... " She licked her dry lips, hoping her voice did not tremble. "As your *family*, to put aside your prejudice until we know more."

The techi snarled. A chill lanced through Ronja, weakening her knees and spine. "My prejudice?" Evie hissed. "You think that skitzer hates me any less than I hate him?"

Ronja felt her patience wane. She folded her arms and hardened her coaxing expression. "Look," she growled. "Jonah might be a threat; he might be an ally. We need him breathing until we know for sure. So pull yourself together. Now."

The final syllable was an ultimatum. It did not need to be explained; it was inherent in her tone. She watched as Evie absorbed it like a blow to the stomach. It was then Ronja felt the true weight of her power. She was the crux of their plan. Their only plan. Without her, everything would crumble. Roark might be their leader, but her word was final.

Evie gave a sluggish shake of her head, as if her muscles were coated in honey. Her eyes never left Ronja, who held her ground despite the voice in her head begging her to back down. As sudden as a match igniting, Evie whipped around and stalked off across the factory.

"Where are you going?" Iris called desperately. Evie waved without turning back, both a farewell and a signal to leave her alone. The surgeon sighed, her petite form sagging. "Come on, Ro," she said quietly.

They made their way to the far side of the factory in charged silence. Ronja focused on counting her footsteps. She kept her eyes down, pretending she did not notice the apprehensive looks the surgeon shot her every few seconds.

1-2-3

2-2-3

3-2-3 ...

Eventually, they reached the terminus of the warehouse where two iron doors waited. Iris opened the one on the left with a grunt of effort. Stale air rolled over them. Ronja wrinkled her nose, tucking deeper into the high collar of her coat. The surgeon reached around the frame, hunting for the light switch. A line of electric bulbs coughed to life, bounding up a narrow stairwell.

Iris stood aside, motioning for her to step through. "After you," she said.

Ronja thanked her, hitched up her bag, and started up the stairs.

It was long haul to the top of the warehouse. With each step, Ronja felt the burden on her shoulders grow heavier. Exhaustion and anxiety were starting to get the best of her. Less than an hour ago, she had wanted nothing more than to dive headfirst into action. Now, all she wanted was to sleep.

"Here we are," Iris said as they crested the landing. "Home sweet home. Good thing Mouse came a couple of days ago and started the heater."

Ronja peered around curiously. The attic was considerably more compact than the main floor. It was little more than a short, dingy corridor framed by nine doors, four on each side and one capping the end. The floors were scratched hardwood, the walls whitewashed. Dust motes stirred sleepily in the unexpectedly warm air.

"Pick a room," Iris said.

Ronja tossed her a surprised glance. "These are all bedrooms?"

"All but the one on the end, that's the bathroom." The redhead offered a tentative smile. "If Evie and I share, which is a big *if* at the moment, there should be enough for everyone to have their own."

"Okay." Ronja smiled tiredly, then made for the closest room on the left.

"Wait," Iris yelped. "Can I talk to you for a second?"

Ronja froze, her boots chafing against the floorboards. "Not now, Iris," she sighed. She shut her eyes, willing the girl to disappear. "Can we do this later?"

"Oh ... ummm ... "

"Sorry, Iris," Ronja sighed, lifting a hand to her temple to massage it. "I just need to sleep."

"Of course," the surgeon replied too quickly. "I completely understand. We can talk later."

Ronja nodded. Her burden felt twice as heavy as she trudged over to her chosen room. She spun the brass knob and stepped inside, tapping the door shut with her heel. Total blackness engulfed her. It was oddly peaceful. In the dark she could be anywhere. She reached back with a sigh, feeling for the switch, then snuffed the dark.

The room was square and plain with white walls and wooden floors, just like the hallway. Two bunk beds with naked mattresses stood on either side and a sink crouched against the far wall. A cloudy mirror hung above it. Nearby was a writing desk and chair, complete with a typewriter blanketed in dust. Her heart leapt at the sight of the machine. She had only used one once before at a library in the outer ring. As soon as the librarian heard the click of the keys and the whir of the carriage he shooed her away. *Mutts should not be using such complicated instruments*, he scolded.

Ronja shrugged off her pack. It landed with a ringing thunk, shaking a plume of dust from the ceiling. The debris coated her hair and shoulders. A neuron snapped in the hollows of her mind. Moving erratically, Ronja ripped off her black wig and coat, chucking both across the room. She shrugged off her top, cursing when it caught on her chin, then kicked off her boots and pants. Naked except for her underwear, she crossed to the sink.

She spun the knob labeled H, found it was busted, then turned to C. The faucet sputtered, the pipes rumbled. "Come on," she ordered crossly. Icy water spouted from the tap. "See," she muttered, running her hands under the stream. "Magic voice."

Ronja made a basin with her palms, allowing water to pool there, then bent toward the sink and splashed her face. Her makeup sloughed off, the peach ribbons spiraling down the drain. She raked her wet fingers through her short hair, teasing out the knots that had formed under the wig. Shivering, she locked eyes with her reflection.

Her pallor had returned along with her freckles. The water made her curls appear longer, darker. They dripped down to her cheekbones. She took a step back to examine her body. It was a battlefield. Or maybe it was a universe. Her freckles could be distant constellations, the white scars on her chest, planets. The branching burn over her heart could be the sun.

Maybe.

"Siren," she tested the word on her tongue, watching to see if it matched the curve of her lips. "Siren."

Mutt.

Ronja gasped, whirling around and bracing herself against the porcelain. The water continued to run, unfazed. She glanced around wildly, terror clawing at her throat. The voice was so close, she had felt a gust of breath at her ear. A reply formed in her mouth. She swallowed it. Speaking to a figment of her imagination was as good as admitting she was losing her mind. She could not afford to do that.

Ronja turned off the faucet and hurried over to her bag. With quaking hands, she dug through her belongings until she found her favorite sweater, the red one that fell to her knees. Tugging the roomy gray socks Georgie had knit for her over her feet, she stumbled to the nearest bunk and curled into a ball on the mattress. She squeezed her eyes shut against the room, against the world, against her own mind. It was too much. She could not handle it, but she had to.

The walls sang her to sleep. They spoke a single line, repeated over and over like a chant, a mantra. *Maybe the stars are alive after all.*

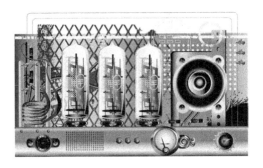

22: CATERPILLAR

Terra

"What does a man have to do to get some food around here, blondie?"

Terra rolled her eyes, shifting against the metal door. They had only escaped the Belly a couple hours ago and she was already back on guard duty underground. While the basement was considerably less pungent than the sewers, the maze of corridors was no less depressing. Half of the lights were busted. The bulbs that did work cast a sickly green glow. And it was cold. Damn cold. The hallways were lined with scores of identical locked doors. She never would have found the storeroom were it not labeled accordingly.

"I could go for some pastries," the prisoner went on, his request muffled by the thick panel between them. Terra breathed in through her nose, out through her mouth. The rogue had entered his cell without a fuss, but once the boredom set in, he refused to shut up. "You still out there?" he inquired after a long pause.

Terra did not answer. She was good at keeping quiet. It was a skill she had acquired early in life.

"When the doctor comes, I need you to keep quiet," her mother used to say, stroking her blonde hair with a tender hand. *Then she would smile, deepening the crow's feet that branched from her warm hazel eyes.* *"Can you do that for me, caterpillar?"*

"Yes, Mommy."

Then she would crawl into the closet, cocoon herself in towels and quilts while the sound of bedsprings shrieking twined with The Music. She would wait in the blackness and the noise, listening for that final creak and groan, waiting for her mother to open the door. "All done, butterfly. How about some tea?"

"Oi, blondie!" Jonah bellowed, slamming on the door with a large fist. Terra flinched as the shock ripped through her spine.

"Keep calling me blondie, see how far that gets you," she shot back.

His laugh dusted her remaining ear through the sheet of metal. Her skin prickled uncomfortably. "Well you never did give me your name, sugar."

"No need to talk to me at all, then."

"Terra."

The agent jumped at the sound of her own name, her hand flying instinctively to the blade at her hip. "Evie," she sighed, unable to keep the relief from her voice. The techi was the one person in the warehouse she could stand to talk to. Terra climbed to her feet, wincing as her stiff muscles creaked. "What are you doing down here?"

Evie smiled vaguely as she approached. She had shed her wig along with her coat and weapons and now wore a loose green sweater and leggings. The curved edge of her Anthem brand peeked over the lip of the fabric. "Just looking around," she answered, coming to a halt before Terra. She jerked her chin at the storeroom. "He giving you any trouble?"

Terra gave a bitter smile. "About as much as you would

expect."

"I can hear you," Jonah grumbled.

Evie nodded, ignoring the Tovairin. She appeared to be wrestling with her words. "Actually, I came to see if you needed any help."

Terra cocked an eyebrow at her. "Watching the locked door? No, not really."

The techi huffed. Her shoulders sagged with an intangible burden. "Look, can I just stay awhile?" She glanced down at her boots, at a loss for words. That was a first. "No one really wants me around right now."

Terra could not resist. She grinned. Her jaw ached at the foreign motion. "Join the club. What did you do?" Evie grimaced. "Come on, Wick. Spit it out." Somewhere in the back of her mind, Terra noted the novelty of the situation. She could not remember the last time someone her own age had confided in her about something other than tactical plans. It was a good feeling.

"I was a bit of a skitzer," Evie answered, shutting her eyes and kneading them with her palms. "This place brings out the worst in me." She let her hands fall limp at her sides. "Last time I was here I was a kid. Sixteen, I think. We came on the anniversary of the day ... you know."

Terra nodded. She remembered the day the Romancheck party left for a mission and never returned. It was the same day Roark arrived in the Belly. "Yeah, I know."

Evie reached out and clapped Terra on the shoulder. The agent strove not to flinch at the gesture. She had not realized how long it had been since someone had touched her in a friendly manner.

Jonah shattered the moment. "Evie, huh? You the Arexian or the cute redhead?"

"Shut it!" the techi barked.

Jonah fell silent. It was the satisfied sort of quiet that oozed through the walls. Terra and Evie copied him for a while, each sifting through their own thoughts.

The techi finally broke the hush. "What do you think of him?" she asked, jerking her head toward the storeroom.

Terra shrugged.

"He has to be Tovairin," Evie went on, speaking more to herself than to her comrade. "He called me ... " She bit down on her lip until it turned white. "He speaks the language. He *looks* Tovairin."

Terra glanced at the stockroom. Jonah was keeping his silence, but that did little to comfort her. Motioning for Evie to follow, she took off down the corridor. The techi fell into step beside her. They did not speak until they were a good dozen paces from the makeshift cell. "His story seems off," Terra said in a low voice. "Usually when something is too good to be true, it is."

Evie nodded. "My mum always told me, never trust a Tovairin."

Terra skated over the comment with a question. "What do you know about the Kev Fairla?"

"Not much," she admitted, scratching her head. "But what he said matches up with what my parents told me. They overthrew their leader, they run the nation now." She gave a considerate tilt of her head. "At least, they did when we left Arexis."

"Do they have any identifying marks?"

Evie cocked her head to the side. "What do you mean?"

Terra crossed her arms, peeking back at the storeroom suspiciously. "I searched him before I locked him up," she murmured. "I had to lift up his shirt to check for weapons. He's covered in tattoos, looks like head to toe."

Evie sucked in a shocked breath that did not match her gruff exterior. Terra lifted a single brow. "Skitz," the techi breathed. She spread her fingers before her, examining them in the sickly light. Terra followed her gaze. She had never paid much attention to Evie's tattoos before. Every Anthemite was branded with the symbol of the revolution, and many chose to decorate their skin with artistic ink. Still, there was something unique about the whirling symbols that spiraled from the tips of her fingers to her wrists. "Well," Evie said. "He has to be Tovairin."

"What are they?"

"*Reshkas*," the techi answered. "I should have thought to check for them before. Tovaire and Arexis have some common traditions." She winced at the admission. "When kids turn fifteen they get their ancestry tattooed on their bodies. My dad is an artist, so I had my ceremony here. I ... " She cut herself off, plunging her hands into her pockets as if to hide them. "Jonah was right. I never learned to read mine."

Terra gave a terse bob of her head. She could tell it was a sensitive subject for Evie, but now was not the time to be gentle. Not that she had much capacity for tenderness in the first place. "His are a lot bigger than yours," she noted.

"Yeah, they're probably in white ink too, right?"

"Yes."

"I remember hearing about this," the techi mumbled, massaging her chin and gazing into oblivion. "The white ink represents ... pitch ... my mum explained this ... "

"Wick, focus." Terra snapped her fingers twice before her vacant face. "Do the Kev Fairla have any specific markings?"

"Not that I know of. Anyway, *reshkas* are mostly just words, not pictures."

An idea sparked in Terra. "How similar are Arexian and Tovairin? The languages, I mean."

The techi eyed her reproachfully. "Not similar at all," she

ground out.

Ignoring the disappointment taking root in her stomach, Terra spun back toward the storeroom, her hands resting on her knives. She imagined Jonah pressing his ear to the face of the door, straining to hear them. That was what she would be doing if she were in his position. She did not care if he heard her next words. In fact, she hoped he did. "Guess we'll just have to do this the old-fashioned way."

"Terra," Evie warned.

The agent rolled her eyes at the low ceiling, groaning so the techi knew. "Get off your high horse, Wick, you almost turned his brains to pudding an hour ago."

"Whatever. Trip said to wait."

"Do you *always* do what Trip tells you?" Evie did not respond, so Terra pounced. She turned back around, her fingers knit pleadingly. "Come on Wick, just stall them for a few hours, tell them I have the watch covered. I can figure out who he is and what he wants. Just give me a chance."

Evie squinted at her, her jaw bulging in her cheek. Terra swallowed her heart as it attempted to climb into her throat. Finally, the techi groaned and raked a hand through her jaw length hair. "Fine. Just keep him alive. If you kill him, everyone is gonna think I egged you on."

Terra grinned darkly. At this rate, she was going to develop a downright sunny disposition. She made a fist, then smashed it into her open palm. "Excellent."

Evie chuckled. "I thought I was supposed to be the pitched one."

"Two can wear that crown, Wick."

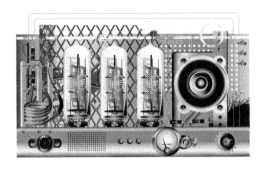

23: ANSWER
Jonah

Jonah smiled bitterly, his ear pressed to the door. The girls had moved off down the corridor. Their exchange was a ghost. He could make out the rise and fall of their conversation, but could not tease apart the words. He peeled away from the panel and turned back to his cell.

It was small but not claustrophobic. He had been in far worse. The only door was the one through which he had entered. No windows, of course. There was a vent in the ceiling. It was scarcely the width of his thigh. There would be no escaping through there.

Not that he was looking to run.

The only furniture was a folding chair blanketed in dust. He crossed to it with grace that did not match his bulky form and sat. He shoved back his long hair and probed his right ear with his pointer finger. Rather than cartilage, he hit metal. He smothered a wince when the communicator shifted in its bed of scar tissue. He had not been pleased when his client insisted the device be placed, but had to admit the little bug was useful.

Static crunched as the communicator came to life. The metal

warmed against his skin. He did not wait for his employer to speak; he knew he was listening. "They took me prisoner, just as you expected," Jonah whispered in Tovairin, his gaze locked to the door. "You can trace my location as soon as the strike team is ready."

"*Nis*," came the mechanical whisper. Though Jonah would never admit it, he found the closeness of the voice unsettling. "*Verta telesk*." The line went dead. He reached up and shut the device down with a touch. He leaned forward, his fingers steepled in contemplation. His employer's Tovairin was flawed, but his command was clear.

Wait.

Jonah was about to get back to doing just that when the door banged open, spilling greenish light over him. He barked a curse in his native tongue and vaulted out of the chair. He had not even heard the key stir the tumblers. Somewhere in the back of his rattled mind, he kicked himself for letting his guard down. He could not remember the last time he had been so startled.

"Still feel like talking, *sugar*?"

The girl, the one with the half-buzzed head and long nose, stood in the doorway. She held two slender throwing knives and wore a smile reminiscent of a wolf drooling over its prey.

Jonah felt his lips curl upward of their own volition. "How about those pastries?" he replied dryly.

She stepped through the door and kicked it shut with her booted heel. She twirled the knives between her fingertips. A pretty trick, but that did not mean she knew how to use them. "Wrong answer," she growled.

"Well ... "

All he felt was the piercing kiss of the blade whistling past his temple. Jonah tried and failed not to flinch when it embedded itself in the far wall with a ringing thud. He peeked over his shoulder, his eyebrows high on his forehead. The blade shuddered in the drywall, trembling like a frightened child. A shocked chuckle pulled itself from his chest as he swung back around to look at the girl.

"Well *fiest* me, what did you want to talk about?"

"How about we start with what you are really doing here."

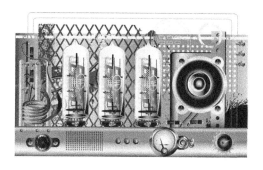

24: FLARE

Iris

A tentative knock at the door broke her concentration. Iris glanced up from her book, her nostrils flaring. The knob jiggled noisily, then stilled. She had locked it the moment she was inside. Evie knew which room she would choose, the same one they slept in last time they were at the warehouse.

"Come on, darling, open up," the techi begged through the panel. Iris creased the page to mark her place and set aside her paperback. It was collection of poetry called *Silence and Noise* her mother had given her on her eleventh birthday. The poor little book was so worn she had twice been forced to reinforce its binding. The paper was the color of butter and smelled like home.

"Can you just open the door?" Evie pleaded.

Iris crossed her arms, her impatience waxing as the girl struggled to find the right words.

"I know I was a pitcher," she finally managed. Iris imagined her resting her brow against the door. The taut threads of her heart loosened. "Please just let me in so I can apologize."

Iris shot to her feet, fuming. White lights cracked in her vision at the sudden change in pressure. "I am not the one you need to be apologizing to!" she yelled.

"Ronja is asleep, or just really good at keeping quiet. I already tried knocking." Iris bit her lip. "Come on, darling," Evie pleaded, an exhausted edge creeping into her tone. "Let me in."

Iris took a breath, forcing out her anger and inviting in composure. She crossed to the door, flipped the lock and yanked it open. Evie stumbled in with a black curse. Rather than catching her, the surgeon stepped back, watching with narrowed eyes as her girlfriend resealed the door.

"Right," Evie sighed, spinning around to face her.

Her muscular form sagged, even her thick hair seemed limp. Bluish circles ringed her eyes. Any other time her appearance would have instilled pity in Iris, but not now.

"Out with it," Evie said.

"What the hell were you thinking?" Iris exploded, throwing her hands into the air. "You could have killed that man, and I know he was Tovairin, but that does not make it okay!"

Evie made a cyclical motion with her wrist, her eyes on the whitewashed ceiling as she waited for her to finish her tirade.

The surgeon felt heat blossom in her cheeks. Her small frame began to quiver with rage. "You could have killed Ronja," she said in a soft voice.

Evie tensed visibly. "Her jacket protected her."

"You could have killed her!" Iris shrieked again, jabbing a finger at the techi. "Then where would we be?"

Evie opened her mouth, then shut it with a snap. She shifted her gaze to the floorboards as shame flooded her features.

Good. Iris scoffed. Her head felt fuzzy, as if it were filled with static. She stalked back to the bunk bed and sat heavily. "Did you even stop to think about what you sound like when you talk about Tovairins?" Iris asked. The sharpness had fled her voice. She sounded tired, weak. "Did you think about how that must make

Ronja feel?"

Evie swallowed, the skin of her throat glistening in the low light. Still, she refused to look up at her girlfriend.

"She grew up with a mutt Singer. For all intents and purposes, she was a mutt. Do you get what that means?"

"I know what it means," the techi barked, finally lifting her gaze from the floor. The whites of her eyes were tinted pink.

"It means she was hated for something she couldn't control," Iris pressed. "Just like you hate Jonah for a war he didn't start. Just like ... just like The Conductor hates people like you and me."

Evie stiffened. Iris bowed her head as her eyes filled with unwanted tears. She missed the feeling of her hair sweeping forward over her shoulders. Her red curls were her favorite thing about her appearance. She had been awake when they shaved her head at Red Bay. Ronja was barely conscious, Henry already had a buzz cut. But Iris fought tooth and nail against the razor. Three Offs had had to hold her down like a terrorized animal while they sheared away her locks.

All at once Evie was next to her on the bed, her arm curled around her frail shoulders. Evie was so warm, so full of life. She was her own sun. She was *her* sun. All the rage rushed from Iris like a great exhalation and she wilted. Evie eased Iris's head onto her thighs.

"I am so sorry," Evie murmured, brushing her finger over the curve of Iris's ear, ignoring the piercings that studded her cartilage. "I never thought about it like that."

"Just ... promise me you'll do better."

"I will, I swear."

Iris nodded against her legs, then shifted so she could look Evie in the eye.

The techi smiled ruefully, the corners of her eyes crinkling like paper. "Guess what?" she asked, poking Iris in the shoulder.

Iris sniffed, her lips twitching into an involuntary smile. She was familiar with this game. "What?"

Evie bent down and planted a kiss on her brow. "I love you," she whispered against her skin. Iris blushed as quick as a lighter igniting. How was it that after all this time those three simple words still made her heart sing?

"I certainly hope so," she replied offhandedly. Before Evie could pout, Iris sat up and gave her a proper kiss, just to remind her that the feeling was mutual.

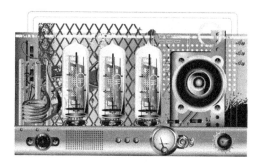

25: HUMAN

She waited in the center of the room, her knees raw against the rough concrete. The nightmare was becoming familiar, almost mundane. The expressionless walls. The stiff prison gown. The impenetrable cell door. Ronja reached to her shoulder absently, feeling for her long hair. Her hand cut through air.

She reached up to her scalp. Her stomach vaulted when her fingers caught her brief mess of curls. Her fingers flashed to the side of her head, hunting for her right ear. There was nothing but a puckered scar.

No.

"Help," Ronja rasped, scrambling to her feet. Her knees knocked. She stumbled to the back wall to steady herself, pressing her burning forehead to the concrete. She was back at Red Bay. Only moments ago she had been at the warehouse with her friends.

Roark. Evie. Iris. Samson. Their names formed on her lips, then wasted away to panicked breaths. Where were they?

"Your friends are here."

Ronja whirled, her fists raised to protect herself. She froze as shock ripped through her. Her jaw dropped, her hands followed.

"Henry," she breathed.

The boy stood with his back to the cell door, his arms crossed, his handsome face expressionless. He was dressed in a white suit, the bleached fabric blazing against his dark skin.

"They are waiting for you," he went on. Ronja felt her pulse atrophy. His voice was all wrong. It was mechanical, like his tongue was acting without the consent of his brain.

"Who is?" she asked carefully.

Henry gave a sinister smile, then pushed open the heavy door with ease. Blistering light crept into the room. Ronja squinted, taking a tentative step forward. There was something on the floor behind him. She could not make it out. Reading her mind, Henry stepped out of her line of sight.

There was no moment of realization, no wave of horror that engulfed her. She simply collapsed, her hands pressed to her mouth to hold back a scream that was never there in the first place. Their bodies were piled on the white tiles, their limbs twisted, their eyes glazed. There were no bullet holes, no knife wounds, no stinger burns. Only the trails of blood that leaked from their ears, forming little rivers in the cracks between the tiles.

A thick arm snaked around her waist and a hand gripped her throat. Ronja flinched. The stench of death leaked from Henry's mouth. She could feel his eyes on her, so close, but she refused to look away from the bodies of her family.

Georgie. Cosmin. Iris. Evie. Samson.

Roark.

"You cannot save them, mutt," Henry sneered. The words were not his own. "How can you possibly, when you cannot even save yourself?"

When Ronja screamed, it was too loud for her eardrums to contain. It ruptured the cell, stormed the halls, burned away the hands on her body.

"Ronja!" Her name slammed into her, fracturing the prison. She shot up, fists flying. Two hands caught her wrists, stilling them with ease. Panic ripped through her and she lashed out blindly with her feet, but they were tangled in something soft. A blanket. "Come back to me, love."

Ronja blinked. Roark leaned over her, his face an inch from hers, his hands holding hers aloft. Genuine fear wracked his angular features. The girl relaxed enough to be embarrassed. "Uh, could you ... " She flicked her eyes up to her trapped wrists.

"Oh, sorry." Roark released her. Without his support, she flopped back onto the mattress, staring blankly at the bunk above her. Someone had carved their initials into the box spring. *S.L.P.*

"What are you doing here?" she finally asked.

"I heard you scream," Roark answered, as if it were entirely obvious. Out of the corner of her eye, she saw him scratch the back of his head anxiously.

"What time is it?" she asked.

"Nearly 6:00."

"In the morning?"

Roark chuckled under his breath. "Guess again."

Ronja sat up far too quickly, her brain lurching against the walls of her skull. "What?" she cried, blinking rapidly to reclaim her sight. "Why the hell did you let me sleep so long?"

The boy shrugged helplessly. "We needed to set up the radio station anyway, and to be honest you looked pretty rough."

"Yeah, well, I still could have helped," she mumbled, lying back down on the hard mattress. It was only in the aftermath of her shock that Ronja realized how cold she was. Her sweater with damp with sweat, her freckled legs studded with goosebumps.

"Here." As if her thoughts were being broadcast, Roark tugged the gray blanket trapped around her knees up to her chest, leaving her hands free. She moved to tuck them under the covers, but he cocooned them in his own.

"Th—thank you," she stuttered. Her eyes darted down to the soft quilt, then returned to his face. "Did you do this?"

"Yeah, sorry," Roark apologized hastily. He grimaced when she shot him a dubious look. "I would have given it to you downstairs if I knew you were going to sleep so quickly. I just figured ... " He trailed off as it became clear she was not angry. The worry in his gaze gave way to tenderness. "What happened?"

Ronja rolled her head to the side, fixed her gaze on the whitewashed wall. The lumps and divots in the plaster read like the patterns in the stars, but she was blind to them. "Nothing."

"Liar," he growled.

"Kidnapper," she quipped weakly.

Roark shook his head in disbelief. His hands were vividly present wrapped around hers. "Did you forget that I am the master of deflection?" he joked. Ronja frowned. Her warning was clear, but Roark barreled on obliviously. "You can tell me, whatever it is. You can trust me."

"I know," she replied, keeping her voice low so it did not shake. "I *do* trust you." It was true, she realized. She did trust him. With her life. "I just ... I am so tired of being weak."

Roark maintained his silence for a long time, regarding her with unflinching eyes. He lifted one hand from hers to cup her cheek. His touch was as gentle as a whisper, as firm as the ground. "How can you not see that you're the strongest of all of us?"

Ronja jerked away and sat bolt upright. "No, I am not!" She ripped her hands away from his, curling them to her chest. Hurt flashed across his face, but he did not protest. "I am angry all the time. I have nightmares every night. I wake up screaming and there's nothing I can do to stop it." She took a rattling breath. The oxygen in the room was suddenly thin. "I'll never be free of it."

"Free of what?"

"Roark," she choked out. "It's—it's my fault. We all blamed Terra. It was easy, but Henry and Layla died because of me. Cos can barely speak because of me. Georgie almost died. You—you were tortured because of me."

"No," Roark said. "If you need to blame someone, blame me. I'm the one who took you from the station that night."

"He still talks to me," Ronja rasped. Hot tears rolled down her cheeks, landing on her blanketed knees without a sound. Somewhere in the depths of her mind she realized how she must look. "I can still hear his voice, his last words, over and over."

"I know." Roark took her face in his hands. This time she did not pull away. His dark eyes tethered her to her bones. He pressed his brow to hers and warmth spread between them. Ronja clutched at his shoulders, digging into him with her fingernails. If it hurt him he did not say as much. "I hear him, too."

"How am I supposed to do this?" she whispered, squeezing her eyes shut to rid them of the sting. "How am I supposed to save this city if I can't even save myself?"

"You're not alone."

"You can't fix me, Roark."

"You don't need fixing. Fear, pain, guilt ... they don't make you weak, Ronja. They make you human."

Human. The word lodged itself in her brain, stanching her tears. She had been called so many names throughout her life. Mutt. Anthemite. Singer. Savior. Traitor. Weapon. Siren. But not once had she been called human. It filled her to the brim, flushing out her terror and her doubt, her guilt and her regret.

Without thinking, without wondering if it was too soon, Ronja leaned forward and kissed Roark.

Her eyes were closed, her lips parted, her soul cracked to the core. His mouth was still for a split second, then he moved against her, slow and sure. She kicked off the blanket and buried her fingers in his long hair. His arms snaked around her waist, pulling her closer. Their heartbeats twined, their breathing sped. Roark leaned back. Ronja panicked, thinking she had done something wrong. Then he pulled her into his lap. He locked eyes with her. "Is this okay?"

Ronja answered him with another kiss, wrapping her slender legs around him. She wanted nothing between them. No space. No secrets. No separation.

He must have felt the frantic flutter of her thoughts, because he yanked off his shirt in a swift motion. He palmed the curve of her cheek, silently asking. She nodded, her eyes glued to the muscular planes of his chest, the proud brand of the Anthem over his heart. His skin was stitched with scars, just like her own. He was the most beautiful thing she had ever seen. Her vision flooded. Roark tensed. "Hey," he murmured, dipping his forehead to touch hers again. "We can stop."

Ronja tugged her thick sweater over her head and threw it aside. Roark stared openly, his lips parted. His glazed eyes hardened when they landed on the knot of scar tissue above her breast. "You did this to save me," he murmured, shame creeping across his features.

"I would do it again," she replied. There was not a trace of doubt in her voice.

Roark reached out tentatively and covered the scar with his hand. She copied him, splaying her cold fingers across his tattoo.

"I love you, Ronja," he whispered. "There and back."

She smiled through her sheen of tears. Her hand slipped from his chest. She curled both arms around him, clinging to him as if he might vanish into the night. He held her with equal ferocity.

"I love you, too," she whispered into his neck. "There and back."

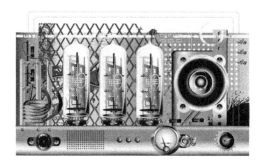

26: CICADA
Terra

"How about we sit down," Jonah suggested, gesturing to the metal folding chair with a large hand. Rather than waiting for Terra to agree, he plopped down in the seat, which groaned beneath the sudden burden. He tossed her a coy smile. "We only have one seat but ... " He patted his thigh and waggled his eyebrows. "Surely we can work something out."

Terra smirked, balancing her throwing knife on the tip of her index finger. Her calluses protected her; she scarcely felt the blip of pain. "Talk to me like that again and I'll put this through your eye."

Jonah laughed, a low rumbling that filled the cramped space. "I believe you," he said. He leaned forward, his eyes at once calculating and amused. "You have a short fuse. I doubt it serves you well."

"And how does your ego serve you?" she asked.

The Tovairin grinned, his white teeth blazing against his skin. "Well enough." Terra narrowed her eyes, scrutinizing Jonah through her lashes. He shared some basic features with Evie, straight black hair and dark hooded eyes. He was taller than

Roark, stronger than Samson with biceps as thick as tree branches. She hated to admit it, but he was also something of a looker.

"We know you're Tovairin," Terra said, letting her blade tumble from her fingertip and catching it in her free hand.

"How astute."

"The rest of your story is up for debate."

"Oh?"

"How about you try telling it again," Terra suggested, leaning up against the metal door. She circled her finger in the air, like a record spinning backward. "From the top."

The Tovairin sighed deeply, reclining in his chair. It moaned again, threatening to cave. Jonah laced his fingers together, then bent them backward. His joints cracked like thin ice under a boot. "Right. My name is Jonah … "

"Jonah what?"

"Just Jonah. We give up our last names when we enter the Kev Fairla. It reminds us that our cause is more important than our blood."

Terra folded her arms over her chest. If Jonah was offended, he did an excellent job hiding it. "What exactly is your cause?" she asked. "Evie seems to think you're just out for power."

Jonah barked a humorless laugh. "The Arexian *would* say that. Truth is, sugar, everyone is out for power, the trick is to use it properly once you have it." He crossed his thick arms to match her pose. "The Kev Fairla has been around for decades. Our goal has always been the same, to protect our country from internal and external threats by whatever means necessary."

"Nice party line," Terra commented blandly. "Do you practice that in the mirror before bedtime?"

"Only on weeknights. Can I go on?"

Terra huffed, then motioned for him to continue with a flick of her fingers.

The man smiled, his eyes glinting. He clearly knew he was wearing on her nerves. "Tovaire is small, we only have one port and one major city, but we do have one thing that every other country wants: coal. A *fiesting* ton of it."

Terra fought to keep her expression level. She did not like being surprised.

"Judging by the smokestacks I saw on my way in here, you lot have plenty of black diamonds stored up." Disdain dripped from his voice. Terra kept her arms locked to her chest in a heroic effort not to sock him in the jaw. "But most of the world used up their coal during The War of the Ages. Tovaire didn't even come close to running out. After the dust settled, everyone was out for us, trying to get control of our supply, especially Vinta." He grimaced, flashing an unexpected dimple on his stubbled cheek. "Your Arexian friend will tell you different, but our war with them had nothing to do with nationalism. They were coming for our coal."

"Move it along," Terra commanded, ignoring the acute sense of discomfort the words instilled in her.

"Like I said in the truck, Vinta is at our shores," Jonah explained. His tone shifted, his arrogance shrinking. Exhaustion crept into his eyes, the kind that was difficult to fake. "They wasted most of their coal winning The War of the Ages. They rule most of the east now. We are the last independent eastern nation."

"So Vinta is a vulture," Terra summarized with a curt nod. "Feeding off the remains of its neighbors."

Jonah laughed hollowly. "Yeah, you could say that."

"Get on with it."

"Patience, blondie."

"Fresh out," she replied through gritted teeth. She raised her blade, allowing the light to collect on its edge. "Tell me why you're here."

"I told you in the truck."

"Tell me again," Terra ground out. She crossed to him in a single stride and jammed the tip of her knife under his chin. He craned back his neck, the thick tendons straining like the lines of a ship. A droplet of blood bubbled up around the point. He just smirked at her. "I need to see your face when you say it," Terra said. "I am *very* good at weeding out liars."

"Are you now?"

"Yes."

"You know I could snap your neck like a twig," Jonah said softly. It was not a threat. It was a fact.

"I know," Terra breathed, bringing her face close to his so their noses almost brushed. Were she not so close, she might never have noticed the hitch in his breathing. "Your first chance to kill me was when I was standing in that door like a pitcher. Your next is right now."

Jonah gave a strained chuckle. A sheen of sweat built on his skin. His pulse was visible in the hollow of his throat, his blood hot as it slithered over her knuckles. "I was wondering why you were taking so long to shut it."

"You aren't here to kill us outright," Terra stated, giving her weapon a gentle twist. Jonah flinched as the little wound widened. "That doesn't mean we can trust you."

"Says the girl with a knife on me," he panted.

"I am not going to ask you again."

"I already told you, I came to get my hands on the arsenal."

"You said *half.*"

"I was speaking in generalities ... *ger pris netram* ... "

Terra grasped a chunk of his thick hair and jerked his head back. He inhaled sharply, his eyes flashing to the ceiling to hide the twinge of fear that had crawled in. "What did you say?"

"I said I was speaking in generalities," he hissed. "You crazy mother ... "

Terra released his head roughly and stepped back. She cleaned her blade on her pants, then slipped it into its sheath with a ringing clang. Jonah wiped away the trail of blood that had crawled down his neck.

"You expect me to believe," Terra said after a while. "That you came all the way across the world to get your hands on a dictator's cache of weapons because you heard the government *might* be unstable."

"Because we heard that the rebels got their hands on a weapon that could take it down."

"Who told you this?"

"A Revinian trader. Calls himself Cicada. He said ... " Jonah trailed off, blinking up at his warden. Terra had gone rigid. Her arms were stiff at her sides, her lips parted as if to scream. "You know that name."

"Yeah," Terra murmured. "I know it."

Jonah might have said something else, but the girl was too far gone to hear. Her head was buzzing; her heart was writhing in her chest. Ignoring all she had been taught, she whipped around and wrenched open the door with a shriek of rusted hinges. "Where are you ... ?"

Terra slammed the door on his confusion. The jarring noise bounced down the hall until it faded altogether. Terra pressed her brow to the metal slab, hoping the cold would subdue her rioting thoughts.

Cicada.

A hand on her shoulder. Before her neurons could spark with fear, she slammed her attacker up against the door and whipped out her closest knife, pressing it to their throat. "Easy! Skitz!" the man yelped.

"Samson," Terra barked, stepping back quickly and sheathing her blade. She shook her long hair over her shoulder, clutching at composure. "What the hell were you thinking, sneaking up on me like that?"

The captain glowered at her, massaging the pale pink line left behind by her knife. "I was thinking I said your name three times and you ignored me."

"I only have one ear, pitcher," she grumbled. "What are you doing down here? Did Evie talk to you?"

"I was coming to see if you wanted me to take over guard duty." He let his hand fall from his neck. His bright eyes narrowed to slits. "Why would Evie have talked to me?"

Dammit, Evie. She was probably upstairs begging Iris to forgive her. That was the problem with attachments. They invariably distracted from the big picture. "Never mind," Terra muttered, glancing down and away. She kicked herself internally. She was off her game.

"Did something happen?" Samson asked, concern inching into his voice. He peeled away from the door. His rugged face muted the false light hanging above them. His eyes cut straight through her. "Did he hurt you?"

"No," she snapped, glowering up at him as if he had just insulted her. "If I was a man would you be asking that?"

"You know what I mean."

"Drop it, Sam."

"No."

Terra made a frustrated noise at the back of her throat. Samson had always been kind to her, ever since she had arrived in the Belly as a child. She had never cared for him much. He was too pure. She had made her feelings clear to him several times over the years. Nothing seemed to faze him. He was blinded by an inexplicable desire to draw her out of her shell. "Fine," he surrendered. "I guess I'll just tell Roark you were interrogating the prisoner after he told you to wait."

Terra clenched her jaw, her nostrils flaring. Well, perhaps he was not all good. "No, just ... " She dragged an exasperated hand down her face, warping her skin. "Wait."

Samson folded his arms over his barrel chest. "Waiting."

"I know how to figure out if Jonah is telling the truth," she admitted in a low voice. The captain raised his eyebrows, his blue eyes flickering with interest. "But I need backup. I need someone to come with me to the middle ring."

The captain regarded her for a long moment, digging for answers in her vacant expression. She waited in the silence of his contemplation, her heart hammering in her ear. "We should wait," Samson finally said. "Until everything is up and running. Nothing else matters if the broadcast fails."

Terra nodded in agreement. She appreciated how quickly he fell into step with her. He was better than all the others combined in that respect. They spent far too much time oscillating on morals, in her opinion. "We can wait a week, two at most." She jerked her head at the storeroom. "Not like he's going anywhere."

"Why the middle ring? Where are we going?" Samson inquired.

Terra smiled hollowly. "To see my father."

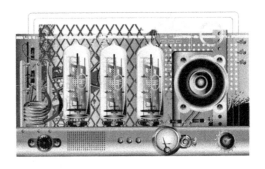

27: THE END OF THE STORY

They spent the better part of an hour locked in a feverish embrace. The city could have crumbled around them and they would not have noticed. Roark winced when he realized he had not packed protection. "I have another idea," he said, his lips on the curve of her ear. "Do you trust me?"

Ronja nodded eagerly, anticipation thrumming in her veins. It was then she learned there were other routes to pleasure. Though she had no one to compare it to, she was quite certain Roark was an unusually good lover. Eventually, they ended up side by side on their backs, crammed together like sardines on the twin bed, their chests rising and falling like pistons.

Ronja laughed breathlessly. Roark shifted to look at her, wearing a self-satisfied smirk. "Got something to say?"

"Not really," she replied offhandedly, scooting over to lay her head on his chest. "I mean, it was all right, I guess."

Laughter rumbled in the hollows of his ribs. He reached up to stroke her damp hair. "Happy to be of service."

Silence settled over them like a fresh blanket of snow. The wind threw itself against the walls of the warehouse, whistling through the cracks in the foundation. They did not feel the chill.

"Can I ask you something?" Roark asked after a while.

Ronja nodded, her eyelids fluttering sleepily. This was a different sort of exhaustion than she was accustomed to. It was easy, sweet as honey.

"That song you sang to get us out of the Belly, where did you hear it?"

Ronja smiled ruefully, the muscles of her face moving against his chest. "Are you asking if I heard it on my own, or if I remember you singing it when I was under The Quiet Song?"

"Well," Roark sighed, his hand stilling in her curls. "I guess that answers that. I was hoping you were brain-dead by then."

"Thanks."

"You know what I mean."

"It was strange," Ronja admitted. She traced the curve of his tattoo with her index finger, allowing the past to wash over her. "The Quiet was so loud. It felt like it was coming from everywhere, not just my Singer." Roark slid his hand down to cup the back of her neck, as if bracing her before a fall. "But your voice helped. It grounded me."

"Are you saying I have your gift?" he asked with a short laugh.

Ronja grinned. She sat up, squinting down at him teasingly. "You want a magic voice, too?"

He reached up and plucked at one of her tight curls like a violin string. "I think sirens are typically female."

"Right, of course."

"I read somewhere they can enchant men to do their bidding," he went on, his brown eyes shivering with mirth. Ronja laughed, an unhindered sound that almost never graced her lips. Roark must have registered its rarity, because he crushed her to his side and continued. "In some stories, they are also devastatingly beautiful."

Ronja giggled, then grimaced sharply. "Ugh," she moaned.

"What the hell did you do to me?"

Roark twisted his grin into a smirk. "Nothing you didn't like, by the sound of it."

Ronja kicked him in the calf. Hard. "Where did you and Terra pick up all these fairy tales, anyway?" she asked. Roark stiffened against her. She propped herself up on her elbow, searching his face for an answer to his sudden tenseness.

The boy forced a smile. "It was part of our training, of course. No self-respecting Anthemite goes into the field without a basic understanding of mythology."

"Roark."

Roark heaved a sigh, a divot of stress forming between his brows. He closed his eyes wearily. Ronja watched them roving behind their lids, searching for something she could not see. A birthmark no larger than the tip of a pen dotted the edge of his left eyelid. She had never noticed it before. It was usually hidden by his fringe of lashes.

"Sigrun."

His voice was so soft she thought she might have imagined it. She leaned toward him. "What?"

Roark opened his eyes. He looked haunted around the edges. "Her name was Sigrun."

"Like your violin," Ronja said with a nod, struggling to make the connection. Her stomach clenched. "Were you two ... I mean ... who was she?"

"She was my sister."

"Oh." Embarrassment took root in Ronja as she studied him. His expression was pinched, as if he were straining beneath a heavy burden. She knew the answer to her next question before it left her tongue. "What happened to her?"

"She died." Roark rolled his head to the side to face the wall. He traced the uneven terrain of the plaster with his pointer finger.

"She was my half-sister, really. She was five years older than me."
He rapped his knuckle against a clump of whitewash with a
hollow crack. "She was everything to me."

"How did it happen?" Ronja heard herself ask. She reached
down unconsciously and brushed a strand of hair off his forehead.
If he felt it, he did not react.

"My father shot her."

Ronja stared at him dumbfounded, her blood stilling in her
veins. She knew she should not be surprised. Victor was a monster.
Both she and Roark bore the scars of his abuse. Still, to murder his
own child, that was something entirely different. After he shot
Layla off the ladder to the airship, Victor had told Ronja he had
been aiming for Roark. Despite everything, she had assumed that
shot was not intended to be fatal. Now, she was not so sure.

"She was the first person to ever say 'no' to him," Roark went
on quietly.

"What do you mean?"

"It started small," he murmured.

His voice was almost inaudible. Ronja had to bend forward
to hear him properly. Her shadow poured over his regal features,
blanketing them in gray.

"He would order her to speak at an event, she would refuse.
She started disappearing. I asked her where she was going and she
told me it was a secret. One night, I caught her sneaking out her
window. She tried to bribe me."

He pinched the coin he wore on a cord around his neck,
holding it up for her to see. Ronja had always wondered about the
strange token, but had never asked. It seemed private, somehow.
Evidently, she was right. Roark continued.

"It didn't work, I told her I would shout if she didn't take me
with her." Roark laughed softly. There was no joy in the sound. "I
swear she almost decked me right there, but she took me with her

in the end."

"Where was she going?"

"To the cottage."

"The one you took us to?"

Roark nodded, his thick hair whispering against the mattress. He blinked sluggishly, still refusing to meet her eyes.

"What was she doing there?" Ronja prompted gently.

Roark gave a ghost of a smile. "Falling in love."

"With who?"

"An Anthemite named Parker."

Ronja's eyes widened as a chill settled over her. Her free hand drifted up to her mouth. "Sigrun was an Anthemite," she whispered through her fingers.

Roark shifted his head side to side, weighing her words. "Yes and no. She never went to the Belly, never got her tattoo. She was less of an agent and more of an informant, providing information and advice where she could. Mostly, I think she just wanted to be with Parker, and to make music."

A thousand questions sparked in Ronja, but she bit them back. Roark was not finished. She could see more words building behind his eyes.

"The cottage belonged to Parker," he said. "I have no idea how he got his hands on it. I don't even know how he and my sister met, only that they spent as much time as they could there, listening to records and making music. When Sigrun took me to the cottage that night, that was the first time I heard real music." His mouth quirked upward at the memory. "They sang a lullaby called *Shoreline*."

Cast your troubles off the shore ...

Ronja inhaled sharply. *Of course*. That was the song. It had to be. Guilt wove through her. She had subjected Roark to hearing it over and over on full blast.

"I had no idea what the pitch was going on, but I loved it," Roark continued. He shifted to look at her, but his eyes cut straight through her, seeking the past. "It was the first and last song I ever heard her sing. She had a beautiful voice, like you."

Roark opened and closed his mouth several times. He was wavering. Ronja took her hand from her lips and rested it on his chest. His heartbeat tickled her nerves. The unspoken words were choking him. She could almost see the noose. He had never told anyone what happened. She knew because she saw the same look in her eyes every time she passed a mirror. The weight of unspoken horrors was suffocating.

"Tell me how it happened."

Roark swallowed, his throat glistening with sweat. He was trembling, yet his voice remained steady. "When Sigrun and I got home, our father was waiting. I remember it so clearly. I know what he was wearing. He was smoking. I had a rock in the toe of my boot. I ... "

Ronja reached across his body and grabbed his hand, anchoring him. He screwed his eyes shut. "He asked us where we had been. We said nothing, so he called me forward and told me to roll up my sleeve."

Ronja clenched her teeth against the bile building in her mouth. She wanted nothing more than to kiss the story from his lips, to make it disappear, but she could not. He needed to talk, she needed to listen.

"Sigrun stepped in front of me. She told him to go to hell. He hit her so hard her tooth came out." Roark opened his eyes. Ronja knew, for him, the story was playing on the underside of the bunk like a moving picture. She could feel it hanging over her, as present as the sky. "I can still hear it bouncing across the marble.

She told me to run, so I did. I was so scared."

"You were a child," Ronja whispered. "He was a monster. There was nothing you could have done."

Roark did not seem to hear her.

"I heard them shouting, but I just kept running. Then I heard the gunshot. I must have passed out. I woke up in my bedroom with the door locked. No one came to let me out for a week. I drank water from the tap. I kept some candies in my desk drawer, I ate those. When my father finally came to get me, I was half dead."

Roark paused here, as if catching his breath. Ronja waited patiently for him to resume. Each second felt like a thousand. When the boy finally spoke again, she felt as if the sun had risen and set twice.

"He dragged me down the stairs. Her body was still on the floor, the smell was ... " He bit his lip until it turned white. "He forced me to my knees and made me look at her. Just look. Then he told me this was what happened when people disobeyed him."

Roark fell silent again. Ronja knew that was the end of the story, but it seemed unfinished, like some sort of retribution should have capped the end. There was none, of course. Sigrun was dead. Victor was dead. Roark would never have his sister back any more than he would have his revenge. The girl struggled to find something to say. She laid her head back on his chest, listening to the echo of his blood charging through his veins. She reached for the coin, covering the cold metal with her warm palm.

"May your song guide you home." The phrase fell from her lips before she could stop it. She winced, knowing she was not using it properly.

Roark pressed his warm hand to the space between her shoulder blades, pulling her closer. He planted a kiss on top of her curls. "I am home."

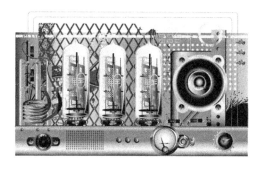

28: COLD STAR

Ronja did not remember falling asleep. One moment she was talking to Roark, the next, he was shaking her awake with gentle hands. "Hey," he coaxed her as she blinked up at him blearily. "Time to get up."

"Why?"

"We have to dismantle a government and free several million people from mental slavery, or something along those lines."

"Right now?"

"Right now. Evie says the radio station is ready."

Ronja sat up, raking her fingers through her short hair. Roark smiled down at her, amusement sparking in his onyx eyes. He was already dressed in his knit navy sweater and black pants, his long hair pulled into a knot at the base of his skull. Sigrun's coin rested against his sternum, glittering dully in the electric light.

Yawning, Ronja reached up an expectant hand. Roark grasped it and pulled her to her feet. Rather than letting her go, he drew her into a tight embrace. She sighed contentedly, slipping her bare arms around his waist as she breathed in his familiar scent.

"You should probably get dressed before we go downstairs," he said after a long moment, his chin resting on the top of her head.

"Mmm," she hummed. For the first time since she could remember, she did not feel self-conscious about her body. They were both scarred, after all. She pulled back so she could see his face. They continued to grip each other by their forearms. Neither wanted to admit they were afraid to let go. "Too bad."

"Truly," Roark agreed with an appreciative downward glance. "Get going, they're probably wondering where we are."

Ronja dressed as quickly as she could. Roark sat on the bunk, his head thrown back against the wall. She could feel his eyes on her, but was not bothered. His gaze was thoughtful, not lewd.

"What are you thinking?" she asked as she yanked her sweater over her head.

"I was thinking how much I wish we could stay in this room."

Ronja snorted, bending down to retrieve her left boot. "Yeah, I bet."

"No, that's not what I meant," he corrected. "I mean," he clarified when she shot him a withering look. "It is, but ... " He faltered, weighing his words. "As soon as we leave this room, we have to go downstairs and broadcast."

Ronja tugged on the laces of her boot. The leather tightened around her calf. "Yeah, unless you have other plans."

"What if I did?"

The girl let out a laugh, glancing around in search of her other shoe, which she had chucked several hours back. She spotted it under the desk and crossed to it. "You got a date or something?"

"Ronja."

She froze half a step from her desk. She kept her eyes locked to her boot, which was waiting patiently under the chair. "No,

Roark," she said in a low voice.

"Well ... "

"No," Ronja snapped, whipping around toward him, her eyes aflame. "We have a responsibility."

"Do we?" Roark got to his feet swiftly and crossed to her in a heartbeat. He tilted his head down slightly to meet her eyes. The panicked spark in his gaze glared down at her like a cold star. "Why does it fall to us to save everyone?"

Ronja floundered, her mouth hanging open on a busted jaw. Shock was etched into her features; there was no need for her to vocalize it.

"I know, I know!" Roark shouted. He backpedaled away from her on unsteady legs and braced himself against the side of the bunk bed. "Sing for the mute. Listen for the deaf. Fight for the powerless. All that pitch." He laughed, an empty sound that sucked the heat from the room. "I never even got a choice. It was fight for the Anthem or die. Wilcox would have killed me if I tried to leave."

"I didn't have a choice either," Ronja reminded him softly.

"Yeah, because I took it from you." He collapsed back onto the mattress with a groan of rusted springs, his head in his hands. Even from across the room, she could see the tremors in his hands. "I should have let you be. I should have left you in the station that day."

"And I am so glad you didn't," she exclaimed, hurrying over to kneel before him. She took his shaking hands in hers. He flinched at her touch, but did not pull away. "If I could have chosen to go with you, I would have. I would rather die with you today than live the rest of my life under The Music."

"Then come with me," he breathed. Ronja felt her heartbeat stumble. The desperation in his voice was palpable. "Come with me. We can leave right now, all of us. We've gotten out of the city before, we can do it again."

"And the Anthem? Georgie, Cosmin, and Charlotte?" she asked quietly. "Who will protect them?"

Roark shook his head, limp strands of hair slipping from their tie. "Wilcox is right, they've hidden down there for half a century. What makes us so sure The Conductor is going to find them?"

"You know it's only a matter of time."

"Do I?"

"I think you do." She gave his fingers a squeeze. "I think you're tired of losing people."

"So what if I am?" he barked, wrenching his hands back as if she had stung him.

Ronja swallowed dryly. She refused to be afraid of him.

He scowled at her, his jaw bulging in his cheek. "What if I can't stand to lose one more person?"

"Who says anyone else is going to die?"

Roark inhaled sharply. The whites of his eyes were tinted red. He looked terrified, almost as scared as he had been in the presence of his father.

As much as she wanted to, Ronja did not look away. "You know before this is over someone else is gonna die," he said, his voice cracking. "You. Me. Iris. Sam. Evie. Mouse. Terra."

Ronja winced internally at the last name. It was easy to forget that despite her recent betrayal, Terra and the others had grown up together. Fought together. Mourned together. There was too much history there to be ignored. She would just have to be okay with that.

"I know how you feel, I do," she told him softly. Roark did not react. He kept his shivering gaze fixed on the rough floorboards. "But the way I see it, we only have two options. We live, or we die. Running or hiding in that pitching tomb ... that is not living. The only way we get to live is if we fight. The only way we win is if we strike first."

Her words washed over Roark in a gentle wave. As she watched, the fear leaked from him. His shoulders drooped. He wilted forward. She laid his head on her shoulder, pressed a hand to his back. "Everyone in this city," she continued in a soft voice, running her fingers up and down his curved spine. "They deserve the chance to live, too. We can give them that."

Roark nodded against her. "I know."

"Where is this coming from?" she asked, stilling her palm at the small of his back.

The boy raised his head to look her in the face. A smile pricked the corner of his mouth. His dark irises shivered like oil in sunlight. Her stomach twisted itself into knots. He looked like himself again. "I guess I have just never had so much to lose."

A loud knock at the door shattered the moment. They both jumped half a foot. Roark was lucky he did not bash his head on the top bunk.

"Oi!" Mouse shouted through the wood. "Put your skitzing clothes on and get out here! We're live in ten!"

Roark and Ronja grinned in unison. Relief welled in the girl as she watched humor climb back into his eyes. "Coming, Mouse," he called. A bit of unintelligible muttering from beyond the door, then the trader traipsed back down the corridor.

"Why are we on such a tight schedule?" Ronja asked as they got to their feet.

"Asks the girl who was going stir-crazy in the Belly."

"First of all," she shot back, raising her finger before his face. He smiled, batting it away jokingly. "You would have gone nuts without your little escapades. Second, what I meant was, why is it so important that we broadcast in exactly ten minutes?"

Roark stretched his arms above his head and yawned before

answering. "Evie says the easiest spot to hack The Music will be during the gap between The Day and Night Songs," he explained, letting his arms fall limp at his sides. "Apparently, it lasts about ... "

"Sixty-three seconds," Ronja finished.

The boy eyed her curiously, his question written on his face.

She smiled ruefully. "When you spend your entire life with noise in your head, you learn to appreciate the quiet bits."

Roark nodded thoughtfully. "I suppose so."

"Come on." She stretched out her hand for him to take, wriggling her scabbed fingers. "Together."

He laced his fingers with hers, all traces of fear and doubt wiped clean from his face. "Together."

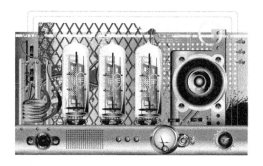

29: LITTLE WARS

Stepping into the hallway was like jumping into a cold river. Ronja actually gave a tiny gasp when she crossed the threshold. The corridor was empty, the rooms silent. *The station must be downstairs*, the girl thought vaguely.

"You all right, love?" Roark asked, laying a coaxing hand on the small of her back. Her skin tingled beneath his touch.

"Yeah," she answered quickly, realizing she had been staring into oblivion. "Fine."

"I hope so. One of us has to keep a level head."

"That would be me."

Roark chuckled. It was good to hear him laugh. Ronja started toward the stairwell. Her hand drifted back and caught his, pulling him forward. A shock sang down her spine. It felt so natural, all of it. Kissing him, touching him, even arguing with him. It would be so sweet to run away, to leave their responsibilities behind and explore the world they were owed. But she wanted so much more than running, and was willing to fight for it. She hoped Roark was, too.

They descended the rickety stairway together, their footsteps clattering like hail on a rooftop. They were forced to release each other before they hit the doorway. *Not that it'll make a difference*, Ronja thought, flushing as they stepped onto the vast factory floor. Trying to hide a secret from their friends was about as pointless as trying to move a subtrain by getting out and pushing.

"Where is everyone?" she asked, glancing about suspiciously. She saw nothing but the arching ceiling and Singer crates.

Rather than answering, Roark gestured at the chaotic maze of boxes. She tilted her remaining ear toward it, focusing. A tangle of faint voices kissed her eardrum. It sounded as if they were arguing. "Come on, Siren," he teased. "Your throne awaits."

Ronja swatted at his arm. He dodged the blow easily and jogged toward the labyrinth. She followed, apprehension creeping up on her like a bad cold. She held her breath as she passed into the tight wooden aisle. It did not take long before she lost track of the entrance behind them. Without Roark to guide her, she would have been utterly lost. Every bend and curve looked the same. The sense of foreboding that leaked from the boxes was overwhelming.

"Almost there," Roark promised, as if sensing her discomfort.

"Almost where?"

Roark winked and turned the corner. Ronja stopped in her tracks. The voices of their friends curved around the bend, meshed with the hum of machinery. Her stomach knotted. She sucked in a deep breath and followed.

"There they are."

"Finally."

"Enjoy your *nap*?"

"Skitz, let them be."

Ronja scarcely registered the teasing as she drank in the bizarre scene laid out before her. Her jaw dropped as she scuffed to a halt next to Roark.

"Not what you expected?" he asked, nudging her in the ribs with an elbow.

She shook her head sluggishly. In truth, she had no idea what she had expected. The only images she could conjure when the Anthemites spoke of the radio station were a handheld communicator and a subtrain station.

She could not have been further off the mark.

They stood at the edge of a ring of crates stacked ten feet high. At their peaks were spindly antennae with stiff metal branches. Red wires dripped from the towers to the ground. Ronja traced them to a massive dashboard on the far side of the circle. It was full of switches and dials and gauges she could not begin to make sense of. The machine rumbled like a distant subtrain. She could feel the whisper of heat radiating from it, even across the ring.

Evie sat cross-legged on an upturned crate before the dash, her back to them. She was either ignoring Ronja or focusing acutely on her task. Probably both. Iris and Mouse were conversing near the nucleus of the ring. The trader looked bored. The surgeon was fizzing with anxiety.

"Ro!" Iris yelped, bounding over to her and snatching up her hands. Roark choked on a laugh as Ronja balked like a skittish horse. He abandoned her to talk to Mouse. She glared daggers at his back, wondering if she could singe him with her gaze alone.

"I am *so* sorry about before," Iris said, peering up at her with watery doe eyes. "I had a talk with Evie, she knows she was a pitcher."

"Forget it," Ronja said hastily, wriggling free of her surprisingly firm grip. "There are more important things."

"Not really."

Ronja looked up. Evie swung her muscular legs over the edge

of the crate. She paused long enough to take a breath, then stood and crossed to her. Iris scooted out of the way, moving to stand with Roark and Mouse.

"I ... uh ... owe you an apology," the techi mumbled. "I was being reckless. I could have really hurt you." Ronja opened her mouth to speak, but Evie held up a tattooed hand to silence her. "Iris said I was being insensitive to your past. I see that now. I hope you can forgive me. You mean a lot to me, mate."

Ronja shifted from foot to foot, focusing on a random spot on the concrete to avoid eye contact. She was still not accustomed to such sincerity. She wondered if she ever would be. "Thanks," she answered, kicking a chunk of stone and sending it skittering across the plain. "We're good."

"Good," Evie exhaled. She clapped Ronja on the shoulder. Her knees knocked under the strain. "Glad we straightened that out."

Ronja nodded and offered a closed-lipped smile. The knots in her back loosened. She had not realized her fight with Evie had affected her so deeply. "Yeah."

"Tick tock," Mouse called loudly. Ronja leaned around Evie to look at him. He now stood beside the whirring machine, bobbing up and down on the balls of his feet like a nervous buoy. "We have three minutes, *three minutes*."

"Right," Evie said, clapping once to emphasize the word. She punched Ronja in the bicep, then hurried back to her station. Wincing, the girl crossed to Roark and Iris, who were still talking at the center of the ring.

"Where are Samson and Terra?" she asked.

"Sam is guarding Jonah," Iris answered. Her nerves apparently pacified after Evie's apology, now she was all business. "We sent Terra out about an hour ago to gauge the response to your voice. She should be somewhere in the slums."

"You mean you sent her to see if it works at all," Ronja said blandly.

The surgeon gave a considerate tilt of her head, tapping her index finger to her lips, "Or if it has any complications."

Ronja blanched, a strangled noise escaping her throat.

"It'll be fine," Iris assured her. "This is just a test. The signal will only travel a quarter mile. Right, darling?"

"Yeah," Evie responded from her seat on the crate. She was hunched over the dashboard, flicking an oscillating gauge with her forefinger. The quivering hand stilled and she grunted in satisfaction. "We're gonna make the field as narrow as possible. It should only affect a couple hundred Singers."

"Great," Ronja groaned. "I might set off The Quiet Song in a couple hundred Singers."

Roark hooked his arm around her shoulders, pulling her to his side and passing Iris a withering look. "It'll be fine," he soothed her.

She grimaced. He sounded as if he were trying to convince himself rather than her.

"All right everyone, back up and shut up," Mouse shouted, clapping a few times to dispel the chatter. "Zipse, stay right where you are."

Iris and Roark peeled away from Ronja. She was left alone in the center of the circle, which felt oddly claustrophobic. Mouse was approaching rapidly, carrying a steel microphone stand across his body like a musket. He parked it in front of her with a ringing clang. Ronja stared at it, curiosity bubbling inside her. She had never seen a microphone up close before. It was beautiful for the same reason a cello or a trumpet was, because of the potential it held. It was terrifying for the same reason.

Before she could reach out and touch it, Mouse slapped a pair of bulky leather headphones over her head. Fear spasmed in her chest. *The headset squeezing her skull as she tore through the halls of Red Bay, a razor-thin barrier between her and The Air Song.* She quieted her mind with a series of deep breaths. Now was not the time.

"When we go live, you'll only be able to hear your voice," Mouse told her. He steadied her head with his hand and plugged a thin cord into the jack in her headphones. "We'll count you in," he went on, walking the long wire back to the dash and handing it to Evie. The techi took it without looking up and plugged it into an outlet in the belly of the beast. Ronja shivered as faint static blossomed in her ear. "Can you hear me?" Mouse called.

Ronja nodded. His voice was muffled, but not inaudible. The trader put his hands on his hips, examining her like an artifact in a museum. His pale eyes seemed to drill straight through her. "Please tell me you have a song in mind," he said.

"Uhhh." Ronja rifled through the reservoir of songs she had learned from dozens of nights spent lingering at the edge of jams. There was only one that felt right. She nodded in affirmation. "Yeah."

Mouse exhaled a relieved breath. "Good," he said. "We'll count you in at the ten second mark."

"You need to start singing right away," Evie jumped in, twisting around to look at her. Her face glistened with sweat from the heat pouring off the machine. "We'll signal you when the gap is about to end."

Ronja nodded again. Her jaw was locked. Her thoughts were whirring louder than the machine she was connected to. Connected. She sucked in an unsteady breath. She was connected to a machine. Just like before. When they switched it on, she would be a breath from The Music. She would not hear it, but it would be there. A shadow she could never catch. Her throat constricted.

"Ronja." She followed the muffled voice to Roark, who watched her from the edge of the ring. He smiled, just a quick twitch of his lips. The panic that had distorted his face only minutes ago was gone. There was only trust, as clear and startling as those gold specks in his dark irises. "You can do this."

"Thirty seconds," Evie announced from her seat. Her fingers flew across the dashboard, coaxing the machine to life. Mouse stood at her shoulder, occasionally pressing a button or muttering something in her ear.

Ronja allowed her eyelids to drift shut. *This is it*, she thought distantly. The moment that would change everything. As soon as she opened her mouth she would be more than just a girl on the run. She would be the weapon she was meant to be.

Unless it was all a mistake. Unless Roark waking up from The Air Song was just a fluke. Unless her voice was not a weapon at all, but a beautiful empty thing that had only affected Roark because he was falling for her.

"Ten."

No. She could not think that way.

"Nine."

She had to believe she was something more.

"Eight."

She had not come so far, lost so much just to fail.

"Seven."

For Henry. For Layla. For Georgie and Cosmin.

"Six."

For Iris and Evie, so their love could see the light of day.

"Five."

For Roark and the burns on his arms. For Sigrun.

"Four."

For herself.

"Three."

Ronja opened her eyes.

"Two."

She gripped the microphone with both hands, stepped so close that her lips brushed the grated metal.

"One."

Ronja began to sing.

The walls of the warehouse did not crumble. The air did not flee the room, nor did the planet tilt on its axis. The shift within Ronja, however, was immediate. Immense.

> *First day you saw me I was way down low*
> *With my hands in my pockets and nowhere to go*
> *You were standing on my neck just to reach so high*
> *Sifting for those diamonds in the sky*

The familiar song ignited before her eyes, swallowing the faces of her friends, the wires, the machine, the arching ceiling of the warehouse. The visual manifestation of her voice was different than any instrument she had ever seen. At first glance, the writhing knots of sound were black as smokestacks. But the harder she stared, the more light she saw within. With each note the masses grew larger, fraying at the edges, spilling like water.

It was not beauty. It was power.

> *Blood in my veins and you say it's cold*
> *But if you cut my skin it will come out gold*
> *The brainwaves are crashing on the shores of my mind*
> *And if you stare too long then you may go blind*

Ronja's brain split, one half stumbling into the past, the other vaulting into the future. She saw where she had come from. A childhood marked by loneliness. An adolescence marred by prejudice and fear. She saw where she might go. A world without borders. A world full of possibility and song.

I got little wars
Little wars in my head
Telling me wrong from right
Out of mind out of sight
Little wars
I am a warrior

The song spun itself shut. No one needed to tell her she was out of time. Her internal clock still remembered the length of the gap. As the final seconds flickered out, her lips parted of their own volition. "This is Siren," Ronja said, her voice sharp as honed metal. "May your song guide you home."

The static fell flat in her ear as the line went dead. The thunderheads built from her song evaporated. Ronja removed the headphones, running her fingers through her hair. She was surprised to find she was not shaking. It felt as though hours had passed, though she knew it was barely more than a minute. "How was ... "

Iris reached her first, throwing her arms around her neck and kissing her on both cheeks. Evie hit her a split second later, slamming into her like a freight train. Ronja felt her eyes pop as the breath went out of her.

Just as the girls released her, Roark swooped in and lifted her from the ground. He spun her once, then planted her on her feet and kissed her full on the mouth. Evie crowed and Iris let out a shriek that could have shaken dust from the ceiling.

When the boy pulled back after what seemed like an infinity, Ronja was beet red. "Did it work?" she asked breathlessly. She looked to Mouse and Evie, who both shrugged helplessly. "How do we know if it worked?"

Static crunched as if in response, the telltale signature of a communicator coming to life. Ronja traced the sound to Evie, who dug a handheld radio out of her pocket and held it out for them to hear. Everyone froze, their breath suspended as they waited for an answer. "This is Medusa," came a familiar female voice, gravelly from the poor connection. "It's working."

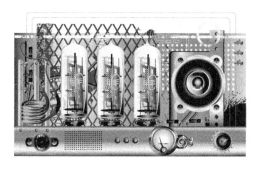

30: THE SHIFT
Terra

The last time she was in the slums, Terra was ten. She had passed through them since, but never stayed. There was no reason for *anyone* to visit the sprawling shantytown, unless they were looking to make a buck in the fighting rings.

The odor of human waste was only overpowered by the stench of garbage. There was no electricity, no plumbing and not a trustworthy soul for miles. Even the Offs steered clear. The Music kept the residents from revolting against The Conductor, but did nothing to protect them from one another.

Terra crouched low in a mud-slick alley between two dilapidated huts. She had tied her blonde braids into a knot under her hood. The last thing she wanted was to draw attention to herself. The radio Evie had given her was warm in her chest pocket. It was raining. Sleeting, really. Any other time she might have cursed her luck, but the rain felt incredible after weeks stuck underground.

The Revinians trudging along the main road did not seem to agree with her. They walked with their heads bowed, their spines bent. But then, that could have been The Music. It withered the soul. The body followed.

Terra stifled a yawn, rocking back and forth in a vain attempt to create a bit of heat. After they laid out the basic parameters of their plan, Samson had insisted on taking her watch. Disgruntled, she had retreated to one of the attic bedrooms to get some shut-eye. Then Evie was shaking her awake, asking her to sneak into the slums to observe the test broadcast.

She sincerely hoped she was not about to watch an accidental massacre. *Though it might be a skitzing mercy*, she thought dryly, watching as a girl a few years younger than her rooted around in a pile of trash for something to eat.

"Oi, you!"

Terra stiffened, slipping her hand inside her coat to brush the cool hilt of her closest blade. She stood fluidly and rounded on the voice, squinting through the sheets of icy precipitation.

Three hulking men barred the mouth of the alley. They were clothed in varying shades of gray and brown. The only bright things about them were their Singers. Even their eyes were as dull as paper. The largest of the trio, clearly the leader, stood at the front of the pack. He carried a knobby club as thick as his massive forearms. His seconds carried rusted blades.

"Nice coat you got there," the leader drawled, grinning to expose rotting teeth. His beady eyes raked up and down her body. "Would like ta see what's under it."

Terra smirked. "You'll have a hard time seeing without your head."

His depraved smile faltered. He whistled through the gap in his front teeth and jabbed a sausage finger at her. "Get her."

"Any other day I would gladly put you out of your misery," Terra said, not budging an inch as the knife wielders prowled toward her. "But now is actually a bad time."

"That so?"

"Yeah." Terra drew the knives at her hips with a ringing hiss. The honed metal glinted in the silver light.

The thugs stopped in their tracks, glancing back at their boss uncertainly. Clearly they had not expected her to put up a fight. He jerked his head at her again and they advanced with caution.

The Anthemite heaved a sigh. "Can we put this off for ... " She squinted at her rain speckled watch. "Ten seconds?"

The boss stared at her as if she were speaking in tongues. His goons froze again, peering back at him over their hunched shoulders. "Sorry?"

"Five."

"Shut her up, would ya?" The order fell on deaf ears. The thugs dropped their weapons. Terra hissed in disgust and surprise when muck sprayed across her boots. The two men reached up to touch their Singers, confusion warping their expressions. Behind them, their boss had let his club slip from his fingers. He was clutching his head as if it were about to burst.

Here we go, Terra thought tensely. She offered a lazy salute, then whipped around and sprinted out onto the main road. Her breath snagged in her ribs. She skidded to a halt, sending up a spray of mud.

Nothing moved but the driving sleet and the burgeoning storm clouds. Never in her twenty-three years had Terra seen such utter stillness. Never had she heard such silence. Hundreds of bodies crowded the slick road, their limbs and faces stiff as iron. She searched their paralyzed features for traces of panic or agony. Not daring to breathe, she took a tentative step toward the closest Revinian, a young man about her age in a heavily patched coat. He stared into oblivion, his lips parted.

It was not fear in his eyes, she realized with a jolt. It was focus. They were not afraid. They were enraptured. It was working.

Terra pulled out her radio, her frigid hands trembling with cold and unchecked adrenaline. "This is Medusa," she said into the speaker, dusting off the code name she had not used in months. "It's working."

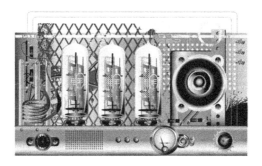

31: SYNESTHESIA

"To Ronja, the Siren!"

Glasses clinked as Ronja drained her fourth shot of whiskey. She winced as the burning liquid slid down her throat, grateful to whoever thought to bring alcohol on a suicide mission. Then again, almost two hours had passed since the broadcast and the Offs had yet to bust down the door.

It took ten minutes for the party to migrate upstairs to Ronja's room, twenty for the whiskey to appear, and sixty for Iris to get entirely too drunk for her own good. She hung off Evie like a rag doll, her cheeks as bright as her hair, her mouth churning out stories none of them could follow. Ronja and Roark sat shoulder to shoulder on one of the lower bunks, watching as Iris tried to convince Mouse to dance with her to a beat that did not exist.

"This feels ... " Ronja started to say. Roark passed her a curious glance, waiting for her to continue. Instead, she just smiled and shook her head. The moment was too lovely to weigh down with words. "Nothing."

"Nothing, huh?" He leaned toward her and brushed his lips against the curve of her ear. Ronja shivered. His breath was sharp with alcohol, but his voice was steady. Controlled. "I was thinking maybe we could slip over to my room later, if you like."

"I ... "

"You two are so cute I could just ... " Iris cut herself off with a hiccup. She giggled. Her hands were braced against Mouse, who was only mildly less intoxicated than she. "Eat you up."

"Huh." Mouse eyed Ronja and Roark with a wrinkled nose. "I just ... nah."

"Seriously?" Roark muttered under his breath.

"Please, like we were going to take it easy on you two," Iris scoffed. Mouse agreed with a fervent shake of his head. "Not after all of that." She puckered her lips in a poor interpretation of their kiss. Roark muttered unintelligibly under his breath as Ronja fought a blush.

"We should get some food in you two," Evie said, wedging herself between Mouse and Iris. She grabbed them both by their shoulders and steered them toward the door. "Lightweights," she sighed.

Just before they reached the exit, the techi shot Ronja a knowing glance. The singer could not help but grin. The door clicked shut, muffling the drunken protests of the trader and surgeon. Roark wasted no time pulling Ronja into a tight embrace. She laughed as he peppered kisses across her face, one for every freckle. "You." He kissed her left cheek. "Were." Her right. "Incredible." His mouth found hers and she sank into the bliss.

"It feels too good to be true," Ronja admitted when they finally pulled apart. "When was the last time something went our way?"

Roark chuckled darkly. "I think maybe we're due."

Ronja flopped back onto the mattress. "Maybe," she conceded doubtfully.

"It'll be a process." Roark wedged himself between her body and the wall. She scooted over a few inches to accommodate him. "We knew from the start one broadcast was not going to be enough to undo a lifetime of The Music. We'll know more once Terra gets back, but she said they felt something, and that in my humble opinion, is worth celebrating."

Ronja snorted, rolling her eyes at the underside of the bunk bed. "You. Humble. Right."

"Oi," the boy growled, clutching her closer. She let out a short laugh, marveling again at the ease with which they fit together, body and soul.

"Count your victories, yeah?" she said.

"Every last one."

They fell silent, their breathing settling into a magnetic rhythm. Ronja let her eyelids fall shut. She was not tired. In fact, she could not remember the last time she felt so well rested. She was simply content.

"I have a question," Roark admitted after a while.

Ronja opened her eyes, her stomach tightening. There was a hesitant ring to his voice she did not like.

"Shoot," she said.

"When you sing, you get this look on your face, almost like ... " He paused, his arm tightening around her torso, to restrain or to protect. She tensed, waiting for the inevitable. "Like you are seeing something."

Ronja felt her heart sink through the mattress, landing with a dull thwack on the dusty floor. She knew she was going to have to tell him eventually, but had hoped to put it off for as long as possible. With a heavy sigh, she rolled over onto her side, facing away from Roark. She did not think she would be able to look him in the eye when she admitted it.

"It started at Red Bay," she began, keeping her eyes locked

on the whitewashed wall. Roark was still against her, listening. For the first time, she found herself wishing he was not so damn attentive. "When I sang to you, I saw something. I thought it was The Lost Song still messing with my head, but when we got back to the Belly, it was still there."

"What was?"

Ronja licked her lips, which were dry as a crust of bread. "It only happens when I hear music, or when I sing. Especially when I sing." She swallowed a wad of nonexistent saliva. "I see colors, shapes. Everywhere. Not just in my head, they look real, like I could touch them. They move with the music."

She waited for Roark to say something, to tell her she was insane or imagining things. Instead, he maintained his silence. Somehow, that was worse. "They ... they go away as soon as the song is over," she babbled, attempting to fill the void. "I ... "

"Synesthesia."

"Sorry?" Ronja flipped over, wondering if perhaps she had misheard him. Perplexed relief washed over her when she found Roark was grinning at her, the corners of his eyes crinkling with wonder.

"I *think*," he continued, stressing the second syllable. "You might be a synesthete."

"A syne — ?"

"A synesthete," he explained through his radiant smile. "It means some of your senses cross over. Some people can taste colors or sounds. Some people see colors when they hear sounds, or in your case music. You said it started at Red Bay, right?" The girl nodded mutely. "I'll bet you anything it was triggered by The Lost Song." Roark itched his shadowed jaw thoughtfully. "You were probably predisposed; a lot of artists are."

"Artists?" Ronja asked with a snort. "I thought I was a weapon."

Roark shrugged against the mattress. "Sirens are both." The girl rolled her eyes again and gave him a slight shove. He threw his hands up in defense. "Hey, you said it, not me."

"Good point. Thought it had a nice ring, though," she muttered, itching the bridge of her nose.

"It does," he agreed, adopting a somber tone. "You needed a code name, anyway." Ronja cocked her head to the side in askance. "We all have code names, just in case," Roark explained. "Actually, yours fits perfectly. Most of ours are from mythos."

"What's yours?"

"Drakon. It's a dragon," he answered with an embarrassed twitch of his lips. "We all picked ours from the book of myths my sister gave me. Evie is Chimera, Iris is Nymph, Terra is Medusa, Samson is Griffin."

"Huh, it does fit," Ronja realized with a little laugh. A thought struck the humor from her. Her brow furrowed. "Who do you think started calling me Siren? And how did word get to the Kev Fairla?"

Roark mirrored her troubled expression. "I wish I could tell you." He sighed. "No one under The Music could have coined it; myths are outlawed."

Ronja nodded. Since being severed from her Singer, she had gotten her hands on multiple books hoarded by the Anthem filled with magical creatures and impossible worlds. They kept her up at night almost as much as her nightmares.

"It had to be someone who knows about your voice, obviously," Roark went on. Suspicion crept into his eyes. He shifted anxiously, the springs of the mattress groaning under his weight. "Maybe it's a warning, someone trying to tell us they know who you are."

"Maybe," she conceded. "Or maybe they are trying to tell us they stand with us."

Roark chuckled, laying a hand on her waist. Her stomach fluttered. She fought to keep her mind from wandering. "When did you get so bloody optimistic?"

"Hard not to be when we keep kicking ass." They grinned at each other and fell into another easy silence. Eventually, Ronja looped back to the inception of the conversation. "So," she began tentatively. "I am *not* going crazy?"

"No more than usual."

"Hilarious."

"Why did you wait so long to tell me?" he asked curiously. Ronja shrugged, breaking eye contact with him. She spotted a bit of lint on the sleeve of his sweater and picked it off absently. "Synesthesia is nothing to be afraid of," he told her, blanketing her hand with his. "Just another thing that makes you so rare."

Ronja felt her throat tighten, her eyes fill. Roark tensed against her, his fingers tightening around hers. She waved him off frantically. "Sorry," she grumbled, wiping her cheeks. "Just the shots."

"I have seen you throw back twice that much without breaking a sweat, love," the boy said dryly. "Come on, what is it?"

I never thought I deserved to be loved. I never thought I was capable of loving someone back.

"Nothing." An unexpected wave of exhaustion rolled over her, weighing down her eyelids. She took a slow breath and tucked her head into his neck. "Can we go to sleep?"

"Of course," Roark said quickly. "Do you want me to go?"

Ronja shook her head. He pulled her close, curling around her to press a kiss on top of her curls. "I love you," she mumbled, sleep sweeping over her like a curtain across a stage.

"I love you, Siren." The words stood guard over her, wardens to her nightmares.

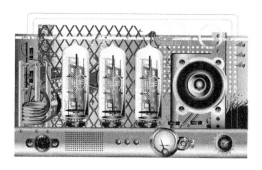

32: JOLT
Jonah

An otherworldly screech jolted him from sleep. Jonah swore and clamped his hand to his ear as the keening gave way. He waited, staring into the endless black of the storeroom, for the voice to hit his eardrum. *"Kal peske ven a ledar. Letraon vein lev mantra."*

Jonah sat bolt upright, white lights popping like firecrackers before his blind eyes. "What?" he hissed. "What do you mean they launched the weapon? There was no explosion, there was no ... " He cut himself off, mindful of the guard outside his door. The girl, Terra, had left hours ago. Her replacement was one of the men, he was not sure which. He was silent as a tomb, but Jonah was certain he was not asleep.

Static crackled like distant thunder in his ear. For a long moment, he thought his employer had walked away from the radio and forgotten to disconnect. Just as he was about to lie back down and try to sleep through the electronic babel, the man spoke again. *"Ger vein pien."*

The line went dead. Jonah frowned and lay back down on his coat, his eyes on the invisible ceiling. For five years he had been an agent of the Kev Fairla. He had fought and killed to protect their island from threats both foreign and domestic. He was accustomed to sudden shifts in plans; if anything they injected a little adrenaline into his blood.

What he could not stand was being lied to.

He rolled onto his side, his brow creased with doubt. *Ger vein pien.* Gain their trust. Why? His original task was to locate the rogues and relay their position to his employer once they were stationary. It was a straightforward mission with a monumental reward: enough weapons and ammunition to give them a fighting chance against Vinta. Jonah had assumed his boss was just gathering the necessary forces while he waited in his cell. It was clear that was not the case.

What is he waiting for? he thought angrily. If the rebels had already launched their weapon, whatever it was, why waste time digging into their ranks? Jonah gritted his teeth and tucked the crook of his arm under his head.

Tovaire would not last much longer. If it came down to it, he would get the weapons on his own. He slipped his hand under his makeshift pillow, touching the cool metal of the blade the blonde had abandoned. He had gotten out of worse binds with less. But he would not use it. Not yet. "What are you doing, Bullon?" Jonah muttered. "What the hell are you doing?"

PART II: SIREN SONG

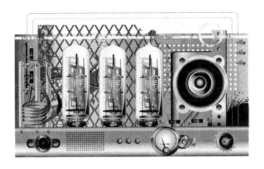

33: ROUTINE

The days fell into a steady rhythm.

Each morning Ronja woke at 4:45 A.M. to the piercing wail of the alarm clock Mouse had given her. The very concept of an alarm was foreign to her. She had never needed one under The Music. The dying moans of The Night Song were enough to rouse her. In the Belly, she was either awakened by the clatter of cookware or the intense urge to run before the compound became choked with suspicious Anthemites.

In the bone-quiet warehouse, an alarm was an absolute necessity. The pull of her bed was stronger than ever. Rather, the person *in* her bed. On their first night in the factory, Ronja and Roark discovered they slept well together, despite the fact that she had now kneed him in the kidney several times. Neither of them had said as much, but they knew sharing a pillow buffered their nightmares.

Roark slept like the dead at her side. There was little that could wake him, even the ungodly screaming of the alarm clock, so the task fell to Ronja. She was always reluctant to rouse him. He looked younger in sleep, unburdened.

"Get up, shiny."

"Hmmm no."

"Come on, time to go."

"No, thanks."

After a few minutes of fruitless coaxing, she would be forced to pinch his earlobe, which through some mishap she had learned he hated. This caused him to sit bolt upright, grumbling and massaging the pink welt left by her fingernails. Forgiving her at once, he would snag a kiss and vault out of bed as if she were the one lagging behind.

By the time they had showered and dressed, it was 5:15 and the gap between The Night and Day Songs was approaching. Yawning and stretching, they made their way down to the radio station. Mouse and Evie usually beat them there. The machine that hacked the Singers, which the techis had named 'Abe,' required almost as much persuasion to wake up as Roark.

Evie and Mouse usually rose around 4:00 with the aid of coffee brewed in Mouse's portable kettle. The little black pot was a godsend. They were eternally grateful that he thought to bring it from his apartment. "My contribution to the revolution," he said with a sweeping bow each time someone gulped down a mug.

Though Ronja was fond of the taste, she did not need the coffee to get her blood pumping in the morning. The promise of singing into the void of The Music was enough to shoot electricity into her veins. It was like standing on the edge of a cliff with her arms spread wide, terrifying and exhilarating. She no longer feared the darkness that blossomed from her mouth. It had expanded and morphed since her confession, freed by her words. Now, the black mass was studded with bullet holes that spilled white light.

She wished she could make the Revinians see what she saw. If they could see beyond the desolate prison they were born into, she was sure she could set them free. The best she could do for now was make them listen. From what her friends told her, they did.

Each day before the sun rose, Samson and Terra clipped on false Singers and ventured out to watch the song of the Siren roll over the city. Besides Evie, the captain was the only one who could stand to be around Terra for extended periods of time. Their personalities were oil and water, yet somehow they worked together smoothly. Iris expected some secret romance. She was alone in this theory. No one else thought Terra had the emotional capacity for a relationship.

During the evening broadcast, Roark and Iris snuck into the city. They had to be considerably more cautious than their counterparts, even skulking around the outer ring in the dead of night. Iris wore a wig. There was always the chance that the Offs had been instructed to keep an eye out for a petite redhead with two inches of hair.

Roark had a harder time with his disguise. He was a celebrity long before his mugshot was plastered to every street corner. Ronja tried to convince him to remain inside to no avail. He suffered from the same cabin fever that had plagued her in the Belly. She knew once he set his mind to something, there was no stopping him. It was a quality they shared. Instead of throwing punches at a brick wall, Ronja coughed up a compromise.

At her request, he swapped his fine leather overcoat for a shabby brown jacket Terra brought back from the slums. He donned a pair of thick rimmed glasses with the lenses punched out and tucked his chin into a woolen scarf to hide his razor jawline. Most importantly, he allowed her to chop off his long elegant hair.

"I look like an Off," Roark complained, glowering at his clean-cut reflection in the mirror. Ronja snickered, setting her scissors on the lip of the sink and brushing locks of inky hair off his shoulders. For all her lack of experience with primping, she was quite good at cutting hair. They had never possessed the money to go to a hairdresser as children, so she gave Georgie and Cosmin trims over the kitchen sink.

"I like it," she replied seamlessly, peeking around him to view herself in the looking glass. She frowned, tousled her brief mess of curls. "I look like I stuck my finger in an electrical socket."

Roark laughed, his grimace giving way to a grin. He spun around and pulled her toward him by the waist. Her stomach vaulted. His eyes were clear and sharp, especially without the shadow of his hair. "It matches your personality," he said, reaching up to pluck at one of her curls.

"Skitzed?"

The boy tilted his newly freed head to the side, considering her with a coy smile. "I was going for pitched, but if you like."

The days became a week. The heart of winter settled over the warehouse like a yoke. Evie was able to keep the radiators running in their bedrooms, though the factory floor was too vast to heat much. Roark and Mouse had managed to smuggle in a month's worth of rations while they were building the radio station. Their bounty consisted mostly of canned goods, but no one complained. They were too focused on the task at hand, sinking into their individual roles with fervor.

Ronja stopped splitting the days between morning and night, instead measuring the passage of time by broadcasts. At 5:30 A.M., she poured her soul into the microphone for a minute, signed off as the Siren, then climbed back into bed with Roark until Samson and Terra returned. Their stories were always the same.

"They float around like the dead until the gap, then as soon as Ronja starts singing, they light up," the captain described one day over a breakfast of lukewarm soup. Despite the lack of a fire, they still took their meals sitting in a circle on the floor of the room Ronja and Roark now shared. "Some people smile, some cry. Some of them hold on to each other. The only thing they have in common is — "

"They go silent," Terra finished, setting aside her own tin can. She tossed her dirty blonde hair over her shoulder.

"They are listening," Ronja said quietly.

Terra surprised her by answering her directly. "Yeah," she said with a blunt nod. "I think they are."

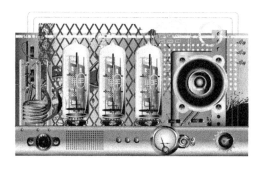

34: BRAWLER

"Good, again."

Ronja groaned, clutching her sore ribs. She lay on her back on the smooth concrete, her eyes screwed shut against the dull pain in her back. Her tank top was soaked with sweat, her leggings too.

"Come on, get up, I know you can." Ronja opened her eyes for the sole purpose of glowering up at Samson. He grinned down at her. He was barely sweating, his hair tied into a loose braid at the back of his neck. The captain stuck his hand out for her to grab. Huffing, she took it and he pulled her to her feet. "All right?" he asked with a laugh.

"Fine," Ronja grumbled, looking anywhere but his teasing blue eyes.

They had been sparring for hours and she had yet to win a single match. She started out confident enough. While she had never had any formal training, a lifetime as a mutt and three years as a subtrain driver in the merciless outer ring had forced Ronja to learn how to defend herself. She was a brawler. She fought ugly with her teeth and elbows and nails.

Samson and the other Anthemites were more than just

fighters, though. They were dancers.

"Go again?" Samson asked.

"Yeah, give me a minute." Ronja ambled over to the crate where she had set her canteen. She unscrewed the top and leaned up against the rough wood. She took a long swig, her eyes on the arching factory ceiling.

"Where did you learn to fight?" the captain asked, stretching his muscular arms over his head. Ronja tried not to notice how beautiful they were. She set her bottle down with a dull thwack, leaving it uncapped.

"Self-taught," she replied, copying him and raising her arms above her. "I had a lot of skitzed passengers when I worked the subtrain."

Samson grinned. "You were a driver."

"Yeah," she replied, letting her hands fall to her sides.

"You know something," he said, turning his gaze to the ceiling thoughtfully. "I have spent my entire life in a subtrain station and I have never *actually* been on a steamer before."

"Seriously?"

"Yeah," Samson laughed. "I do most of my work in and around the Belly, I can walk everywhere I need to go."

"Huh," Ronja said. Her lips split into a grin. "When this is all over, I'll take you for a ride."

"Really?"

"Yeah," she said eagerly. "It'll be great. We'll steal an engine and I'll take you on a loop around the city."

"Wow," Samson ran his fingers through his sweat-damp hair, beaming at her. "I would love that."

"Great, but I have one condition."

"Which is?"

Ronja raised her fists before her, hopping side to side on the balls of her feet. "Teach me how to flip somebody over your shoulder, like you just did to me."

Samson let out another ringing laugh. His humor was infectious. "You got yourself a deal, Siren. Here, come stand by me."

Ronja dropped her arms and sidled over to stand next to him. Heat radiated from his muscular form. "If you can learn to do this, you can flip just about anybody," he told her. "In this case, size doesn't matter."

"Never heard that one before," Ronja quipped.

Samson grinned. "All right, bend your knees, feet a bit more than shoulder width apart, good. Assume somebody comes up behind you, like this." He paused before stepping behind her, arching an inquisitive brow. "Can I?"

"Oh, sure."

The captain moved to stand behind her. Her skin tingled as he pressed himself against her, then slowly wrapped his arms around her neck. The smell of sweat and musk overwhelmed her senses, and she fought to keep her head. "There is no way in hell I am going to be able to flip you," Ronja said.

"Iris can."

"She *cannot.*"

"Okay," Samson conceded. "Iris can flip *Trip.*"

"You have fifty pounds on Roark," Ronja seethed, shifting in his snug grip.

"To be fair, you have a good thirty on Iris."

Ronja grumbled unintelligibly. She felt rather than heard Samson laugh, his chest vibrating against her back. "All right," he said. "Bend your knees, feet a bit further apart, then I want you to grab my right forearm and lift me onto your back ... "

"Are you kidding me?"

"Then roll me over your shoulder."

"There is no way in hell ... "

"Ronja, you are in the process of freeing several million minds from mental slavery by singing into a transmitter. I think you can flip me over your shoulder."

Ronja sucked in a deep breath, then bent her knees as he had instructed her and grabbed his thick forearm with both her hands. It was slick with sweat. "Okay," she said. "One, two, three." She heaved with all her strength, dipped forward and slammed Samson into the ground. His eyes popped with shock as he struggled for breath on the concrete. Ronja let out a noise of distress and crashed to her knees next to him. "Are you okay?" she gasped.

"Fine," Samson said, with a winded laugh. "I just didn't think you would actually throw me the first time."

Ronja grinned as pride replaced her concern. She stuck out her hand for him to take, then yanked him to his feet. He looked down at her with bright eyes, kneading the muscles of his right shoulder. "Again," she said.

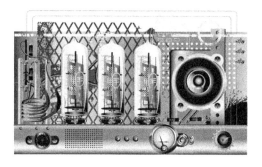

35: PARADOX
Roark

"H—how much longer?" Iris asked through chattering teeth. Roark squinted at his watch in the dim light of the alleyway. "Three minutes," he replied.

The surgeon made a distressed noise at the back of her throat and stomped, sending up a spray of slush. Roark tossed her a scathing look, then unwound his scarf and passed it to her. "Ro—Ronja would kill you," she said as she took the garment and wrapped it around her neck. She crossed her arms to hold the heat in.

"Probably," he agreed, peeking out onto the main road. They were staked out on the inner edge of the outer ring, several miles from the warehouse. It was nearing 9:00 P.M. and the streets were still full of Revinians. They moved mechanically, their Singers glinting like flint in the aura of the gas lamps. Across the avenue, Roark could just make out a wanted poster bearing his face nailed to a storefront. "But I doubt a scarf is going to keep people from recognizing me, anyway."

Iris grumbled under her breath, then sank deeper into the wool. The tip of her nose was as red as her natural hair, which was currently obscured by an ashen brown wig.

"Trip."

Roark looked down at the girl questioningly. She heaved a sigh, her breath mushrooming in the air, then leaned against the wall. She looked even tinier than usual in her padded overcoat and mousy wig. "I'm worried."

"When are you not?"

"I'm serious," she said sharply "This is taking longer than we thought."

"We knew from the start it would take time to make a lasting change," he reminded her, a hard edge creeping into his tone. His defenses were up and he knew why. Iris did, too. "We have to get them to feel before we get them to rebel."

"The problem is, the change does not hold," Iris explained gently, as if he had not thought of this himself. She placed a gloved hand on his arm. He did not return the gesture, nor did he pull away. The wind gusted, stirring their coats and hair. "They feel something when she sings, but as soon as The Music comes back, it dissipates. I was worried about this when we came up with the plan. I hoped if they heard her enough, it would effect a permanent change in their minds ... "

"It might," Roark cut in.

"It might," she agreed with a somber dip of her chin. "But ... we're running out of time."

"Give her another week," he implored her. He stood up straighter despite the biting wind. "I believe in her voice."

"I know you do," Iris said, her chapped lips twitching upward. "I do too. But we have to be realistic. You were never very good at that."

"Realism is overrated."

"Surviving is not."

Roark shushed her, tapping the face of his watch with a

leather-clad finger. "Ten seconds."

Iris huffed indignantly, turning her brooding eyes on the street. She had stopped shivering, though the tip of her nose was still ruddy.

"Iris," he said tenderly. "You know this is our only shot."

"I know. That's what scares me."

Roark looked down at his watch just as the minute hand clicked into place. Over the past week, he had grown accustomed to the sudden hush that enveloped the neighborhood each time Ronja's voice flooded the Singers. It no longer unnerved him. Instead, it instilled awe in him. The paradox of silence and noise, the knowledge that fully autonomous thoughts and emotions were stirring in the minds of the Revinians, perhaps for the first time in their lives.

That was why it was particularly shocking when a blood-curdling scream lanced through the streets.

Roark and Iris looked at each other. For a split second they stood rigid. Then they shot out of the side street, kicking up slush in their wake. The Revinians, who were usually static as pillars by now, were looking around wildly, calling out to each other in confusion.

Another tortured shout.

Roark poured on more speed, leaving Iris in the dust. Thoughts of The Quiet Song swelled in his head, forcing out his better judgment. His hood flew back, revealing his cropped hair. His glasses bumped against the bridge of his nose. Swearing, he ripped them off and stuffed them in his pocket.

"Hurry up!" a masculine voice shouted from the alleyway ahead. "Forty-five seconds!"

Roark skidded to a halt, the traction of his boots keeping him from sprawling across the slick cobblestones. Iris slammed into him a moment later, gasping for air. She clutched his arm as they stared into the shadow-drenched alley. Four pairs of eyes stared back, three blazing with adrenaline, one shivering with fear. Three men were crowded around one, pinning him to the wall. The victim was rail thin with a greasy ponytail and a proudly glinting Singer. Unbridled fear flashed in his murky brown eyes.

Roark started forward, his hand flying to his stinger, but Iris yanked him back. "Wait," she hissed. "Look." He squinted into the dimness. A speck of white latched his gaze, the white emblem of The Conductor glaring at him from the chest of the apparent victim. He was an *Off*.

"Keep moving, pitchers," barked one of the aggressors, a boy about their age with soot dark hair. He stepped back from his prisoner, trusting his friends to hold him steady. The Officer struggled in vain, reaching for his high-powered stinger lying on the ground.

"What are you doing?" Iris asked carefully.

"This bastard raped my sister," the boy spat, his eyes still on the Off. He delivered a solid blow to his gut. The man wheezed, his eyes popping in their deep sockets. "Now I can make him pay."

"Thirty seconds, Lou," one of the boys warned, checking his watch as if he could squeeze more time out of it.

Lou reached into his coat and drew a serrated blade. Iris clapped her hand over her mouth. Roark stepped in front of her protectively. His eyes never left the scene. "My sister says she can still feel your hands on her," Lou spat, saliva flying from his lips. The Off whimpered, thrashing against the two boys restraining him. "She couldn't say no to an Off, not that you would have listened."

The captured Officer wriggled like a leech on a hook. The boys held him steady. Their eyes were trained on Lou, unflinching and unquestioning. One of them was muttering something under his breath, but Roark could not make out the words.

"Y—you cannot do this," the Off stuttered, his oily head whipping back and forth between the young men who restrained him. "The Conductor will protect me ... The Music will ... "

"May the Siren give me strength," Lou proclaimed, his cracked fingers tracing the curve of his Singer.

Then, without a moment of deliberation, he cranked his arm back and stabbed the Off in the gut. The man went rigid, shuddered, then slumped against the wall. Blood bubbled up over his lips, spilling down the front of his uniform. He choked out a laugh, spraying Lou with gore. The boy blinked rapidly, but did not move to clean it off.

"Should have check—ed my pock—ets," the Off managed to say. His eyes rolled back into their sockets. As the life fled him, the boys released his body. Iris flinched when the corpse hit the ground with a jarring thud. Lou crouched next to his body, patting down his pockets. Feeling something, he dug in and yanked out a portable radio. A pinprick of red light flashed from its face. It was on.

Lou dropped the radio and crushed it beneath his boot. He looked up at the Anthemites. "Westervelt," he said quietly. "Victor Westervelt III, the traitor."

Roark tensed, his hand flashing back to the stinger hidden in his coat. He cursed himself internally for abandoning his disguise. The broadcast would be over any second now. The Offs would arrive on the heels of The Music. The voice of the Siren would fade, and with it their only cover.

"Lou," one of the boys whimpered. Roark shifted his gaze to him for a split second. His eyes were wide, his skin drained of color. His trembling hand covered his Singer.

"I hear it," Lou growled, tearing his gaze from the Anthemites and looking down at the lifeless Off. His hands were slick with blood, which was almost black in the shadows of the alley. Out on the main road, the Revinians were beginning to go about their business again, the echoes of their emotions suffocated beneath the hands of The Night Song. Roark put up his hood.

Lou collapsed with a soft cry. His friend, the one who had spoken, crashed to his knees in a puddle of sludge. The other was absolutely still, his shoulders hunched and his hands clamped over his ears. Iris stepped out from behind Roark.

"Stay back," Lou barked through gritted teeth. "You gotta get outta here." He lifted his chin. Two ribbons of blood slithered from his nose, settling between his lips. "If you stay much longer I'll ... " He slammed his eyes shut, sagging toward the ground.

Iris glanced back at Roark fearfully. He barely noticed, his gaze trained on the three teenagers. The one on his knees had bowed his head, his fingers twined in his shaggy hair. The other was still on his feet, paralyzed. "Remember what she said," Lou ground out. "Remember what the Siren said. Say it with me ... "

"Little wars ... "

"Little wars ... I am ... "

"I am ... "

Shouts rang out from the street, mingled with the thunder of militant footsteps. "Roark," Iris whispered shrilly, using his real name for the first time in a long time. "We have to go."

"Go," Lou cried, slamming his fist into the bricks. Iris glanced over her shoulder at the passing crowds. Any second now they would be discovered. Still, Roark refused to look away from Lou. The teenager wiped his nose with the back of his wrist, then looked up. He was grinning, his teeth stained with his own blood. "Get outta here. Tell the Siren, tell her ... we're fighting for her."

"I will," Roark promised, snagging Iris by the hand and backing away. "I swear."

He and Iris spun and launched back into the throngs, their

faces angled toward the ground. Shouts of surprise flew up as they jostled shoulders and stomped on feet, but no one stopped them. They reached the side street where Roark had hidden his motorcycle under a tarp. Working as one, they ripped the damp fabric off the vehicle and climbed on.

"Go, go," Iris begged as he popped the kickstand. "Come on."

Roark revved the engine, sending up a spray of slush. As they shot out of the alley, the sound of gunfire ripped the night. They did not stop. They did not look back.

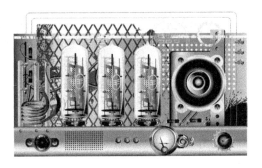

36: AIM

"And then we came home," Roark finished anticlimactically. He glanced over at Iris to see if she wanted to add anything. The surgeon shook her head. Her milk white skin was tinged green. She appeared dangerously close to vomiting.

Samson whistled through his teeth. "Skitz."

Ronja nodded in silent agreement. *Skitz* was about the only word she could think of to describe the situation. They were gathered in the bedroom she and Roark shared. She sat with Evie and Samson on the right-hand bunk. Mouse was perched above them, his skinny legs kicking back and forth hypnotically. Terra refused to sit still, electing instead to pace. Roark and Iris were seated across from them, still wearing their disguises. At least, one of them was. The boy had discarded his glasses and scarf. Ronja vowed to chew him out for it later.

"We haven't seen anything like that on our runs, right Terra?" Samson asked, glancing up at the blonde as she carved a trench down the middle of the room.

"No," she replied tersely, spinning on her heel when she hit the far end of the room.

"What are you guys moping about?" Evie demanded. "This is

great, people are fighting back!"

"And dying for it," Samson pointed out darkly.

Evie snapped and aimed two fingers at the captain, rather like a pistol. "But not by The Music."

"Evie's right," Iris said softly. All eyes shifted to the surgeon, who was staring at her knees, her mousy wig like curtains drawn around her face. She slipped it off absentmindedly, revealing tussled red locks. "They triggered The Quiet Song, they were bleeding from their noses and ears." She looked up, locking eyes with each of them in turn. "But they were fighting it off."

"I've never seen anything like it," Roark said with a slow shake of his head. "Not even when Ronja went into The Quiet. They could talk, they could move. They were in a ton of pain, but I doubt it would have killed them." A shadow passed over his features. "Until the Offs arrived."

"You say they were fighting it off," Terra spoke up. She was facing the door, her callused hands twined behind her back. "How?"

Roark smiled, a spark igniting in his rueful face. "They were singing. Well," he amended. "They were *speaking* lyrics. *Little Wars*, the first song Ronja broadcasted. Before he killed the Off, Lou asked the Siren to give him strength."

Six pairs of eyes fell on Ronja, who wanted nothing more than to sink into the mattress. Her thoughts warred. She knew she should be ecstatic. This was what she wanted, for the people to rise up against The Conductor and his men. Against violence and injustice. Part of her was proud that her voice had allowed Lou to do what had to be done to avenge his sister. A sliver of her soul reveled in the knowledge that an abuser had been killed in her name. Still …

"This is … " Ronja began, trailing off as her thoughts slipped through the cracks in her mind. Her head sagged. She cradled it in her hands. Samson reached out and laid a tentative hand on her shoulder. She did not react. "Dangerous." She lifted her head and let her hands fall. Everyone watched her intently save for Terra, who had returned to pacing with increased fervor. "If we're not careful, we'll create anarchy."

Terra froze mid step, this time facing the cracked porcelain sink. Ronja braced herself as the agent turned slowly, her hands still clasped behind her. Her long blonde hair was braided back, revealing the brutal scar behind her right temple. "What did you think was going to happen, Siren?" she asked softly. "Did you think you were going to sing and make everyone hold hands?"

"No," Ronja answered curtly. Across the room, Roark shot her a warning look. Her fingers curled into fists against her thighs. Her scabs had mostly healed from her last altercation with Terra, but her knuckles were still capped with pink. "But we want to start a rebellion, not a bloodbath."

Terra barked a humorless laugh. Her hazel eyes were as sharp as the blades sheathed at her sides. "Did you think there was a difference? Are you really that naive?"

"Look," Ronja snapped, getting to her feet. "It sounds like that Off got what was coming to him. If I was Lou I probably would have done the same thing. But what about next time? What if next time we broadcast, someone takes revenge on the wrong person, or kills someone innocent?"

"I agree," Roark interjected.

"Of course you do," Terra snarled, tossing him a black look. He opened his mouth to retort, but Iris beat him to the punch.

"They are new to emotion," she said, splaying her hands before her thoughtfully. Her skin had lost its greenish tint. She looked as she did before she was going to perform an operation. Focused. Pragmatic. "We've given them the ability to feel, but not the tools to control those feelings."

"No." Ronja shook her head as a slow epiphany rolled over her. "No, we don't want them to hold back."

"We want them to direct their rage at the right target."

Roark was on his feet. She had not seen him move. Their eyes locked as understanding passed between them. "The Conductor," she said. "We've given them the ability to rebel. Now, we need to remind them who to rebel against."

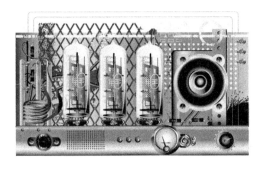

37: THE CALL

"Are you ready?"

Ronja looked up from the microphone. Roark stood before her. Lost in the forest of her thoughts, she had not heard him approach. Bluish shadows ringed his eyes, his short hair stuck out in all directions. She knew she did not look much better. Their meeting had not ended until after midnight, meaning they only got a few hours of sleep before the morning broadcast pulled them downstairs.

"Yeah," she lied. She crowned herself with the headphones that wreathed her neck. "Ready."

Roark gave her a reassuring smile then stepped back, his footsteps muffled through the leather pads. Ronja fixated on the dashboard. Mouse and Evie sat side by side before the machine, their fingers flying across the field of switches and buttons. Her gaze travelled upward, climbing the red wires to the metal towers that flung her voice across the city. Static filled her as the machine came to life.

"Ten seconds," Evie called over her shoulder. "We'll signal you when you're halfway through."

Ronja stuck out her thumb, too focused to vocalize her

response. Singing had become second nature to her, as easy as breathing. This was different. This was more than just a vague concept she was exhaling into the microphone. This was a call to arms, a declaration of war.

"Ro," came a distant voice. She flicked her gaze to the side. Roark stood with his back to the wooden walls, his arms folded across his chest. He smiled. Her pulse crescendoed. "You can do this."

Evie stuck her hand in the air. She let a finger fall with each passing second. "Five, four, three, two ... " The techi made a fist. Ronja sucked in a deep breath and sang.

Blood in my veins and you say it's cold
But if you cut my skin it will come out gold
The brain waves are crashing on the walls of my mind
And if you stare too long then you may go blind

The song tasted different on her tongue, now that she knew it had been used to stave off The Quiet Song after a killing in her name. That difference was reflected in the black clouds that grew from her words. Ronja kept her eyes on them as she sang, searching for meaning in their depths. Today, they were heavier. There were no gaps to let the light in.

May The Siren give me strength.

She could almost see it, could almost hear the dull thud of the body hitting the ground. The bullets of the Officers cutting down the rebels. She did not feel guilty, not exactly. Rather, she felt the weight of an awesome responsibility. She had to be more than just the ammunition. She had to be the scope that aimed the rifle. Ronja gripped the microphone and poured out the chorus.

I got little wars

Little wars in my head
Telling me wrong from right
Out of mind out of sight
Little wars
I am a warrior

Evie raised her fist again, signaling that the first part of the minute was gone. Ronja took another breath.

"People of Revinia. For decades The Conductor has robbed us of the ability to think, to feel. He has tortured us, killed us, turned us into mutts and slaves. He has divided us." She gripped the neck of the microphone. Her palms were slick with cold sweat. Above her, the black clouds had dissolved without her music to sustain them. It did not matter. Their energy was inside her. "Now, I call on you to rise up against Him. Rise up against The Music. Remember who your enemy is." She took a deep breath, drawing on the resolve that had always been in her, just waiting to blossom. "This is the Siren. May your song guide you home."

The line went dead.

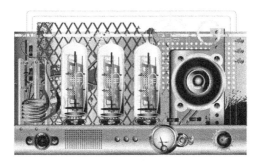

38: DISTRACTIONS

Ronja had endured torture. She had survived both The Lost Song and The Quiet Song. Still, there was little that compared to the agony of waiting for Terra and Samson to return after the morning broadcast ended. The captain had radioed a few minutes after they shut down to tell them they would be lingering in the middle ring until early afternoon, watching for signs of unrest.

"How did they react during the broadcast, though?" Ronja inquired, holding the portable communicator up to her mouth. Her hands were still trembling in the afterglow of her adrenaline. She and the others stood in a knot in the center of the radio station, crowded around the microphone.

Samson took his time responding. With each second that passed, the Siren felt her hopes shrivel. "No major changes yet," he admitted. "But we'll be watching. Right, Terra?"

The agent did not answer, surprising no one.

"Anyway," the captain said pointedly. "We'll be watching, Ronja."

The Siren swallowed dryly, then nodded. Realizing he could not see her, she wet her lips and spoke. "Thank you, Samson." Out of the corner of her eye, she noticed Roark purse his lips.

"We should save the battery on this thing," Sam told them regretfully. "We'll radio later this afternoon when we're headed back. Hang in there."

"You too," Ronja replied, though she did not know exactly what she was referring to. Perhaps just spending an extended afternoon with Terra.

The captain signed off with a crunch of static. Ronja shut off the communicator, dejected. Roark laid a hand on her shoulder and squeezed gently. She scarcely registered it. Logically, she knew Samson and Terra were making the right choice. But she had not expected their revolution to be filled with so much waiting.

It was going to be a long day.

"Maybe it was a fluke," Mouse suggested later over their breakfast of canned fruit. He crammed another spoonful of syrupy pears into his mouth, chewing thoughtfully. "Maybe this is as far as we go." Evie swatted him on the back of the head with an open palm. He returned the blow and they launched into a squabble worthy of two toddlers fighting over sweets. Iris made a halfhearted effort to separate them, then gave up and returned to nibbling on her crust of bread anxiously.

Roark leaned toward Ronja. His smell, something between rain and smoke, tickled her nose. "We'll figure this out, love," he murmured. "We always do."

The Siren just stared into her tin of pears sightlessly. Where she came from, they were a delicacy. The others seemed neutral to them. She could not imagine growing accustomed to such luxuries. A warm hand graced the back of her neck, massaging the stiff tendons. She sank into the touch with a heavy sigh. "Thanks," she murmured.

Roark nodded, smiling down at her ruefully. "You were

incredible," he said, leaning down to kiss the top of her head. "Truly."

"What if it fails?" she asked.

"It won't." He set his half-eaten tin of pears in her lap for her to finish. Her canister and his clicked together softly. Ronja found herself nodding mechanically, absorbing the words but not taking them to heart.

The rest of the morning passed in a sleepy haze. Once breakfast was finished, the Anthemites went their separate ways. Iris holed up in her room, exhausted from the previous night. Evie and Mouse disappeared downstairs to work on Abe. Apparently, something was wrong with one of its circuits, or maybe it was the capacitor. Ronja could not remember and did not particularly care.

She and Roark tried to sleep the day away, but quickly found it impossible. The girl could not lie still for more than half a minute before her skin startled to prickle, prompting her to fluff her half of the pillow or flop onto her stomach. "All right," Roark finally groaned after an hour, rolling over to face her. He rubbed the sleep from his heavy-lidded eyes. "Out with it."

Ronja glared up at the underside of the bunk. "Out with what?"

He kissed the curve of her shoulder through her sweater. "Talk to me."

"Make me," she grumbled childishly, digging her face into the pillow they shared.

"Ro ... "

"What if Mouse was right? What if Lou and his friends killing that Off was just a fluke? If Terra and Sam had noticed any changes, they would have reported back by now."

"Give it time," he implored her. "Did you think they were going to form a civilian army the second the broadcast was over?"

Ronja rolled over to face the wall with a huff. "No." It was not a lie. The problem was that her head and her heart were out of alignment.

"Come on," the boy said suddenly, getting to his feet and tugging on her arm. She groaned and gripped the bed frame with her free hand. "I am going to distract you."

Ronja grumbled unintelligibly, snuggling deeper into their deflated pillow. Roark released her arm. It flopped back down to the mattress, useless. "All right," he said with a weighty sigh. "You leave me no choice."

"What ... " The boy slipped his hands under her shoulders and knees and lifted her from the bed, still tangled in the quilt. Ronja let out a shriek of shock, which quickly dissolved into bewildered laughter as he carried her out of their room. "What the hell are you doing?" she demanded breathlessly as they breezed down the hall. They were headed for the showers.

Oh.

"If you would be so kind," Roark quipped, nodding at the brass knob. Ronja reached down awkwardly and opened the door. The first time she had entered the communal bathroom, she was surprised by how pleasant it was. With the blankets and pillows Mouse had brought from his apartment, their bedrooms were comfortable enough. Still, they were cold and spartan. Her room in her old row house in the outer ring had been more inviting, dirt floor and all. The bathroom, conversely, was almost luxurious.

It was tiled pale blue from floor to ceiling. The walls were heavily insulated, blocking the tendrils of winter air from creeping in. Three toilets hidden by white stalls stood in the far corner, well away from the four large shower heads that jutted out from the wall. Iris had already scrubbed the floors twice, prompted partially by her boredom between broadcasts and partially by her relentless fear of germs.

Roark set Ronja on her feet on the cool tiles, kissed her cheek smartly, then padded over to the nearest shower head. He moved like music. Easy as a melody. He was dressed in a pair of loose drawstring pants and a sweater. His feet were bare, his hair tousled from sleep. Or rather, lack of sleep.

Glancing back at her with a teasing smirk, he spun the knob. The pipes in the wall shuddered and groaned, then steaming water spouted from the shower head. Roark jumped out of the way, but he was not quick enough. The edge of the spray caught his shoulder, soaking the fabric of his sweater.

Ronja laughed, raising her fingers to her lips. Roark looked from his sleeve to her, his expression neutral, then slowly tugged the garment over his head and cast it aside. That effectively shut her up. Her mouth went dry. He was so beautiful. His muscular abdomen, his smooth tawny chest punctuated with the symbol of the Anthem.

And he loved her.

Ronja stepped forward, shedding the husk of her responsibilities. She crossed the room in three quick strides, then slammed into Roark, crushing him against the wall under the cascading stream. He laughed in disbelief, then kissed her back, his hands slipping under her sweater. It caught under her chin when he tried to yank it off, causing the girl to dissolve into a fit of giggles utterly unlike her.

"I have a question for you," Roark murmured when the sopping garment was tossed aside. Ronja squinted up at him through the spray, asking with her eyes.

"I had Samson run an errand for me a couple days ago," he said.

"Errand?"

"To the pharmacy."

Ronja blinked. Roark watched her with a little smirk, waiting for understanding to click into place. "Oh!" she gasped, clutching him by the forearms as her heart rioted in her ribs.

"Yes," he laughed. "I have them in our room."

"Then why the hell are we in the shower?"

"I was cold, and this is fun."

Ronja laughed, then sobered. Roark followed suit, gazing down at her through the lifting steam. He raised a hand to her face, cupping her cheek.

"We can save them for later," he said softly. "Or not at all."

"You promised me a distraction," she replied, raising up on her tiptoes to kiss him. His sinewy arms snaked around her waist, drawing her closer. The combined heat of their skin and the falling water was almost dizzying. She pressed her lips to the curve of his ear. "Distract me."

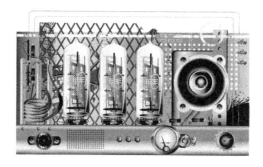

39: FALLING OUT
Terra

"I hate lying to them," Samson muttered under his breath for the third time in twenty minutes.

Terra took another deep breath, her knuckles bleaching around the steering wheel. The windshield wipers swung back and forth hypnotically as the grayish snow threw itself against the glass. The city streets were scarcely visible through the sheets of snow. Thankfully, the hulking beast of a truck Mouse called his 'baby' would crush just about any other vehicle that came in their path.

"We're not lying," Terra reminded him with an exasperated huff. She flicked her gaze to the captain. His face was arranged into a queasy mask. "We *are* examining the middle ring for signs of rebellion. Keep looking out the damn window."

"I can't see anything."

Terra shrugged. "Not my problem."

"Remind me why we didn't just tell them what we're up to?"

"Because we agreed they have too much on their minds. Plus, this will be easy. They'll forgive us when we come back with intel on Jonah."

As she said the words, doubt festered in Terra. She knew it was a risk, going to see Cicada without telling the others. None of them trusted her, not even Evie. This would not help bridge the gap, but they would try to stop her if they learned how untrustworthy her adoptive father was. She had already waited long enough to get answers about Jonah, she was not going to wait another day.

"Are you sure you know where you're going?" Sam asked, squinting out the windshield at the hazy streets. Terra did not reply, so the captain tried again. "How much further?"

"Do you ever shut up?"

"No. Are you always this cross?"

"Yes."

Terra jumped in her cracked leather seat when he barked a laugh. "Should have guessed."

The girl smiled tightly at the windshield. The storm seemed to be moving with them as they wove deeper into Revinia. It was a thirty-minute drive from the lip of the outer ring to the middle ring where Cicada lived in his townhouse. Of course, that was assuming no traffic and no inclement weather. A half hour had already stretched into forty-five minutes. Of course, that could also be attributed to her intentionally slow pace. Though Samson was wearing on her nerves, Terra was not looking forward to arriving at their destination.

"How long has it been?"

She glanced over at the captain. He had given up squinting out the fogged window, apparently. His blue eyes were trained on her. "Since?"

"Since you saw your father."

The girl clicked the turn signal as they rounded a sharp corner onto 31st Street. The tires skidded and she gripped the wheel to steady them. "Seven years."

Samson blew a low whistle through his teeth. "Falling out?"

Terra smiled grimly. "Something like that."

"I need to know what we're heading into. Should I keep my stinger on me?"

"Always."

She fell silent, watching the world crawl by. The street lamps were live, though it was the middle of the day. They had faded from gas to electric twenty blocks ago, a telltale distinction between the outer and middle rings. It was difficult to see the buildings through the snow, but Terra knew they were growing taller and finer. The blurred figures braving the elements were dressed in opulent clothing, their heads bowed beneath bowler hats and hoods, their hands wrapped in fur.

"Okay, elaborate," Samson prompted after a time.

Terra heaved a sigh, rolling her eyes skyward. "You know I grew up at Red Bay." It was not a question, but the captain nodded anyway. Most Anthemites knew the first part of her story. Few were familiar with the next. "When I was six, my mother was killed by Victor Westervelt II."

Sam shifted in his seat, the only physical manifestation of his shock. Evidently, his rambling mouth *did* have an off switch.

Terra made a left on Canal Street, which ran along one of the manmade rivers that wove through the middle ring. Its waters were frozen solid, cradled by snow-covered bricks. She might have found it beautiful were she not blinded by her memory.

"I knew they would kill me next," she went on. "Scientists were forbidden to have children. They were a liability. My mother paid a heavy ransom to keep me hidden." She could feel Samson watching her from the passenger side, his handsome face full of pity she did not want. "I escaped through the sewers, ended up in the forest. I was dying of The Quiet Song when he found me."

"Cicada," Samson interjected.

"Yes."

28th Street crept up on them like a migraine. *Here we go,* Terra thought dully. She sucked in a breath through her nose and blew it out through clenched teeth. She signaled right, then eased the truck into a parking space on the side of the street. Avoiding eye contact with the captain, she put the auto in park and yanked the key from the ignition. The engine died with a whine. Silence engulfed them, fractured only by the faint whisper of snow hitting the windshield. It was starting to slow down, though it would still be a pain to walk through.

"Cicada was a black-market trader," Terra explained. "Like Mouse, only he traded in information. He cut off my Singer to save my life, then he took me home and nursed me back to health. When I was well again, he started to train me."

"Train you?" Samson asked, his eyebrows shooting up his forehead.

Terra nodded absently. "To be his spy. Who would suspect a child?"

"Who were you spying on?"

"Anyone he asked me to. Offs, other traders, private citizens. Information is a dangerous commodity. He got a lot of people killed." She paused. "I got a lot of people killed. But he was the only father I ever knew. I would have done anything for him."

"What happened?" Samson asked quietly. There was no judgment in his tone, only sympathy. She would have preferred the former.

"He sent me to spy on Ito." Terra smiled ruefully at the memory. "She knew I was trailing her immediately. She caught me, took me to that safe house in the outer ring, the one on Winchester."

The captain nodded, doubtlessly picturing the little flat above the bodega.

"I thought she was going to kill me, but instead she recruited me. It was easy. I was angry, I needed revenge, and Cicada wasn't going to give me that." She shrugged, pocketing the keys to the truck and glancing over at Samson. He was pensive, his blue eyes sparking as the gears of his mind spun. "The rest is history."

"So," he began tentatively. "You just left."

"Yes," Terra answered tersely.

The captain raised his hands to pacify her. "No judgment, just ... how is he going to react to seeing you after all this time?"

Terra popped her door. The wind rushed in, making her eyes water. "Guess we'll find out." She hopped down from the high compartment and landed on the veiled cobblestones with a splat. Thankfully, her waterproof boots rose to her knees. She slammed the auto door with a muted rattle. Every sound was dulled by the snow. Shivering in her thick coat, Terra leaned up against the auto and cast her eyes around the quiet street.

Her old neighborhood was just as she remembered. White stone row houses with cast iron railings. Warm electric street lamps with intricately carved posts. Clean, wide streets, free of potholes and cracks. The houses were full of large families with mothers and fathers who took their children to the parks on the weekends. They would be harder to wake than the people of the outer ring and the slums. They were peaceful under the fog of The Music.

Samson slammed the auto door and rounded the engine to stand next to her. He peered around curiously as if trying to see what she saw in the unremarkable scene. "Come on," she muttered, jerking her head to the right. "We have five blocks to go."

"Five?"

"He'll go mad if we park out front."

"I think one would have done it."

"Sorry, do you know him?"

The captain grunted, his breath ghosting in the frigid air. Terra made a satisfied noise in the back of her throat, then started down the street. Samson quickly fell into step beside her. They kept their heads bent against the wind. Their boots carved deep trenches in the accumulating snow. A distant thought brushed the surface of her mind. Terra scraped to a halt, her eyes on the frozen ground. Samson trudged forward for a few more steps before he noticed. He circled back around to her, his brow furrowed. "What?" he asked. "You okay?"

"The streets ... " she murmured, her eyes shifting back and forth as her thoughts hummed. "Why are they covered in snow?"

Samson opened his mouth, then closed it. He chuckled uneasily. "Uhhh ... probably because of the blizzard. Just my guess."

"They clear them the second snow falls," she continued, ignoring his sarcasm. "A team of workers from the slums. I remember watching them work from the window."

Hunched figures in pure white uniforms, nearly invisible in the swirling snow. Once, one of them was struck by a passing auto. His body had flown twenty feet before coming to rest in a pile of snow. The auto roared away. Terra ran outside barefoot, her bathrobe flying behind her like a banner. She skidded to a stop before the victim, at the edge of the spreading pool of blood. His features were warped with agony, sunken with malnutrition. He had died before she worked up the courage to step into his steaming blood.

"Where are they?"

The captain frowned, glancing around the empty street. It was perfectly still, save for the falling snow. "Do you think ... ?" He never finished his thought. His eyes flew wide; his mouth went slack. He crashed to his knees.

"Sam!" Terra shouted, shock ripping through her. The captain looked up at her, his lashes fluttering with lethargy. Then his eyes rolled back into their sockets and he collapsed forward. Terra launched forward and caught him by the shoulders before he smashed his head on the bricks. "Sam," she cried, shaking him violently. "Come on, Sam, open your eyes!"

A blip of pain at the base of her neck. Terra stiffened as heat flooded her veins. Footsteps whispered toward her, growing steadily closer. A sardonic smile unfurled on her lips. "Cicada ... " she whispered. "You bastard." Sleep washed over her just as a shadow engulfed her.

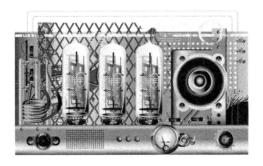

40: DIRECT LINE

Ronja woke like frost melting at dawn. For a long time, she lay motionless listening to Roark breathe deeply next to her. Their legs were twined; their hair still damp with water and sweat. Their sopping clothing was scattered across the room, collecting mildew. A lazy smile surfaced on her lips.

As if sensing the shift in her mood, Roark opened his eyes. He smiled at her blearily, his hair rumpled and his lashes sticky with sleep.

Her heart swelled, so big her ribs could scarcely contain it.

"Good morning, love," he said.

Ronja laughed. "It is ... " She rose on her elbow to check the alarm clock on the desk. "3:30 in the afternoon."

Roark groaned, rubbing his eyes with the heels of his hands. "Samson and Terra are probably back. We should get up."

"Yeah." She heaved a sigh. Everything seemed so distant, buffered by the dopamine high she was still riding. As soon as they got out of bed, the weight of the world would settle on their shoulders. For now, she was lighter than air. "That was a pretty good distraction."

"Pretty good," Roark repeated with a laugh. "I hope it was a bit better than that."

"A bit."

"Whatever you say." He nuzzled her neck, slinging an arm over her belly to draw her closer.

She sighed contentedly. Her fingers drifted up to knit with his hair of their own accord.

"We really should go," Roark murmured after a while. "The neighbors will talk."

Ronja nodded. She did not have to say what she was feeling; it radiated from her.

"Come on, Siren," he murmured, his breath tickling the delicate skin of her neck.

"Fine," she sighed. She sat up and heaved herself out of bed before she could be tempted to linger for another minute. Her muscles groaned as she stood. She stretched her long arms over her head, yawning, then peeked over her shoulder to find Roark watching her. His expression was glazed, his jaw slack. "I thought we were leaving," she teased.

"I take it back," he answered with a slow shake of his head.

"What about the neighbors?"

"If they saw you, they would understand."

Ronja snorted, then padded over to her bag to retrieve her clothes. She put on a moderately clean sweater and leggings, stifling a series of yawns that threatened to drag her back to bed. Roark joined her as she was tugging on her socks.

"Hey, Roark," she began as he was pulling on his pants. He cinched his belt and tossed her a questioning look. "What are we going to do, if the broadcast failed?"

The boy squatted down to retrieve his socks from his knapsack with a sigh. "I thought we went over this."

"Actually, I tried to talk to you and you literally swept me off my feet."

Roark paused to wink at her, then continued rifling through his belongings. Ronja crossed her arms, an eyebrow arched as she waited for a real answer.

"We'll see what Terra and Samson have to say, shall we?" he soothed her. "Ah, here we go." He yanked out a pair of matching socks triumphantly and pulled them on. When he straightened up, she was still watching him sourly.

Roark gave a rueful smile, then stuck out his hand for her to take. "Worrying won't save the world, love."

Ronja let up with a sigh, then clasped the offered hand. Their fingers knit with ease. "Neither will your ego," she replied.

"I beg to differ."

They stepped into the hallway, bickering. Their banter fizzled and died when the hum of another conversation dusted their ears. It was coming from the room Iris and Evie shared. They shared a glance. Ronja released Roark and crossed to the door. She knocked tentatively. The conversation cut off at once, which only heightened her suspicion. "It's us," she called out softly.

"Yeah, come in," came a strained voice.

Ronja opened the door, her brow creased and her stomach knotted. Roark was on her heels. His apprehension was palpable, stirring the air behind her. Evie, Iris, and Mouse sat in a tight knot on the right side of the room. The girls were perched on the edge of the bunk, shoulder to shoulder. The boy sat cross-legged on the floor, brooding.

"We were just about to come get you," Iris said quietly.

Ronja felt her throat tighten. She did not like the dejected tint to her voice. "What happened?"

"Do you want the bad news, or the bad news?" Evie inquired dryly.

The Siren crossed her arms as if to protect herself from a blow to the stomach. "Try me."

The three Anthemites shared a loaded glance, then Mouse spoke up. "Abe is ... giving us trouble." He leaned back, supporting himself with the heels of his hands. "Your voice is getting through to people, but the signal is damp, like something is blocking it "

"Imagine listening to music through a window," Evie added helpfully, spreading her palms to symbolize the glass.

"It might be why it's taking so damn long to get a response out of people," Mouse said.

"How long has this been going on?" Roark asked. His voice was sharp enough to cut through bone. Ronja snuck a glance at him. His face was arranged into a mask of calm, but his eyes sparked like match heads.

"We dunno," Evie admitted. "Maybe the whole time."

"And you're just noticing it now?" he demanded.

The Arexian tensed, her eyes narrowing to slits. Iris tapped her on the knee discreetly, reminding her to keep her head. "Careful, Trip," Evie warned in a low voice.

"Do you know what it is? The interference, I mean?" Ronja cut in hurriedly.

Mouse and Evie shook their heads.

The Siren took an unsteady breath. She flexed her fingers at her sides, forcing herself to remain calm. "How do we fix it?"

Evie scratched the back of her head, squinting up at the ceiling in search of answers. Mouse drummed his pale fingers on the hardwood, chewing on his lip. Iris stared at her knees. It was Evie who finally worked up the courage to answer her. "I don't think we do, mate."

The room slipped from focus. Ronja felt as if all the oxygen had been yanked from her lungs. She swallowed dryly, begging her mind to remain steady.

"What do you mean?" Roark growled, shouldering past her to stand in front of Evie. Mouse scooted aside like a crab across the sand.

"This is the best signal we can get so far out," the techi told him levelly. "If we want a more potent signal, we would need to pick up and move closer to the core."

"Which is sort of impossible," Mouse added with a wince. "Abe is delicate. If we hit one pothole, he'll fall apart."

"Okay, theoretically, where could we go in the core? Do we have a safe house there?" Ronja asked. Her voice sounded distant, as if she were hearing it through a tube. She wondered if that was how she sounded to the people of Revinia.

"Yeah, but ..." Roark began.

Ronja's thoughts drifted to the core. She blinked as the past washed over her, veiling her vision. When she was a child she would scale the fire escape of her elementary school to catch a glimpse of the radiant heart of Revinia. The golden clock tower. Sometimes, when The Conductor spoke to them through their Singers, she would hurry up to that same rooftop to view the tower. It made her feel closer to Him. "What are we going to do?" she heard herself ask, peeling away from her memories.

"Move Abe by airship?" Evie joked darkly.

No one laughed. The radiator hummed away in the corner, oblivious. Outside the wind howled, throwing itself against the bricks.

"Whoa," the techi backpedaled, throwing up her hands. "You guys know I love a challenge, but moving Abe really is impossible. Right, Mouse?" She jabbed her thumb at the trader, who nodded fervently. "Even if we could get him to the core, it would take too long to get up and running. Not to mention, the safe house on 11th doesn't have nearly enough space."

"What if we didn't have to use Abe?" Roark twisted around to look at Ronja, an epiphany flaring in his dark face. The others leaned around him curiously. She scarcely noticed. "Evie," she said suddenly. The techi jumped, drawing a little whine from the rusted mattress springs. "What if we could get a direct line to The Conductor's radio station? The one he uses to broadcast His speeches."

"Uhhh." The techi raked her fingers through her silky hair.

"Could we free the city in one shot?" Ronja pressed.

Evie bit her lip. She glanced first at Mouse, then at Iris. Both shrugged helplessly. The techi returned to Ronja, her expression caught between interest and uncertainty. "I dunno. Maybe." She leaned forward and steepled her fingers, resting her chin on her thumbs. "When you sang directly to Roark it worked immediately."

"Yes," Ronja confirmed.

"But I had only been under The Air Song for a few minutes," Roark pointed out.

"Yeah," Ronja allowed. She itched the bridge of her nose as her thoughts took shape. "But The New Music is way more powerful than The Night and Day songs."

"Right," Evie agreed with an affirming nod. "It evens out."

Ronja blinked as if she could reset the world around her. "If we could find that station, we could start an uprising in one broadcast."

"Maybe," Evie interjected quickly.

Both Ronja and Roark pretended not to hear her.

"Terra and Sam haven't called yet," Roark pointed out. "Maybe we've already started one."

Ronja rolled her eyes, though she knew it would only egg him on. "Come on. If anything had happened they'd be back by now." She stretched out a tentative hand to touch him on the elbow. He did not react. "We are running out of time," she reminded him, her voice barely more than a whisper. "We have to make a move. Every day we wait is a day they could launch The New Music. Who knows if I'll be able to bring people back from that. Not to mention, it's only a matter of time before it breaches the Belly."

The words planted the seed of nausea in her stomach. As hard as she tried, she could not push away the image of Georgie and Cosmin struggling under the waves of The New Music. Would The Conductor use The Air Song, simply wringing emotion from them? Or would he torture them first with The Lost Song?

Roark stared at her for a long time. Tension radiated from his taut muscles. Ronja held her ground, unflinching. "Even if we could find the station," he finally said. "How would we get in?"

The Siren released his arm, knowing he would recoil as soon as she answered. She glanced at Evie out of the corner of her eye. The techi nodded, her mouth pressed into a grim line. She knew. "Maxwell."

Roark blinked. "Maxwell," he repeated blankly.

"We know where he is," Ronja reasoned. "We can trade access to the station for his freedom."

"Terra said he was insane," Iris said, speaking up for the first time in a while.

"Right," Roark agreed with a grateful glance her way. "Samson said he does nothing but pace around the cell and talk to himself in another language, a language he shouldn't even be able to *speak*."

"To be fair, I would probably talk to myself too if I was locked up in a room alone for months on end," Mouse pointed out.

"I'm not saying we should trust him," Ronja said with a huff. "I'm saying we should *use* him."

"No," Roark snapped. The Siren flinched at the harsh syllable, then clenched her jaw. "No, this is too dangerous."

"Yeah, damn right it is," she said. "But we already know Maxwell will do whatever he has to do to save his own skin, even if that means going against The Music."

"Ronja is right," Evie chimed in thoughtfully. Roark whipped around to glare daggers at her. She slapped her hands to her knees, then got to her feet and moved to stand beside Ronja. The Siren felt her heart swell.

"This is insane," Roark said, his eyes flashing back and forth between them in disbelief.

Ronja shrugged and cast a glance at Evie. The techi flashed her signature grin, which only stoked her confidence. "So is using my voice as a weapon," she replied. "But here we are."

"You want to get the son of The Conductor to lead us to the radio station his father spits propaganda from." He shook his head. The coin he wore around his neck shifted against the fabric of his sweater. The silhouette of Atticus Bullon regarded Ronja haughtily. She fought the urge to snatch it from his neck and bury it. "What makes you think he'll betray his father?"

"Technically, he already did by helping us get out of Red Bay," Evie reasoned.

"That was different," Roark shot back. "This would be a direct betrayal."

"No one knows about Maxwell," Ronja reasoned. "He was hidden away at Red Bay for who knows how long. He has a Singer, which given his status is downright bizarre."

"Maybe his father was trying to control him," the techi hypothesized, rubbing her jaw with her finger thoughtfully. "Or hide him."

Ronja shrugged. "Either way, he was able to resist The Music enough to get us out, which means something was driving him." She paused, wondering if her next statement would be taking things too far. She was already in deep; there was no sense holding back now. "I think, for whatever reason, he wants to make things hard on his father."

To her surprise, Evie agreed with her at once. "That would make sense," she muttered, nodding to herself. "Bastard kid gets mad when Daddy slaps a Singer on him and hides him outside the city."

Roark gawked at Ronja and Evie as if they had just announced their engagement. "Someone help me out here," he groaned, turning to Iris and Mouse, who were watching the exchange with eyes flown wide.

"Well," the surgeon began in a tiny voice. "I actually think it sort of makes sense."

"Pitching hell," Roark muttered, craning his head back toward the ceiling. He took a deep breath and brought his eyes down to Ronja. She crossed her arms, a challenge. "Samson and Terra should be back soon," he finally said. "We should wait to hear what they have to say. Then we'll talk."

"Fine," she snapped.

"Fine."

Roark spun on his heel and marched from the room without another word, leaving the door wide open behind him. Ronja stood perfectly still, listening to his footsteps sing down the staircase.

Evie leaned toward her. "Do you really think that could work?" she asked out of the corner of her mouth.

The door to the factory floor slammed, the crack radiating up the stairwell. "Yeah," Ronja answered, her eyes fixed to the place Roark had been. "Yeah, I do."

"Then if it comes to it, we're with you."

"Yes," Iris agreed fervently from her seat on the bed. She kicked Mouse in the knee when he said nothing.

"Yeah, yeah, sure," the trader grumbled.

"We'll see what Sam and Terra have to say," Ronja said absently. They all nodded, knowing the words were hollow.

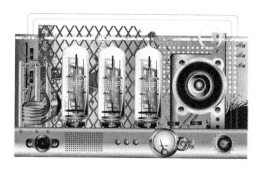

41: RADIO SILENCE

Ronja paced back and forth across her room, her fingers laced behind her back. The perpetual motion was starting to make her dizzy, but she knew if she sat down her fears would swallow her whole. Iris, Evie, and Mouse had left half an hour ago, leaving a trail of reassurance.

She glanced at the bed she shared with Roark as she strode past. The sheets were rumpled, creased. For some reason, the image tugged at her heart. He was just downstairs, she reminded herself. Probably thinking about her too.

He's right, a nagging voice at the back of her mind whispered. Her plan was insane. In some ways, more dangerous than their mission to Red Bay and infinitely more likely to fail.

The Siren scraped to a halt. The world tilted. The image of the clock tower was seared into her brain like a brand. She could still feel the wind combing through her curls as she stood on the rooftop, gazing out across the smoke-stained city at the golden behemoth. Somehow, it sharpened the voice of The Conductor, as if his lips were pressed to her ear.

Passion is perilous. Emotion is treacherous. Disobedience is destruction. This is The Conductor. Remember, I am watching.

Ronja felt her knees buckle. She crashed to the floor, her head in her hands. White hot pain exploded in the walls of her skull, scattering her vision. Chills wracked her body as memories coursed through her. The Music, the voice in her head, the face of the clock baring down on her from above. Larger than Carin, darker than an eclipse.

A knock at the door, louder than a gunshot.

"Just ... just a second ... " Ronja called.

"Ro, are you all right?"

Skitz. "Coming," she called, striving to keep her voice steady. Ronja clambered to her feet, wiping the cold sweat from her brow. She stumbled over to the door, fiddled with the lock, then yanked it open.

Evie stood in the gap, her eyes narrowed suspiciously.

Ronja flushed. "What?"

"Did you and Trip make up?" The techi leaned around her, searching for the boy in the spartan room.

"No."

"Were we fighting?" came a voice from down the hall.

Ronja peeked outside. Roark was approaching from the stairwell. She glowered at him through the fog of her migraine. Her blood simmered beneath her skin. He smiled apologetically as he arrived outside her door. "Well," he said, itching the back of his head. "If we were, I am quite sure it was my fault."

Ronja felt her migraine recede, her blood cool. She rubbed the bridge of her nose and looked down at the floorboards, smiling vaguely. His gaze rested lovingly on the top of her head. "What did you need, Evie?" she asked.

"Right," the techi said, settling into a solemn tone. "Sam and Terra have gone radio silent."

Ronja snapped her head up, her eyes wide. "What?"

"When?" Roark asked.

"They were supposed to check in hours ago," Evie answered, holding up her portable radio and giving it an indicative shake. "I radioed them three times, got nothing."

"Maybe it died," Ronja suggested halfheartedly

Evie pressed the red button on the face of the communicator. Static rushed to fill the silence. "It works," she said grimly. "They're just not answering."

The trio fell into an uneasy silence as the reality of the situation set in. Ronja rested her hand on her stomach as it lurched with nausea. She cared for Samson like a brother. He reminded her of Henry. Terra, she would be happy to punch in the face any day of the week. That did not mean she wanted to see her dead.

"We should go after them."

Evie and Roark looked at Ronja, surprised.

She gave a firm nod, settling into her words confidently. "They could be in danger. Not to mention we need to know what happened with the broadcast before we go hunting for Maxwell."

"That would be swell, except we have no way of finding them," Evie said dryly.

"Yes, we do."

The three Anthemites rounded on the voice, surprise plastered across their faces. Iris stood in the doorway of her bedroom, wearing her green pajamas and a smug expression.

"How?" Ronja asked.

"Easy." Iris examined her nails, leaning up against the doorframe. "We ask Jonah."

"Jonah?" Evie exclaimed.

The surgeon glanced up at her friends, dark amusement glinting in her hazel eyes. "Did you really not notice?"

"Clearly not," Roark replied, his voice dry as bone.

"Terra and Samson kept disappearing. At first I thought they were going at it," Iris said, tapping a manicured finger to her lips. "But then I realized if they were fooling around, they would just do it one of their rooms."

"You think they were questioning Jonah," Ronja gathered.

Iris nodded. "Yeah, I think so. Maybe he told them something, something they felt they had to keep from us."

"Terra isn't exactly known to be forthcoming," Roark admitted, itching his jaw thoughtfully. "But Samson? He hates lying."

"They *have* been acting off, now that I think about it," Evie interjected, folding her muscular arms over her chest. "Were they friends before all this? They spend an awful lot of time together, now."

"Terra doesn't have any friends," Iris answered, regret shading her voice.

"Only one way to figure this out," Ronja said. She locked eyes with the surgeon, who nodded in return. "We talk to the Tovairin."

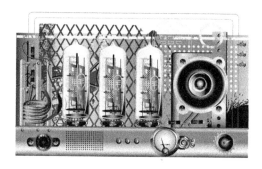

42: GOOD WILL

In the end, it was decided that Ronja and Roark would speak to Jonah alone. Evie was still working out her personal issues with the Tovairin. Iris was too anxious to do anything but fret. Mouse was just Mouse. As soon as they hit the narrow staircase to the basement, Roark put a hand on her shoulder to stop her. "About before," he began.

Ronja waved him off. "Forget it."

"Ronja ... "

"No need to apologize," she muttered, shrugging him off.

"There is," he asserted, seeking her gaze. She glared down the wooden steps. They reminded her of the stairs to her bedroom at her old row house aboveground. "You know I trust you, right?"

Ronja looked up at Roark, her eyes hard and her lips pursed. Normally, the genuine flicker in his gaze would have melted her heart. Not today.

"I need you to understand something," he said, taking her stiff hands in his own. She did not pull away, nor did she return the gentle squeeze he gave them. "Before I met you, there was nothing more important to me than taking down The Conductor and my father."

"What about Evie and the others?" Ronja asked, her eyebrows shooting up her forehead.

"Of course," he agreed. "But they were part of that goal. We all agreed a long time ago that we were willing to die in order to free ourselves and the city."

"I am too," Ronja reminded him, her voice dipping low. She tightened her fingers around his, but it was not a loving gesture. "I *did* die."

Roark gave a ghost of a smile. "I know, love. I know. But listen to me. I love you because you are so much more than a weapon. You are music. You remind me of everything I am fighting for, and I know how selfish it sounds but every time I think about losing you I ... " He trailed off, swallowing his words. Ronja waited in silence for him to continue. "Your plan," he finally said, "is incredibly stupid, and dangerous."

Ronja opened her mouth, wrath bubbling up on her lips. Roark shushed her gently. She bit the inside of her cheek to keep from shouting.

"It is also a good plan," he continued earnestly. "Stupid, but good. My kind of plan."

"So you *are* with me?" she asked after a while.

Roark grinned, the volatile energy she loved rushing back into his eyes. She could not help but mirror his expression. "There and back," he said.

"Then come on," she said, taking her hands back from his and jerking her head toward the basement. "We have an interview."

By the time they arrived at the iron door to the storeroom, they had settled back into their usual rhythm. "No torture," Ronja muttered as they regarded the makeshift cell.

"Have a little faith, love," Roark replied, fishing his key ring out of his pocket and selecting a small brass one. "Besides, I doubt it'll be necessary." He inserted the key into the lock and twisted. The tumblers clicked and he nudged open the door with the tip of his boot, drawing his revolver and aiming it around the corner. It creaked open on a dimly lit room. Ronja winced as the smell of body odor leaked out. Three times a day someone escorted Jonah to the bathroom after his meals. Apparently, those trips did not include time for showers.

"Ah, freckles and pretty boy, what can I do for you?"

Jonah sat in the shadow-drenched corner of the room, ignoring the folding chair only a few feet from him. The pillow and wool blanket they had given him were folded into a neat pile. His dishes sat nearby, scraped clean and stacked into a small cairn.

"Jonah," Roark greeted him politely. He opened the door further and stepped back. Ronja shot him a disbelieving look, but said nothing. "You smell like you could use a shower."

"I usually prefer to take my dates to dinner first," Jonah answered, climbing to his feet with a grunt.

Ronja swallowed the stone in her throat. He was even taller than she remembered. His long hair was tied into a loose knot at his crown. He had stripped off his shirt, exposing his impressive muscles and ...

"Wow," Ronja murmured.

Jonah smirked at her, sliding his hands into his pockets. Roark, on the other hand, looked like he was about to punch him.

"Well ... " she defended herself as color flooded her face. "It *is* interesting."

Winding around his arms and torso like creeping vines were dozens of intricate white tattoos. They reminded her of soaring flocks of birds against a dark sky.

"*Reshkas*," Roark said aloud.

"Very good," Jonah purred. "Unlike the Arexian, I can read

mine."

"She has a name," Ronja snapped, her fascination evaporating.

"Most do," Jonah answered with a solemn dip of his chin.

The girl bristled. Roark tapped her between the shoulder blades, reminding her to keep a level head.

The prisoner bent down to collect his clothes, then straightened up with a coy smile. "What about that shower, huh?"

"Surely I don't need to tell you that if you try to run, I'll shoot you," Roark said breezily, opening the door a shred further.

Jonah grinned, exposing an unexpected dimple on his right cheek. "Not at all."

"All right, then." Roark took Ronja by the hand firmly. She arched an eyebrow at him as he pulled her aside to allow Jonah out. The Tovairin groaned with relief, stretching his long arms over his head, his bundle of clothes still in his big hands. His fingertips almost brushed the low hanging ceiling. Ronja struggled heroically not to look at his straining muscles.

"Get going," Roark ordered, a hint of a warning in his voice. Jonah smirked at him, but dropped his arms and started toward the exit, his bare feet whispering across the concrete.

Ronja did not notice how uncomfortable she had been underground until they surfaced on the factory floor. She breathed in the vast space, her fingers loosening and her shoulders dropping. Roark did not seem to notice, his attention trained on their prisoner, who was looking around with mild interest.

"What do you have in all these boxes?" he asked.

"None of your concern," Roark said. Ronja glanced up at him. His tone was calm, but the muscle in his jaw was bulging as it did when he was stressed. She cut her gaze toward the winding aisle of crates, a frown tugging on the corners of her mouth. They could not hold Singers anymore, could they?

She released his hand. He glanced at her questioningly, but did not protest.

They marched up the stairs, one after the other. Jonah led the way, clearly taking his time. He hummed under his breath as he trudged along. Roark went after him. Ronja brought up the rear. When they reached the attic, Roark gestured with his revolver down the hall to the bathroom. "You have five minutes, we'll wait outside."

"Sure you don't want to join me, freckles?" Jonah inquired, glancing back at Ronja. Roark tightened his grip on his gun. Neither of them cracked a smile, stony faced. "Tough crowd," the Tovairin muttered, then turned on his heel and padded down the hall to the showers.

"What are you doing?" Ronja asked out of the side of her mouth as Jonah shut the door. A moment later, the muffled hum of the pipes warming up graced their ears, followed by the gentle patter of falling water.

"Earning some good will," Roark replied without taking his eyes off the bathroom door.

"We don't have time to get him to like us," she replied in a clipped tone. "Sam and Terra could be in danger."

"It'll go a lot faster than breaking him."

As he said this, a door creaked open on the right side of the hall and a fiery head poked out. Iris looked first at the bathroom door, then twisted around to glare at them. "Did I just hear *Jonah*?"

"You did," Roark replied lightly.

"And you thought this was a good time to let him clean up?"

Ronja shot Roark a pointed look, signaling her agreement with Iris. The boy sighed heavily, reaching up to knead the bridge of his nose with his thumb and forefinger. "Just — trust me, would you?"

Iris and Ronja rolled their eyes at the same time, then the surgeon ducked back into her bedroom and shut the door. The whisper of a tense conversation seeped through the wooden panel. Evie, most likely.

Five minutes felt like fifty as Roark and Ronja paced back and forth along the hallway. Finally, the water turned off beyond the bathroom door. Roark stilled, as did she. He checked his watch. "Five minutes, on the dot," he muttered. Ronja narrowed her eyes at the door. She could not remember if Jonah had been wearing a watch or not.

The door banged open as if in response to her thoughts. Steam ballooned into the corridor and Jonah parted it with his large body. He was fully clothed, even wearing his shoes and canvas jacket. Weighed down with water, his black hair fell past his shoulders. He was grinning ear-to-ear.

"That," he said, kicking the door shut with his heel. The steam rushed away from the sudden slap. "Was incredible."

"Glad you enjoyed it," Roark said with a half-smile.

"So what is it you want?" he asked. The two Anthemites shared a quick look. "Oh, come on," Jonah snorted, rolling his eyes at the ceiling. "I know what this is about. Something has changed, you need my help. So out with it."

"Two of our own have gone missing," Roark answered honestly. "We were wondering if you had spoken to them."

Jonah stuck his little finger in his ear, then wiped a bit of earwax on his pants. "The Blondie Twins, right?" Ronja bit her lip to keep from laughing. "Yeah, we talk occasionally on my bathroom excursions. Sometimes they even say 'hi' when they bring me my food." He smiled a bit too wide. "We're the best of friends."

"Ever talk any more than just the occasional greeting?"

Jonah stroked his stubbly chin thoughtfully, making a contemplative noise at the back of his throat. "Well," he said slowly. "There was the one time she busted into the storeroom and lobbed a knife at my head."

"That sounds like Terra," Ronja muttered darkly.

"Ah, Terra," Jonah sighed melodramatically.

"She likes it when you call her blondie, actually," Ronja piped up.

Roark elbowed her in the ribs. She blinked up at him innocently.

"Did you give her any information?" the shiny pressed. "Something that might have prompted her to leave?"

Jonah smiled, a slow creeping twist of his lips that gave Ronja chills. "Well," he said. "She *did* leave me this." He reached into his coat and drew out something silver and narrow.

Several things happened at once. Roark shoved Ronja backward, whipping his revolver out of the waistband of his pants. The door to Evie and Iris's room banged open and a dark blur shot out and crashed into Jonah. The pair went flying into the far wall, slamming into the plaster with a crack. The Tovairin swore profusely as Evie twisted his arm behind his back, pressing his head into the wall with her free hand.

"DROP IT!" she roared in his ear.

"Dropping it," Jonah said, wincing as he let the little blade fall from his fingers. It landed on the hardwood floor with a ringing crack. Ronja darted forward to retrieve it. It was heavier than she had expected.

"How did you get that?" Evie growled, twisting his arm with increased ferocity. Ronja glanced to the right as movement caught her eye. Iris was peeking out into the hallway with eyes flown wide.

"I told you," Jonah grunted. "Terra left it behind when she

came in to question me."

"That doesn't sound like Terra," Ronja commented uncertainly. Evie glanced up from her prisoner. Her eyes were partially obscured by her raven hair. The singer felt her gut twist. She had never seen her friend look so unhinged.

"She freaked about something I said," Jonah answered, his voice straining. A droplet of sweat rolled down his forehead, which was pressed to the wall.

"What?" Evie hissed, leaning forward

"Let me up and I'll tell you."

The techi released a puff of breath to blow her hair out of her eyes. She glanced over at Roark and Ronja, who were watching the scene unfold with equally stony expressions. Evie released the Tovairin, moving to stand in front of Iris protectively.

"Damn," Jonah groaned, peeling away from the wall and massaging his shoulder. "What was that, *Kenv Likan*?"

It might have been her imagination, but Ronja was fairly sure Evie cracked a half smile. It disappeared quickly, if it had been there at all. "*Kenv Mekan*, actually," the Arexian corrected him. "My mother taught me."

"You know *Kenv Likan* is more powerful," Jonah said, crossing his arms and observing the techi with an amused expression.

"Maybe for someone your size," Evie shot back. Her eyes settled on his injured shoulder. "And I would not be so sure of that."

"All right," Ronja said, exasperation breaking into her tone. "You two can talk about this another time." She held up the little blade and rounded on Jonah. "Why did Terra give this to you?"

The Tovairin shook his head, his wet hair flopping against his shoulders. "She lobbed it at my head and it got stuck in the wall."

"Terra doesn't miss," Evie said accusatorially.

"Then she was just trying to scare me. Go check the storeroom," Jonah suggested, nodding at the floor. "You'll see the mark on the wall."

"What did you say to her that caused her to leave one of her knives behind?" Roark pressed.

"A name," Jonah said. "Cicada."

A soft yelp from the bedroom Iris and Evie shared made them all jump. Half a moment later, Mouse stuck his brilliant head out into the hall. He looked as if someone had just slapped him. "Cicada? I know him!"

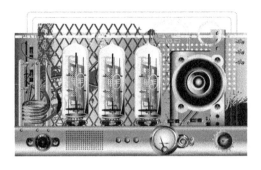

43: SEVEN YEARS
Terra

Terra woke up seven years in the past. It was the smell that gave it away. Fresh laundry and mothballs. Soft white sheets were pulled up around her shoulders. She squinted at the ceiling. It was painted deep purple. She remembered when she picked that color.

The Anthemite sat up slowly, the covers slumping around her. She was fully clothed save for her heavy winter coat, which was folded neatly in the upholstered armchair next to her bed.

Her bed.

Terra shivered, though the bedroom was just as cozy as it was in her memories. She took a few steadying breaths, then ripped off the white sheets and got to her feet. The ceiling traded places with the floor. She swayed, gripping the top of the armchair with a labor-hardened hand.

The vertigo faded. Terra looked around, drinking in her past.

A large queen bed sprawled beneath the window. The drapes were drawn, shutting out all but a sliver of light. If she were to pull them open, they would reveal a snowy lane. The picture of tranquility. Three small paintings hung above the headboard, each featuring a slightly different image of the ocean. A white vanity stood next to the closet. Terra crossed to it carefully. Her booted feet were silent against the pillowy carpet.

The mirror grasped her reflection. Her black clothes were rumpled from sleep, her long hair mussed. Her mascara ran down her cheeks in rivets. She must have landed face first in the snow when the drugs overwhelmed her system. The Anthemite smirked at herself in the looking glass. She would have been less out of place at an opera house.

A distant thump pricked her ear. Her eyes darted toward the white door. It was not locked; she did not have to try it to know that. That was not how Cicada did things.

She snatched her coat off the armchair, tugging it on as she stalked to the exit. Sure enough, when she twisted the brass knob the door creaked open on a familiar corridor. Pristine white carpet, electric lamps mounted on the beige walls between the rows of closed doors.

Without giving herself time to wallow in nostalgia, Terra plunged into the hallway and marched toward the stairway at the end. She knew where her father would be waiting. Down the staircase, silent as a wraith even on the oak steps. Past the study and the dining room with its long table and hulking marble fireplace. Around the corner, past the bathroom and ... Terra scuffed to a stop. The door to the parlor was cracked. Warm light tumbled across her boots.

"Come in," a gravelly voice called.

Terra tensed, her hands flying to the blades still strapped to her hips. Of course, he had heard her. She pushed open the door and stepped through, leaving it open behind her.

"Cicada," she said flatly.

"My daughter." The parlor was just as she remembered. High-ceilinged with evergreen walls and a semicircle of armchairs arranged around a low coffee table. Built-in shelves overflowing with priceless artifacts from distant lands, and books so dangerous the Anthem would think twice before including them in their collection. The drapes were drawn across the arching window. The only source of light came from the electric lamps scattered about the room. "To what do I owe the honor?"

Terra zeroed in on the source of the voice. Her stomach hit the carpet. Cicada sat in his favorite armchair, one ankle resting on his knee, a glass of wine in his hand. He had aged since they last saw one another. Of course he had. His cropped brown hair was streaked with silver. Deep crow's feet decorated the corners of his gray eyes. Yet he held himself with the confidence of a younger man.

"Where is my friend?" Terra inquired tonelessly.

"Safe," Cicada answered. He gazed up toward the ceiling. "In the guest bedroom. The door is unlocked."

"What did you dose us with?"

"A variation of the sap. One of my contacts gave it to me as a gift. Perfectly safe, I assure you."

Terra grunted. "Did you dart us, or was it one of your students?"

"You mean to ask if I have a new you," Cicada said with tilt of his head. Terra pursed her lips. He took a sip of his wine, watching her over the lip of the crystal glass. "Adulthood suits you," he said. "That hairstyle does not."

"I am not here for a chat, Cicada," she snapped.

"Clearly," he answered in a clipped tone. He set his wine aside and got to his feet, straightening his navy suit coat with a snap. He prowled toward her, his eyes never leaving her face.

Terra regarded him with a stony expression. Unruffled, uncaring.

"I looked for you, for years," he said.

Terra swallowed. "I know."

"I thought you were dead."

"You taught me well."

Cicada smiled, just a quirk of his lips. "Too well, it seems."

"I knew you would never let me go."

"I would have let you go," he corrected her. "Once your debt was paid."

Terra did not reply. The skin on the back of her neck prickled. She fought the urge to grasp the hilt of her blade.

"Where did you go?" he asked, changing the subject.

Terra sighed wearily. "You already know that."

"I would like to hear you say it," Cicada replied with a tight smile. He slipped his hands into the pockets of his slacks.

"I went to the Anthem," she said, unconsciously straightening her spine. She was almost as tall as he was, now. Still, she felt he was looking down on her.

"Why?" The word was pinched with the sting of betrayal.

"I needed revenge, you know that."

"Oh, my dear girl," Cicada murmured, reaching out with a ringed hand to caress her cheek. Terra stepped backward, her fingers flying to the hilt of her closest blade. The trader let his hand fall to his side. "I thought we were beyond all that."

"You know I'll never be beyond it."

Cicada shook his head, clicking his tongue admonishingly. "Such a waste," he murmured. "You would have been my successor."

"I need your help, Cicada," Terra snapped. "I need you to tell me what you know about a Tovairin man named Jonah."

Cicada rolled his eyes. The Anthemite bristled silently. He strode back to the coffee table and took a generous swig from his wine glass, smacking his lips in satisfaction. "And what would you offer me, in exchange?"

"My debt to you, paid in full."

Cicada fell silent. His jeweled fingers tightened around the stem of the goblet. "There was a time that you would have swayed me," he said softly. "But things are different now. Soon, none of this will matter."

"What are you ... ?"

The doorbell chimed from the hall. Terra whipped out two of her blades, which flashed in the warm electric light. Cicada snapped and pointed at the closet in the far corner of the room. The agent did not need to be asked twice. Sheathing one of her knives, she darted over to the door and wrenched it open. She ducked inside. Cicada slammed the door in her wake. Darkness engulfed her. She squatted among the coats and folded towels and pressed her eye to the keyhole.

Caterpillar, a distant voice whispered.

She ignored it, watching with muscles coiled as Cicada disappeared out the door. His footsteps sang down the corridor, mingling with another barrage of knocks. "One moment," he called, his voice distant. A reverberating bang caused Terra to reel backward, landing silently on a tower of pillows. She scrambled back to the keyhole, for once thankful she was alone in the dark.

"Ah, Visser, what can I do for you?" Cicada greeted his guest warmly.

"This is not a social call, Cicada," The voice was deep and monotone, dripping with distaste.

"Of course, but do come in out of the cold." The distant clunk of heavy boots, then a rush of air and a sharp clap as Cicada closed the front door. Terra wound up like a spring as the footsteps drew nearer. They were coming into the parlor.

Pitch you, Cicada.

Two figures walked through the door, one after the other. Terra swallowed the stone in her throat. Cicada, who was of average height, seemed tiny in comparison to the man behind him. Still, his size was not what unnerved her. It was the black uniform he wore, and the white eye of The Conductor that clung to his lapel.

Skitz.

"Brandy? Wine?" Cicada asked smoothly.

"No."

"Suit yourself." Cicada poured himself another full glass and sank into his armchair with a sigh. He gestured at the chair next to him. The Off just stared.

"What is this about?" the trader inquired, taking a sip from his glass.

"Bullon has moved up the release of the improvements to The Music. If all goes as planned it will go live tomorrow evening. He is waiting on one last requirement."

Terra inhaled sharply, then clapped her own hand over her mouth. At the same moment, Cicada choked on his drink, sputtering and coughing. The Off watched him, unmoved.

"Why?" the trader floundered, trying in vain to dab the red wine from his ruined button-down.

"None of your concern," the Off snapped, showing his first trace of emotion. "We need you to speed things up on your end."

Cicada set his glass on the table. His discomfort was almost palpable. "Ah ... you see ... my contacts are already working as fast as they can. The best we can do is four weeks."

"Have everything ready in three."

"I ... "

"No exceptions." Visser smiled, a slow curve of his lips like the bend of a scythe. "You do wish to continue living without a Singer, correct?"

"Yes, quite." Cicada bowed his head. "They will be here in three weeks."

"For your sake, I hope that is true." Visser reached down and patted Cicada on his stubbly cheek. The trader flinched. "I'll return tomorrow to check in on your progress. Do *not* fail me, Cicada." He puffed his chest out, pride flickering in his dull eyes like a banner. "Bullon has promised me command of the Offs. I am free to do what I wish with ... unnecessary assets."

"Of course," Cicada said quickly, getting to his feet and sticking out his jeweled hand. "I'll wait for your call."

Visser nodded brusquely, then turned on his heel and marched from the room. Cicada let his hand fall limp at his side and collapsed into his armchair.

Terra waited until she heard the bang of the front door before slipping out of the closet. Her hands trembled around her blades, but she managed to keep her voice steady. "Cicada, what have you done?"

Her father got to his feet slowly. The wine he had spilled was like a spray of blood on his pristine white shirt. His eyes were bottomless. "Forget the debt," he said softly. "Or consider it paid. You need to get out of the city. Take your boyfriend and run."

"Cicada," Terra growled in a low voice.

"This is ... more complicated than I imagined it would be."

"*Father.*"

Cicada froze, paralyzed by the word. He slicked back his hair with his fingers, straightened his suit. Not looking at her, staring at the carpet. "I negotiated a contract for new ships with the Vintian government."

Terra knew the answer before she asked. "For what?"

"For the conquest."

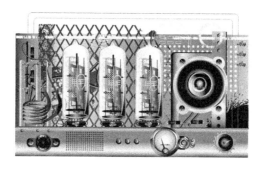

44: DRAWING STRAWS

"**S**o," Mouse began, his voice an octave higher than usual. "How do we decide who goes to go get them? Do we draw straws?" He fell silent when he received a barrage of dirty looks from the irritable Anthemites. The trader sagged in his chair, whining like a dying animal. "Why do I have to go?"

"Because you know Bug," Roark explained.

"Cicada," Ronja corrected him halfheartedly. He waved her off.

"Do all traders have animal related names?" Iris asked, sounding genuinely curious.

"No," Mouse said absently. "But about the trip ... "

"Mouse, you have to go," Roark said with a shake of his head.

The boy sank deeper into the desk chair, muttering under his breath about hypothermia. Ronja and Roark shared a glance loaded with dark humor. The silent exchange warmed her insides, despite their increasingly complicated situation. They had gathered in their bedroom with the rest of the crew. Jonah was locked in the bathroom. After ten minutes of waiting, he had apparently gotten bored and was now taking another shower.

Evie was still playing with the knife she had wrestled from

him, attempting to balance it on her fingertip the way Terra did. "I'll go with Mouse," she offered, the blade wobbling on her pointer finger. Iris snatched the weapon away from her with an indignant huff and set in on the desk.

"Can you drive my bike?" Roark asked.

"I taught *you* how to drive, shiny," the techi said sweetly.

Ronja covered her mouth with her hand to hide her smile. Roark shot her a withering look, which she met with a smile.

"If we leave now, we can make it before the broadcast tonight," Evie said, hopping to her feet. She stretched out a hand for Mouse to grasp. He eyed it like a picky child staring at a plateful of raw vegetables. "Seriously, kid," the techi warned. "I will come down there."

Static. Frantic breaths.

The Anthemites went rigid, the blood draining from their faces in the hush that followed the outburst.

"This is Medusa! Over! Pitching hell ... left, left, Sam ... I mean Griffin! Mother — !"

The audio cut off. Ronja shot to her feet and leapt over Iris, who let out a squeak of shock. She snatched the black communicator off the desk and slammed her thumb into the button.

"Medusa!" she shouted unnecessarily, whipping around to face her friends. "This is Siren, where are you?"

"Siren!" Terra barked a laugh. "Never thought I would be glad to hear from you."

Ronja grinned up at her comrades, her eyes flashing like oncoming headlights. Everyone was on their feet now, even Mouse. They crowded around her. She held out the radio so they could all hear. "Where the hell have you been?" she asked.

"Forget it. Left — make a *left!*" Terra bellowed. "Siren, The Conductor is releasing The New Music tomorrow night."

Ronja felt the breath leave her lungs. Her vision faded to gray. She blinked rapidly, trying to clear it. Somehow, she maintained her grip on the communicator. Her brain kicked into high gear.

"Medusa," she said in a voice that did not match her reeling body. "Are you coming back?"

"Yeah, if Griffin and this stupid truck can get us there."

"Oi!" Mouse cried, wounded. Iris shushed him.

"Medusa, listen to me," Ronja implored. "The prisoner, the one we pulled from Red Bay, do you know where he is?"

Silence. She imagined Terra in the passenger seat of the auto, gaping at the windshield as Samson careened through the city streets. "Yeah," she finally replied, uncertainty dripping from her tone. "Yeah, I do."

"Get him," Ronja commanded. "Bring him to the clock tower at midnight." She flinched as she said the words, hoping against hope that the line was still secure.

"What? Why?"

"Medusa," she begged. "Please. I need you to trust me, just for today. Find him. Bring him to the clock tower. We'll meet you there." Ronja tightened her grip around the communicator, as if she could wring the response she wanted from Terra. She felt her comrades shifting uncertainly around her, waiting.

"We'll be there," Terra finally said.

The line went dead.

"The clock tower," Roark asked at once, bewildered. "Why?"

"Because," Ronja answered levelly. "His radio station is there."

"Wait," Evie interjected, throwing up her hands to halt the conversation. "How do you know?"

"I just ... I know." Ronja shifted uncomfortably on her feet as her family stared at her like she was speaking in tongues. Even

Mouse, who was practically born bored, looked thunderstruck. "Look," she said, lacing her fingers before her pleadingly. "I know it sounds skitzed, but I am sure the radio station is there. When The Conductor would broadcast messages into our Singers, I felt its pull. We just need Maxwell to get us in."

"She is right," Iris said. Her cheeks were flush with color. She looked left at Evie, who was nodding slowly.

"Makes sense to me," the techi exclaimed. Her dark eyes were on fire, her lips split into a manic grin. She looked to Roark. "In fact, it is obvious. It is the perfect place for a radio station."

Roark did not react.

"Do I have to go?" Mouse squeaked, glancing back and forth between Roark and Ronja desperately.

"No," the Siren sighed. "There are only two seats on the damn motorbike, anyway."

Mouse snatched Roark by the arm. "I believe her, I believe her." He might as well have been a buzzing mosquito, as the Anthemite had eyes only for Ronja.

"You never had to convince me," he said. "I trust your instincts."

"Wait, wait," Iris said, stepping toward the Siren. "Even if we can free them from The Music, what's the game plan? I mean, we had some time before to see how it unfolded, but now ... "

Ronja swelled up, standing taller. She locked eyes with Roark. "We free them with a song," she began.

" ... then call on them to destroy the mainframes that produce The Music," he finished for her through a radiant grin.

"We don't know where the mainframes are," Iris pointed out, her voice sparking with apprehension.

"Someone does," Ronja replied. "Someone protects them, maintains them. If we can reach those people, they will destroy them. The revolution will unfold from there."

"We have to warn Ito," Roark said at once. "If this goes south and we get caught, it could mean the discovery of the Belly."

"Thanks for the vote of confidence," the Siren muttered under her breath.

"I got it," Evie said, glancing first at Roark, then Ronja. "You two get to the tower, I'll contact our lieutenant."

"She is gonna be *pissed*," Iris murmured.

"Better pissed than dead," Ronja answered.

Before she could push them down, the faces of her cousins, of Charlotte, buoyed to the surface of her mind. Her throat constricted. She hated risking their safety like this, but it was their only shot at freedom. If they did not interfere now, eventually the Belly would be found. The New Music would flood the compound, drowning minds and lives.

"All right," Roark said, clapping his hands together to dispel the moment. "Ronja, get your stuff."

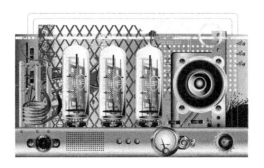

45: NIGHTMARE

There was no debate on who would accompany the Siren to the clock tower. Roark simply started packing and no one stopped him. Iris and Evie hovered while they prepared for the mission. The surgeon was dripping with melancholy. Her girlfriend did a better job of hiding her fears with mocking jokes. Mouse had disappeared. Evidently, he was not one for sappy goodbyes.

"When have we ever failed a mission, Iris?" Roark asked as he shrugged on the holster that held his revolver. He fiddled with the buckle, swearing when he lost hold of it. Ronja made a noise of annoyance and moved to help him with it. He glanced down at her, amused and warmed by the gesture.

"When have we ever done anything like this?" Iris muttered darkly.

"Well, technically," Evie said, tapping her chin in mock consideration. "We aren't doing anything."

"Maybe if Roark hadn't hocked his auto we could all go," Ronja grumbled, shooting him a biting glance.

"Even so," Evie taunted. "It is an *awfully* big bike. Compensating for something?"

Roark cracked a lopsided grin as he threw on his overcoat. "Ronja can confirm there's no need." Ronja blushed as Evie dissolved into a fit of cackles. Even Iris mustered a vague smile.

"But really," the surgeon went on, worrying the hem of her sweater. "We should bring Terra and Samson back here first, then take the truck in together. Safety in numbers."

"There's no time," Roark said gently.

They all fell silent. Ronja went to her bag to collect her wig, then crossed to the mirror that hung over the sink. She was dressed in black, down to her socks. The stingers Evie had given her were strapped to her hips. A small knife was tucked into her boot and an automatic with a full clip was in a holster under her arm. Around her neck were a pair of riding goggles. She pulled her wig over her curls with ease, shifting it back and forth on her scalp until it settled properly.

"Here." Ronja spun around just in time for Evie to toss her a black stocking cap. "It'll keep your wig from flying off on the ride over."

She smiled at the techi in thanks, then pulled the hat over her false hair. It squeezed her scalp, but her wig was certainly not going anywhere.

"Almost perfect," Roark said, appraising her with a satisfied nod. "One more thing." He held up a small black tin the size of his palm.

Ronja gasped softly, her eyes flaring wide. "Really?" she asked. "Should we?"

"Soon enough, it won't matter if we attract attention," he reasoned.

Ronja grinned as Roark tossed her the black tin of war paint. She turned back toward the cloudy mirror, popping the container with trembling hands. She dipped two fingers inside, shivering as the cold paste kissed her skin. She locked eyes with herself in the looking glass and raised her fingers to her brow. She hesitated.

The first time she wore war paint was at a jam in the Belly. It was only a few months ago, though it seemed like a lifetime. That night, she danced without ever being taught how. Roark played his violin, reviving something in her that had almost withered beneath The Music. If she could replicate that feeling, cast it from the highest tower so that it rained down over the city, she could free them. She felt it in her bones, storming through her like a drumbeat.

Atticus Bullon, she thought as she pressed a blackened finger to her forehead. *I am coming for you.* She drew a line down the center of her brow.

For Henry.

Two lines branching from the first, crawling diagonally toward her scalp, disappearing beneath her false bangs.

For Cosmin and Georgie.

She shut her eyes, drew two columns from her eyebrows to her cheekbones. The paint was cool and damp sliding across her lids. She paused for a moment, allowing them to crust, then opened her eyes. Sawyer had said she looked like a nightmare. Ronja had not understood what she meant, until now.

A long stroke running the length of her nose.

Her family, her Anthem.

A black line straight through her lips.

Roark.

She set the canister on the edge of the sink with a quiet clatter. Her hands were no longer shaking. In fact, every cell in her body felt steady, concrete. She turned slowly to face the people she loved.

"I'm ready."

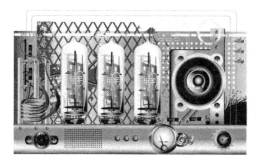

46: DRAWN

R onja clung to Roark as they roared through the middle ring. She kept her cheek pressed to his leather-clad back. Her eyes watered against the sting of the frigid air whipping past, but she forced herself to keep them open. It was a beautiful night, uncommonly clear and bright. A part of her was acutely aware that it might very well be her last.

Carin and Calux were high in the sky, pouring their light through the haze of winter clouds. The houses whipped past, silent and watchful. They were magnificent, tall and pale as cream. When she was a child she used to imagine herself sitting in the parlor of one such home, reading by a roaring hearth, Cosmin and Georgie eating their fill in the kitchen. Henry was there. Charlotte, too. Usually bickering on the sofa or playing a board game.

It was a lovely image, marred only by the Singers clinging to their ears. That was not the life she wanted, not anymore. She wanted something better for all of them. She tightened her grip around Roark.

"We're coming up on the core," he called back to her, his voice buffeted by the wind. "Should be right on time."

"Where's the tower?" Ronja shouted.

Roark made a hard left onto Central Avenue. Ronja slammed her eyes shut against the nausea that spiked in her stomach.

"Look up."

She opened her eyes, lifting her chin.

It was more massive than she ever could have imagined. Her view from the outer ring rooftop was deceptive. The tower sliced through the clouds, its golden crown veiled by the haze. The two faces of the clock she could see were wrought of glass and metal, blazing against the dark sky.

Yes, something in her whispered. The radio station had to be there. She set her jaw, craning her neck back to keep her eyes on the time. The avenue was empty, though it was not yet midnight. "Where is everyone?" Ronja called forward.

"Curfew," Roark shot back.

"What?" she shouted over the roar of the engine.

"Most of these people do not have Singers." He lifted a gloved hand from the handlebars to gesture at the sleeping mansions flying past them.

Ronja followed his hand, her long wig fluttering behind her like a banner. The houses were all stone with spectacular front doors lined with pillars. Their windows were as large as their entrances. All of them were curtained, though shards of warm light slipped out through the cracks.

"The Conductor has to control them somehow," Roark added.

Ronja nodded against his back, her jaw tightening. How many bowed to Atticus Bullon without the aid of a Singer? What would they do, when the revolution knocked on their doors? They were about to find out.

They ran out of road before they were ready. A sprawling concrete square surrounded the behemoth clock tower, dotted with cast iron lamps and stone park benches. Roark slowed to a virtual crawl, rolling them into a narrow alley between two mansions before she had time to take it in. Ronja dismounted on unsteady legs, pulling her hood up over her head. Roark switched off the engine and got off the bike. He patted the handlebars fondly, an expression that did not match the fierce black war paint on his features. With a final glance at his beloved motorcycle, he took Ronja by the hand and led her toward the avenue.

"Walk fast, head down," he murmured as they approached the mouth of the alley.

"We'll be exposed," she whispered, slowing her pace so that he was practically dragging her forward "Completely. Someone could look out their window any second."

"Trust me, Ronja," he assured her as they reached the lip of the street. "I know these people. They keep their eyes and blinds shut. No one will be looking." The girl nodded, suddenly incapable of speech. Roark checked his watch. "We have two minutes to get to the north side of the tower. Knowing Terra, she'll be right on time."

"What about Offs? Guards?" she asked, still wavering on the edge of the street. "Where are they?"

"Most of the security is concentrated around the palace a few blocks from here. The tower itself is a fortress," Roark explained patiently, giving her hand a firm squeeze. "If anyone is inside, we'll take them out."

Ronja nodded, forcing herself to breathe through her nose. The eyes of the clock tower seared her skin. She rolled her fingers into fists, setting her jaw. She would burn it to the ground. Without another word she stepped out onto the avenue and started toward the clock tower, taking Roark with her.

The square was as still and silent as a graveyard. Their

footsteps echoed as they neared the tower, their shadows elongating across the plane of concrete. Ronja kept her eyes trained on the tower. The great clocks themselves were now obscured by cloud, their glow scattered by the vapor. As she drew nearer to the base of the building, pressure began to build in her skull. It was like a drumbeat, one she could not escape. She swallowed in an attempt to relieve it. Nothing happened.

"You all right?" Roark murmured, glancing over his shoulder to check that they were still alone.

"Fine," Ronja lied through gritted teeth. White spots were eating into her vision. "Fine."

They slowed their pace as they approached the edge of the great tower. A massive stone door stared them down from its niche in the wall. Its face was engraved with swirling patterns. They were almost artistic in nature, Ronja realized with a jolt. There was no knocker, no handle, no keyhole. "Maxwell will be able to open it, right?" she whispered, not taking her eyes off the door.

"He has to," Roark replied grimly.

"He certainly does."

Ronja and Roark whipped around, their hands flying to their weapons. The Siren breathed a sigh of relief, sagging slightly as her pulse slackened. "Terra," she exhaled. "You made it."

The agent offered a bleak smile as she came to a halt before them. She wore her overcoat open, revealing the leather hilts of the knives at her hips. Her blonde hair was knotted, her cheek bruised. Ronja frowned at the sight, opening her mouth to ask what had happened. "Not now," Terra said, lifting a hand to stop her.

"Where are Samson and Maxwell?" Roark inquired.

Terra jerked her thumb behind her just as two forms rounded the corner of the tower, silhouetted by the glaring streetlamp behind them. One was muscular and sure footed, the other waifish and awkward.

"Maxwell," Ronja breathed.

They stood in silence as Samson approached with the prisoner. The captain did not lead Maxwell as they walked, though his hand was hidden in the folds of his leather jacket, doubtlessly resting on the handle of his automatic. "Ro, Trip," Samson greeted them as he arrived.

Roark replied with as much warmth as he could muster amidst their peril. Ronja, on the other hand, could not take her eyes off their captive.

She had only seen Maxwell Bullon once. It was just in passing as they were moving him from the Belly to the safe house Terra and Samson had broken him out of. He had been wearing a bag over his head then, so all she saw was his wiry body and large hands and feet. His face did not match the rest of him. His blue eyes were sharp as tacks, his black hair slick with grease. He sported a patchy beard a shade lighter than the hair on his crown. He was paler than she was. When he grinned, her blood stilled in her veins.

"I do not believe we have met," he said in a strange, whispery voice. "My name is Maxwell Bullon, but you already know that." He offered his unusually large hand for her to shake. Samson grabbed him by the arm, his tan fingers encircling his bicep. The prisoner looked up at his warden, his smile stretching wider. "Now, now, I was just being polite to the girl."

Ronja fought the urge to spit in his face.

"You know why you are here, I presume," Roark said, stepping toward Maxwell in silent warning.

"Yes, yes," the prisoner exclaimed, clapping his hands together excitedly. Ronja glanced over her shoulder as the sound bounced around the square. The houses were still, the drapes remained drawn. Roark had been right. "The bargain, the lovely bargain. I let you into the tower and show you where my dear father broadcasts his messages and you let me walk free." His too wide smile slipped a fraction of an inch, replaced by a genuine spark of interest. "How did you know that his station was in the tower?" he asked, gazing around at them with shining eyes.

Ronja shifted on her feet, wincing as pain knifed through her skull. "Just let us inside," she ordered through her teeth. "Now."

Maxwell zeroed in on her. Behind that manic spark was something else, something calculating and sinister. She lifted her chin, forcing herself to hold eye contact with him. It was easier said than done. Her vision swam, her brain throbbed.

"You heard her," Terra snapped, giving Maxwell a shove toward the sealed door. "Get it open, now."

"Of course, of course." Maxwell crossed to the tower, his feet slapping against the hard ground. They watched as he pressed his palms to the stone door and began to run them across the twisting designs, hunting for something. "They make it so remarkably easy," he commented, his hands stilling at the center of a diamond pattern near the edge of the entrance. There was a hiss as a hidden panel rolled open to reveal a board full of faded brass keys. "Those with Singers revere the tower, those without are terrified of it."

He might have said something else, but Ronja was no longer listening. Her feet moved forward of their own accord. Her arms were loose at her sides, her lips parted slightly. Her bones hummed, her skin tingled. The drum in her head grew louder with each breath she took. Somewhere in the back of her mind, she heard someone call out her name. She ignored it. She reached the door. It was whispering to her, calling her. An old friend.

She raised her right palm and placed it at the nucleus of a sprawling circle. Heat flared beneath her skin. The door caved with a hiss.

"Oh!"

Ronja crashed back into her body. Maxwell stood next to her, his index finger hovering over the keypad. They locked eyes. A chill passed through her. He was looking at her as if seeing straight into the bottom of her soul.

"It worked," he said, not tearing his eyes away from her. He let his hand fall. "You can go in now."

Ronja turned around just as Roark came to stand beside her. He put a hand on her waist. "Are you all right?" he asked quietly. "What were you doing?"

"Nothing," Ronja replied, looking back at the door. Her palm was still hot from touching it. The designs seemed to revolve before her eyes. "Nothing."

"No time to waste," Samson said, stepping up behind them. He had drawn his gun and held it up before him, his jaw clenched.

Terra whipped out her machetes as Ronja reached into her coat and drew her stingers. They were heavy in her hands, comforting. She ignited them with a twitch of her wrists. Their tips flared blue. Roark gave her waist a comforting squeeze, then reached out and pushed open the door with a large hand.

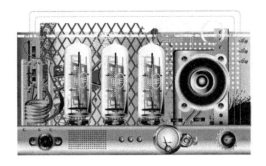

47: MAINFRAME

Ronja squinted through the portal, her knuckles bleaching around her stingers. It was pitch black inside. Heat and sound poured through the entrance, a constant clicking and humming that raised goose bumps on her arms. Around her, the Anthemites tensed, ready for an onslaught. It never came. She glanced over at Roark, a question in her eyes. He responded with an offhand shrug, then passed over the threshold, gun up.

They followed single file. As soon as the last of them passed through, the door slid shut smoothly, plunging them into near total blackness. Ronja fought to keep her breathing steady as she held her stingers aloft, trying to snuff the black with the pale light. The humming seemed to come from everywhere, wrapping around them. It was thicker than the darkness.

"Maxwell, get the lights," Samson growled from somewhere in the shadows.

"Certainly," came the cheery reply. A moment later, bright light flared from above. Ronja felt the blood leave her face.

"What the hell is that?" she breathed.

"Oh, that?" Maxwell smiled genially. "Mainframe number three, of course. Did you not know it was here?"

The rebels were silent, momentarily forgetting their mission. Ronja blinked rapidly, gathering her vision. Her stomach bottomed out. Her knees buckled and she struggled to remain standing. She wanted to call the darkness back. In the dark she could be anywhere. Anywhere but here.

When she imagined The Music, it was always some disembodied creature, formless, weightless, able to slip between the folds of the brain in the blink of an eye. It was the stain no amount of soap could scrub away. The chill no clothing could bar. But it was not. It was a physical entity, a black beast of wire and metal and coal. It scaled the inside of the tower, stretching further than the eye could see. It whirred and hissed and throbbed like an inorganic heart.

"Beautiful, beautiful."

Ronja cut her eyes to the side, where Samson was holding Maxwell by the arm. The son of The Conductor stared up at the machine, shaking his head in awe.

"Take us to the station," Roark ordered him. "We'll deal with it later."

Maxwell heaved a sigh, then tore his gaze from the machine. "The elevator is this way, I believe," he said.

"You believe?" Terra hissed, her voice dangerously low.

"I have not been here for many years," Maxwell admitted, glancing back at the mainframe with adoration.

"Just take us to the damn elevators," Ronja demanded, lifting one of her live stingers to his face.

He squeaked and elongated, terror flashing in his ever-shifting eyes. "Fine, fine, this way." He turned his back on the machine reluctantly and started toward the south end of the tower. There was a spring in his step, as if he were a child on his way to a picture show.

The Anthemites held back for a moment, tension growing

between them. "No guards," Terra muttered, her sharp eyes shifting around the massive room.

"Could be a trap," Samson agreed.

"How?" Roark asked, desperation ringing in his tone. "How could he set a trap? He's been a prisoner for almost three months. He had no idea we were coming here."

"This is our only shot," Ronja said firmly, setting her sights on the odd man ten steps ahead of them. Maxwell gave a little skip, then his hand twitched up to touch his Singer. "We'll never have another."

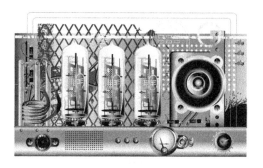

48: RISING

Ronja had endured several awkward elevator rides over the course of her life, but none quite as charged as the trip to the top of the clock tower. Maxwell seemed incapable of standing still for more than a couple seconds at a time. He stood at the center of the capsule, fidgeting as the cables outside the cherrywood compartment creaked and groaned. Ronja pressed herself against Roark, trying to put as much distance between her and the madman as possible. Terra followed suit, shooting him disgusted looks from the opposite corner. Samson maintained his grip on Maxwell, though he looked like he would rather be yanking out his own teeth.

When the elevator finally shuddered to a halt after the long crawl, Ronja could not resist a sigh of relief. It was quickly extinguished, however, when Terra reached out and slammed a red button with her fist. Ronja slapped her hand over her ear as an alarm flared outside.

"Terra, Sam," Roark said, jerking his head at the far side of the elevator. The captain released Maxwell and went to stand with Terra. Moving as a unit, they crouched low, their respective weapons held at the ready. The prisoner moved to follow them, but Roark snapped his fingers at him. "You stay right there," he ordered, pointing at the center of the compartment. "If anyone is gonna get shot, it'll be you."

"No one will be in," Maxwell told him. "No one comes up here except my father and his aides."

Ronja twitched, her fingers tightening around her weapons. Something about the statement itched her. Before she could place it, Roark tapped her on the elbow and crouched down, his gun trained on the polished elevator doors. She copied him, twisting her stingers to life again and raising them before her.

"Ready?" Terra asked from the opposite side of the compartment. A series of nods rippled through them. Ronja glanced up at Maxwell, who was the last one standing. He was gnawing on his lower lip, shifting from foot to foot. Her brow furrowed. His personality was constantly in flux. He was as volatile as a wet stick of dynamite.

Fear cut through Ronja. Her lips parted, forming around a word of warning, but it was too late. Terra hit another button and the elevator doors rolled open with a polite peel of chimes. Ronja tensed and felt her friends do the same.

Silence.

"I told you," Maxwell said in a singsong voice. He stepped out of the elevator confidently, his long arms swinging at his sides. "Come in, come in."

The Anthemites shared a loaded glance, then slowly rose to their feet, peering out into the unknown. "Whoa," Ronja breathed.

"Yeah," Roark agreed.

There was almost no furniture in the sprawling room, save for a high-backed leather chair that stood before a hulking dashboard. It was painted deep red, full of dozens of gold switches and levers. There was no freestanding microphone, but a pair of brown leather headphones with a mouthpiece lay at the edge of the machine. As impressive as the setup was compared to their makeshift station, what was truly impressive was the room itself.

The floors were white marble, the ceiling gilded gold. An intricately carved door stood opposite the elevator, likely leading to a staircase. The walls were not walls at all. They were the glass undersides of the great clocks. Through them, the metal gears of the machines revolved in perfect synchronization. The eight hands of the clocks crept in steady circles.

Ronja stepped from the elevator, the world falling away behind her. She crossed to the nearest clock, her heart thundering in her chest. Her head still throbbed, but the pain seemed distant now. She pressed her palm to the cool glass. The hum of machinery tickled her skin. The city sprawled beneath her for miles. She could see the core, the middle ring, the outer ring, all the way to the slums. The onyx wall was almost invisible save for its many watchtowers that flung glaring searchlights over the shantytown. What they were searching for, she would never know. Perhaps nothing. Perhaps they were only there to instill fear.

"Ronja."

Ronja peeled her hand from the glass and turned around. Terra had taken a seat at the dashboard. Samson stood before the elevator doors, his hand on the gun strapped to his side. Maxwell roamed the room aimlessly, a faint smile hanging off the corner of his mouth. Roark stood before her, watching her curiously.

"It looks so small," she said, jerking her head at the city beneath them.

"It does," he agreed. He jerked his head at the machine behind him. "Come on, no time to waste."

Ronja nodded and swept past him. She shrugged off her heavy overcoat, letting it crumple on the floor. Terra was staring at the dashboard from her seat. Her eyes roamed across the field of switches and dials.

"Do you know how to work it?" Ronja asked.

"Yes," Terra answered flatly. "Evie taught me."

"What are you waiting for, then?"

Terra glanced up. To Ronja's surprise, the cross expression Terra typically reserved for her was gone. There was a vulnerability flashing in her eyes she had never seen before. Terra Vahl was afraid. "Terra," the Siren said quietly, leaning down toward her so the boys would not hear. "Remember at Red Bay, when you told me to keep walking, after I almost got incinerated."

Terra snorted. "Yeah."

"Well ... walk."

For a moment, the agent did not react. Ronja kicked herself internally. *You had to go and say something*, she chastised herself. Then Terra smiled. Not a quirk of the lips or a sardonic smirk, but a grin.

"All right, Siren," she said, cracking her knuckles and rolling her shoulders. "Here we go."

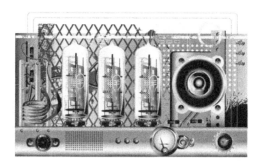

49: CLARITY

"That should do it," Terra said. She exhaled sharply, then climbed to her feet. Ronja and Roark pressed toward the console eagerly. It was far quieter than Abe. Heat did not pour from it, either. Ronja might not have known it was on were it not for the flashing red light on the corner of the switchboard. "Ronja," Terra said, sidestepping out of the way. She inclined her head toward the impressive leather chair. "All yours."

Ronja nodded mutely. Her mouth felt like it was filled with sawdust. She stepped in front of the chair, her eyes fixed on the humming machine before her. This was where The Conductor sat. It was His throne. He never made public appearances; there was no need when he had a direct line to the minds of His citizens. A sliver of her mind, the part that still responded to the word *mutt*, bucked against the thought.

She crushed it in the palm of her hand and lowered herself onto the throne.

The tower did not crumble beneath her. The glass walls did not shatter. Ronja closed her eyes, bracing her hands against the slick leather arms of the chair.

"How long do you need?" Terra asked.

"Three minutes?" Ronja said, opening her eyes and blinking up at the girl. "Can we do that?"

"Yeah," the agent answered, nodding and turning a dial on the far side of the dashboard. "We can. This is different, though. We are not hacking the gap. We are cutting straight through The Music."

Ronja took a steadying breath. "Will I be able to hear The Music?"

"No," Terra shook her head.

"As soon as you finish, we need to split," Roark spoke up to her right. He smiled crookedly, dark humor flaring in his gaze. "Unless we want to go down with the tower."

"Will we be able to make it out in time?" Ronja asked, looking from him to Terra anxiously.

"This was your plan," the boy pointed out with a low chuckle.

"True, but to be fair, I didn't know we were going to be at the top of the bloody tower, and I didn't know about the mainframe."

"Almost no one in the core is going to hear you," Roark reminded her, laying a hand on her shoulder. "It'll take time for the people of the other rings to make it up here."

"Not to mention, we'll have to open the door for them," Samson pointed out. Ronja twisted around in the chair, peeking over the winged back to lock eyes with the captain. He still held his automatic in his gloved hand. Maxwell hovered near him, bouncing from foot to foot and gazing around the room with childlike interest.

"True," Ronja said with a forced laugh. "All right. Put me through."

"Headphones," Terra said, nodding at the pair on the edge of the switchboard.

Ronja crowned herself with the headset, adjusting the mouthpiece so it hovered an inch from her lips. The device quelled all sound but the gusts of her breath in the microphone. She looked up at Roark blankly. His lips were moving. "What?" she asked, peeling off one of the pads. The world came screaming back.

"I asked if you knew what you were going to sing," he said.

"Yeah, I do."

Roark cocked his head to the side. "And?"

Ronja let the earpiece slap back down over her scar. "It's a surprise." She winked up at him, settling herself on the edge of the throne. She locked eyes with Terra. "Go," she said. It was strange to have her voice projected directly into her ear. It felt almost too close.

Terra leaned over the dashboard, her long hair sweeping forward to obscure her features. She paused for a moment, her tan fingers hovering over a gold-trimmed lever. Then, in one swift motion, she slammed it down.

Ronja closed her eyes.

Silence erupted. The absence of The Music played on her skin, though she could not hear it. She was with them, all of them, as it jolted them from sleep, stopped them in their tracks on their way home from work. Their fear and confusion were reflected back at her through the wires. They were expecting The Conductor, wondering why he was contacting them at such a late hour. Ronja began to sing.

When the day shakes
Beneath the hands of night
When your page is ripped
From the Book of Life
When your knees crash
Into the ground
And your desperate lips

Won't make a sound

With each word the shackles of her past fell away. All the fear, all the rage, all the agony, extinguished. Red Bay receded, swallowed by the waters it was named for. Her mother was laid to rest on a hillside. Henry waded through the stars.

When you're all alone
And the night is deep
When you're surrounded
But you want to weep
When the morning comes
And it's all but bleak
When you want to scream
But instead you're meek

Ronja raised her eyes to the ceiling. Hot tears spilled over her lids, hitting the dashboard without a sound. The thunderheads that blossomed from her voice were no longer black. They were clear as glass. They crackled with energy as if charged by stingers, shedding sparks that would never burn their skin.

Sing my friend
Into the dark

Sing my friend
Into the deep

Sing my friend
Into the black

Sing my friend
There and back

Ronja climbed to her feet, her clammy hands clutching the edge of the dashboard for support. Though her song had ended, the white clouds did not rupture. They remained above her, guarding her. "People of Revinia," she began. Her words echoed as if bounding down a long corridor. "My name is Ronja Fey Zipse and I am the Siren. I spent most of my life a prisoner of The Music, made to serve The Conductor with every breath I took, just like you. Three months ago, I was freed from my Singer. I saw Atticus Bullon for what He really was, a liar and a coward. He has enslaved us, taken everything that makes us human. He divides us. He manipulates us and warps us.

"Tomorrow, He will release a new form of The Music. It will drain you of all emotion and take away the last shreds of your free will. But you can stop it. You must help us destroy the mainframes that generate The Music. Some of you know where they are. Seek them out and destroy them. The rest of you, head for the palace. I will meet you there. This is the Siren, signing off for the last time. May your song guide you home."

Ronja fell silent. She drew a deep, shuddering breath and slipped off the headset. The quiet hum of the machine, the unsteady breathing of her friends, came roaring back. She turned around leaned up against the dashboard. Roark was watching her with full eyes. Samson and Terra were grinning ear-to-ear. "Do you think it worked?" she asked.

Before any of them could respond, Maxwell began to laugh.

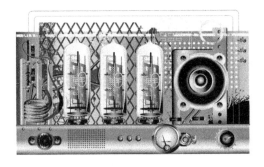

50: ENCORE

"**B**ravo!" he shouted, applauding fervently. He bobbed up and down on the balls of his feet. "That was incredible, truly inspired."

Ronja glowered at him. Roark stepped between her and the madman, beaming. "Ignore him," he said, offering his hand. He jerked his chin toward the glass clock nearest to them. "We have more important things to worry about."

Ronja reached out and took his hand. His skin stilled the tremors coursing through her. They hurried over to the window facing north. Samson followed, his heavy boots thumping across the marble. Terra stayed back, holding Maxwell in place, her machete ready to skewer him from behind.

Ronja held her breath as they approached the towering face of the clock. The great gears slowed as she approached, their groans fading to silence as she pressed her brow to the cold surface. Her breath fogged as she squinted down at the distant city.

The Siren ceased to breathe.

Revinia was on fire.

Electric lights and blazing torches sliced through the night.

Every window, every door, every streetlamp was illuminated. Snow had begun to fall. It was painted orange, sparks drifting down from burning clouds.

"What the hell is that?" Samson asked from behind her.

"What?" Roark asked, squinting down at the metropolis. "What are you seeing?"

"That," Ronja breathed. She pressed the tip of her finger to the glass, her lips parted with shock. Amber light shivered in his dark irises as Roark followed her gaze to the boulevard that ran from the tower to the middle ring. It had come alive, a fiery river inching toward them step by step. "The Revinians," Ronja breathed. Her breath formed a halo on the glass, veiling the march. "They're coming."

Samson let out a whoop, jamming his fist into the air. A female voice joined his cries: Terra. Ronja turned around just in time to see the captain knock Maxwell out of the way and sweep the agent off her feet into a passionate kiss. Terra blinked rapidly, her mouth pressed to his, then sank into the moment, twining her fingers in his long hair.

"Well," Roark said with laugh. "I, for one, am not about to be upstaged by those two."

Ronja smiled through a sheen of tears as he took her face in his hands and pressed a kiss to her brow. "You did it," he whispered against her skin. "You did it."

"We did it," she murmured, slipping her arms around his waist. The future curled around them, expanding as far as they could see. Further than they had ever been.

"All right, all right, enough!" Ronja and Roark looked around to see Terra step back from Samson. Her cheeks were flushed with color, her lips puffy. The captain ran his fingers through his shaggy hair, his eyes wide with internalized disbelief. "We have a mainframe to destroy, then apparently, we have to get you to the palace."

Ronja barked a disbelieving laugh, wiping away her tears with the heels of her hands. She stepped back from Roark, still holding him by the hand. "All right," she said in a firm voice. "You heard the woman, time to go."

Terra smiled, her hazel eyes crinkling around the edges. Ronja returned the gesture.

"Ah, about that." Maxwell lifted a single finger.

Ronja rounded on him, her hand drifting toward her stinger. "You know," she snapped. "Maybe we should just leave you up here."

"I second that," Terra said, prowling toward the chemi. Her knives were back in her hands. Ronja had not even seen her draw them. Maxwell just smiled, exposing far too many of his teeth.

"We'll all be leaving this tower," he assured them. "But you will not be going home."

Ronja glanced over at Roark. His war paint was smeared with sweat, the black lines mingling with the orange glow of the mob drawing steadily nearer. His free hand was on his revolver. The Siren shifted her gaze back to Maxwell. His eyes were on her. In the aura of the revolution below, they were almost red. His lips formed a single word.

"Now."

Ronja did not even have time to scream. The door burst open and a flood of Offs rushed in. Roark swore and knocked her backward. She cried out when her shoulder struck the unforgiving floor and she heard a sickening pop. Clutching her arm to her side, she scrambled to her feet and drew her gun.

Chaos reigned. Roark had already emptied his revolver and was fighting with his twin stingers. He was a storm, twisting and striking with deadly precision. But he was not untouchable. Blood gushed from his nose and a thick gash on his brow. Samson had one Off in a headlock. When another jumped on his back, with a roar the captain slammed him into the eastern clock. The glass spidered behind them just as Terra let one of her blades fly, nailing the Off Samson was suffocating between the eyes.

Terra was fighting from the top of the dashboard, a ring of bodies at her feet. She was down to her last two knives, fending off multiple attackers at once. She did not notice the man sneaking up behind her, black stinger rippling with deadly electricity.

Ronja did not even think. She shut one eye, aimed at the Off and fired. The bullet lodged in his shoulder. Dark blood oozed from the wound, soaking his uniform. The Off blinked, glanced down at the wound as if it were a mosquito bite, then struck Terra with his stinger.

Her scream of agony filled the clock tower just as Ronja was forced to her knees. Her vision was flooded with Offs. She twisted and bit at her captors as her revolver was ripped from her hands, her stingers from their holsters. They crossed her arms behind her back. She roared as white hot pain flared in her dislocated shoulder. Somewhere over the din, Roark was shouting her name.

Terra was silent.

"Enough," came a lazy command.

The hands restraining her disappeared. The Offs backed away. Ronja scrambled to her feet, clutching her throbbing shoulder. She took stock of the room. It was filled to capacity with Offs. At least, at first glance they looked like Offs. Their uniforms were dark and lined with silver buttons, but the symbol over their hearts did not belong to The Conductor. Three red pillars against a black backdrop. Many of them were bleeding, including the one she had shot, but none of them appeared to register the pain.

Samson and Roark had both been forced to their knees and remained there, guns pressed to their temples. They were covered in blood, their own mixed with that of their enemies. Ronja tasted rust in her mouth and knew she looked the same. Terra was crumpled on the floor, lifeless.

"Do you understand now, Siren?" Ronja tore her eyes from Terra. Maxwell stood at the center of the room, bathed in the inferno of the approaching revolution. He no longer bobbed up and down on his feet. The manic smile had slipped from his mouth, replaced by a smirk.

"Whatever you have planned," Ronja said through her teeth. "It's too late. The Revinians are free. They'll destroy this tower with us in it, we'll all go down."

"How poetic," Maxwell purred. "What an end to the story that would be."

"What story?" Roark growled.

Maxwell snapped his fingers without taking his eyes off Ronja. The Off holding Roark at gunpoint cranked his arm back and slammed the butt of his automatic into his skull. Ronja screamed, clamping her hand over her mouth as the boy cried out in shock and pain.

"How I hate being interrupted," Maxwell sighed, shaking his head.

"You've got a big one coming," the Siren spat.

"Ah, yes, thank you for reminding me." Maxwell raised his pallid hand to his Singer, then spun a tiny dial between his thumb and forefinger. "Begin the countdown," he said.

Ronja felt her heart still in her ribs. Her body went numb, yet somehow she remained standing. She slid her gaze to Roark. His face was dripping with blood and war paint. It did nothing to hide the panic flaring in his eyes.

"The best thing about being mad," Maxwell said, shifting the little dial again, "is that when you appear to be talking to yourself, people assume you are."

"Your Singer is a transmitter," Ronja whispered.

Maxwell smiled absently, still fiddling with the device that bracketed his ear. "My Singer is a lot of things, Siren." He raised a long finger to shush her. "*Fel nevin.*"

A chill lanced through Ronja. "Tovairin." She swallowed. "The language you were speaking in your cell, it was Tovairin."

"How astute. If only my guards had been so keen." A knock at the door. Ronja took an involuntary step backward, turning her back foot to the side as Samson had taught her. "Come in, come in," Maxwell called.

The door swung open. Jonah filled the frame, a pair of hulking Offs at his back. His lip was split, blood was crusted on his chin. He locked eyes with Ronja.

"Allies," she snarled. She spit on the marble floor. "I should have let Evie kill you."

The Tovairin flinched, then shifted his gaze to Maxwell.

"Yes, you should have," Maxwell agreed. "Your heart is far too good for war, my dear."

"Tell that to the guards I killed at Red Bay," Ronja hissed.

"Jonah," Maxwell said, ignoring her. "Where are they?"

The Tovairin stepped aside and motioned for the pair of Officers to do the same. They parted ways, pressing their backs to the walls of the corridor. Ronja felt her knees buckle. Somehow, she maintained her balance. Evie, Iris, and Mouse stood in the gap, hands cuffed behind their backs and headphones clamped over their ears.

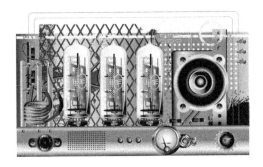

51: MUZZLE

"So glad you all could make it," Maxwell said smoothly, beckoning the three Anthemites. When none of them moved, the Offs grabbed them and half-led, half-dragged them inside. "Put them with young Mr. Westervelt and the other one," he continued, gesturing at Roark and Samson. He locked eyes with Ronja, who snarled at him like a feral dog. "I want the Siren to have a good view of her friends."

Ronja quivered with rage as Evie and the others were forced to their knees next to Roark and the captain. Evie was bleeding from a nasty gash on her forehead. Iris was sporting a split lip and Mouse a black eye.

"We are still waiting for a few guests," Maxwell said, glancing around at them all as if they were an audience waiting for a play to begin. "I do hope they are on time. I would rather not delay."

"Delay?" Ronja asked through gritted teeth.

Maxwell sighed, casting his eyes to the gilded ceiling. "Yes, dear girl, delay. Delay the launch of The New Music. It has been finished for weeks, I have only to apply the final piece. "

"And what is that?" Ronja growled.

She tried not to flinch when Maxwell let out a laugh that

could shatter glass. "My dear little bird, what do you think? *You* are the final piece. *The Siren.* The weapon. You did what my father tried and failed to do for decades, you united the people organically."

The room slipped from focus. Ronja steadied herself against the back of the leather chair.

"You," she breathed. "You were the one who named me." Her gaze darted to Jonah, who stood at the edge of the room between two Offs. He refused to meet her eyes.

"Yes," Maxwell answered with a smirk. "I am."

"Why wait?" Ronja demanded. She jabbed a finger at Jonah, who shifted awkwardly under the spotlight of her gesture. "You knew where we were. What the hell have you been waiting for?"

Maxwell giggled behind his hand, waiting for her to put the pieces together. A moment later, she did.

"You were playing with us," she murmured. "You wanted us to believe we had won."

Maxwell grinned, his eyes flashing like broken bottles in sunlight. He strode over to her swiftly. Roark swore and began to struggle against his captor. Ronja kept her eyes on the enemy. All traces of his awkwardness were gone. He was still erratic, but was pulsing with power and authority. He stopped a breath from her. She lifted her chin defiantly as he peered down at her.

"Yes, little bird," he breathed, lifting a large hand to her face. Ronja tightened her jaw as he ran his thumb across her lips. "I was playing with you. I wanted to see how far you could take it, and look!"

He jerked her head to the side, toward the inferno leaking through the glass. Roark swore, elbowing his guard in the gut to no avail. Maxwell pressed his lips to her ear. "Look how far you have come. Truly, you are the best opponent I could have asked for. More than I could have dared to hope. Your father would be proud."

Ronja snatched his wrist and bit down on his thumb with all her strength. Hot blood spurted in her mouth as Maxwell roared in agony. The Offs flew forward, struggling in vain to restrain her. She lashed out blindly with her feet as one Off lifted her from the ground. She released her jaw and spat at Maxwell, spraying his own flesh and blood across his contorted features.

"YOU BITCH!" he howled, cradling his hemorrhaging hand to his chest. He rounded on the nearest Off, snarling. "You," he commanded. "Bring me what I asked for. This girl needs to keep her mouth shut."

Ronja twisted in the grip of the Off. Rather than trying to still her, he lifted her higher then smashed her into the ground. She landed on her back, her head ricocheting off the marble. Her vision fled along with her breath. Before she could collect herself, she was dragged to her knees, her skull held in place by two massive hands. She struggled feebly as something metallic was slipped under her tongue, then locked around the back of her head.

"Much better," Maxwell hissed. The Offs supporting Ronja retreated and she sagged toward the ground. "Stay with me, little bird," he hissed, snatching her by her hair and dragging her upward. "Look at me. Look at me."

Ronja blinked up at the madman. Her vision was spotted with gray and black. "Useless," Maxwell hissed, releasing her. She collapsed to the ground, limp as a rag doll. Her own blood was pooling beneath her head. Her mouth tasted like rust. She raised her trembling fingers to her lips but struck metal. Her frayed neurons struggled to connect, to understand what was happening.

Then it slammed into her with the force of a subtrain.

Maxwell had muzzled her.

Rage ignited in her chest, sending adrenaline singing through her veins. She rolled onto her stomach, pressing her palms to the marble. The blood pooling in her mouth dripped from her lips, oozing through the bars of her muzzle. She rose to one knee, then two, then clambered to her feet. The tower swayed. "Good, good," Maxwell murmured from far away. "I want you to see this. Our final guests have arrived."

Ronja blinked, her eyes drifting toward her family. Iris was crying through her gag, her shoulders trembling with soundless sobs. Roark was shaking, his eyes flown wide with horror and rage. The eyes she loved.

The elevator chimed. The doors rolled open, spilling golden light.

Ronja stumbled, catching herself on the back of the leather armchair. "No," she tried to say through her muzzle. All that came out was a broken wail.

Two men were inside the compartment. One sat hunched in a wheelchair, his balding head bowed. An oxygen mask strapped to his sagging face. An IV bag dangled above him from a metal rod. He was dressed in a fine bathrobe and matching slippers. He seemed to be asleep, or comatose.

The other man was young. Tall and handsome with dark eyes and skin to match. He was dressed in a elegant suit with a high collar and intricate gold clasps running down the front. His gaze was set dead ahead, as if he were not really seeing the room. A gold-trimmed Singer clung to his right ear.

Maxwell smiled. "Thank you for bringing my father to me, Henry. Well done."

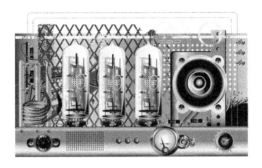

52: ALEZANDRI

Atticus Bullon. The Conductor. The orchestrator of her nightmares. The tyrant that had drained the life from her city was only feet from her. Ronja barely noticed him. He was a speck of dust caught in her eye. All she could see was Henry. The longer she stared, the more she expected him to fade away, a figment of her rattled imagination.

She had heard him die over the radio. The Offs pounding on the door. His resolve to take his own life before they reached him. His last words ushering in the gunshot.

"Come in, Henry, bring my father to me."

Ronja snapped her attention back to Maxwell, who radiated glee. Henry did as he was told. He moved mechanically, wheeling The Conductor toward his son with dead eyes.

Henry, Ronja tried to call. It came out as a mangled groan.

Maxwell shot her an amused look. "Sorry, were you saying something?" he asked, tittering slightly. He pointed down at his father, who was still slouched in the wheelchair, his eyes on the floor. His breath rattled through the oxygen mask. "Not what you were expecting, hmmm? You probably thought he looked like his portraits, even after all these years. Do you know how old he is?

Ninety. Can you believe it?" He let out a harsh laugh, then squatted down next to The Conductor.

"Hey," Maxwell whispered. He reached up a hand and patted his creased face. "Hey," he said more forcefully. The Conductor stirred feebly, his drooping eyelids flickering. Maxwell rolled his eyes, as if this were nothing more than a minor inconvenience. He reached up and rolled a dial attached to the IV bag that dangled above the wheelchair like a lantern. For a moment, nothing happened.

Then The Conductor sucked in a shuddering breath, rising up in his seat, then crashing back down. His bloodshot eyes darted around the room, landing on Ronja. They widened as he drank her in. His lips parted. For a moment, only his ragged breathing could be heard. Then he spoke, a single word.

"Alezandri."

Confusion ruptured the fear swelling in Ronja.

"Yes, Father," Maxwell said quietly. "A story for another time." He switched his attention back to Ronja. "You don't understand, little bird, I see it on your face." He got to his feet and patted The Conductor on the shoulder. The old man squirmed, wheezing as adrenaline barreled through his veins. "My father has not been active for years. The voice you heard through your Singers was just a recording. Certainly, in his prime he was an adequate dictator," Maxwell sneered, his white teeth dripping with malevolence. "Now, the only thing keeping him in power is the suggestion of The Music." He reached down and tugged the oxygen mask over his head. "And this."

The Conductor went rigid. His hands curled toward his throat in a vain attempt to coax more air into his lungs. Henry stood over him, detached. "Your days as The Conductor are over, Father," Maxwell hissed, bending down toward the old man, who was twitching erratically. "You hid me away, called me a freak, put a Singer on me. You should have known Singers only work on those weighed down by emotion."

The Conductor convulsed, his eyes darting over to where Ronja stood, then back to his son.

Maxwell shook his head. "You set your sights too low, Father. You were a coward, locking yourself inside these walls, hidden from the outside world. I will do so much more. I will be a conqueror."

He glanced at his watch, as if he were checking the time on his way to dinner plans. "Excellent timing," he cooed, patting The Conductor on the top of his bald head. The old man was growing quiet in his seat, his chest rising and falling rapidly as he struggled for breath. "The New Music will go live any second. Look out the window, Siren. I want you to see your revolution die."

Ronja gritted her teeth behind her bit, kept her shivering eyes on Maxwell. "Do it," he ordered quietly. "Or I will have Henry here kill your friends, one by one."

The Siren slid her gaze toward her brother. Her pulse stumbled. He was looking at her. His eyes were black holes. He was not angry. He was not afraid. He was nothing. Ronja forced herself into motion, crossing to the north window with leaden feet. She felt the eyes of her family on her as she moved. She could not look at them. If she did, she would crumble.

Ronja came to a stop before the glass wall. The resistance was still approaching, marching up the central avenue, their torches aloft. The city was still shining. For a split second, hope flared in her chest. Then the first wave of lights winked out in the core. Ronja pressed her hand to the glass as if she could call it back. The darkness spread, engulfing the neighborhoods in devastating waves. The revolutionaries stopped in their tracks.

They put out their lights. They bled apart, drifting back to their homes without a sound.

Behind her, it was absolutely silent. The Conductor was dead.

"What a show," Maxwell said. "Now, little bird. Where were we? Yes. Your voice. I will be needing it."

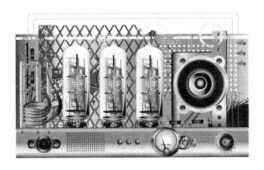

53: CHOOSE

Ronja turned around slowly. The Conductor's haggard form was slumped in his wheelchair. Maxwell still held his oxygen mask in his hand like a trophy. Her eyes shifted up to Henry. His expression remained unchanged, cold and indifferent.

"Look at me, little bird."

Ronja flashed her gaze to Maxwell. Her blood roared in her skull. She could barely hear him over the sound.

"I want you to know that I have learned from listening to you," he said.

Ronja coughed, all she could manage through her metal bit.

"Oh, but I have," Maxwell assured her. "You have taught me that there *is* power in emotion, as much as I hate to admit it. Those people out there," he said, gesturing to the nearest window. "Right now, they feel nothing. And they will stay that way for as long as I want them to. But soon they will need to feel. Can you guess why?"

Ronja glared at him, quivering with rage.

Maxwell sighed. "You know, this would be more interesting if you could speak."

Take this off me and I'll destroy you, Ronja thought.

"But no," he said, waving a dismissive finger. "Better safe than sorry. Little bird, I am done hiding from the world. Down below, I now have an army three million strong. Beyond this city is a world ripe for the taking." He gave a considerate tilt of his head. "I could always just order them to do it, but you have shown me that when people burn for a cause, they are far more effective.

"Very soon, a fleet of ships will be delivered to me. I will fill them with my subjects to lead a conquest across the ocean. I will take this world for all it is worth. And *you*." He smiled. "You will sing to them until their veins are burning with the fire of a thousand suns, until they want only to kill in my service."

Never, Ronja screamed in her mind, but she was silent. She just shook her head, slow and sure.

"You will," Maxwell said. "I promise, by the time I am done with you, you will. Henry." The boy snapped to attention. "Kill one of her friends."

Ronja screamed through her bit as Henry turned his back on her, drawing a gilded automatic from his hip. She launched forward before the guards could restrain her and leapt onto his broad back, throwing her one good arm around his neck. He drove an elbow into her stomach and shook her off, unfazed. She crumpled to the floor, trembling and sobbing.

She looked up, her eyes roving across the faces of her friends. Evie had moved in front of Iris, using her body to shield her from the barrel of the gun. Mouse was cowering in a ball on the floor, crying silently. Samson was motionless, his eyes trained on Terra, who still lay limp on the floor.

Roark stared at Ronja as she wept, heaving sobs tearing themselves from her chest. He smiled through the blood and the war paint. "I love you," he mouthed. "I love you." He closed his eyes, tranquility washing over his features.

No, no, no.

"Henry," Maxwell snapped. "Choose."

Ronja let out a piercing wail as a single shot ripped through the room.

His body struck the floor. His blood spread across the marble, blazing bright against the pale surface. Iris and Evie were screaming. Mouse was still tucked into a ball, shaking. Roark let out a roar of agony, his head tipped back toward the ceiling.

Samson was dead, his blue eyes open, a perfect entrance wound at the center of his brow.

Ronja was no longer crying. She was empty, the bottom of her soul scraped clean. Maxwell dragged her to her knees by her hair. She looked up at him with glassy eyes. "The next time you say no to me," he shouted over the cries of her family. "Another one will die. Do you understand?"

Ronja nodded.

"Are you ready to come with me?"

Another nod.

"Good. Sedate her."

Pain pricked the back of her neck. Maxwell released her and she slumped forward. She blinked, clinging to the last shreds of her sight. Roark was screaming her name, struggling to reach her. His voice followed her as she descended into blackness.

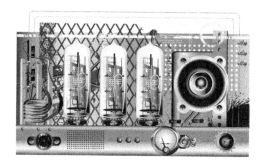

54: IN THE GLASS

It was the cold that woke Ronja, not the ache in her jaw or the searing pain in her head. She lay on the floor of a room that stretched for miles. There was another girl on the slab of concrete next to her. She took a breath. The girl breathed with her. Ronja sat up slowly, blinking through the drug-induced haze that veiled her brain.

Looking around blearily, she realized the room was not massive at all. It was claustrophobic, barely four paces in every direction. A hole in the concrete floor served as a toilet; it was the only real landmark. There were no windows, no visible door. The walls were sealed with floor to ceiling mirrors, cocooning her in a false infinity. A million versions of herself regarded her from the looking glasses. They all seemed to have different expressions.

Her face was a war zone of black and red. Blood and war paint. Cuts and bruises. Her curls were matted, her eyelids swollen with salt. The muzzle still clung to her mouth, wrapping around her skull. Her overcoat, shoes, and weapons had been stripped. She was left with only her tank top and ripped pants.

She did not search for an exit. She did not try to pick the lock at the back of her bit. She simply tucked herself into a ball and let

oblivion wrap around her. When she closed her eyes, she felt her
many reflections watching her.

Sometime later, a tiny portal opened in one of the mirrors.
Harsh white light poured inside. Ronja scrambled over to it,
leaving logic in the dust. As soon as she reached the opening, a
crackling stinger shot through and snapped at her fingers. She
cried out, cradling her burnt hand to her chest. The stinger
disappeared. A moment later, a gloved hand appeared and set a
small tin and straw on the concrete. The hand retracted and the
portal sealed.

Ronja scooted the dish closer. It was filled with cloudy broth.
With trembling fingers, she peeled the paper from the straw and
poked it through the bars of her muzzle. She drank the broth
without tasting it, then set the dish aside and tucked herself into a
ball.

Time bled out of existence. There was no way to track it. The
guards brought her food at irregular intervals. She slept as much
as she could. There were no dreams, no nightmares, only the
endless black of her withering brain. When she could not sleep,
she alternated between pacing and watching the girls in the glass.
There were so many of them.

It was not long before they started to talk to her.

*First Layla and now Samson too. And Henry, look what you
did to poor Henry. Sweet Henry. You knew he loved you and you
pretended not to. And now look where he is, a slave, just like you.*
No. *Slave! Mutt!* Shut up! *Useless! Freak!* SHUT UP! *You are alone,
no one is coming for you. Roark and the others are dead. Dead.
Dead! The Belly will become a tomb because of you, because you
were not strong enough.* NO! *You are nothing.* STOP! *Nothing!
Nothing! NOTHING!*

Ronja did not remember attacking the glass. She only
remembered the pain that followed, the tiny shards that stuck out

from her bleeding knuckles like jagged peaks. There was no epiphany, only instinct. She took one of the larger fragments in her hand, brought it to her throat.

Do it. Do it. Do it.

Ronja squeezed her eyes shut, salt tears crawling down her cheeks. *I will not be your weapon*, she thought. *I will not be your weapon.* Her hand trembled violently, the edge of the glass shivering against her rice paper skin.

Do it, you coward! Do it!

The smell of sulfur tickled her nose. She peeled her eyelids open, her grip loosening around the glass. Hot blood oozed from the undersides of her fingers. Drowsiness rolled over her. Her knees buckled and she crashed to the ground. *No*, she tried to whisper. The air was choked with white smoke. Her vision leaked away. She released the shard of glass. It shattered on the floor as her consciousness wilted. *No.*

Ronja awoke lying on her back in a different cell identical to the first. Her hands throbbed, crusted with her own blood. The shards of glass had been removed, but the wounds had not been cleaned or bandaged. She shifted on the hard floor. The telltale clink of metal chain links scraped her eardrum. She looked down, already knowing what she would find. Metal cuffs were locked around her wrists and ankles, chaining her to the ground. She knew she could stand, there was just enough slack for her to make it to the toilet. But there was no energy left in her blood. There was no will.

There was nothing.

She was no one.

Not Ronja.

Not an Anthemite

Not the Siren.

No one.

When she closed her eyes, she felt the girls in the glass watching her.

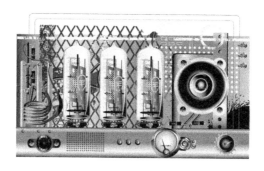

55: PRAYER
Roark

The first night, Roark did not stop moving. He paced the perimeter of his cell like a caged animal, running the pads of his fingers across the concrete in search of a weak point that did not exist. He tried the door next. It was welded iron. He did not truly expect to escape, but movement was the only thing that kept his mind from falling into chaos. If he stopped, reality would catch up to him.

Samson was dead. His friend, his comrade. They had known one another since they were children. Fought together, mourned together, laughed together. How many times had they played music together at jams? How many pranks had they pulled on the girls when they were young?

The Conductor was dead. He had not really been alive for some time. The thought made Roark sway. So many years of fighting, raging against a man who was nothing more than a puppet held aloft by the echoes of The Music.

How long? How long had they been at war with a ghost?

Henry Romancheck. His best friend, his brother, was alive, a shell of himself. A slave to Maxwell and The New Music. He would rather he was dead.

Ronja. Her name bubbled up on his lips like a prayer. He bit it back, afraid it would vanish if he released it. The image of her kneeling on the marble, a cruel bit in her mouth, her blood and the blood of Maxwell mixing with her war paint, was seared into his brain. He knew it would never leave him.

He knew he would never stop trying to get her back.

The days stretched and warped. The guards delivered his food and drink through a slot in the door. They did not speak to him, no matter how he egged them on. No one came to question him. Of course not. He and the others had not been imprisoned because of the information they possessed, but so Ronja would follow orders.

And for that reason, they would be kept alive.

Roark was asleep when the door clicked open. At first he did not notice. The crack of light that fell across his face felt like a dream, distant. It took a human voice to pry him from his stupor.

"Hey, fella."

Roark launched to his feet, his fists raised before him, his back foot pivoted to secure his stance. The door was only opened a crack, spilling bluish light across the concrete floor. A dark eye peeked through the narrow opening.

"Jonah," Roark spat.

Jonah pushed the door open further, ignoring the venom in his voice. Surprise lanced through Roark. The Tovairin was dressed from head to toe in night-dark furs. Two broadswords were strapped to his back, rising above the back of his head like horns. In his hand was a portable communicator. It looked familiar.

"That radio," Roark growled. "Where did you get it?"

Jonah tossed the communicator at him. He caught it by the tips of his fingers. He flipped it over. His stomach vaulted. A tiny

E was scratched into the back of the metal.

"I swiped it from the Arexian when Maxwell's men converged on the warehouse," Jonah explained. "Thought it might come in handy."

"How's that?" Roark asked through gritted teeth.

Jonah shrugged. "Had a feeling Maxwell might not pay up. Radio your people, tell them I am getting you and Alezandri out of here."

"Alezandri. You mean Ronja?"

Jonah nodded, just a quick dip of his chin. "Yes, Ronja."

"What about the others?"

"No time, I'm only here for Alezandri and I need *you* for a little backup getting out of here."

"No," Roark snapped. "Absolutely not. I will not leave my family, neither will Ronja."

Jonah shook his head. "Ronja is *fiested.* If you want her to live, you'll do exactly what I say. Now, call your people, tell them I am taking you to Tovaire, and you'll be back with reinforcements as soon as you can. I am *not* going to let that bastard Maxwell invade Tovaire or any other damn country on this godforsaken planet."

Roark shook his head slowly. "How do I know this is not a trap?"

The Tovairin cocked his head to the side, observing him with oil-dark eyes. "Do you really have another choice?"

Roark glared at Jonah, then brought the familiar radio to his lips. He rolled the dial with his thumb, switching it to Channel 3. He pressed the button on the face of the device. Static blossomed. "This is Drakon," he murmured. "Does anyone copy?"

Silence. Jonah shifted uneasily in the doorframe, checking over his shoulder for signs of life in the hallway.

"This is Drakon," Roark tried again. "Does anyone copy?"

Silence.

"This is Drakon," he tried again. "Does anyone read me? The Siren has fallen. I repeat, the Siren has fallen."

"Drakon!"

Roark felt his heart lurch. He cupped the radio to his mouth. "Harpy?" he breathed. "Is that you?"

"What the hell is going on up there?" Ito demanded, fear coursing through her voice. "Where have you been?"

"Harpy, the Siren has fallen. Nymph, Chimera, Medusa, and Mouse have been made. They're below the palace. I'll get the Siren. Blow the Belly."

"Roark, what are you — "

Roark clicked the radio off. Before he could stash it in his pants pocket, Jonah yanked it from his hand and set it on the concrete.

"Wait!"

The Tovairin crushed the device beneath the heel of his boot.

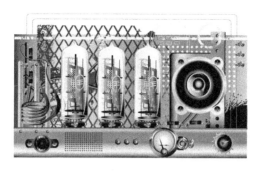

56: INTO THE STARS

When the door to her cell opened, the prisoner did not react. She registered the flush of fresh air, the stir of voices over her head. They meant nothing to her. She kept her eyes sealed shut. She was not even sure she remembered how to open them.

Ronja.

The name pricked her brain. It was familiar. Where had she heard it before? The prisoner stirred feebly in her skin. Her chains clanked hollowly.

Ronja, love. Come with me.

The prisoner smiled, her first smile in what felt like years. Death had finally come for her. She had stopped drinking, stopped eating, hoping to call him. His voice was in her ear, his hot breath on her face. He had taken her once before, in a different life.

We're out of time. Carry her.

Time. The prisoner frowned. What an unwelcome intrusion. Time implied attachment, purpose. There was no time, not anymore. The world heaved. Her oblivion tilted. White lights erupted behind her sealed eyelids, stars spinning overhead. It was like they were dancing. It was like they were alive.

Maybe the stars are alive after all.

The prisoner twitched. Her mouth curved around the words, straining against the bit that was at once vividly present.

"Ronja, can you hear me?" That voice. She knew it. It did not belong to Death. "Give me that key, now."

Pressure at the back of her head. Then, release. The iron crown lifting from her matted curls. The bar sliding out from beneath her tongue. She ran it over her cracked lips, tasting the rust caked there.

"Ronja, love, I'm here." The voice was desperate, raw. Loving.

"Ro — ark," the prisoner rasped. All she wanted was to see him. His face would heal her. She struggled to open her eyes. She let out a sob of frustration when she found she could not. It was like her lids were sealed with dried wax.

"Yes, love. Yes."

"My name ... what is it?"

"Ronja. Your name is Ronja. You are the Siren. You are my world."

"Ronja ... " the prisoner repeated. "My name is Ronja."

"Yes," Roark repeated. "Yes."

Another voice struck her. "Westervelt, we have to go. Now."

"Help me get these shackles off her."

Ronja faded into the stars.

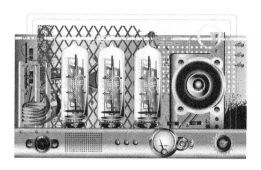

57: EXILE

Ronja woke to the smell of salt and rain. The world heaved steadily, as if it were breathing with her. Her eyelids cracked. She shut them quickly. The light was almost too much to bear.

"Ronja."

The girl shifted her head to the side. Stiff fabric crinkled beneath her head. A pillow. She was resting on a pillow. Perhaps she had died after all.

"Ronja, open your eyes."

The gentle command ignited something deep in her chest, flooding her with energy. She opened her eyes. At first there was nothing but whiteness. Then, slowly, the blank slate began to recede, unveiling her surroundings. She lay on a comfortable cot in a cramped, wooden room. A single oil lamp hung from the low ceiling and a round window displayed a gray sky.

Roark sat on a wooden chair inches from her bed. Warmth flooded her body as she drank him in. His face was a patchwork of bruises. His beautiful dark eyes were shot with red. But he was alive, here, with her. That was all that mattered. He bent forward and pressed his brow to her own. Ronja reached up with a trembling hand to caress the back of his head. That was when she noticed her knuckles were wrapped in clean bandages.

"Where are we?" she whispered. She coughed. Her throat was dry as bone.

"Here," Roark said hastily, helping her to sit up, then grabbing a canteen from the floor. He unscrewed the lid and pressed it to her lips. The cold water slithered down her throat, hitting her like a kick in the gut. But she was so thirsty. "Slowly, now," he murmured. "Slowly."

When she had finally finished drinking, he took the bottle away and laid her back down.

"Where are we?" Ronja asked again, her voice slightly clearer. "What happened?"

"We're safe," he soothed her, petting her curls gently. "We were imprisoned below the palace."

"Georgie and Cosmin?"

"Safe, with Ito, I am sure of it."

"How could you know?"

"I should have told you before," he murmured. "Ito, Samson, and I worked out a backup plan in case everything went to hell."

"You promised no more secrets," Ronja rasped. Her eyes grew hot with unwanted tears. "You promised."

"I was trying to protect you," Roark said, a hint of a plea in his voice. "You had to believe we were confident in your voice."

"Were you?"

"I still am."

Ronja fell silent. The boy followed suit. The weight of his gaze was almost too much to bear. She cast her eyes to her knees, blanketed in cream sheets.

"What was it?" she finally asked. "The backup plan."

Roark shook his head. "Not now. You need to rest."

"What about Evie and the others? What about..."

Henry.

"There was no time." Roark bowed his head, taking a deep shuddering breath. "Ito will get them out."

"Are you sure?"

Roark did not respond

"How long were we there?" Ronja pressed, switching the subject.

"Two weeks, give or take a few days."

Ronja turned her eyes to the ceiling as they flooded. Two weeks. It felt like months, years, she had been trapped in that terrible room. "Where are we, now?" she finally asked.

"On a ship," Roark replied, blinking at her with glazed eyes. "Leaving Revinia."

"A ship?" she asked, her eyebrows flying up her forehead. That explained why the room was rocking back and forth. She had figured it was just her exhausted brain playing tricks on her. "Whose ship?"

"Mine."

Roark and Ronja looked up, startled. The girl let out a noise of shock and fear, pulling her covers up higher as if they would protect her. Jonah stood in the low doorway, stooping slightly to avoid hitting his head. His usual arrogant smirk was gone. He looked haunted.

"Jonah helped us get out," Roark murmured, laying a soothing hand on her knee. "He set your shoulder, too."

As he spoke, Ronja registered the receding pain beneath her skin. "Why?"

The Anthemite fell silent, looking back at Jonah expectantly.

"Because," Jonah said quietly. "Before The Conductor died, he recognized you. He called you by a name."

"Alezandri," Ronja filled in, her tone guarded. "I remember."

"I should have noticed before," the Tovairin went on, his eyes shifting across the planes of her face. "You look so much like him.

Your eyes, your hair, even your nose."

Ronja looked to Roark, seeking answers. His face betrayed nothing. "Like who?" she asked, turning back to Jonah.

Jonah straightened up. The top of his head nearly brushed the doorframe. "Your father, His Royal Highness, Darius Sorin Alezandri II, King of Revinia in exile."

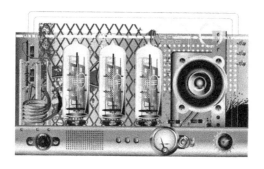

EPILOGUE: SHORELINE

R onja stood at the bow of the ship, her arms limp at her sides. The frigid ocean air stung her eyes and cheeks. She scarcely registered it. Her body was warm in the fur cloak Jonah had presented to her. "Wolf pelt," he had told her as he laid it in her arms. "The best we have on the ship. You'll need it when we reach Tovaire."

The ocean bucked beneath her feet, trying to bring her to her knees. Her lips quirked into a humorless smile. She was a subtrain driver, it would take more than that to throw her off balance. Ronja craned her neck back to view the sky. It gleamed silver, like the belly of an oyster, or a Singer in the sunlight.

"TELES REN LIER PEN VAS!"

Ronja rounded on the female voice, her gray furs stirring. The mast of the sleek ship rose from the wooden deck, cutting through the low hanging clouds. Jonah was scaling the pillar with bare feet, his long hair wound into a knot at the top of his skull. His first mate, a young woman named Larkin, stood below him, her hands on her hips as she watched him climb. Her black hair was tied into two braids. Her intricate white *reshkas* crawled up her neck, ending in a sharp point below her jaw.

"TELES!" she shouted, cupping her warm brown hands around her mouth.

"TOVAIRE VES LAN!" Jonah called down to her, pointing out across the gray waves.

Larkin threw her hands up in the air, then turned to leave. As she did, she caught sight of Ronja watching her. The Siren raised her hand in a halfhearted greeting. The Tovairin woman gave her a curt nod, then stalked toward the stern of the ship and disappeared below deck.

Ronja returned to watching the waves. They were a few shades darker than the sky. The ocean was not as she had imagined it. It was dark and violent, unpredictable. Then, she was becoming accustomed to the unexpected.

When Ronja was finally able to haul herself out of bed several days into their voyage, she had found her way to the captain's quarters at the stern of the little ship. She cornered Jonah at his simple writing desk and pressed him for information on the supposed royals. "If Revinia had a royal family, someone would know about it," she insisted, frustration and disbelief straining her vocal cords. "There would be some sort of written record."

The image of the bare shelves of the library in the outer ring had slinked into her mind. Thumbing through the sparse volumes, the passages obscured with generous amounts of black ink.

"Someone would know about them," she had persisted.

"Maybe someone does," Jonah replied with a shrug. "According to your father —"

"That man is *not* my father."

"According to *Darius*, when The Conductor overthrew King Alezandri, he tried to wipe out his entire bloodline and burned all their records. He tried to obliterate them from history."

A troublesome bit of logic had pricked her brain. *He could have used The Music to wipe the royals from our memories, too.* She pushed the thought away firmly.

"Gregorio —"

"Who?" Ronja snapped.

"Ger pris netram," Jonah sighed, rolling his eyes at the wooden slats on the ceiling. "Your grandfather, King Gregorio, was the only survivor. He was smuggled into Tovaire as an infant. The Kev Fairla have been protecting him and what remains of his bloodline ever since."

"Why?"

Jonah rubbed his thumb and forefinger together. "We protect the Alezandri line, they fund our war with Vinta. How do you think I got this gorgeous ship?"

Ronja folded her arms over her chest, ignoring the dull pain that flared in her healing shoulder. "If Darius has been with you all these years, how the hell could he be my father?"

Jonah offered a tight smile. "That is not my story to tell, princess."

"Convenient," Ronja snarked. "You can't prove a thing."

The Tovairin shrugged again, backing away from her to attend to his duties. "Not my job to make you believe it. Just wait until you meet Darius, you'll see."

"Ronja Alezandri," she murmured to herself. The vicious wind swept the name from her lips, sending it out over the dark waves. It did not sound as if it belonged to her. "Ronja Zipse." But no, that did not sound right, either. She had moved beyond that name, beyond the agonizing years it stood for.

"Ronja."

The girl turned around again. Roark stood a few feet behind her, watching her intently. He was dressed in a long fur cloak that matched his dark eyes and hair. His long nose was capped with pink. Without speaking, she extended her chapped hand to him. He took it, his skin still warm from being inside.

"You'll catch your death out here, love," he murmured, moving to stand beside her.

"Death seems to have trouble keeping up with me," she replied, her eyes on the horizon. Roark chuckled, a low rumbling sound that heated her insides. Ronja pressed closer to him. He brushed his lips against her temple. "Roark," she said after a while. "Do you think Ito can get them out of the palace?"

"I have to believe she will," he replied quietly, curling her closer with his strong arm. Ronja looked up at him, squinting through the frigid bite of the air. His eyes were watering. She knew it was not from the cold. "She'll find a way."

Ronja nodded. She had not allowed herself to think about their friends, much. The possibilities were too bleak, the chances that Ito and the Anthemites were able to free them from the prison below the palace too slim.

"I still don't understand," Roark said quietly. "Why Jonah picked me."

Ronja looked up at him, her brow cinching. "What do you mean?"

"He took you because he knew thinks you're the daughter of this Alezandri, and because he knew Maxwell would eventually use you to invade Tovaire. He needed someone to help get you out, but he could have chosen Terra, or Evie. He should have freed one of them. He should have..." Roark trailed off, gritting his teeth to choke back a sob.

"I know why he picked you," Ronja said quietly. She returned her eyes to the sea. Her stomach fluttered. There was something on the horizon, a black rip in the gray fabric of the sky. The craggy shores of Tovaire. "Because he knew I couldn't survive without you."

Roark was quiet. He wrapped his arms around her shoulders and rested his brow on the crown of her head. She let him, watching with steady eyes as the black shores of the island crept closer over the roiling waves. Behind them, Jonah and Larkin were shouting at each other in their native tongue, their voices buffeted by the wind. Ahead, there was nothing but silence.

"May our song guide us home," Ronja whispered.

"I am home," Roark replied.

ACKNOWLEDGEMENTS

Writing acknowledgements is always tough. There are so many people to thank. It is often hard to quantify or qualify the positive impact they have on my life and art. I'll give it a shot, though.

First, I want to thank my mom, who is there for me through thick and thin. Not only is she my biggest fan, she is my business partner and one of my most trusted editors. If it were not for her, I doubt *The Vinyl Trilogy* ever would have left my computer. I have no idea what I would do without her. Thank you, Mom. I love you.

Dad, I love you dearly. Thank you so much for being there to support me when everything goes wrong. Even better, thanks for sticking around when everything goes right. Thanks for reading my poems and stories, for listening to me ramble about the complex subplots rattling around in my head. Most of all, thanks for being an incredible father.

To my editor, Katherine. I am so lucky I found you. Thank you for combing through the pages of *Vinyl* and *Radio* with speed and candor. Thank you for caring about this series and for going above and beyond to make it right. I cannot wait to send the third installment of this series your way.

Heather (Cyberwitch), my formatter. You have been incredible. I know I asked for a lot this time around, which makes your work twice as amazing. I would not trust anyone else to make my books beautiful. Thank you so much.

Jennifer, Dela, and Amanda. You three ladies are some of my closest friends in the wild world of writing and publishing. Your love and support mean the absolute world to me. You are all crazy talented and I cannot wait to see what you do next!

Jo Painter, thank you for bringing my characters to life. Your illustrations make me smile every time I see them. It has been such a gift to watch you grow as an artist and to work with you.

My friends, family, and loved ones. Bryan, Maya, Mackenzie, Grace, Kosta, Lucy, Jill, Dani, Aban, Ella, Darlene, Masha, Allie, Sylvie, Eniola, Annmarie, Brandon, Amelia, Jeffrey, Lucy Q, Emma, Margaret, Skylar, Grandpa Tom, Grandma Wanda, Grandpa Wayne, Grandma Sharon, Lisa, Tony, Katie, Jackson, Leah, Sanzida, Jessa, Rebekah, Sophie. Thank you for making my life bright. I love you all.

Lastly, to my readers. I do not think I have the words to describe how much you mean to me. I love you all. Without you, this series would not exist. Thank you. Thank you. Thank you.

May your song guide you home,
Sophia

ABOUT THE AUTHOR

Sophia has been writing novels, short stories, and poems since she was still losing her baby teeth. Throughout her high school career, she amassed an impressive 35 Scholastic Art and Writing Awards including two National Gold Medals for science fiction short stories. As a Scholastic alumnus, she joins the ranks of many great authors including Truman Capote, Sylvia Plath, and Joyce Carol Oates. Her critically acclaimed debut novel, *Vinyl: Book One of the Vinyl Trilogy*, spent many weeks in the number one position on Amazon. Her first book of poetry entitled *hummingbird* was released in early 2017. Sophia grew up in Iowa with two dogs and two fantastic parents. She now resides in New York City as a student at her dream school, NYU. She loves pigeons and Star Wars. To learn more, see Sophia's blog at: www.sophiaelainehanson.com or follow her on Instagram and Twitter @authorsehanson.

Amazon reviews are so important for indie authors, if you enjoyed *Radio*, please consider leaving one today!

Made in USA - North Chelmsford, MA
1101064_9780692854198
05.07.2020 1106